John Lanchester was born in Hamburg in 1962. He has worked as a football reporter, obituary writer, book editor, restaurant critic, and deputy editor of the *London Review of Books*, where his pieces still appear. He is a regular contributor to the *New Yorker*. He has written three previous novels, *The Debt to Pleasure*, *Mr Phillips* and *Fragrant Harbour*, and two works of non-fiction: *Family Romance*, a memoir; and *Whoops!: Why Everyone Owes Everyone and No One Can Pay*, a book about the global financial crisis. His books have won the Hawthornden Prize, the Whitbread First Novel Prize, the E.M. Forster Award, and the Premi Llibreter, been longlisted for the Booker Prize, and been translated into twenty-five languages. He is married, has two children and lives in London.

Further praise for *Capital*:

'Intelligent and entertaining.' Claire Tomalin, *Observer*

'The great London novel of the early 21st century.'
Jonathan Derbyshire, *New Statesman*

'A novel that is as readable as it is clever.' *Evening Standard*

'A big book about contemporary London, there's lots here about property prices, while the characters include a Premier League footballer, a traffic warden and a banker. Might seem clichéd if it weren't so damn good.' William Skidelsky, *Observer*

'A complex and gripping tale of London life, a pre-crash portrait of greed and fear and money.' *The Times* Book of the Week

'Searching, expert, on the money. I loved it.' Joseph O'Neill

'An elegant state-of-the-nation novel [whose] large, colourful cast is expertly choreographed by Lanchester.' *Mail on Sunday*

'*Capital* comes in a great tradition of novels which are filled with the news of now, in which the intricacies of the present moment are noticed with clarity and relish and then brilliantly dramatized. It is clear that its characters, its wisdom, and the scope and range of its sympathy, will fascinate readers into the far future.' Colm Tóibín

'As a state-of-London novel, *Capital* succeeds magnificently and, by avoiding the temptation to show us any way out of the current moral and monetary crises, captures the malignant mood of the post-property age.' *Time Out*

By the Same Author

fiction
THE DEBT TO PLEASURE
MR PHILLIPS
FRAGRANT HARBOUR

non-fiction
FAMILY ROMANCE
A Memoir
WHOOPS!
Why Everyone Owes Everyone
and No One Can Pay

Capital

JOHN LANCHESTER

faber and faber

First published in 2012
by Faber and Faber Ltd
Bloomsbury House, 74–77 Great Russell Street
London WC1B 3DA

This open market paperback edition published in 2013

Typeset by Faber and Faber Ltd
Printed and bound by CPI Group (UK) Ltd, Croydon CR0 4YY

A CIP record for this book
is available from the British Library

ISBN 978–0–571–29031–4

For Jesse and Finn
and Miranda

Prologue

At first light on a late summer morning, a man in a hooded sweatshirt moved softly and slowly along an ordinary-looking street in South London. He was doing something, though a bystander would have been hard put to guess what. Sometimes he crept closer to houses, sometimes he backed further away. Sometimes he looked down, sometimes he looked up. At close range, that bystander would have been able to tell that the young man was carrying a small high-definition video camera – except there was no bystander, so there was no one to notice. Apart from the young man, the street was empty. Even the earliest risers weren't up yet, and it wasn't a day for milk delivery or rubbish collection. Maybe he knew that, and the fact that he was filming the houses then was no coincidence.

The name of the place where he was filming was Pepys Road. It didn't look unusual for a street in this part of town. Most of its houses were the same age. They were built by a property developer in the late nineteenth century, during the boom that followed the abolition of the tax on brick. The developer hired a Cornish architect and Irish builders and the houses were built over a period of about eighteen months. They were three storeys high, and no two were identical, because the architect and his workmen created tiny variations in them, to do with the shape of the windows, or the chimneys, or the detailing of the brickwork. In the words of a guidebook to local architecture: 'Once this is

1

noticed, it is pleasing to look at the buildings and detect the small differences.' Four of the houses in the street were double-fronted, with twice as much space as the others; because space was at such a premium, they were worth about three times as much as the single-fronted properties. The young man seemed to take a special interest in filming these bigger, more expensive houses.

The properties in Pepys Road were built for a specific market: the idea was that they would appeal to lower-middle-class families willing to live in an unfashionable part of town in return for the chance to own a terraced house – a house large enough to have room for servants. For the first years they were lived in not by solicitors or barristers or doctors, but by the people who worked or clerked for them: the respectable, aspirational no-longer-poor. Over the next decades, the demographics of the street wobbled up and down in age, up and down in class, as it became more or less popular with upwardly mobile young families, and as the area did well or less well. The area was bombed in the Second World War, but Pepys Road was unaffected until a V-2 rocket hit in 1944 and destroyed two houses in the middle of the street. The gap stayed there for years, like a pair of missing front teeth, until a new property with balconies and French windows, looking very strange amid the Victorian architecture, was built there in the fifties. During that decade, four houses in the street were lived in by families recently arrived from the Caribbean; the fathers all worked for London Transport. In 1960 a small irregularly shaped patch of grass at one end of Pepys Road, vacant since the previous structure was destroyed by German bombs, was concreted over and a two-up-two-down corner shop was built there.

It would be hard to put your finger on the exact point when Pepys Road began its climb up the economic ladder. A conventional answer would be to say that it tracked the change in

Britain's prosperity, emerging from the dowdy chrysalis of the late 1970s and transforming into a vulgar, loud butterfly of the Thatcher decades and the long boom that followed them. But it didn't seem quite like that to people who lived in the street – not least because the people who lived in the street changed too. As house prices slowly rose, the working classes, indigenous and immigrant, cashed in and moved out, usually looking to find bigger houses in quieter places, with neighbours like themselves. The new arrivals tended to be more middle-class, with husbands who worked at decently paid but not spectacular jobs, and wives who stayed at home and looked after the children – because these houses were still, as they always had been, popular with young families. Then, as prices rose and times changed, the new arrivals were families in which both parents worked and the children were in childcare either in the home or out of it.

People began to do up the houses, not in the ad hoc way of previous decades but with systematic make-overs in the knocking-through, open-plan style that became fashionable in the seventies and never really went away. People converted their lofts; when the council veered to the left in the 1980s and stopped giving permission for that, a group of residents banded together and fought a test case for the right to expand their houses upwards, and won it. Part of their argument was that these houses had been built for families, and that loft conversions were entirely in keeping with the spirit in which they were built – which was true. Someone in the street was always doing up a house; there was never a time when there weren't skips outside, builders' vans hogging the street, and all the banging, crashing, drilling, pounding, roaring, and turned-up transistor radios of builders and scaffolders that came as part of the package. The activity slowed down for a little after the housing crash of 1987, but began to pick up again ten years later. By late 2007, after many more years of a new boom, it was usual for two or three houses in the street to be undergoing some sort of major renovation at the same time. The fashion was for people to install basements, at a cost usually starting around £100,000 a time. But as more than one of the people digging out the foundations of their house liked to point out, although the basements cost hundreds of thousands of pounds, they also added at least that much to the value of the house, so looked at from a certain point of view – and because many of the new residents worked in the City of London, this was a popular point of view – the basement conversions were free.

All this was part of a big change in the nature of Pepys Road. Over its history, almost everything that could have happened in the street had happened. Many, many people had fallen in love and out of love; a young girl had had her first kiss, an old man had exhaled his last breath, a solicitor on his way back from the Underground station after work had looked up at the sky, swept blue by the wind, and had a sudden sense of religious consolation, a feeling that this life cannot possibly be all, and that it is not possible for consciousness to end with the end of life; babies had died of diphtheria, and people had shot up heroin in bathrooms, and young mothers had cried with their overwhelming sense of fatigue and isolation, and people had planned to escape, and schemed for their big break, and vegged out in front of televisions, and set fire to their kitchens by forgetting to turn the chip pan off, and fallen off ladders, and experienced everything that can happen in the run of life, birth and death and love and hate and happiness and sadness and complex feeling and simple feeling and every shade of emotion in between.

Now, however, history had sprung an astonishing plot twist on the residents of Pepys Road. For the first time in history, the people who lived in the street were, by global and maybe even by local standards, rich. The thing which made them rich was the very fact that they lived in Pepys Road. They were rich simply

4

because of that, because all of the houses in Pepys Road, as if by magic, were now worth millions of pounds.

This caused a strange reversal. For most of its history, the street was lived in by more or less the kind of people it was built for: the aspiring not-too-well-off. They were happy to live there, and living there was part of a busy and determined attempt to do better, to make a good life for themselves and their families. But the houses were the backdrop to their lives: they were an important part of life but they were a set where events took place, rather than the principal characters. Now, however, the houses had become so valuable to people who already lived in them, and so expensive for people who had recently moved into them, that they had become central actors in their own right.

This happened at first slowly, gradually, as average prices crept up through the lower hundred thousands, and then, as people from the financial industry discovered the area, and house prices in general began to rise sharply, and people began to be paid huge bonuses, bonuses that were three or four times their notional annual pay, bonuses which were big multiples of the national average salary, and a general climate of hysteria affected everything to do with house prices – then, suddenly, prices began to go up so quickly that it was as if they had a will of their own. There was a sentence that rang down the decades, a very English sentence: 'Did you hear what they got for the house down the road?' Once, the amazingly big figure under discussion involved sums which just crept into the ten thousands. Then they were in the multiples of ten thousand. Then they were in the low hundred thousands, and then in the high hundred thousands, and now they were in seven figures. It began to be all right for people to talk about house prices all the time; the topic came up in conversation within the first minutes of people speaking to each other. When people met they held off the subject of house prices with a conscious sense of restraint, and gave in to the desire to talk about them with relief.

It was like Texas during the oil rush, except that instead of sticking a hole in the ground to make fossil fuel shoot up from it, all people had to do was sit there and imagine the cash value of their homes rattling upwards so fast that they couldn't see the figures go round. Once the parents had gone off to work and the children off to school you saw fewer people in the street in the daytime, except builders; but the houses had things brought to them all day. As the houses had got more expensive, it was as if they had come alive, and had wishes and needs of their own. Vans from Berry Brothers and Rudd brought wine; there were two or three different vans of dog-walkers; there were florists, Amazon parcels, personal trainers, cleaners, plumbers, yoga teachers, and all day long, all of them going up to the houses like supplicants and then being swallowed up by them. There was laundry, there was dry-cleaning, there were FedEx and UPS, there were dog beds, printer ribbons, garden chairs, vintage film posters, same-day DVD purchases, eBay coups, eBay whims and impulse buys, mail-order bicycles. People came to the houses to beg and to sell things (towels for the homeless, utility company salesmen). The tradesmen and trainers and craftsmen disappeared into the buildings and came out when they were finished. The houses were now like people, and rich people at that, imperious, with needs of their own that they were not shy about having serviced. There were builders in the street, all the time, servicing the houses, doing up lofts and kitchens and knocking though and adding on, and there was always at least one skip parked in the street, and at least one set of scaffolding. The new craze was for doing up basements and turning them into rooms – kitchens, playrooms, utility rooms – and the houses going in for this craze had conveyors of dirt flowing into skips. Because the earth was compressed by the weight of the houses above it, as it was dug up it expanded to five or six times its original size, so there was something bizarre, even sinister, about this digging, as if the earth was spreading, vomiting, rejecting its own excavation, and far far too much of it seemed to come out of the ground, as if it were fundamentally unnatural to reach down into the earth to take up more space, and the digging could go on for ever.

Having a house in Pepys Road was like being in a casino in which you were guaranteed to be a winner. If you already lived there, you were rich. If you wanted to move there, you had to be rich. It was the first time in history this had ever been true. Britain had become a country of winners and losers, and all the people in the street, just by living there, had won. And the young man on the summer morning moved along the road, filming this street full of winners.

Part One

December 2007

1

On a rainy morning in early December, an 82-year-old woman sat in her front room at 42 Pepys Road, looking out at the street through a lace curtain. Her name was Petunia Howe and she was waiting for a Tesco delivery van.

Petunia was the oldest person living in Pepys Road, and the last person to have been born in the street and still be resident there. But her connection with the place went back further than that, because her grandfather had bought their house 'off the plan', before it was even built. He was a barrister's clerk who worked at a set of chambers in Lincoln's Inn, a man who was both conservative and Conservative, and in the way of barristers' clerks he passed on the job to his son, and then, when his son had only daughters, to his grandson-in-law. That was Petunia's husband, Albert, who had died five years before.

Petunia did not think of herself as someone who had 'seen it all'. She thought she had had a narrow and uneventful life. Nonetheless, she had lived through two-thirds of the whole history of Pepys Road, and she had seen a great deal, noticing more than she ever admitted and judging as little as she could. Her feeling on this point was that Albert had done enough judging for both of them. The only gap in her experience of Pepys Road was when she was evacuated during the early years of the Second World War, spending 1940 to 1942 at a farm in Suffolk. That was a time she still preferred not to think about, not because anybody was cruel to her – the farmer and his wife were as nice as they could be, as nice as the constant labour of their physically active lives allowed them to be – but simply because she missed her parents and their cosy, familiar life, with the day shaped by her father's arrival home from work and the tea they took together at six o'clock. The irony was that despite being evacuated to miss the bombing, she had been there the night in 1944 when a V-2 rocket landed ten doors down the street. It had been four o'clock in the morning, and Petunia could still remember how the explosion had been a physical sensation rather than a noise – it pushed her firmly out of bed, like a companion who had got tired of sleeping with her but wished her no harm. Ten people died that night. The funeral, held at the big church on the Common, had been awful. It was better to have funerals on rainy days, with no sky, but that day had been bright and clear and crisp and Petunia hadn't been able to stop thinking about it for months.

A van came along the road, slowed and stopped outside. The diesel engine was so loud that the windows rattled. Perhaps this was it? No, the van re-engaged its gears and moved off down the street, making an up-down banging as it went over the sleeping policemen. They had been supposed to reduce the amount of traffic in the street but seemed only to have made it more noisy, and also more polluted, as traffic slowed to go over the bumps and then accelerated away afterwards. Since they were put in there had not been a single day on which Albert did not complain about them: literally not a single one from the day the road reopened to traffic until his sudden death.

Petunia heard the van stop further down the street. A delivery, though not of groceries, and not to her. That was one of the main things she noticed about the street these days: the deliveries. It was something which happened more and more often as the street grew posher, and now here was Petunia, awaiting a delivery of her own. There used to be a term for it: 'the carriage trade'. She remembered her mother talking about 'the carriage trade'. Somehow it made you think of men in top hats, and horse-drawn vehicles. Part of the carriage trade, at my age, thought Petunia. The idea made her smile. The shopping was her groceries, and it was an experiment on the part of her daughter Mary, who lived in Essex. Petunia was starting to struggle with the trip to the shops, not in a major way but just enough to feel anxious about the round trip to the high street and back with more than a single basket of shopping. So Mary had set up a delivery of basics for her, with the idea being she would get all her bulkier and heavier staples sent once a week, at the same time, Wednesday between ten and midday. Petunia would much, much rather have had Mary, or Mary's son Graham who lived in London, come and do her shopping with her, and give her some help in person; but that option hadn't been offered.

The van noise came again, an even louder rumbling this time, and then the van moved off, but not far: she heard it park just down the road. Through the window she saw the logo: Tesco! A man came up to her front garden carrying a pallet, and cleverly managed to unlatch the gate with his hip. Petunia got up carefully, using both arms and taking a moment to steady herself. She opened the door.

'Morning, love. You all right? No substitutions. Shall I take it through? There's a warden but I told him don't even think about it.'

The nice Tesco man took her shopping through to the kitchen and put her bags on the table. As she had got older Petunia more and more often noticed when people made displays of unthinking health and strength. An example was here in the ease with which this young man lifted the heavy pallet to dump it on the table, before taking the bags out of it four at a time. His shoulders and arms stretched out sideways as he lifted the bags: it made him look enormous, like a body-building polar bear.

Petunia did not go in much for being embarrassed about things being out of date, but even she was a little self-conscious about her kitchen. Linoleum, once it started to look tatty, somehow looked extra-tatty, even when it was clean. But the man didn't seem to notice. He was very polite. If he had been the kind of workman you tipped, Petunia would have given him a nice tip, but Mary, when she set up the delivery, had told her – irritatedly, as if knowing her mother well enough to be annoyed at what she was thinking – that you didn't tip supermarket delivery men.

'Thank you,' Petunia said. As she closed the door behind the man she saw there was a postcard on the doormat. She bent over, again carefully, and picked it up. The card was a photograph of 42 Pepys Road, her own house. She turned it over. There was no signature on the card, only a typed message. It said, 'We Want What You Have'. That made Petunia smile. Why on earth would anybody want what she had?

2

The proprietor of 51 Pepys Road, the house across the road from Petunia Howe's, was at work in the City of London. Roger Yount sat at his office desk at his bank, Pinker Lloyd, doing sums. He was trying to work out if his bonus that year would come to a million pounds.

At forty, Roger was a man to whom everything in life had come easily. He was six foot three, just short enough to feel no need to conceal his height by stooping – so that even his tallness appeared a form of ease, as if gravity had, when he was growing up, exerted less effect on him than on more ordinary people. The resulting complacency seemed so well-deserved, and came with so little need to emphasise his own good fortune relative to anyone else, that it appeared like a form of charm. It helped that Roger was good-looking, in an anonymous way, and had such good manners. He had been to a good school (Harrow) and a good university (Durham) and got a good job (in the City of London) and been perfect in his timing (just after the Big Bang, just before the City became infatuated by the mathematically gifted and/or barrow boys). He would have fitted seamlessly in the old City of London, where people came in late and left early and had a good lunch in between, and where everything depended on who you were and whom you knew and how well you blended in, and the greatest honour was to be one of us and to 'play well with others'; but he fit in very well in the new City too, where everything was supposedly meritocratic, where the ideology was to work hard, play hard, and take no prisoners; to be in the office from seven to seven, minimum, and where nobody cared what your accent was or where you came from as long as you showed you were up for it and made money for your employer. Roger had a deep, instinctive understanding of the way in which people in the new City liked reminders of the old City as long as they showed that they also accepted the new City's way of doing things, and he was very adroit at signalling his status as someone who would have been at home in the old world but who loved the modern one – even his clothes, beautifully made suits from a wide-boy, Flash Harry tailor just off Savile Row, showed that he understood. (His wife Arabella helped him with that.) He was a popular boss, who never lost his temper and was good at letting people get on with things.

That was an important skill. A skill worth a million quid in a good year, you would have thought . . . But it was not straightforward for Roger to calculate the size of his bonus. His employer, a smallish investment bank, did not make it straightforward, and there were many considerations at work to do with the size of the company's profits overall, the portion of those profits made by his department, which traded in foreign currency markets, the relative performance of his department when compared with its competitors, and a number of other factors, many of them not at all transparent, and some of them based on subjective judgements of how well he had performed as a manager. There was an element of deliberate mystification about the process, which was in the hands of the compensation committee, sometimes known as the Politburo. What it boiled down to was, there was no way of being confident about what the size of your bonus was going to be.

Sitting on Roger's desk were three computer screens, one of them tracking departmental activity in real time, another being Roger's own PC, given over to email and IM and video-conferencing and his diary, another tracking trades in the foreign exchange department over the year. According to that they were showing a profit of about £75,000,000 on a turnover of £625,000,000 so far, which, although he said it himself, wasn't bad. Simple justice, looking at those numbers, would surely see him awarded a bonus of £1,000,000. But it had been a strange year in the markets ever since the collapse of Northern Rock a few months before. Basically, the Rock had destroyed itself with its own business model. Their credit had dried up, the Bank of England had been asleep, and the punters had panicked. Since then, credit had been more expensive, and people were twitchy. That was OK as far as Roger was concerned, because in the foreign exchange business, twitchy meant volatile, and volatile meant profitable. The FX world had seen a number of fairly self-evident one-way bets against high-interest currencies, the Argentinian peso for instance; some rival firms' FX departments had, he knew, made out like bandits. This was where the lack of transparency became a problem. The Politburo might be benchmarking him against some impossible standard of profitability based on some whizz-kid idiot, some boy racer who had pulled off a few crazy unhedged bets. There were certain numbers which couldn't be beaten without taking what the bank told him to think of as unacceptable risks. The way it worked, however, was that the risks tended to seem less unacceptable when they were making you spectacular amounts of money.

The other potential problem was that the bank might claim to be making less money overall this year, so that bonuses in general would be down on expectations – and indeed there were rumours that Pinker Lloyd was sitting on some big losses in its mortgage loan department. There had also been a well-publicised disappointment over their Swiss subsidiary, which had been outcompeted in a takeover fight and seen its stock price drop 30 per cent as a result. The Politburo might claim that 'times are hard' and 'the pain must be shared equally' and 'we're all giving a little blood this time' and (with a wink) 'next year in Jerusalem'. What a gigantic pain in the arse that would be.

Roger moved around in his swivel chair so that he was looking out the window towards Canary Wharf. The rain had cleared and the early-setting December sun was making the towers, normally so solid-looking and unethereal, seem momentarily aflame with clean gold light. It was half past three and he would be at work for another four hours minimum; these were the months during which he would both leave the house before the sun had risen and get home long after it had set. That was something Roger had long since stopped noticing or thinking about. In his experience, people who complained about City hours were either about to quit, or about to be sacked. He swivelled back the other way. He preferred to face inwards, towards 'the pit' as everyone called it, in honour of the trading floors where people yelled and fought and waved papers – though the foreign exchange trading department couldn't be less like that, as forty people sat at screens, murmuring into headsets or at each other but in general hardly looking up from the flow of data. His office had glass walls, but there were blinds which could be lowered when he wanted privacy, and he had a new toy too, a machine generating white noise, which could be turned on to prevent conversation being overheard outside the room. All department heads had one. It was genuinely cool. Most of the time, though, he liked having the door of his office open so he could feel the activity in the room outside. Roger knew from experience that being cut off from your department was a risk, and that the more you knew about what was going on among your underlings the less chance you had of unpleasant surprises.

He knew this partly because of the way he had got his job. He had been deputy in the very same department when the bank suddenly brought in random drugs tests. Four of his colleagues were tested and all four failed, which was no surprise to Roger, since the tests were on a Monday and he knew perfectly well that all the younger traders spent the whole weekend completely off their faces. (Two of them had been taking coke, one ecstasy, and one had been smoking dope – and it was the last guy who worried Roger, since in his opinion marijuana was a loser's drug.) The four had been given final warnings and their boss had been fired. Roger could have told him what was going on if he had asked, but he hadn't, and his way of letting Roger do all the work for him had been so arrogant, so old-school, that Roger, who was too lazy in interpersonal relations to be a nasty or scheming man, was not sorry to see him go.

Roger was not personally ambitious; he mainly wanted life not to make too many demands on him. One of the reasons he had fallen for and married Arabella was that she had a gift for making life seem easy. That, to Roger, was an important talent.

He wanted to do well and to be seen as doing well; and he did very much want his million-pound bonus. He wanted a million pounds because he had never earned it before and he felt it was his due and it was a proof of his masculine worth. But he also wanted it because he needed the money. The figure of £1,000,000 had started as a vague, semi-comic aspiration and had become an actual necessity, something he needed to pay the bills and set his finances on the square. His basic pay of £150,000 was nice as what Arabella called 'frock money', but it did not pay even for his two mortgages. The house in Pepys Road was double-fronted and had cost £2,500,000, which at the time had felt like the top of the market, even though prices had risen a great deal since then. They had converted the loft, dug out the basement, redone all the wiring and plumbing because there was no point in not doing it, knocked through the downstairs, added a conservatory, built out the side extension, redecorated from top to bottom (Joshua's room had a cowboy theme, Conrad's a spaceman motif, though he had started to express a preference for all things Viking, and Arabella was thinking about a re-design). They had added two bathrooms and changed the main bathroom into an en suite, then changed it into a wet room because they were all the rage, then changed it back into a normal (though very de luxe) bathroom because there was something vulgar about the wet room and also the humidity seeped into the bedroom and made Arabella feel chesty. Arabella had a dressing room and Roger had a study. The kitchen had been initially from Smallbone of Devizes but Arabella had gone off that and got a new German one with an amazing smoke extractor and a co-lossal American fridge. The nanny flat had been done up with a separate pair of rooms and kitchen, because in Arabella's view it was important to have that feeling of cut-offness when she, who-ever she was, had boyfriends over to stay; the nanny's quarters had a smoke alarm so sensitive that it would go off in response to someone lighting a cigarette. But in the event they didn't like having a live-in nanny, that sense of someone under their feet, and there was something naff and seventies about the idea of having a lodger, so the flat was empty. The sitting room was un-derwired (Cat 5 cabling, obviously, as all through the house) and the Bang & Olufsen system could stream music all through the adult rooms of the house. The television was a sixty-inch plasma. On the opposite wall was a Damien Hirst spot painting, bought by Arabella after a decent bonus season. Considering the Hirst from aesthetic, art-historical, interior-design, and psychological points of view, Roger's considered judgement about the painting was that it had cost £47,000, plus VAT. Leaving out the furnish-ings but including architects', surveyors' and builders' fees, the Younts' work on their house had cost about £650,000.

The Old Parsonage in Minchinhampton, Gloucestershire, had

also not been cheap. It was a lovely building from 1780, though the outside impression of Georgian airiness and proportion was undermined by the fact that the rooms were smallish and the windows admitted less light than one might expect. Still. Their offer of £900,000 had been accepted and then gazumped for £975,000 so they had had to regazump and it had become theirs for a cool £1,000,000. Renovation and general tarting up had cost £250,000, some of it in lawyers' fees fighting the utterly pointless minutiae of the listing restrictions (it was Grade Two). The tiny subsidiary cottage at the end of the garden had come up for sale and they felt it was essential to buy that, given that as things stood it was a little too cosy when friends came to stay. The vendors, a surveyor and his boyfriend who were second-homers themselves, knew they had the Younts over a barrel, and with prices surging everywhere had gouged £400,000 for the tiny cottage, which turned out to need another £100,000 of work for structural issues.

Minchinhampton was lovely – you can't beat the English countryside. Everyone agreed. But going there for your year's major summer holiday was a little bit dowdy, Arabella felt. It was more of a weekend place. So they also went away for two weeks in the summer, taking a few friends and, on alternate years, inviting either Roger's or Arabella's parents for one week out of the two. The going rate for the sort of villa they had in mind seemed to be £10,000 a week. Any flights would be taken business class, since Roger thought that the whole point of having money, if it had to be summed up in a single point, which it couldn't, but if you had to, the whole point of having a bit of money was not to have to fly scum class. They had on two separate occasions, on good bonus years, hired a private jet, which was an experience from which it was hard to go back to queuing for your luggage . . . Then they would go away again, sometimes at Christmas – though not this year, mercifully, Roger felt – but more often either in the middle of February or for the Easter holidays. The exact dates depended on the timing of Conrad's break at Westminster Under School, who were ferocious about only taking breaks during approved times – a little too ferocious, Roger thought, about a five-year-old boy, but that was what you paid your £20,000 a year for.

The other costs, when you began to think about them, added up too. Pilar the nanny was £20,000 a year out of net income – more like £35,000 gross once all the pissy employment taxes were allowed for. Sheila the weekend nanny was another £200 a time, adding up to about £9,000 (though they paid her in cash and they didn't pay her for holidays, unless she came with them, which she often did; or they would get another nanny from an agency). Arabella's BMW M3 'for the shops' had been £55,000 and the Lexus S400, the principal family car, which was used in practice by the nanny on the school run and play dates, was £75,000. Roger also had a Mercedes E500 given him by the office, and on which he paid only the tax of about ten grand per annum; though he hardly ever used it and made a point of preferring the Tube, which, leaving the house at 6.45 a.m. and returning at about 8 p.m., was bearable. Other things: £2,000 a month on clothes, about the same on house stuff (shared between the two homes, obviously), tax bill of about £250,000 from last year, a need to make a pension contribution 'well into six figures', as his accountant put it, £10,000 for their annual summer party, and then the general hard-to-believe expensiveness of everything in London, restaurants and shoes and parking fines and cinema tickets and gardeners and the feeling that every time you went anywhere or did anything money just started melting off you. Roger didn't mind that, he was completely up for it, but it did mean that if he didn't get his million-pound bonus this year he was at genuine risk of going broke.

3

It was late afternoon. Roger sat on one of the sofas in his office, opposite the man who more than any other was going to help him earn his million-quid bonus, and the man who was going to play the single biggest role in deciding whether or not he was paid it.

The first man was his deputy, Mark. He was not quite thirty, a full ten years younger than Roger and pale from all his time indoors sitting in front of a screen. Mark had the habit of constantly, and almost invisibly, shifting: he moved his weight from foot to foot, touched his watch, checked that something was in his pocket, or made small twitching facial movements, as if to adjust the way that his glasses were sitting on his nose. The effect was a little like that produced by people who in conversation constantly use the first name of the person they are speaking to: you can go years without noticing this but once you do it is hard not to become distracted by it – hard, in fact, not to feel that it is specifically intended to drive you mad. That was how Roger felt about Mark's fidgeting. At that very moment he was fiddling with a Montblanc ballpoint pen.

In many respects Mark was a perfect deputy. He worked hard, never made a mistake, was not too obvious about wanting Roger's job, and if you left aside the question of his non-stop fidgeting, never seemed flustered. There was a slight sense that he kept things too tightly under control, and he was the kind of person who might turn out to have a secret vice: if he turned out to be a paedo or bondage freak or to have a chopped-up body under his floorboards or something, Roger would be surprised, but he wouldn't be all *that* surprised. He would have been very surprised indeed if he had known what Mark really thought of him, and also what a close and personal interest his deputy took in his boss's life – in where Roger lived and where he'd gone to school, in his children's names and birthdays, in his wife's spending habits and in the way he spent his free time. Roger would have been completely freaked out by that, but he didn't know anything about it, so that wasn't why Mark made Roger uneasy.

Roger's discomfort with Mark was based on the fact that he, Roger, had come to work at Pinker Lloyd in the time when the City was more about relationships and less about maths. He had prospered, thrived, in the intervening decades but it was no longer true that he had kept up entirely with the changes in the underlying nature of the work. Foreign exchange trading was based on the manipulation of immensely complicated mathematical formulae, which allowed the bank to take subtle, lucrative positions that amounted to betting on both sides of the trade at the same time. As long as anything not too wildly untoward happened – anything outside the parameters and predictions built into your bets – and as long as your algorithms were correct, you were guaranteed to make money. It was a law of the business that you could not make money without taking some risk, but it was also true, thanks to the wonders of modern financial instruments, that you could manage the risk almost out of existence. And of course the bank did every little thing it could to help itself. Some of the trading was algorithmic, done on a purely mathematical basis to benefit from the way prices had momentum: when they moved in any direction, they were more likely than not to move in the same direction the next day. So they had traders using software to profit from that. Some of the trading was 'flash' trading, done to profit from the split seconds between an order being placed in the markets and the order being executed. Some of the trading drew on databases of what customers had paid in the past, and used that to predict what they would pay in the present, in real time, so that the bank could quote a price that the customer would accept, but which would also lock in a guaranteed profit for Pinker Lloyd. That was all fine, and the broad principles were well understood by Roger – but it was not the same thing as understanding the maths itself. That was by now well beyond him. Mark, on the other hand, did understand it; he had abandoned a Maths PhD to come and work at Pinker Lloyd. Roger did not love the fact that his footing was no longer entirely secure, and that he could no longer explain, right the way down to the finest grain of detail, exactly what was going on in the trading his department supervised. But then, hardly anyone else could either. That was just the nature of the work that went on in the City these days.

'OK to bring up one more issue?' asked Mark, putting down the first set of figures he'd brought, and picking up another file. 'I've got the next run at that software thing. I thought you might like to have a look?'

Mark here was using upspeak, ending on an upward inclination, making what he said nearly a question but not quite. He held the file aloft in a way which invited the third man in the room to take a look at it if he wanted to. That man was Roger's ultimate boss, Lothar Billinghoffer. Lothar was a forty-five-year-old German who had been headhunted from Euro Paribas a couple of years ago. Companies have styles in personal comportment; the style at Pinker Lloyd was calm and level, and no one embodied that better than the German Chief Executive Officer. He looked super-fit and uncannily healthy for a man who worked twelve to fourteen hours a day, though when you got close up he seemed older than he did at a distance. Lothar was a fanatic about outdoor sport, and spent his weekends walking up mountains or skiing down them or hanging off the sides of yachts. His face was often reddish with a touch of sunburn or windburn and his eyes were lined from outdoorsy squinting. Lothar beside Mark was like a colour chart for men's faces: this is what happens when you go orienteering in the Black Mountains v. this is what happens when you never voluntarily look up from a screen.

Lothar would not normally be here. Dropping in on people was a new thing he did; he'd read some book about 'deconstructed' management techniques. Since no one in the world was less deconstructed than Lothar, he had formulated a strict policy of spending half an hour a week wandering around the building talking to people and going into meetings at pretend-random. So here he was pretend-randomly at Roger's daily check-in with his deputy.

Roger might have been nervous at going over the software problems with Lothar in the room. Everyone in business knows that everything to do with new software is a guaranteed nightmare. But Mark never approached Roger with a problem to which he did not have, if not a solution, then an idea about where a solution might possibly be sought. The department was working with the IT department and an external contractor to develop a new, custom-made software package to display information on traders' screens: the holy grail was the maximum amount of information with the minimum clutter, and the greatest amount of individual customisation (since the traders all had their own views about how they wanted their screens to look) combined with the shortest learning curve. This didn't interest Roger particularly, but then not much of his work did, and he was always ready to take a view in his amiable, even-tempered way. That didn't seem to be necessary here. In this instance, Mark's tone implied that he knew Roger was busy, that it was not all that urgent a query, and that it would be entirely legitimate for Roger to wait for a new, improved version of the software before he deigned to look at it. So he was making it clear that his enquiry was pro forma, except that if it was too obviously pro forma it might look as if he did not value Roger's opinion, which he did, he deeply did. All this was part of the way Mark was a perfect deputy, almost uncannily so. Lothar made no move to take the file. For a moment Roger thought it would be more expressive of confidence in his deputy, and therefore a better example of Deconstructed Management, if he didn't look at the papers, but then a bat-squeak of instinct told him to play it the other way.

'Let's have a shufti,' said Roger. Mark slid some screenshots in front of his superior. Sure enough, the screenshots were a little cluttered and busy. One of them displayed eight different graphs. Roger and his deputy looked at each other. Neither of them looked at Lothar, who in Mark's case was his boss's boss.

'No,' said Roger. 'Still too much.'

Mark bowed his head slightly. Because he was at the same moment doing something to his pen, this made him seem as if he was wringing his hands in a gesture of self-abasement.

'I'll bounce it back to them and tell them you said so.' He nodded and backed out of the room towards the trading floor.

'Good,' said Lothar – one of the only things he ever said which came across with a faint flavour of German: 'gut'.

Roger got up, stretching to his full height, and moved towards the door, which Mark had closed as he went out. He pressed the button that made the blinds go up and looked out into the space where his colleagues were all in their various work postures – leaning into their screens, slouched and tilted backwards, or occasionally standing and moving as they talked into their headsets. The sun had gone down and the lights in the other tower of Canary Wharf seemed brighter; but the only people looking out the window were simultaneously on the phone, buying and selling. One or two of his people nodded or grimaced at Mark as he walked past. Roger momentarily found himself thinking about his million pounds, before wrenching his attention back to Lothar.

'They're a good bunch,' he said. 'Work hard play hard, same way all kids are these days.'

'Figures look pretty gut,' said Lothar in a neutral tone.

Roger thought: yes!

4

Ahmed Kamal, who owned the shop at the end of Pepys Road, number 68, came awake at 3.59 in the morning, one minute before his alarm clock was set to go off. Through long habit he was able to reach out and press down the button on top of the digital clock without coming fully awake. Then he rolled back and lay snuggled up behind his wife Rohinka, who he could tell was still a long way down into sleep.

Ahmed was used to waking up early and did not mind it all that much, but he didn't like getting out of bed when Rohinka was so warm and the house was so cold. In the distant epoch before they had kids, the heating would have been timed to come on as he was getting up, but the house was small, with two rooms upstairs and two down, and their children's bedroom was immediately over the tiny downstairs kitchen. When the boiler came on, it made a noise which, though not loud, through some dark magic of sound conduction woke their son Mohammed as if it were a backfiring motorbike. Mohammed, who was eighteen months old, could then be guaranteed to wake four-year-old Fatima, who would march straight into the bedroom and wake Rohinka, and the day would be well on the way to disaster by one minute past four in the morning. The solution was to leave the heating off until later in the morning, and wear more clothes. This Ahmed did. But before getting up he lay in the warmth of the marital bed and counted slowly to a hundred.

Exactly on a hundred – this was part of the drill, because he told himself that if he waited a second longer he wouldn't get up at all – Ahmed climbed out of bed. He put on two Gap T-shirts, one medium and the second extra-large, a thick cotton shirt his mother had sent him from Lahore, a cashmere sweater Rohinka had bought him for Christmas, a pair of boxer shorts, two pairs of socks, a pair of thick brown trousers, and finally a pair of fingerless gloves. Rohinka thought these hilariously tatty, but they were a big help with accomplishing the first task of the day, getting in the newspapers, cutting the wrappers and plastic tape off them, and getting both the deliveries and the daily displays ready. Ahmed went downstairs slowly, stepping over the third, fifth and eighth steps, all of which creaked, and making it to the kitchen without waking Mohammed. The preacher at Wimbledon mosque sometimes talked about the jihad against your smaller temptations and lazinesses, the jihad to get up and say your prayers in the morning. Ahmed, by the time he got downstairs before the dawn, felt that he knew what the imam meant.

He made tea, took some of yesterday's naan out of the bread bin and went through to open the shop and bring the papers in. Ahmed loved his shop, loved the profusion of it, the sheer amount of stuff in the narrow space and the sense of security it gave him – *The Daily Mail* and *The Daily Telegraph* and *The Sun* and *The Times*, and *Top Gear* and *The Economist* and *Women's Home Journal* and *Heat* and *Hello!* and *The Beano* and *Cosmopolitan*, the crazy proliferation of print, the dozens of types of industrially manufactured sweets and chocolates, the baked beans and white bread and Marmite and Pot Noodles and all the other inedible things that English people ate, and the bin-liners and tinfoil and toothpaste and batteries (behind the counter where they couldn't be stolen) and razor blades and painkillers and the 'No Junk Mail' stickers which he'd only got in last week and had already had to reorder twice, the laser-print-quality 80 g paper and the A4 envelopes and the A5 envelopes which had become so popular since they changed the way postal pricing worked, and the fridge full of soft drinks and the adjacent fridge of alcohol, and the bottles of Ribena and orange squash, and the credit card machine and the Transport for London card-charging device and the Lottery terminal – it all felt snug and cosy and safe, his very own space, and never more so than first thing in the morning when the shop was his alone. Mine, he thought, all mine. Ahmed turned down the volume on the CD player behind the counter and then pressed play: Sami Yusuf's 'My Ummah' came on at low volume. Later in the day he would turn to Capital Gold, because not everyone liked Sami Yusuf, but nobody disliked oldies. Then came the day's first irritation: that little bastard Usman had done it again. The shelves beside the counter where the shop's alcohol was on display were covered by a blind. So was the section of the fridge devoted to beer and white wines.

Usman was Ahmed's younger brother, a not very grown-up (in Ahmed's view), argumentative (in everybody's view) 28-year-old who divided his time between working in this very shop and studying (in Ahmed's view that should be 'studying') for an engineering doctorate. Either Usman was going through a devout phrase or – Ahmed's view – he was pretending to. Whichever it was, he was making a big deal of his dislike of selling alcohol and magazines with naked women on their covers. Muslims were not supposed to blah blah. As if everybody in the family were not well aware of these facts and also well aware of the economic necessities at work. There was no reason for the blind to have been pulled down. The only reason to pull it down was to make it clear that alcohol could not be legally sold outside the licensing period; but last night the shop had been shut at eleven and they had a licence to sell alcohol until eleven. The last person inside the shop the night before was Usman, and his latest trick was, when Ahmed was absent, pulling down the blind so that it would not be clear whether or not his scruples had on this occasion allowed him to sell alcohol to the unbelievers. It was a wind-up.

Ahmed unlocked the front door and pulled up the bottom of the shutter, which was always the hardest bit; then he shoved it up under the shop awning, as gently as he could. It was a cold day and his breath steamed freely. From just around the corner he could hear the whirr of the electric milk cart. He must have just missed it. Ahmed dragged the papers inside, puffing slightly, and pulled the door to. On a bad day when Rohinka was busy with the children and he was minding the shop all day, that would be the only exercise he would get in the whole twenty-four hours.

While he got on with the business of unpacking and setting out the newspapers, and then putting together the bundles for the three delivery boys who would be arriving at any time after six o'clock or so, Ahmed grumbled to himself. He loved Usman, of course he did, but there was no question that he was an annoying little bastard. If his precious conscience wouldn't allow him to serve alcohol he should plainly say so, and then Ahmed could give him a bollocking and – this of course was the real reason Usman wouldn't come out and say so plainly – get on Skype to their mother in Lahore. Hah! That would be a good one. That would be a classic. Mrs Kamal would scream. She would yell. She would denounce every single bad thing Usman had ever done, omitting nothing and minimising nothing, and then describe every single good thing that had ever been done for him, and then would invite Allah to inform her of what she had done, given the extraordinarily total contrast between his badness and his family's goodness, what they had done to deserve such a thing. She would invite Allah to strike her dead rather than witness any further displays of ingratitude. She would go into orbit. And that would be just the warm-up. That would be her just getting going. She would give Usman such a bollocking there would be a real chance he'd drop dead right there on the spot. The world would realise that Pakistan had no real need of its nuclear deterrent since they already had the elder Mrs Kamal.

The thing which most irritated Ahmed about his younger brother was the self-righteousness. Usman could not prevent it from being clear that he thought he was a better Muslim, a better person, than his two brothers, thanks to his new religious scruples. That was hard to take, all the more so because it was written on his face and in his body language rather than said out loud where it could be shouted down. His expression when he was putting magazines like *Zoo* or *Nuts* on the shelf, or giving change to a customer who'd just bought a bottle of wine – he looked like a Rottweiler chewing a wasp. On some days when Usman had been on in the evening, or when he'd done the first shift at the weekend, Ahmed would find the men's magazines hidden at the back of the shelf, behind the car and computer mags. It was obvious when Usman had done it, though when Ahmed had asked him about it he had blamed the customers. It was supposed to be a shop, you were supposed to sell people things, not try to see how many people you could deter from buying Special Brew by the sheer force of your scowling. Usman stood behind the counter with his shoulders hunched and his stupid unkempt new beard, looking like something from a Wanted poster.

On the subject of scowling, Ahmed could hear footsteps thumping down the stairs. From the weight of them and the determined way they were being whacked down on the steps he knew it was Fatima. He looked at the clock: it was six; she often woke around now. And sure enough his daughter came into the front of the shop, cross, and stood with her hands on her hips.

'Daddy! Daddy! What is the time!'

'Early, darling, very early. Wouldn't you like to go back to bed? It's cold down here and Daddy's working.'

'Daddy! No! I want breakfast!'

'It's a little early for breakfast, my flower.'

'I'll wake Mummy! She'll give me breakfast!'

'No, darling, you mustn't do that.'

'I'll wake Mohammed and he'll wake Mummy and then she'll give me breakfast but it will be Mohammed's fault that she's awake!' explained Fatima.

'OK, darling, I'll give you some breakfast. You can have some tea, too,' this being a new special treat, and something that made Fatima feel especially grown-up. Ahmed took his daughter by the hand and led her into the kitchen. When he went he took the last few papers, the batch for Pepys Road, to scribble addresses on them so that they'd be ready for the delivery boys. As he picked them up he saw something on the floor of the shop, a card which must have been pushed through the postbox while he'd been working. Some idle bastard wanting an ad put up on the noticeboard and too lazy to give it in by hand or too stupid to realise that the shop was already open, thought Ahmed. But then he looked at the card, still holding Fatima's hand, and saw it was a photo of the shop, and written on the back were the words 'We Want What You Have'. For about three seconds Ahmed wondered what the significance of the card was, and then his daughter, holding his hand and leaning at forty-five degrees, giving herself entirely over to gravity in an attempt to force her father to follow her, succeeded in dragging him away.

5

Shahid Kamal, who was due to work a shift at the family shop between eight o'clock in the morning and six o'clock in the evening, walked down the street at a brisk clip. He was early, and had several things he could be doing with this extra half-hour: he could have stayed in bed; he could have sat in the café downstairs from his flat reading a book; he could have spent half an hour on the net catching up on the news and his Myspace page and his discussion boards; but instead he chose to take a brisk walk. Five years ago their father had died suddenly in Lahore, struck down by a heart attack at sixty-two, and his brother Ahmed was already beginning to look a little like their dad: paunchy, tired, unfit, indoorsy. Shahid could read the omens and knew the family body type; now that he was in his thirties he was going to have to take exercise if he was not to turn into yet another ghee-fattened South Asian with a gut and high blood pressure. So here he was, going the long way round, and at speed. There was lots of traffic on the pavement, most of it people on the way to work, heads down in the cold, most of them carrying briefcases and shoulder bags or handbags. Shahid had no bag, he liked to move unencumbered.

Just before the corner of Pepys Road, Shahid crossed to the other side of the street – to reduce the chance that Ahmed might see him and call him to come and help with the pre-work rush – and turned towards the Common. He still had twenty minutes.

It was cold, but Shahid had nothing against the cold as long as he could keep moving. He came out on the Common, passed the Church and its billboard of advertisements for itself, and headed out for the bandstand; there and back would be about twenty minutes and he'd be bang on time. Commuters came hurrying towards the Tube station from every point of the compass, with cyclists weaving in and out among them. Although he too was heading to work, Shahid was glad he wasn't dragging himself off to some office job. Shahid's view: anybody who had to wear a suit to work died a little inside, every day.

Shahid was the free spirit of the Kamal family: a dreamer, an idealist, a wanderer on the face of the earth – or, as Ahmed would put it, a lazy fuckwit. He had been offered a place at Cambridge to read physics but cocked it up by missing his required A-level grades, owing to a bad case of not doing any work at all for his final school year. He'd gone to Bristol instead but dropped out after a year and went on a mission to save his brothers in religion in Chechnya. He'd been gone for four months. Although no member of the Kamal family ever referred to this as anything other than a joke, it hadn't felt like a joke at the time to Shahid. Chechnya itself had been horrible, a brutal disillusionment – Shahid mainly remembered being shouted at, a permanent sense of moral ambiguity where he'd expected to find a shining light of virtue, a feeling that it was hard, among the good guys, to tell who the good guys were, and being cold and hungry and frightened, right up until he came down with diphtheria and was smuggled back out the same way he'd come in. But the trip there had been sensational, the best time of his life: he'd set out on his own, hooked up with some fellow idealists in Brussels, and then they travelled out by cadging lifts and bumming rides all the way to the Russian border, before blagging their way onto a convoy and riding the scary, exhilarating trail through Russian-held territory, through Chechen lines into the besieged homeland. He hadn't really had a clue what he was doing, other than expressing a vague sense that his brothers were in danger and that Muslims were being killed and no one was doing anything about it, so it was his duty to do something – but it was a rule of life that you were allowed to do silly, half-baked, idealistic things when you were eighteen. The best thing about it had been the sense of purpose, of a shared goal and larger meaning, that they'd all had on the trip there, he and two blokes from Birmingham, a French-Algerian called Yakoub, and three Belgian Muslims, two of whom were converts, all of them high on the sense of purpose and discipline and willingness to fight for a cause. He almost never thought about Chechnya but he often thought about the trip there. Shahid was also aware of the irony that he who prized his freedom and willingness to seek truth had been happiest when he had a defined purpose, a sense of duty and obligation, and a specific destination in mind.

Since then he hadn't done anything much, or nothing which would look like much on a CV. He spent a couple of months recovering from his stomach bug, and one large irony was that his system could no longer tolerate alcohol – it instantly gave him the runs. So after giving up on his mission to save the *umma* he was now doomed to be a lifelong teetotaller. Not that he had ever been a heavy drinker but he did like a glass of cider every now and then . . . After getting better he'd worked in the shop and pursued a series of interests, many of which had looked like turning into jobs: he'd been a martial arts bum, learning first t'ai chi, then wing chun, then karate, and had spent every conscious non-working moment for several years in one dojo or another. He liked the discipline and the implicit spirituality of the martial arts, and the way respect and courtesy were built into their fabric: it had the rigour of religious practice but no supernatural or political baggage. Also you learned to kick the shit out of people. But his interest in karate faded just at the point when he'd taken and passed his karate black belt exam; that would have been the moment at which he took up teaching, and something about the idea of being in authority over people, telling them what to do, bossing them about – that, to Shahid, just wasn't him.

After his martial arts phase Shahid got interested in computers. This was the end of the nineties and the internet was starting to take off. He taught himself HTML and began helping people to make websites – first friends and friends of friends and then gradually building up a word-of-mouth business. It was a time when you could make a living by having read roughly two books about writing code, so he did, and earned more money than at any other time in his life. Perhaps that was the problem. Somewhere deep in Shahid's sense of himself was the idea of being a seeker, a drifter, a man not tied down; he could feel the cash, four-figure sums in a good week, starting to tether him. Shahid could tell that it wouldn't be long before he wanted the life to go with the money, so on the day he was offered a proper, full-time job – setting up a website for a friend's cousin, who'd made a shedload importing cloth, and was planning to make several shedloads more – instead he just stopped writing code. These days he spent very little time surfing the web, which now seemed, on reflection, a giant collective conspiracy to waste time. Given infinite freedom of intellectual movement, it turned out that what people mainly want to do is look at pictures of Kelly Brook's tits. Shahid enrolled at Birkbeck and did another year of physics before dropping out again – as Ahmed pointed out, at this rate he was well on course to graduate in 2025. It was the daily slog across London, more than the work, which made the educational fight go out of him. After that, Shahid mainly read books and worked in the shop. He was OK with that. He felt full of potential.

Shahid came to the shop and checked his watch: bang on time. More and yet more commuters were scuttling past, the morning rush building up, a few of them taking a sharp turn sideways to go into the shop, preferably without breaking step or losing speed. Bless them, every one. He followed one of them through, and saw that a queue had already built up at the counter. He came through and grunted a greeting at Ahmed in return for the fact that Ahmed had done no more than grunt one at him. Ahmed was doing that thing of wearing every piece of clothing he owned. Together they served ten customers, the typical morning crowd, buying newspapers and energy drinks and topping up their Oyster cards, the queue to pay on the right side of the central shelves and the queue to exit on the left. Then there was a lull.

'Cup of tea?' said Ahmed, thawing slightly. He gestured behind him towards the living quarters with his soft right hand. Shahid nodded his thanks and went through.

Ahmed did not know this, but Shahid was not free of envy at the domestic side of his brother's life, and he felt a jab of it as he saw Rohinka stirring something on the stove while Fatima, looking prim and businesslike in her school uniform, sat at the kitchen table drawing a flower on a piece of paper with a yellow marker pen. Mohammed sat in his high chair in a bright red Babygro, looking with deep, reverent concentration at the palms of his hands. He had what appeared to be mashed banana on his nose.

'Mohammed, say hello to your uncle,' said Rohinka.

'Nun-nun,' said Mohammed, without looking up from his hands. Something about them was possessing him; it was as if he'd never seen them before. He began turning them from side to side. 'Un-un,' he added.

'So what's new?' Shahid asked his sister-in-law. There was a sexy gentleness to Rohinka that Shahid approved of very much. She was so much nicer than his stiff brother, it was ridiculous. Rohinka could tell that he liked her and in turn liked him back.

'Nothing in my life is new,' said Rohinka. 'Why would anything be new? Where would such newness come from?' The words were those of complaint but the tone was happy. Rohinka was happy and did not feel any need to keep the fact secret. 'And now – time for school. Mohammed, we're off to get changed. Fatima, it is time to do your toilet business. Shahid, see you later.'

Fatima lifted up her drawing and said: 'Finished!' As with everything else she said, this came out sounding proud and fierce.

'What a lovely flower! And the drawing is lovely too,' said Shahid, who was shy with girls but flirted effortlessly with children. Fatima put her hands on her hips.

'Fatima!' warned her mother. Rohinka went upstairs carrying Mohammed, who was still looking at his hands, Fatima went into the loo, and Shahid went into the shop to take over from his grumpy overweight brother.

6

At number 51 Pepys Road, Mrs Arabella Yount, who had once read a book about how women were better than men at multitasking, was doing four different things at the same time: she was putting up some shelves in the tiny storeroom she liked to call her pantry; she was looking after her two lovely children, Joshua and Conrad; she was shopping for clothes over the internet; and she was making plans to give her husband a nasty fright.

Two of those tasks Arabella had subcontracted to other people. The shelves were being put up by her Pole, Bogdan the builder, whom she had started using after a recommendation from a friend and had now adopted as her own. He worked twice as hard as a British worker, was twice as reliable, and cost half as much. Something similar could be said about Pilar, their Spanish nanny, who was looking after her two boys, Conrad and Joshua. Arabella had got Pilar through an agency. She had a qualification in childcare (in fact had a degree), a valid driving licence, could cook, didn't mind doing her share of the housework, got on famously with Maria the cleaner, which was good because otherwise it could be a bit embarrassing on the two days they were both in the house, and, most importantly – it went without saying that it was by far the most important – was just heavenly with her two boys. Conrad and Joshua positively doted on Pilar. They loved the games she made up for them, the Spanish nursery rhymes she taught them, and her willingness to submit to local custom and cook them two different meals three times a day, since they were inflexibly committed to never liking the same food. At the moment, Conrad would eat nothing that wasn't doused in soy sauce, and Joshua would eat no vegetables, and Pilar was an absolute genius at dealing with all that.

There was only one problem with Pilar, which was that she was going to be leaving them to go back to Spain. That was scheduled to happen just before Christmas. Pilar had told Arabella weeks before, very decently giving a full three months' notice. She was going back to a job at a nursery school in Spain. A new nanny would begin work in the new year, but the Younts would be without any childcare over the holidays. When she had realised that and begun to think about it, Arabella had the initial flickering of an idea.

For some time now, almost everything about her husband had made Arabella cross. It had begun with the birth of Conrad, eased off a bit after he got to his second birthday, then got much worse when she was pregnant with Joshua, and worse still after he was born. Joshua was now three years old and Arabella was as cross with her husband as she had ever been. The shorthand term for what she felt was 'competitive tiredness'. She felt she was so tired that she could not think or see straight; she felt that she began the day tired, thanks to the broken and shallow sleep she had been having now for, literally, years, and got more tired as the day wore on, and that there were times when she was running on, as she put it, 'sheer adrenalin'; but that when her husband came home from work he had the temerity to act as if he was the one making all the effort, as if he was the one who had, by the time he got home, the right to sigh and put his feet up and talk about what a tiring day he had had! Blind! Oblivious! He didn't have a clue! As for weekends, in some ways they were even worse. Sheila the Australian weekend nanny was very helpful (though she was no Pilar – for one thing she couldn't drive) but there was still masses to do, and her husband did very little of it. He didn't cook, except show-off barbecues on the occasional summer weekend at his silly boy-toy gas grill, and he didn't wash clothes or iron them or sweep the floor or, hardly at all, play with the children. Arabella did not do those things either, not much, but that did not mean she went through life acting as if they did not exist, and it was this obliviousness which drove her so nuts.

The idea Arabella had had was quite simply to vamoose and leave Roger to it for a few days, with no warning. He could learn about looking after the children and the house by doing it for a few days, solo. While he was doing it, Arabella would be at x. x was nowhere specific, not yet, and yet Arabella had very specific ideas about x. It was going to be a luxury hotel, somewhere not exhaustingly far from London, with a spa.

Arabella was not contemplating running away for ever. She couldn't possibly leave Conrad and Joshua. The point was to give her husband a nasty shock. Ideally, the shock of his life. He had no idea, *no idea*, of the burden actually involved in looking after the children and running the house. No idea. Well, this would bloody well give him an idea. Arabella was going to go away, without warning, for three days and during that time she was going to be completely out of contact with home. Her husband would have no idea where she was – she could be in Reykjavik, she could be on Mars.

Beside Arabella on the floor was a pile of perhaps twenty hotel brochures. If her husband had noticed them – which assumed that he ever noticed anything – he would have thought she was planning to nag him about holidays. This would teach him. In addition the web browser on her computer had six different screens open. The current most promising candidate was a hotel in the New Forest which offered a residential package starting at £4,000 for the two of them, though the nicer-looking package, which included a daily massage and pampering, was £5,300, not unreasonable, Arabella felt, for what it was. The idea of luxury, even the word 'luxury', was important to Arabella. Luxury meant something that was by definition overpriced, but was so nice, so lovely, in itself that you did not mind, in fact was so lovely that the expensiveness became part of the point, part of the distinction between the people who could not afford a thing and the select few who not only could, but also understood the desirability of paying so much for it. Arabella knew that there were thoughtlessly rich people who could afford everything; she didn't see herself as one of them but instead as one of an elite who both knew what money meant and could afford the things they wanted; and the knowledge of what money meant gave the drama of high prices a special piquancy. She loved expensive things because she knew what their expensiveness meant. She had a complete understanding of the signifiers.

The tricky thing could be friends: you needed friends who felt the same way. And who had the money to act on the feeling. Luckily, Saskia was one of them. She had been dumped by her shit of a husband eighteen months before but had cleaned him out in the divorce so she was more than good for her share of it. For this sort of adventure she was perfect. Clicking around the website, Arabella thought this New Forest package looked by far the strongest candidate yet. They had availability. She picked up her mobile phone, flipped it open, and said 'Saskia'. The phone rang four times.

'Babes!' said Saskia, who was thirty-seven.

'Darling!' said Arabella, who was also thirty-seven. 'I think I've found somewhere down south. Shall I read you all the porn or just book?'

'Darling, you know I trust you.'

'Cool,' said Arabella, who without thinking about it had stood up and moved across to the mirror in what she called her dressing room. She often went to look at herself when she was speaking on the phone; when she was in the street and took or made a phone call she would stop in front of a shop window and consult her reflection. Although Arabella was conscious of her appearance, careful with her clothes and her blonde highlights and tentatively interested in cosmetic surgery, her skin always the same very faint golden colour to set off her hair, this habit was not vanity but an occasional, sudden, vertiginous loss of self, brought on by the experience of talking to a voice over the airwaves, and not a person in the flesh. When talking on the mobile she needed these occasional reminders that she was still actually there, and it was this unconscious need which underlay this habit of needing to look at her reflection. 'I'll go ahead and book,' she said, turning her face from side to side and keeping eye contact in the mirror. 'I'll send you the deets. Big kiss.'

'Love you lots,' said Saskia, who then broke the connection. Arabella moved back to her computer and started to fill out the hotel booking form. From downstairs she could just hear the sound of three voices, in three familiar tones: Conrad was making an accusation, Joshua was raising his voice to drown him out, and Pilar was interceding between them. But it was not a 'go to' noise and Arabella had no difficulty in ignoring it. Then Arabella heard something which got her full attention: the flap of the letter box opening and closing, and a thump of mail landing on the doormat. It sounded as if there were some catalogues there; and Arabella loved her catalogues. She opened the door of her dressing room and came down the stairs as quietly as she could, making a mental note to have Bogdan look and see if there was a way to make it less creaky. Catalogues! Arabella bent and picked up brochures from two different travel companies – that was in case she finally got her husband to agree to go to Kenya for February half-term. There were a couple of uninteresting-looking letters for him, a credit-card bill for her, and a postcard with no addressee other than their house number. Her first thought was that this was an unsolicited offer from an estate agent: these came through at the rate of two a week and she enjoyed being irritated by them and the compliment they paid to the desirability of her house. Arabella noticed the postcard carried a second-class stamp; no one she knew used second-class stamps. The printed text on the card said 'We Want What You Have'. The postcard was a photograph of their front door. It must be a viral ad thing. There would be a follow-up and then another card finally revealing the point of the exercise as some semi-criminal estate agent finally confessed to a wish to sell her home for her. Arabella took the catalogues and the card upstairs, the catalogues to read and the card to keep for the rainy day when they decided to sell up and get somewhere bigger.

7

At ten o'clock Shahid was stacking unsold men's magazines behind the counter, prior to returning them to the wholesaler,
when the only customer in the shop fainted. She was a little old
lady who had come in and was looking at the dairy products in
the fridge. Or at least that's what she was doing one moment.
The next thing Shahid knew, there was a thumping sound and
she had fallen sideways in the right-hand aisle. It was not a loud
noise but it was an unnatural one – the unmistakable noise of
a body falling over. Ahmed, who had been in the kitchen doing
paperwork, came running through and joined him as he lifted
the counter flap and hurried to her.

The old lady was already stirring where she lay; she couldn't
have been out for long. Perhaps she hadn't even lost consciousness. Shahid didn't think he'd ever seen her before, but he had
the young man's obliviousness to the old – to him, everyone over
the age of sixty looked the same. Ahmed on the other hand did
seem to know her, because as he bent down to help, he said, 'Mrs
Howe!'

'I'm all right, dear,' said the old lady, not sounding the least bit
all right. She was doing that thing people do when they have accidents, of pretending nothing had happened and that they were
completely fine. 'Don't trouble yourself. Wobbly for a second but
I'm fine. Right as rain!'

'Take your time,' said Ahmed. 'Sit for a moment.' He sat beside her with his arm on her shoulder, looking a little uncomfortable at the intimacy he had offered. Shahid went behind the counter. On the CCTV camera underneath the till, Ahmed and Mrs Howe looked strange, like something out of a *Crimewatch* reconstruction: the Asian man crouched on the floor next to the old white lady, neither of them moving. If it had been a film you would have soon tired of it. For the next quarter of an hour Ahmed sat talking to the old lady while Shahid served three customers with a *Daily Mirror*, an Oyster top-up, and five scratchcards respectively. It was a strange lull, Shahid carrying on normally while his brother squatted beside the ill woman like a paramedic. Ahmed was a pompous dickhead in many respects, but Shahid had to admit, it was his brother's good side that he knew who the woman was and didn't treat her just as a nuisance to be cleared up as briskly as possible.

'I'm going to help Mrs Howe home,' said Ahmed, coming behind the counter to pick up his jacket. 'She's just around the corner. Back in five.'

'I'll hold the fort,' said Shahid, saluting. Ahmed didn't seem to think that was funny.

Ahmed gave Mrs Howe his arm and helped her lever herself up off the floor. Old people were right to dread falls. His first thought when he saw that she had fallen was that she must have broken something, a leg or a hip, which at that age could be the beginning of the end, but she seemed to be physically intact. Ahmed picked up her bag and, with Mrs Howe still holding on to his arm, the two of them headed for the door. Ahmed knew that Mrs Howe lived in Pepys Road but didn't know in which house.

'I'm about halfway down the road,' Petunia said. A couple of hundred yards. At the rate they were travelling, that was going to take a while. 'I'm so grateful and so very very sorry.'

'It is me who should be grateful. If I weren't with you I would have to be doing my accounts. I hate doing my accounts.'

'I don't know what came over me. Everything just started whirling. Next thing you know I was on the floor. Do you know, that's the first time I've ever fainted. Managed to get to eighty-two without doing it. Bad luck for you, eh?'

'I won't hear of it,' said Ahmed.

The day was clear and cold. The light was so bright that Ahmed had to hold up his hand to block it out when they crossed the road. He could feel Mrs Howe's thinness; he could feel her trembling, either with cold or shock or fatigue or a little of all three. Petunia knew that he could feel her shaking and was also conscious that this was the first time she had touched a man other than her son-in-law and grandsons since Albert died.

For Ahmed, who felt that he was always in a rush, that any given day was at its heart an equation with too many tasks and too few minutes, the list of things to do never shrinking while the time in which to do things constantly contracted, there was something very strange about moving so slowly. It was like one of those exercises where they make people walk backwards, or wear blindfolds in their own houses, to make the familiar feel different. He could feel – he couldn't help himself – a wave of the irritation he so often felt, at so many different things, in the course of an ordinary day. At the same time he managed to slow himself down and check the irritation, by telling himself that there was no point in doing a good deed if all it made you do was feel bad-tempered.

'Just suddenly everything was going round,' said Petunia, still on the subject of her first-ever faint. Then she said, 'Here we are,' and opened the gate of number 42. The window had some old-fashioned coloured glass in it, an abstract circular pattern. Ahmed – he couldn't help himself – wondered for a moment what the house was worth. If it was tatty on the inside but structurally sound, which would be his best guess, one and a half million.

'I'm fine from here,' said Petunia.

'Let me see you in,' said Ahmed. He helped her over the threshold. His guess had been right. There was clean but old carpet and ugly wallpaper with a flower pattern, and a telephone in the hallway. One million six. Ahmed reprimanded himself and gave Mrs Howe his full attention. There was some back-and-forth about whether he should call her daughter for her, or call a doctor, and her saying she wouldn't hear of it, and then to get rid of him Petunia had to promise that he could bring the newspaper around on days when she wanted it – she didn't get a daily delivery because she didn't want a daily paper. They were mostly full of rubbish and why would she want to keep up anyway?

'OK, OK,' said Ahmed. 'Let me write the telephone number down.' He had a biro but no paper, and went to look for some in the scraps on the table beside the doorway, next to the telephone. There were leaflets for pizza and curry; he took one up and wrote the number on the back.

'I'll put it by the phone,' he said. 'Call!' As he was replacing the leaflet on the hall table he noticed that Petunia too had a card with a picture of her house on it.

'We had one of those this morning,' he said. '"We Want What You Have."'

'When you're my age, nobody wants what you have,' said Petunia, and Ahmed laughed.

'We older people have to stick together, Mrs Howe,' he said. Normally she would have made a joke back, but she was too preoccupied, too deep inside herself, to properly register what he had said.

8

The most unpopular woman in Pepys Road walked slowly down the pavement, taking her time, spreading fear and confusion. She looked from right to left, she looked ahead and back, and no detail escaped her. She seemed to have all the time in the world yet also to be possessed with a sense of mission and purpose. She did not look conscious of the fear and confusion she spread and yet she was, deeply so.

Quentina Mkfesi BSc, MSc (Political Science, University of Zimbabwe, thesis subject: Post-Conflict Resolution in Non-Post-Colonial Societies, with special reference to Northern Ireland, Spain and Chile) was on the lookout for non-residents parked in residents' parking areas, for business permit holders parked in residents' areas and vice versa, for expired permits of both types, for people who had overstayed their paid parking or – and this was a particularly fruitful issue in Pepys Road – for people who had misinterpreted the parking signs and paid for parking but were not parked in the dual-use, residents' or paid-parking area, but were instead parked in the residents-only area. She was alert to cars parked carelessly, protruding into the public thoroughfare or with one wheel on the pavement. She could also issue tickets for out-of-date vehicle duty. She was not a cruel warden – she regularly allowed a period of grace for out-of-date residents' permits and unpaid road tax. But she was a very sharp one. She was dressed in a dark green uniform accessorised with webbing in a paler shade of green, trousers which had white strap-like detailing on the bottom of the legs, and a peaked cap. She looked like the Marx Brothers' idea of a colonel in the Ruritanian customs service from 1905.

The government, the council, and the company Quentina worked for all publicly and repeatedly denied that there was a quota for issuing parking tickets. That was, as everybody knew, a flat lie. Of course there was a quota. Quentina's was for twenty tickets a day, yielding £1,200 in revenue if all the violators paid within the two weeks' grace period, and usually more because many of them did not. If there were no appeals upheld – and Quentina, who was good at her job, had the lowest level of upheld appeals of any current employee of Control Services – the revenue in practice would be worth about £1,500 a day. If she worked 250 days a year that meant Quentina was generating revenue of £375,000 per annum. In return for that she was, in theory, paid £12,000, with four weeks' paid holiday and no health or pension benefits.

Today was showing signs of being a good day. Not because she had already written ten tickets, all of them rock-solid valid, and it wasn't yet ten o'clock in the morning – no, that was easy, that was, for a warden of Quentina's talents and experience, routine. It was showing signs of being a good day for another reason. Quentina and four other of the African employees of Control Services played a game whose rules were simple: the person who gave out a ticket to the most expensive car was the winner. Photos were required for proof. Sometimes the prize involved a free drink or a £5 bet, sometimes it was played for honour alone. Quentina had been on a losing streak. But now it seemed her luck was on the move. 27 Pepys Road was, Quentina happened to know, owned by a solicitor who worked for a Premiership football club based in West London. The club sometimes rented the house from him; it had properties nearer their training ground in Surrey but people occasionally wanted to live in town. Quentina had long thought this might be a good place to find a very expensive car without a resident's permit, so she made a point of regularly visiting Pepys Road, which was otherwise only an averagely productive area from a warden's point of view. But not today. In the visitors' parking section there was a Range Rover with only twenty minutes left and a silver Golf with '05 licence plates which had to move in the next hour – nothing much of interest there. But three parking spaces along from the football solicitor's house there was the car of Quentina's dreams, an Aston Martin DB7, a James Bond car with an on-the-road price of £150,000. What made it even better was that the man driving it had bought a parking ticket but – clearly he didn't know the most recent set of changes in Pepys Road – he had parked in the residents-only area, not the residents-and-visitors area. He had made the classic Pepys Road parking mistake.

With no one in the street and no reason to think she was about to be interrupted, Quentina would normally have gone straight up to the car, written the ticket and taken the pictures and been done. Sometimes, though, it paid to be cunning. She was not a warden who often resorted to tricks but sometimes you had to be street-smart, and so Quentina walked another fifty or so metres past the car, making a mental note of the number and make and model, and then as-if-absent-mindedly tapped the data into her PDA. People were less likely to come running out shouting if they didn't see you standing right there by the car. The invalid ticket on the car had another hour to run so she should have had plenty of time before the driver came out but you could not be sure; it paid to be careful. Quentina printed the ticket out and wrapped it in the plastic envelope. Now it was game on. She turned, moved briskly to the gleaming, recently washed silver car, snapped up the windscreen wiper – even that felt expensive – and stuck down the violation notice, then, stepping up and down off the kerb and moving backwards to get the relevant parking sign into shot, snapped off four digital photos. As the locals would say: Result!

Everybody hated being ticketed, just as everyone hated all the traffic on the roads except themselves. Everyone knew that the city would grind to a halt without restrictions on where cars could and couldn't park, and everyone knew that everybody would disobey all the laws without compunction if they weren't enforced. It was just that nobody wanted the laws to apply to them. Part of the problem, as Quentina had been told several times, was that 'the laws against drivers are the only fucking laws that are ever fucking enforced'. But that, Quentina felt, wasn't her problem. She had no fear of confrontation, which was just as well as it was a very unusual workday that did not feature at least one or two altercations with upset or furious or hysterically weeping or racially abusive or threatening or not entirely sane freshly ticketed motorists. Still, it was better for everyone to avoid ugly scenes, and Quentina was in a good mood as she moved off down Pepys Road. Because she was in a good mood, and because it would have no effect on the quota either way, she merely noted a ten-days-out-of-date resident's permit on an '03-reg A-class Mercedes, and magnanimously took no action. Quentina went to spread fear and confusion somewhere else. It was going to be fun after work, showing the photo of the Aston Martin. Quentina planned to tell people she'd personally ticketed James Bond himself. In his tuxedo. And that he'd been with the woman from *Casino Royale*.

9

Michael Lipton-Miller, 'Mickey' to his friends, stood in the investment property he owned at 27 Pepys Road with a clipboard under his left arm, a BlackBerry held to his right ear, an iPhone vibrating in his left jacket pocket, a dehydration headache, a solicitor's letter setting up an appointment to discuss his divorce terms in his right jacket pocket, and a briefcase at his feet. Of all these things, the one which caused him to feel least thrilled with life in general was the clipboard, which held a list of all the things which should have been done at the house to make it ready for a new arrival. Mickey was a qualified solicitor who no longer practised the law but instead worked full-time as a factotum, fixer and odd-job man for a Premiership football club. He loved his work and loved the sense of himself as a man who got things done, whose approach to life was a bit flashy, a bit wide – but had the other connotations of the word 'wide' too, a sense of breadth, of generosity, of largeness of spirit. His ideal sense of this did not involve checking over an itemised list of crockery, DVD equipment and toilet paper, but he had sacked his assistant last week (the search for a replacement would be what the vibrating phone was about – there were times, Mickey liked to joke, when putting the phone on vibrate was the nearest thing to sex he got all week) so here he was mired in the daily detail of making spoilt footballers happy. He was fifty years old.

In front of Mickey was the woman from the contract cleaning

agency, whose job it had been to supervise the cleaners. She was tall and lean and had high cheekbones: fit. To Mickey's eye she looked East African. She had that disconcerting African patience as she stood there while Mickey ranted and bollocked somebody else over the phone; she did not look like someone waiting for a verdict to be passed on her work. Standing next to her, Mickey had a thought he often had about good-looking young women: he was amazed that more of them did not sell their bodies for sex. It would surely be easier and much more lucrative than working – certainly than this sort of work – and could it really be so bad? People would pay hundreds of pounds to have sex with this woman, so why on earth would she instead want to clean houses for £4.50 an hour or whatever the sodding minimum wage was? Maybe he should put in an offer. And then Mickey, in the privacy of his own head, told himself: only joking.

'Right right, sorry sorry,' said Mickey. 'Shall we have a look? I'm sure it's all fine, darling,' Mickey said, being Good Cop, 'but you know the powers that be . . .'

The cleaner was not falling for any charm. She just gave a minimally polite nod.

Mickey started taking the tour. Because the house was not usually lived in for more than about three months at a time, often less, and because the people who lived there came from all over the place, it was decorated in a semi-expensive version of Hotel-Room Neutral. The players often came from families with no money and their only encounters with affluent style came from hotels, so that was a style they felt was aspirational. The walls were a complicated shade of Swedish white, the furniture was a mixture of modern stuff, the video and sound system were some Japanese make Mickey had never heard of but were also wired under the floorboards so that no one could accidentally forget that they belonged to the landlord and not the tenant. This time it was an African kid who was coming to London and was going to bring his dad. 'Kid' really did mean kid – he was seventeen. The boy was going to be starting on twenty grand a week with options to go higher or break the contract after a year. Mickey, who was fluent in money, who had grown up wanting to make money and thought that everything about making shed-loads of money was fine, was admirable, was a high and noble goal – even Mickey sometimes felt ill when he thought about how much money was knocking around in football these days.

Why had the kid chosen to live here and not somewhere nice and suburban? Who knew? In any case it hadn't been the boy but his father who had made the choice. Mickey thought the dad had probably been freaked out by the whiteness of the suburbs and preferred to live somewhere he might occasionally see the odd black face. It would not last, it never did. Klinsmann had lived in London and so had Lineker, and one or two of the European players still did, but by and large they all moved out to the Surrey rockbroker belt as soon as they could. Mickey himself lived in Richmond, not far from Pete Townshend and Mick Jagger.

Floors scrubbed – check. Windows so clean they're invisible – check. Loos you could eat your dinner off – check. TV system with more buttons and lights than the flight deck of the Space Shuttle – check. TV actually working – check. Wireless broadband working – check. Carpets clean, beds made, windowsills dusted – checkety-check. The fridge was stocked, though whether it was stuffed with things Africans ate Mickey didn't know, and didn't care since that was the club-appointed housekeeper's problem; the dad spoke some English but the kid didn't, only French, so the club had lined up a translator, a French-speaking housekeeper, and an English teacher. All that was someone else's worry so that was fine by Mickey.

It all seemed OK. Mickey had kept his game face on throughout. As he finished he felt like relieving his feelings a little, so he turned to the housekeeper.

'You understand about confidentiality?'

She nodded but did not speak.

'No, I mean you really understand?'

She nodded again. He had planned to do a version of the confidentiality bollocking he gave people, about how they were not allowed to say anything to anyone, ever. The housekeeper was so blank and seemed so indifferent, not in an incompetent am-I-bovvered? way but as if her real being was deeply buried somewhere else, that he lost the impetus to go on with it. It was a bit like losing an erection. Too bad. Mickey liked the confidentiality bollocking, because it gave a sense of importance and drama to the work; and the fact was, there was something glamorous about even the mundane aspects of Premier League football. Checking the supply of loo rolls: because a Premiership player was involved, it was important and interesting. Mickey knew plenty of things that people were desperate to know – most of them variations on the theme of 'what is X really like?' – as if there were a special category of knowledge called 'really likeness' – as if it were somehow the ultimate question.

'It seems to be OK,' he told the cleaner. She nodded again. Obviously this was Nod at Mickey Day. Well, two can nod. So he nodded back and headed for the door. There were a couple of bits of post, which he picked up on the way out – an electricity bill and a card which said 'We Want What You Have'. Mickey had a flash of divorce-paranoia – Dinah's brief was out to get him! – and then realised it was actually to do with 27 Pepys Road, because the other side of the card was a photo of the front door. This, Mickey thought, was almost certainly something to do with a newspaper staking out the house; maybe it was something specifically to do with the African kid. There were rumours that he'd been poached from Arsenal, or something. Maybe this was loopy Arsenal fans threatening the kid or trying to spook him. Bugger! Mickey thought that the last thing he needed today, as his phone started vibrating again, was a tricky what-should-I-do?

He was wrong about that. Something else turned out to be the last thing he needed. When Mickey came out onto the street he found that his car had been ticketed and clamped.

10

Two weeks before Christmas, Petunia sat in her doctor's surgery, waiting for her name to appear on the electronic screen behind her. It was a Monday, and the surgery was even busier than usual. There were no seats available facing the screen, so every time she heard the beep indicating that another patient was summoned, she had to turn and look and see if her turn had come.

Petunia didn't much like that she had to do that. When her name came up she would get up and go through to see her doctor and then everyone would know that she was Mrs Petunia Howe, whether she wanted them to know who she was or not, and her name would then stay up there until the next name came up in lights on the board. She was no spring chicken and to turn her neck enough to see she had to swivel the whole top half of her body, and although every other person in the facing-away seats was doing this too, including the ones who were listening to earphones and talking on their mobiles – two of the people doing that were sitting directly beneath a 'No Mobile Phones' sign, which was so awful it was almost funny – it still made her feel self-conscious. There was also the fact that the whole reason she had come to see the doctor in the first place was because of these funny dizzy spells, her 'turns' as she called them – she had had several more since that time in the newsagent's, though mercifully all the subsequent episodes had been at home, which was one blessing, and never when she was on the stairs, which was another. But twisting her neck every minute or two was starting to make her feel funny and the last thing she wanted was to keel over here in the surgery. And all to save the doctor the ten seconds' effort involved in getting up, walking to the door, and calling out the patient's name – not going over and actually addressing the patient, of course, since there was no chance the doctor would have any sense of who they were. In the last half an hour – the half an hour since her appointment was scheduled to start – Miss Linda Wong, Mr Denton Matarato, Miss Shoonua Barkshire, Mr T. Khan, and Master Cosmo Dent had gone through to see their doctors, but Petunia was still sitting there. She had long since finished the copy of the *Daily Mail* she'd found on the table beside her and was agonising over whether it would be bad manners to fill in the quick crossword in a communal newspaper; she rather thought it was.

Although Petunia was not a grumbler and a complainer-about-modern-life – Albert had done enough for both of them, for several lifetimes – there was nothing much about her doctor's that she liked. For one thing, she did not like that it wasn't really her doctor at all – there wasn't such a person as 'her' GP. In the last twenty years, though she had at one time or another seen more or less every doctor at the practice, she had never seen the same doctor twice in a row. There was something diminishing and impersonal about that and it certainly did not reduce the amount of time that the doctor would spend looking at the computer screen and reading about her, as opposed to looking at her and listening to what she had to say. Petunia disliked feeling such an alien, such an exotic, sitting here in the surgery, where everyone was in Lycra, or crop tops, or T-shirts, or texting, or nodding to just-audible music, or wearing headscarves (two women) or in full concealing hijab (one) or speaking Eastern European languages to each other or over their mobiles. We're all in this together: Petunia was the right age for that once to have been a very important idea, a defining idea, about what it meant to be British. Was it still true? Were they in it together? Could she look around the surgery and truthfully say that?

Finally, finally, 'Ms Petuna How' came up on the board. Close enough. Petunia carefully got to her feet – that was something she was more and more wary about now – and moved through. She could feel people looking at her, never her favourite sensation. A man moved his legs out of the way to let her through but the fact that he did it without looking up from his newspaper or in any other way acknowledging her presence made it even ruder than ignoring her would have been. Albert would have had something to say to him.

The doctor's door was open. When Petunia knocked to let him know she was there, he said, 'Hi! Come in,' while reading something on his computer screen. She went in and sat down. He turned towards her, smiling, and she knew what he was going to say:

'Petunia, what can I do for you today?'

Dr Canseca, this was. Petunia had had him a couple of times before. His name was Latin but he wasn't, not in any way you could notice: he had fair hair combed sideways and always wore a tie and pale V-neck sweaters which looked as though they were made of cashmere, even though the surgery was never under-heated and often boiling. If pressed, on the basis of appearances, Petunia would have put his age at about seventeen, though she supposed he must be thirty or so.

She began to describe her symptoms, the dizziness and fainting and general sense of being under the weather, and after she had spoken for about fifteen seconds, during which time he was nodding and making encouraging noises, Dr Canseca turned to his keyboard and, still nodding, began to type. Petunia had worked as a secretary in her youth and it was interesting how things had changed so that the person doing the typing was now the more important one.

Petunia came to the end of saying what was wrong and stopped talking. The doctor typed on in silence for a minute.

'Any weakness on one side or the other? Funny tingling feelings?'

Petunia shook her head. Dr Canseca asked some more questions. Then he asked if he could take Petunia's blood pressure and listen to her chest. She had dreaded this but had also prepared for it by wearing, under her coat and jacket and cardigan, a blouse which was easy to unbutton. She took off the various layers and was suddenly glad of the overheated room. Funny to think her breasts had once been her prize asset. Her skin felt as if it wanted to goose-bump and mottle, but did not. Should have asked for a woman doctor, she thought – but asking for things at the doctor's did not come naturally to Petunia, she was the wrong type and wrong age. Dr Canseca did not ask her to take her top off but instead slid the stethoscope up inside her blouse. The metal was freezing of course but at least she still had her top on. She breathed in and out, her breaths sounding a little rackety and thready even to her. Then the doctor took her blood pressure. Then he took it again. Then he sat looking at his computer screen for a little while.

'You're not on any medication, are you?' It wasn't really a question so Petunia didn't answer. He began typing. While he did that Petunia read the poster behind his head, about safe sex. There were also posters about the different health risks you could be exposed to travelling to far-off parts of the world. Then he turned to Petunia.

'Well, you seem all right, but I'm just going to send you off for a couple of tests. When somebody faints, sometimes it's a sign that everything's not right with their ticker. Their hearts, your heart. Your blood pressure is on the low side. That's a good thing! You lot live for ages! So, I'm writing off to Tommies, and they'll send you a letter, and you call and make an appointment, and we'll get it all fixed. All right?'

And that was it. Petunia only ever went to the doctor reluctantly, and her motive in doing so was always the same: she did it in order to feel less anxious about things. The doctor was supposed to make the worry go away; she did quite enough worrying without actually having something to worry about. When she came out feeling no less anxious, as this time, something had gone wrong. The basic contract had been broken. Petunia came out through the surgery, again feeling slightly self-conscious – too self-conscious to go into the loo, on the other side of the room beside the door, even though she could have done with a pee before the walk home in the cold. She braced herself and went out through the two sets of sliding doors into the December afternoon, with the air cold and damp and the traffic roaring past. It would take about fifteen minutes to walk home. Petunia pulled her hat down, tightened her scarf around her neck, checked that her coat was properly buttoned, adjusted the way her handbag lay over her shoulder, put her hands into her pockets, and set out.

Albert had not been a big fan of her worrying. It was one of the things he would lecture her about, which was no help at all, since all that did was make her less free to express her worries, so she kept them to herself, which had the effect of magnifying them. Which made her more fretful, which in turn irritated Albert more. And it had been hypocritical of Albert too, since he had so many bees in his own bonnet, especially about money, and tax, and savings, and the untrustworthiness of banks and insurance companies and credit-card companies and the government and everybody else, and the way that you couldn't be too careful. He wouldn't even have a cashpoint card, because he didn't trust machines or PIN numbers; after his death their daughter Mary had had to teach her how to use one. That was one of the many, many things she had had to learn to do for herself after Albert dropped dead.

A lot of those things had been to do with money. What it came down to was that Albert, like lots of people, had had a streak of madness running through his character, like a seam running through a rock. He was not, in general, mad; but when the subject was money, he could not be relied on to be sane. For him, money was out of perspective, both all-important (because it at times seemed to be all he thought about) but also completely out of step with reality, so that he wouldn't do normal things like use a bank or have a pension; he would never pay a bill before, not the reminder, and not the final reminder, but the threat of legal action. It was exhausting; it was mad. But even someone like Albert, obsessively miserly though he became, had to pay gas and electricity bills. He had once mentioned the possibility of getting one or other of these utilities put on a coin-operated meter, and that was one of the few times Petunia had put her foot down with him, telling him no very firmly and then putting up with two weeks' silence while he sulked. And then after a fortnight's huff he had got up in the morning perfectly calm and behaving as if none of it had ever happened. One of the effects of this was that she now missed him in particular when she had to do the practical things that he had taken all on himself, the water bills and the rates and checking that her pension had been paid and worrying about the plumbing. All of these were a bore and a burden in themselves and they also made Petunia miss the man who was missing.

It was funny that most of the specific stories she could tell about Albert made him sound awful – the money stuff, the arguments he'd get into with people, his sheer impossibility. He could make a point of principle about absolutely anything. The things that had been good about him, his warmth and kindness and unpredictable sensitivity, the way he'd do good deeds for people and not tell her about them (loans of cash, a lift home, writing letters when people were bereaved), the sense that he was basically a loving man – those translated much less well into stories that you could tell. His good side had been fully on show only to her.

Petunia was now passing the posh butcher's in the high street. There was a queue, as there often was – the new people who lived in the area, unthinkingly rich. In the window a turkey had been decorated with a gold ribbon and a crown. At its feet was a sign saying 'Order Me'.

Walking past the bright lights and tat of the imminent holiday, Petunia thought about the way that Albert had loved Christmas. You would have expected him to be Scrooge, but he loved every bit of the ritual, from the advent calendar to the hymns to the hats to the Queen's Speech (which he enjoyed being rude about: 'the amazing thing about that family is the way every single member of them gets slightly stupider every year'). He loved seeing Mary and her children at Christmas, even though the holiday made their daughter revert to being a stroppy fifteen-year-old again, silent and grumpy and always judging everything. She couldn't blame Mary for moving away to Essex. She needed to get away. She didn't have to be quite so far away now that her father was dead and her mother lived alone in a big house, but that was her choice and Petunia understood it without liking it.

Albert had been a difficult man, there was no denying that. She had spent more time and energy coping with her husband than a person ought to do. When he died, part of that energy ought to have gone into something else. Her life should have opened up a bit, if only in a private feeling of being a little freer. It hadn't and that, Petunia had to admit, was her own fault. She had blamed Albert for a certain narrowness in the way they lived, but she did not live any more broadly in his absence. Perhaps the problem was that she hadn't had a clear idea of what that broader life might have been: travel, or going out more often, or, or . . . what, exactly? Petunia had always liked colour but she didn't feel she had had much of it in her own life. Or rather she felt she had had all too much of one single colour, grey. Since Albert's death, Petunia would sometimes have the feeling that she could look back over her life and see nothing but grey. From a moral point of view, it is not possible to be too good; but from the point of view of daily living, making your way in the world and demanding your share of its good things, there is a way of being good which does not help you. Petunia had some of that too-quiet, too-undemanding goodness. Given a choice between someone else's needs and her own, she would always opt to put the other person's needs first. And this was one of the things which now made her sometimes feel that everything about her life had been spent in a narrow range of monotones.

Now she was at the end of her own street, Pepys Road, where she had been born and where if she had any say in it she would die. She must have taken this trip ten thousand times in her life. She had done it in a thousand different moods; in fact one of the happiest days of her life had been when she made this very same walk, back from the doctors', on the day she found out she was pregnant. She had gone in the door sad, she had gone in exhausted, she had gone in feeling flat, fat, sexy, giggly, furious, absent-minded, tipsy from holiday sherry, in a flat rush to get to the loo, in every physical or mental state possible. She had gone through a phase of being frightened that robbers would rush up behind her as her attention was on opening the door, and grab her bag or force their way into the house; but that fear, and others like it, had long since passed. It was still the same house and still the same door and still the same her walking through it.

We want what you have. Petunia thought about that strange

67

card for a moment. She still found it hard to imagine anyone saying those words to her face.

11

Bogdan the builder, whose name was not really Bogdan, sat at the kitchen table in the Younts' house. He was drinking strong tea from a mug; he had come to like tea and fully understood why the English took it seriously. In front of him was a sheet of paper with numbers on it and a pen and a plate with a biscuit which he had taken out of politeness but did not intend to eat. Across from him sat Arabella Yount, who was drinking weak Lapsang Souchong out of a cup and adjusting her hair behind her ears. She was wearing make-up, tiny diamond earrings, and what she called 'non-going-out clothes': a pink velour tracksuit.

'Don't spare me, Bogdan. Is it horrible? Just how bad is it? I can't bear the suspense. Is it truly awful? It is, isn't it?' said Arabella happily.

Bogdan, whose name was Zbigniew Tomascewski, put his pencil next to the first line of items on his list and said:

'It is not too bad.'

Arabella sighed in relief.

'But it will not be cheap.'

Arabella picked up her cup of tea, sipped it, and shrugged. Zbigniew said:

'I find some things cheap, I am careful but not too careful, eight thousand. I buy new, everything top-spec, five-year guarantee – you know me Mrs Yount, my personal guarantee – twelve thousand.'

'Does that include the thingies, the electricity thingies?'

'The wiring. Yes, it includes everything we discussed.'

Arabella was having some alterations made to her dressing room and to Joshua's bedroom. The lighting in the dressing room was unsatisfactory. Arabella felt that the bright lights around the mirrors flattened the planes of her face and made her look like an Eskimo.

'I should probably check with Roger. I should, but I can't be bothered. That's fine. When did you think you might be able to start?'

Zbigniew was a sharp student of his British customers and knew that in this country builders had a reputation for specific things: they were expensive and lazy; they were never available when you wanted them; they took over your house and behaved as if it were theirs during the work; and they left things half-finished and went off to another job so that the last phase of the work dragged on for months. He set out always to be the opposite of all those things and to stick to this policy at all times. So although he had a few things due to start, he said, 'Next week.'

'Oh, fantastic,' said Arabella, adjusting her hair behind her ear. 'Fabulous! That's so great!'

Arabella had a habit of overstating things, one that she had so much internalised that it was not always easy for she herself to tell when she was mildly pleased about something and when she was genuinely delighted. Gresham's Law was at work: the cheap money of overstatement was gradually driving out the good money of true feeling. But she was in this case genuinely pleased. She wanted the changes made to her room and she wanted them soon and was pleased that Bogdan would be able to do them, because, beneath the hyperbole, she liked and trusted him.

'I think I should go now,' said Zbigniew/Bogdan. He took up his pad and pencil and put them in his bag. 'Next week?'

'Thank you so much. Next week it is. Crack of dawn. Lovely! Thanks, Bogdan.'

He slung his bag over his shoulder and went out into the street. It was raining but not cold in a serious Polish way. Some of the houses had Christmas decorations up; a couple of them were places where Zbigniew had done some work over the past year. He liked walking past places where he had done things. He never forgot a work project, the bathroom conversion over there and the loft conversion where they'd put a shower in against all advice and then had to run cables up to the top floor to power the immersion heater. The memory of the work on these places was a muscle memory, a physical sensation: he could feel it in his bones, the effort, the exertion, the tired fingers and aching back at the end of the day. But it wasn't an unpleasant feeling. Real work never left you feeling worse.

His first job in London had been on a crew in the next street, Mackell Road, and someone had recommended them to number 54 in this street; the job was for one man and his old friend Piotr had let him take it, for which Zbigniew was and always would be grateful. That was when he had acquired his London nickname, too, because there was a Bogdan on the crew and the man in Pepys Road had got the names mixed up, and Zbigniew had never corrected him. He quite liked being called Bogdan because it left no doubt in his mind that he did not really live in London, that his life here was a temporary interlude: he was there to work and make money before going home to his real life in Poland. Zbigniew did not know whether that would be in a year's time or five years or ten, but he knew it was going to happen. He was Polish and his real life would be in Poland.

Arabella would have been disappointed if she had known what her Bogdan thought of her, because the truth was, he thought very little. He didn't have a negative impression of her, or a positive one; he neither fancied her, disliked her, was interested in her, or had any other feeling about her at all. She was a client and that was it. Zbigniew thought of all his clients the same way: they were people who paid him to do work and had certain expectations which he set out to fulfil. There was no more to it than that.

As for their wealth – Arabella's wealth, the wealth of all his clients – he did not dwell on it but he did notice it. A boy who grew up in a tower block on the outskirts of Warsaw could not fail to notice marble worktops, teak furniture, carpets and clothes and adult toys and the routine daily extravagances that were everywhere in this city. You also couldn't fail to notice the expense, the grotesque costliness of more or less everything, from accommodation to transport to food to clothes; and as for going out to have some fun, that was almost impossible. The feeling of this cash leaking away just in ordinary life depressed Zbigniew. But in another sense it was the reason he was here: everything was so expensive because the British had lots of money. He was there to earn it from them. There was in Zbigniew's opinion something fundamentally wrong with a culture that had all this work and all this money going spare, just waiting for someone to come in and pick it up, almost as if the money were just left lying around in the street – but that was not his concern. If the British wanted to give work and money away that was fine with him.

His mobile rang. It was Piotr.

'Your turn to cook tonight,' Piotr said in Polish. 'I got some kielbasa from the shop, they're in the fridge. Don't eat them all before I get back, OK?'

Zbigniew, Piotr, and four friends lived in a two-bedroom flat in Croydon. The flat was sublet from an Italian who in turn sublet it from a British man who rented it from the council, and the rent was £200 a week. They had to be careful about noise because if the other residents reported them they would be kicked out – but in fact the polite, well-built young men were popular tenants in the flats, whose other occupants were old and white and, as one of them once told Zbigniew in the hallway, 'just grateful you aren't Pakis'.

'You're seeing Dana,' said Zbigniew – Dana being Piotr's latest potential love interest, a Czech girl he'd met in the pub. 'If you're not back by ten, no kielbasa.'

'If I'm not back by ten . . .' said Piotr.

'*Czekaj, tatka, latka,*' said Zbigniew. You can wait until the cows come home. He laughed. He had known Piotr since they were both tiny children, and his friend was a chronic romantic who constantly made the mistake of falling in love with women before sleeping with them. Zbigniew prided himself on avoiding this error.

Now there was the wait for the Tube. Five minutes, said the board, but that meant nothing. One thing about London which was like Warsaw was the difficult transport and the grumbling stoicism of the people who used it. The other guys at the flat were all out on the same job today and would be coming back in Piotr's trashed Ford van, which he had bought for next to nothing and had sort-of fixed up; Zbigniew hated using the van because there was such a strong feeling there was no reliability about getting to where you wanted to go. Zbigniew liked to feel in control.

A crowd of black kids arrived on the platform. Zbigniew had nothing against black people but after three years in England he had not yet got to the point where he did not even register their presence. He had a tendency to assess whether or not they looked likely to be trouble. These kids, seven or eight boys and girls, were loud – the girls more so than the boys, as if proving a point, which in this country often seemed to be the way. They were all simultaneously teasing each other about something.

'You never—'

'He never—'

'Batty man—'

But Zbigniew could see that these were good kids being noisy rather than bad ones on the verge of causing trouble. The old lady beside him, who had been waiting on the platform when he got there, wasn't happy. She would be thinking about her journey in the company of these shouting children. She was probably also wondering about walking off down the platform to somewhere else and worrying about that looking too rude. She wouldn't want to seem racist. Zbigniew knew that it was a big thing in this country not to seem racist. In his opinion people made too much fuss about it. People did not like people who were not like them, that was a plain fact of life. You had to get on with things anyway. Who cares if people don't like each other because of the colour of their skin?

The train came, heading for Morden. The rowdy children got on first, pushing past people who were trying to get off. There was nowhere to sit. The kids went to the other side of the compartment and a couple of them took seats. The others were standing around them and they were all still talking and yelling and showing everybody their high spirits. Most people in the train succeeded in ignoring them. Another of the ways in which London was like Warsaw was the way in which people occupied their own spaces, went inside themselves, on public transport.

Zbigniew got off at Balham and crossed to the train station. Miracle – a train was on the platform and about to move off. He got on. There were no seats but so what? All the people on the train were heading home from work, wrapped up in newspapers or themselves. Zbigniew leaned against the partition and swayed and bounced as the train racketed along. It was hot and crowded and uncomfortable in the compartment, but again, so what? Zbigniew was well aware that people here complained about public transport a lot. In his view they should just shut up. Yes, the transport was shit, but lots of things about life were shit.

None of them was improved by complaining. They should live in a place where life really was hard, for a while. Then they would begin to have an idea.

These thoughts made Zbigniew turn to wondering about his father. He, Michal Tomascewski, was a mechanic. He had worked for thirty years repairing buses for the city of Warsaw: hard and honest work. At the age of fifty he was too young to have much sense that the future would bring any pleasant surprises and nowhere near old enough or rich enough to retire – but there was, thanks to Zbigniew, the glimpse of a plan. Michal had for most of those thirty years had what amounted to a second job, looking after the lifts in their block of flats. Not quite every day, but never less than once a week, he would do some work on one or other of the three small metal boxes which were the lifeline and support mechanism of everyone in the block, especially the families who lived on the upper floors and especially especially the ones who had very old or very young members. News of his expertise in this area – and just as important, but perhaps even rarer, of his willingness to take responsibility – had got around and friends in other blocks had sometimes asked him to help them too. But there were only a finite number of hours in the day and Michal was now in his sixth decade and although he was willing to help people he was no sucker, so he did what he could comfortably do and no more.

Zbigniew's plan was as follows: to make enough money in London to go into the lift-maintenance business with his father. Warsaw was going to grow rapidly, anyone could see that, and modern cities grew upwards, and that meant lifts, which were – he could hear his father saying the words – 'the most reliable form of mechanical transportation in the world'. With capital they could set up together: his father would work less, earn ten times as much money, and within a few years he would retire or semi-retire in comfort. He could buy a cottage somewhere and shuffle around doing things in the garden and wearing slippers and on warm days he could have lunch outside with Zbigniew's mother. His father did not complain – Zbigniew had never heard him complain about anything, not one time – but he knew that his father loved the countryside, loved getting out of Warsaw to his brother's house in Brochow, loved the country air and the space and looking at farm animals instead of cars and trucks and buses. So he was going to earn his father the chance to enjoy that. Instead of sending the extra money he was earning home, Zbigniew was saving it, about half his sterling income, against the great happy day when he could turn up unannounced at his parents' apartment and tell them his news and his plan. That was a scene he often played in his head.

The train came to a stop at South Croydon and Zbigniew got off. The next leg of his journey was the M bus for about two kilometres, then the walk home. Kielbasa to cook and then he would play a few games of cards with whoever was hanging around the flat. Or if everyone was out he might get to use the PlayStation 2 and do a couple of missions of *San Andreas*. Some of them would go out to the pub but that was so horribly expensive that Zbigniew only allowed himself to do it one night a week and then went to one of the bars which had a 'happy hour' offering two drinks for the price of one. 'Happy hour': that made him laugh. There would be girls there; he had met his last girlfriend in a place called Shooters during happy hour. She eventually broke up with him after complaining that he never wanted to go anywhere and never wanted to do anything. That, Zbigniew still felt, was not fair. He had never wanted to go anywhere and never wanted to do anything *that cost money* – an important difference.

Today the stars were in alignment or his patron saint was smiling down on him or something, because the bus came immediately. He got on and found a seat about halfway back beside a girl who was listening to her iPod, smiling and nodding with her eyes closed. This was Zbigniew's least favourite part of the journey: although the trains could be frustrating they did at least tend to move, once they came, but the bus could take any amount of time at all. They could be home in two minutes or he could still be right here half an hour later. On some days, it was quicker to walk. This close to home, he started to think about sitting down and stretching his legs, having a shower, and all that. Today he should have bought a lottery ticket because the bus shot through the traffic like a fish heading downstream, and before Little Miss iPod had opened her eyes he was pressing the button for his stop.

The last part of the journey, on foot, was about ten minutes. Many of the houses had Christmas decorations on display in the windows, and wreaths on the front doors. They looked good to Zbigniew, comfortable and, in the way that so much of London did, rich, polished, shiny, finished. Then he was at their house. The tenants downstairs were still at work. He ran up the stairs and let himself in to find Tomas and Gregor, two new members of Piotr's crew, sitting on the sofa playing *God of War*.

One thing to do before he could relax. Zbigniew went into the bedroom he shared with Piotr and took his laptop computer out from under his bed, where it had been charging. He flipped it open and booted it up. This flat was not perfect, and sharing with five others was not perfect, and sharing a bedroom with one metre ninety of old friend who snored was particularly not perfect, but one great thing about it was that two neighbours had unencrypted wireless connections. Zbigniew logged on and went to check his portfolio. He was not day trading at the moment – he couldn't, he wasn't working at a house with broadband – but he still had £8,000, his entire savings, invested in stocks. At the moment he was mainly in tech, with half of his portfolio in Google, Apple and Nintendo, all of which had more than doubled in the past year. Today GOOG, AAPL and NTDOY had mainly gone sideways and his net position was £12.75 ahead of where it had been the day before. This was not significant and it seemed to Zbigniew that no action needed to be taken, so he put the computer to sleep and went to have a shower and cook the sausages.

12

Smitty, the performance and installation artist and all-round art-world legend, stood looking out the window of his studio in Shoreditch, waiting for his new assistant to come back with a triple-shot cappuccino and the daily papers. He had a black suit and white shirt on for visiting his nan, and could just see in the reflection that he looked, though he said so himself, pretty sharp: if his mum could have seen him, she would have been pleased. So that was good. Other things were not so good. He wasn't impressed by the performance of his new assistant, who had gone out twenty minutes ago, and who only needed about a quarter of that amount of time to get out and back, and who would therefore be returning with a cup of frothy coffee which was odds-on to be cold.

Looking out the window, Smitty surveyed the London scene: oldsters struggling with carrier bags on their way back from the supermarket, a crack whore topping up with Tennent's, pram-faces from the estate and their grub-white babies, immigrants from who knew where, Kosovo probably or wherever it was the latest lot came from. The street was noisy with distant traffic and drilling and people had put their orange recycling bags out, piled and spilling, but they hadn't been collected yet, so the pavement was a military-grade obstacle course. Smitty loved and approved of all he saw. London, life, London life. He felt an idea coming on. At the other end of the road, a group of workmen in bright orange safety jackets were standing around a hole they had dug about a week before. Two of them were smoking, the third was laughing, the fourth was drinking something from a thermos, and to one side of them their mechanical digger stood with its scoop pointing downwards. The way they were all grouped around the hole made it look as if the hole were their focus of attention, as if they were admiring it. That was what gave Smitty the idea: make a work of art about holes. Or, make holes the work of art. Yes, that was better. Dig some holes and make the hole the artwork, or rather the confusion and chaos the hole caused – people's reaction, not the thing itself. Yeah – bloody great hole, for no reason. Let the tossers argue about who fills it in. That's part of the artwork too.

This was how Smitty had made his name: through anonymous artworks in the form of provocations, graffiti, only-just-non-criminal vandalism, and stunts. He was famous for being unknown, a celebrity without identity, and it was agreed that his anonymity was his most interesting artefact – though the stunts made people laugh, too. He had a crew who he had known since for ever, and who helped him when he needed helping. Last year, the sale of signed works and his own book about himself had taken his earnings over £1,000,000 for the first time.

Smitty disliked writing things down – a dislike which meant he had struggled at school and been directed to what were regarded as non-subjects such as art, which had led him to art school, which had led him to where he was today, thanks – so he preferred to use a crappy hand-held dictaphone. He liked the way the object, which seemed so much a tool of corporate subjugation, so much the kind of thing which would belong to the kind of man who would murmur the kind of thing like 'Take a memo, Miss Potter,' was in his hands an instrument of subversion, of creativity, of chaos. Also his assistant would transcribe it later and then send him a text message, to his pay-as-you-go mobile which couldn't be traced, since a large part of Smitty's work, and an even larger part of his allure and his fame, was the fact of his total anonymity. No one knew who he was, or how he got away with what he did. In the case of the hole project, getting away with what he did would be a big part of it. A certain sort of artist would get council permission for the hole, would apply for a fucking grant for it. Not Smitty. He pressed Record and said:

'Bloody great hole.'

The assistant came up the stairs, put a slab of daily newspapers on the table and brought Smitty his cappuccino. It was half-hot, not quite cool enough to complain about, and he was out of breath so he had obviously been hurrying, which added together meant Smitty didn't feel quite justified in giving him a bollocking. All the same, he was a little displeased. The assistant was a middle-class boy pretending to be a streetwise working-class kid, which in itself Smitty didn't mind, since he had once been like that himself – but he did prefer his cappuccino piping hot. Then the boy took out the day's mail from the pocket of his manbag, and Smitty cheered up, since one of the things instantly recognisable among the letters was a fat packet from the clippings agency. His favourite reading, his favourite viewing and listening, was anything about himself, or his work. The coverage usually turned on the amazing thrill given to all by his anonymity.

Smitty tore open the envelope and a bunch of clippings fell out. Some of them were about the paperback of his book, a couple of them were reviews of a new piece he had made on an abandoned building site in Hackney. It had been called *Bucket of Shit* and had involved putting ten abandoned toilets around the rubble – only instead of being filled with shit, the toilets had been full of cut flowers, crunched together and spray-painted to look like oversize turds. He and his crew took photographs and sent press releases out by email. The council's contractors had cleared the piece within forty-eight hours but the harvest was here in the clippings, most of it favourable. Urban renovation and the ease with which we passed by, unseeing, the urban underclass; that was, apparently, what this latest 'guerrilla intervention' had been about. One or two of the usual twats didn't get it, but so what? It wasn't a popularity contest.

'Can I have a look at the clips?' asked the kid. He was – this was one of his better points, perhaps even his best – visibly excited by Smitty's fame and danger and aura. Smitty lobbed the cuttings onto the table in front of the boy and went back to looking out the window. Calmed and buoyed by his reading, Smitty felt himself become expansive.

'You've got to be a brand, man. Then you find some shit to flog, yeah? That's the way it works. A stunt like that, *Bucket*, takes effort to think through and set up and it's harder still when you've got to do it hands-off, so no one can trace it back. Got to be careful, got to cover your tracks, like those Indian dudes walking backwards in their footprints, yeah? And there's not a penny in it either. Nada, sweet FA. Which doesn't mean there's nothing in it, no forward movement. The stuff which can't be sold, that's the stuff which makes everything else seem real. You can't commodify this shit. Which is the whole point. But it adds to your mojo, to your aura. And that allows you to make shit you can sell. See? So that thing which cost whatever it was, four or five grand, by the time it was all in, the long run, it's what's paying for those papers and this cappuccino.'

The assistant, who had heard other versions of this speech before, nodded. But he did not look as fully alert or on the ball as he might do, and Smitty disapproved. He was, truth be told, a little tired of all the people who wanted to be him. Whose admiration was expressed as envy. He wasn't old, nowhere near – he was twenty-eight, for fuck's sake! – but he was already thoroughly familiar with young kids who thought that making your name was easy, that all that needed to happen was for the old-sters to budge up and make way and then it would be their names all over the papers. Achievers who hadn't achieved any-thing yet. Hanging out a shop sign with nothing written on it. That kind of would-be up-and-comer was half in love, half in hate with the people they wanted to be, fizzing with envy they hadn't diagnosed in themselves. This boy was like that, and was showing signs of insufficient respect. He liked Smitty's fame but didn't seem to appreciate that Smitty came attached to it. More interested in his own work than in his employer's – even though he didn't have any work of his own to speak of. He had come recommended by Smitty's art dealer and agent, a bright kid re-lated to somebody or other, freshly graduated from St Martin's or Clerkenwell or wherever it was. The kid was bright and on his better days had a hungry look that Smitty approved of, but the boy also needed to be careful. He had the air of someone who liked to take a few pills of a weekend. Smitty liked to talk about living large and caning it, but his attitude to drugs was, beneath the rhetoric, cautious and epicurean: small amounts, meticulously chosen, at the right time and in the right company. He took as much trouble sourcing his drugs as a different kind of person would take sourcing organic meat. If his assistant was getting off his face Friday-to-Sunday to such an extent that his concentration was wavering at work, he was soon going to find himself being an ex-assistant. An ex-assistant with a watertight confidentiality clause in his contract.

A beeping noise went off. The boy fished his phone out of his pocket.

'You asked me to tell you when it was half eleven,' he said.

'Yeah, OK,' said Smitty. He picked up his mobile and his wallet and his car keys. 'Got a thing to go to. My nan.'

'Sorry,' said the boy with a hint of something in his tone Smitty didn't like, an only just detectable irony of some kind. OK, that's it, he told himself. You're fired. He headed out the door to his car in a genuinely shitty mood.

13

Smitty would have been the first to admit that he was a rubbish grandson. He lived in Hoxton, his nan lived in Lambeth, and he visited her, what, about three times a year? They both stayed with his mum at Christmas. And that was that, out of a typical 365 days.

Smitty's mum had been young when she had him – twenty-one – and Petunia had done quite a bit of looking after him when he was small, childminding and babysitting and the rest. He had been very keen on her then. She was good at looking-after, keen on cuddling, and had never once lost her temper – in fact, at the age of twenty-eight, he'd still never seen her angry. He'd got on well with his grandfather too, Albadadda as he was known (Albert plus dadda). His grandfather had been a mixture of grumpy and hilarious, the kind of grown-up who gets on well with small children because he is close to being one himself. When Smitty's parents moved out to Essex, he saw much less of his grandparents; hardly saw them at all, in fact. He went through the usual teenage thing of thinking his grandparents were smelly and boring and made loud noises when they chewed, and was only starting to come out of that phase when his grandfather suddenly died. That was the year he went to art school. He was at Goldsmiths so it wasn't far away, and he could easily have made a regular habit of visiting his nan. His intentions were good. It was just that he didn't do anything about them.

But Smitty and his grandmother Petunia got on well for all that. When he did see her he was able to be relaxed, his guard down, with none of the wariness he was never quite able to put aside with his mother. That was partly because of his work. His mum would ask questions and he would fend her off with talk about being an artist, deliberately leaving the impression he was some sort of commercial artist, in the sense of a graphic designer or something like that – and she could tell, with her maternal antennae, that he was doing pretty well at it, though not that he was genuinely minted. (Of course, some of Smitty's art-world mates would have said that he was absolutely a commercial artist in a larger sense. That was OK by him.) His father didn't know the details of what he did and didn't particularly care, since he could tell that Smitty had an entrepreneurial streak and would turn out fine. 'He's a natural barrow boy, like me,' was what he always said to Smitty's mother, often in Smitty's hearing. That too was a description Smitty didn't mind at all. His mum, though – he instinctively didn't want her knowing what he was up to. As for his nan, saying to her 'I am a conceptual artist who specialises in provocative temporary site-specific works' would have been like telling her he was the world heavyweight boxing champion. She would have nodded and said 'That's nice, dear' and felt genuinely proud of him without needing to go into any further details. She was good at accepting things; a bit too good, maybe, in Smitty's view.

Anyway, here he was. Pepys Road. Smitty had taken the Tube, because although he could easily have driven, and deeply loved his Beemer, he found he got more ideas when he took the Tube and spent the trip looking at people and wondering about how to get into their heads. That was a big part of what art was about – getting into people's heads.

Before Smitty rang the doorbell, he could hear his nan pottering about inside. One of her signature moves was to put the kettle on before coming to the door, so it would be boiling within seconds of the guest sitting down. Then the door opened and there she was.

'Nan!' said Smitty.

'Graham!' said his nan, because that was Smitty's real name. He handed over a box of chocolates – a fantastically expensive box of chocolates that his soon-to-be-ex-assistant had 'sourced' (the soon-to-be-ex-assistant's word) from a poncy shop in West London. His nan would not notice that the chocolates were incredibly fancy, which is why Smitty felt free to give them to her. If he'd given them to his mum, she would have subjected him to Abu Ghraib-style interrogation about how much they had cost and whether he could afford it.

'I've put the kettle on,' said his nan. They went through to the kitchen, Smitty's favourite room in the house and possibly in the whole world, because it was exactly like time travel to 1958. Linoleum – Smitty loved lino. A Coronation biscuit tin. A proper kettle, one you put on the stove, none of that electric rubbish. The world's most knackered fridge. No dishwasher. His granddad had been too tight to buy one, and then after he'd died and his nan was living on her own there wasn't enough washing-up to justify the expense.

His nan wasn't moving quite as well as she might have been. She was what, eighty-three next year? Nan had never taken up much space, but she had always seemed pretty robust, physically. That ran on both sides of the family. But she seemed thinner, frailer, and now that he was looking closely, slightly less steady on her pins. Probably just age, pure and simple. You heard people say forty was the new thirty and fifty was the new forty and sixty was the new forty-five, but you never heard anybody say eighty was the new anything. Eighty was just eighty.

Smitty was tempted to put out an arm to help her down the single step into the kitchen but resisted the impulse. Nan was talking about how she got most of her shopping done over the internet now, how his mother had set it up for her, and what a blessing it was, though she didn't like the fact that they used up so many plastic bags, sometimes a whole plastic bag for a single item, but his mother had told her that they took away the bags too and she had asked and it was true and that was a blessing. Smitty semi-listened to all this.

'You can get anything over the internet now, Nan. Friend of mine moved to Los Angeles. In America, six thousand miles away. Before he goes he sells his flat, sells his car, and dumps his girlfriend. Then he goes online and rents a flat, rents a car, and gets a new girlfriend, all over the internet and all before he's set a foot in the place. True story.'

'It's a different world,' said his nan. She was fussing about with the teapot and cups. His nan was a bit of a tea snob and liked the whole ritual, warming the pot, doing it with leaves and not tea bags, proper cups. While she was doing that, Smitty picked a postcard up off the table. It was a black and white photograph which he took a couple of seconds to realise was the front door of 42 Pepys Road, shot in an arty style with a camera held low and tilted upwards so the top of the door frame loomed over the rest and the angles looked funny. The kind of photo which would be crap if it were a normal photo but would be OK if it were consciously artistic. Smitty turned the photo over. On the back it said, in printed black ink, 'We Want What You Have'. There was no signature and the postmark was indecipherable.

'You seen this, Nan?' Smitty asked.

'I've gone back to English Breakfast. It's a bit stronger. Oh, that! It's one of these postcards I've been getting. One every fortnight or so for a couple of months. All pictures of the house with the same thing written on them. I've kept them. They're all over there by the dresser.'

Smitty went over to the dresser. Sure enough, beside photos

of his nan with Albadadda, and of his mum and himself and his brother and sister at various phases of development, there was a stack of postcards, all of them pictures of 42 Pepys Road. All of the pictures were different. One of the photos was an extreme close-up of the door number, another was shot from right down the street, as far away as you could go and still pick out the front of number 42. Another was shot from head height, looking straight down at the front doorsteps. Another, from more or less the same angle, looked sideways across the front bay window. One of them had four different pictures cropped into quadrants. Underneath the postcards was a jiffy bag addressed in the same handwriting. Smitty opened it and took out a DVD, with a label which also said 'We Want What You Have'.

'Have you had a look at this, Nan?' he asked, knowing what the answer would be. No point sending a DVD to Mrs Howe.

'No, of course not darling, I don't have one of those thingies.' She put the cup down in front of him. 'I always think English Breakfast is nicer with milk, but I've got some sliced lemon here if you need it.'

'Sure. Thanks. Listen, Nan, can I borrow this? Do you mind if I borrow all these cards?'

'Of course you can, darling. Drink up, it's much less nice when it goes cold.' She put a plate of biscuits beside Smitty, and began unwrapping the posh chocolates so she could offer them back to him.

14

The Younts had gone away for the weekend. It was ten days before Christmas and seven days before Roger was due to find out about his bonus. Their host was a client of Roger's at the bank, a man called Eric Fletcher, who owned a house in Norfolk. This is where the Younts were.

Eric's house had a barn, which he had had converted into a spa, for the use of his wife Naima – he liked to joke that building her a spa was the only way he was able to get her out of London. Opposite it he had built another barn, so that the house was now framed on both sides with a courtyard in the middle. The second barn was given over to the business of entertaining children: the downstairs was full of toys and games for small boys and girls, Lego and Barbie and Bratz and Nintendo Wii and Action Men and Brio; the upstairs was equipped for older ones, PS3 and Xbox 360 and pool table. Both rooms had flat-screen televisions and DVD libraries. There were two nannies. 'The whole point of this place,' Eric would say, solemnly, 'is that it's supposed to be playtime for *everybody*.'

All this had come as a very welcome surprise for Arabella. She had not met Eric before and had not known what to expect. Roger had said that he was a yob but that the house would be lovely, and to give Roger his credit, which she was not especially in the mood to do, he had been right. This was a treat; and Arabella had a deep and sincere love of treats. You could not have too many treats. It was perfectly all right to live from treat to treat. Also, Mrs Eric was simply heaven. She was a shortish, plumpish, very chatty half-Asian woman of about forty who at this precise moment was sitting back on the marble seat next to Arabella in the hammam, stark naked except for a towel wrapped around her head to protect her hair from the steam. Arabella, feeling a little shy, had gone into the hammam with her dressing gown but had now joined in by casting it off. Of the other wives, two were now getting massages, one was still in bed, and one was showing off by swimming laps in the pool. Arabella and Naima had already bonded over their shared obsession with *The X Factor* and their mutual determination to watch all the weekend's episodes.

'I think it's time to go and get my nails done,' said Naima, 'but I don't want to move.'

'Moving. Always bad,' said Arabella.

'Anyway,' Naima went on, continuing what she had been saying before she lapsed into silence five minutes before, numbed by the heat, 'I've stopped going to Selfridges. It's just too overwhelming. The personal shoppers are great and I love the range of stock and they have such an eye for brands, when you see a new label there it's always lovely, but after a couple of hours you're *exhausted*, it's like going round some colossal bazaar. The thing about Liberty's is . . .'

Arabella made noises to show that she was listening and in full agreement. Who would have thought that 'Eric the barbarian', who according to Roger was simply revolting on the subject of women and sex, would still have been married to his first wife, the cuddly little dumpling from wherever she was from (Arabella didn't feel she yet knew her well enough to ask, and was also aware that Naima might have told her once already while she wasn't paying attention). And for all her rabbiting on, you could tell she had very good taste; or the good taste to employ people who had very good taste, which was the same thing. Arabella recognised pieces of serious collectors' modern furniture. The bathrooms and spa were stocked with expensive cosmetic products. Obviously it was a bit like a boutique hotel but so what? What was not to like about boutique hotels?

It was particularly delicious to be lying in the wet, saturating heat when you knew it was so cold outside. Bitingly cold; country-air-in-winter cold. Arabella was especially sensitive to cold and found it difficult to relax entirely when she had to be on alert against a draught; but there was no risk of that here, the house was beautifully finished and insulated. She could properly relax and let herself be pampered. Conrad had been a little mutinous at the idea of the weekend in the company of other children he didn't know, but he and Josh had taken one look at their play barn and instantly been in ecstasy. There was a little whiteboard on which they were allowed to write down what they wanted for their tea (subject of course to parental vetting). Conrad had taken the blue felt tip and in the most adorable way written 'spegeti + chips'. Arabella had been at least as sceptical as the boys about coming here but she had to admit that Roger had been right that it would be good fun – 'even if it's awful in one way, it'll still be fun', he had said. Overall this had to be one of his better ideas in a long time. Not that that was high praise.

Arabella was having moments of feeling, not exactly guilty about the nasty surprise she was planning – because Roger was still a lazy and clueless husband who had no idea what she did, no idea at all – but the faintest stirrings of preliminary unease. This was not to do with Roger, who deserved what he was going to get. Even lying in forty-plus-degree heat, her every pore open to the steam, massaged to the point where she was a giant floppy noodle, sitting on the comfortable seat with her new best friend Naima gossiping about which shops' perfume counters employed off-duty whores, and bitching about Lothar's too-skinny wife swimming round and round in the pool like a huge German goldfish of showing-offness – even there, she could feel a toothache-twinge of pure rage at Roger. She was at home all day, coping, stressed out, while he sat in his comfy office, and then when he came home he had the nerve to act like the tired one, like the big hero! And because the children were pleased to see him at weekends, which was based on little more than the fact that they never saw him at any other time, indeed saw as little of him as if he'd been a white-collar criminal in some prison that had a weekend-release scheme – because the children were happy to see the invisible man, he gave himself airs as if that meant he was Banking Father of the Year. While also complaining about how tired he was, of course.

No, Roger would eat what he was given. He would start to appreciate her, or else. The issue causing Arabella some concern was more to do with the children, who might be upset. Who, let's face it, would be upset. But if she spoke to them and explained that Mummy was having to go away for a day or two, 'one or two sleeps', but would be back very soon, and had left presents for them, and that there would be more presents when she got back – basically, as long as she made a really huge deal about presents – it would be all right. It would be fine. It was all about the presents.

'. . . which is why it was so sodding fantastic,' said Roger's host. 'They just got straight in there. Kit off in two seconds flat. I thought Tony was going to have a heart attack. I thought *I* was going to have a heart attack. No doubt they were sixteen or eighteen or whatever you have to be in Korea but anyway they looked about twelve, except with tits. It was mental.'

Roger was walking a short distance across a field in Norfolk, carrying his Purdey shotgun with the barrel cracked open, with a bag of shells over his shoulder. He was wearing all the gear: a flat cap, Barbour jacket, Burberry corduroys, and green Hunter wellies. In his opinion he would have fit in very well at Balmoral. He'd been shooting a few times before, always on work freebies, and that was when he'd bought all this gear. Roger had the habit, one he wanted to grow out of but was well aware that he hadn't, of buying lots of expensive gear when he thought of taking up a new hobby. This had happened with photography, when he'd bought an immensely, unusably advanced camera and set of lenses, then taken about ten pictures before getting bored with its complexity. He had taken up exercise and bought a bike, treadmill and home gym, and then a debenture to a London 'country club' which they hardly ever used because it was so laborious to get there. He'd taken up wine, and had a high-tech fridge-cum-cellar in the converted basement, full of expensive bottles that he'd bought on recommendation, but the trouble was you weren't supposed to drink the bloody stuff for years. He'd bought a timeshare on a boat in Cowes, which they had used once. He had bought this hunting gear about twenty-four months ago, along with the Purdey which he had ordered when he got his first proper bonus fifteen years before, but by the time it came he'd more or less lost interest in shooting. It was a beautiful gun, though, the aged walnut stock thrillingly textured, and there was something almost pornographic about the thought that it had been made specifically for him, for his body, his eyesight, even the aiming of the gun weighted to allow for his personal shooting technique. Thirty thousand pounds well spent, was how it felt today.

He was also glad about his footwear. His host, Eric – 'Eric the barbarian', as he tended to introduce himself – was wearing Gucci trainers, because wellies made his feet smell. Eric was worth several hundred million pounds and was one of Pinker Lloyd's best clients. At the moment, with things in the City a little edgy and credit getting more expensive, Eric was particularly good news, because he seemed constitutionally incapable of being bearish. He was a born optimist and bull; a perma bull. Pinker Lloyd loved him. Eric was lavished with corporate hospitality all year round, and once a year paid some of it back in the form of an invitation to his 'shooting lodge' in Norfolk. His motives in inviting them were less to do with generosity and more to do with showing off. The guests this year were Roger and Lothar and four of their colleagues. They had come to this field in three matching Range Rovers, which had then gone back to Eric's place to collect their picnic lunch and the staff to serve it. Roger was betting that the 'picnic' would be pretty spectacular.

The short winter day had begun wet, but it had stopped raining at about nine, and by now – ten o'clock – was starting to clear. Lothar had gone for a ten-kilometre run before breakfast and was making his usual fuss about how much he liked being out of doors in the fresh air. Eric had not, as far as Roger could tell, stopped boasting for a single moment, except when he was eating or drinking, and even then he would pause only long enough to clear his airways.

'. . . and then he said afterwards, shaking my hand at the airport and bowing and doing all that shit they do – then he says, "What happens in Seoul stays in Seoul." I almost shat myself laughing.'

Eric was the most tremendous yob, no question. He had that absolute certainty of being right about everything which often came with having made a lot of money in the City. Because every trade involved a winner and a loser, making a great deal of money through trading involved being proved repeatedly right, time after time. That had an effect on people who for the most part had not been shy or unconfident in the first place. They tended to think, genuinely and sincerely, that they were the next-best thing to God. Given that, it was interesting the way people with new money copied the people with old money; interesting that Eric, instead of thinking of things he might like to do for himself, or nicer versions of the things he had used to do before he had money, now did all the things other people with money did, like go shooting and own yachts. He even sponsored charities, not out of charitable feeling – Roger was well placed to know that he had not an atom of charitable feeling of any kind, not for anybody – but because it was what you did if you were that rich. It was as if there was a rule book. Still, Roger didn't care. It was nice to get out of London and before long Eric would tire of boasting at him and go off to boast at somebody else.

People said that Norfolk was flat, but it didn't seem at all flat to Roger. The hills were not high, but there were quite a few of them and he had felt distinctly carsick on the drive here. They had walked across a ploughed field and were now walking up the other side towards a copse of trees at the top. It was about ten minutes' brisk walk on soft ground that sucked at the footsteps and Roger, he was embarrassed to notice, was slightly out of breath. Not as badly as Eric, mind you. He was actually panting; he was pale and fleshy and wobbly.

'. . . didn't even . . . want to . . . shag her . . . that much . . . to be honest . . .' Eric was saying, '. . . but . . . no choice . . . held to . . . ransom . . . by my . . . own cock.'

Roger realised half a second too late that he was supposed to laugh. So he made a sort of half-gasping noise on an indrawn breath that was designed to indicate he would be convulsed with merriment if it weren't for all this manly exertion. It was hard to tell if that placated Eric. He had stopped to catch his breath, with his arms on his hips. With the baseball cap and shooting jacket, his shotgun over the crook of one arm, puffing heavily in mud-caked trainers, he looked like someone who had set out to impersonate a country squire but then about halfway through putting on his costume had suddenly stopped caring.

'. . . don't wait for me . . . go on up . . . I'll have a word with the others,' said Eric. The other Pinker Lloyd men were straggling across the field towards them, with Lothar in the lead. He was wearing advanced-looking outdoor clothes, as if he were going orienteering or the like. His outer garments were brightly coloured Gore-Tex and carried the suggestion that if he felt like it he might jog back to London when they'd finished for the afternoon. They all seemed pretty jolly. Shooting was very much in fashion in the City and this weekend brought bragging rights.

The beaters, who had gone out in advance, were waiting in the next field. The idea was to stand around near the copse and kill the pheasants which the beaters would drive up into the air. The pheasants were tame for the most part, and it was some work getting them to take off in order for them to be shot; so many of them would then be killed that there was no market for their meat. The majority of the pheasants were simply buried. A tractor would come and plough them under the earth. Roger felt it was hard to feel that that was anything other than a slightly revolting sign of excess, of waste. But the shooting itself was good fun.

The four Pinker Lloyd men had now caught up with Eric and the group was standing around talking animatedly about something. Eric was waving his arms about, telling a story. The bankers were either enjoying it or doing a good job of pretending to. Roger used the moment to stand and look around, the first time all day he had been entirely on his own. It wasn't windy where he stood but the winds higher up must be strong, as the clouds were both big and quick-moving, and now they were white: no more rain. In the distance he could see a pattern of light and shade moving across the field, which had been set aside from agricultural use and was knee-deep in grass. The copse, which looked from a distance like a single big tree, was a tight clump of ten oaks and beeches, denuded by the winter. The atmosphere beneath the trees was dark and still. A rabbit stood sniffing at the exposed roots of one of the oaks and then lolloped off into the grassy field where Roger could see the beaters standing about half a mile away, waiting for the signal to begin driving the pheasants.

The Range Rovers had returned at the far side of the ploughed field, and were now being unpacked by a team of Eric's people. What looked like two enormous hampers were being lifted out of the backs of the cars, and the last one was disgorging what looked like portable furniture. If the hampers contained food and drink, they would have enough to keep them eating and boozing well into the new year.

Eric was still talking. Roger found it hard to imagine what the story must involve – two hookers, three Ferraris, ten thousand in cash . . . no, ten hookers, twenty Ferraris, a hundred grand . . .

He did not feel sorry to be missing out. Roger, in this break away from work, felt relaxed enough to have a thought about ethics: the thought occurred to him that it was hypocritical to like his host's hospitality while also letting himself enjoy his dislike of the man. Well, tough. That was how he felt.

The rabbit, or a different rabbit, came back out of the grass and returned to the copse, where it continued sniffing around the roots of the same oak tree. Roger kept still; he could see its little nose twitching. There must be an interesting smell. The rabbit was moving its head one way and another, as if trying to get into just the right angle to sniff the leaf or nut or seed or pheasant turd or whatever it was. Then it walked over the root and began sniffing from the other side. Roger felt a surge of feeling that he for a moment could not recognise. The sensation was like a shiver. He realised that he was free. He was on his own and in the open air and he was still young enough, strong enough, to do anything he wanted with his life. He could just walk off now, get a lift to Eric's house, pick up Arabella and the kids, drive back to London and announce that from now on they would all be living a different life, a simpler and economically smaller life, that they would go round the world for a year and then he would retrain as a teacher and they would move out of London, somewhere like this where you could walk and breathe and see the sky, and the kids would go to the local school and Arabella would look after them and they would pick out good-value cuts at the local butcher and he would drink tea from a mug while helping the kids with their homework. And every day he would go for a long walk, even when it was wet and windy, and he would come in smelling of the outside, the way the children sometimes smelled of the outdoors when they'd been playing on the Common, and then one day he would look at himself in the mirror and see a different man. These thoughts belonged to Roger but he also felt that they came from the air around him, from the fact that he was standing next to a copse in a field in Norfolk on his own, watching the grass sway and the clouds race, being ignored by a rabbit.

The rabbit heard the others coming before he did. It raised its head, twitched its nose, and then with three hops was gone in the long grass. Then Roger heard the voices coming up the hill.

'. . . had her . . . every which way . . . so I said . . . which way . . . is every which way?'

16

Freddy Kamo grew up in a two-room shack on the outskirts of the Senegalese town of Linguère. The shack had electricity, sometimes, but not running water. For water, the Kamos would have to take a jug to the well, a hundred metres away. The floor of the shack was made of packed earth and each room had a single bare electric bulb; the beds, thanks to a gift from a relative, had mosquito nets, the family's sole luxury.

Freddy was the only son of Shimé and Patrick Kamo. Both Shimé and Patrick were Wolof, members of the largest tribal group in Senegal; they were believing but undevout Muslims; Patrick had done well at the lycée and could both speak and read French. He married at the age of fourteen and at the same age left school to begin work, first for his father-in-law delivering gas canisters, and then, when he was eighteen, in the police force. Patrick took a second wife, Adede, when Freddy was four, and had three more children with her, and then Shimé died in childbirth, along with a baby who would have grown up to be their second son. Freddy held no resentment towards his stepmother, who was kind to him, impeccably so, but she was very wrapped up in her own daughters, and in the years after Shimé's death he grew very close to his father.

Patrick Kamo was two people: a stern and unforgiving man at his work, and a soft, gentle, anxious parent. He was sometimes taken aback by how much he loved Freddy, but did his best to hide it from everyone except the boy himself. He worried about his son, a lot, especially as Freddy seemed to be such a dreamer, such a drifter, lacking the hardness the world demands. He was slow in his lessons and disliked school. All he ever wanted to do was play football. He was admittedly very good at football – or at least that's what he was, right from the start, at about the age of five. As he got older, things changed. Football became the only thing Freddy ever spoke or thought about, and it became clear that he wasn't merely good at football, but something else altogether. Patrick realised that Freddy was touched with something a long way beyond mere talent.

Today, Freddy was seventeen, and even people with no interest in football, even people who had never been to a proper football match, even people who actively disliked the game, could see something special about Freddy Kamo with a ball at his feet. This wasn't because Freddy looked at his ease with the ball; on the contrary. Even at the best of times Freddy looked awkward, clumsy, and as if he were about to trip over, with the gangly, jangling awkwardness of a teenage boy who has recently had a big growth spurt and hasn't yet got used to the new disposition of his own limbs. He knocked things over and spilled things. He splashed Coke on himself and bumped into doorways.

With a football at Freddy's feet, it was much, much worse. On a football field, he just looked wrong. Shorts made his skinny legs look not only long and awkward, but also as if they were a telescopic implement with one segment too many, like an overextended radio aerial. His upper body, in a football jersey, was slope-shouldered and narrow-chested. His head was large, which made everything else look even more out of proportion than it already was. When he ran with the ball he looked as if he would at any moment step on it and fall over, or stumble as he tried to catch up with it, or trip over his own feet, or let it get away from him, or bounce it off his shin or knee or ankle. His arms flailed sideways as he ran so that he looked like a windmilling, falling, catastrophically ill-coordinated kid, or an octopus, or a vaudeville routine. But then, as he ran with the ball, and if the spectators kept looking, after about five seconds they might notice something, which was that the ball did not get away from him. The ball looked as if it was always about to be out of his reach – but it never did get out of his reach. He did not trip or stumble or miskick, even though he always seemed on the verge of doing so. By now, in a football match, at least one defender would have lunged at the ball, usually at the point when it was furthest out of Freddy's reach, but he would somehow, magically, have got to the ball just before them, as if his telescopic legs had extended themselves, and he would have slalomed past the now immobile defender, awkwardly, but easily too. Then another opponent would appear in front of him and he would do the same thing, always about to trip and fall and flail and lose the ball, but never actually doing so. And then he would do it again, and again, and the person watching would realise that this weird-looking boy was not just a not-bad football player, not just a good or even very good football player, but a prodigy, a miracle of balance and timing and speed and coordination, a dancer, an athlete, a natural.

Freddy had his big growth spurt at thirteen. He had always had the skill but now the size and speed came too. Before that, other kids would get bored of having him go round them as if they weren't there and would simply kick or push him off the ball. Then it all changed. When Freddy was only fourteen, playing a game of football near his home at Linguère, a mother pushing her pram past the kickabout would stop to watch him. A bus driver would lose concentration and miss the change of lights. Other kids would stop their game and come over to watch. The effect on people who did know about football was more pronounced still. They would blink, wonder if they could quite believe what they were seeing, rub their eyes. The scout who spotted Freddy was rung by a contact who had seen him play in a schools tournament in Louga, the provincial capital. The scout lived in Dakar and there was nothing convenient about getting up-country while the three-day tournament was still running, but his contact told him he would never speak to him again if he didn't go, so he did, and felt that on his deathbed he would still be able to remember, first, his nausea, lasting for about ten seconds, that he had been dragged several hundred kilometres inland just to watch this badly coordinated freak falling over his own feet, then a slow sense that he wasn't watching quite what he thought he was watching but something else, giving way to the certainty that today, for the first time in his twenty years of scouting two or three or five matches a week, and perhaps once a year spotting someone who would go on to play professional football, he was watching a genuine genius, a talent on the world scale. Freddy Kamo: there would be a day when everyone in the world with the slightest interest in football, amounting to billions of people, would know that name.

After the game, the scout had virtually bankrupted himself making calls on his mobile, trying to get through to his most important contact of all, the director of the Arsenal scouting network who reported directly to Arsène Wenger. He also went to meet the boy, to sniff around and see if he had the field to himself, and found two things: first, that he didn't – two or three of his competitors had already approached Freddy to discuss terms; second, that talking to Freddy was not a question of approaching Freddy, who was low-key and at ease with himself off the field, but of talking to his father, who was a dignified, unsmiling, strict-seeming police sergeant of forty. Patrick Kamo spoke fluent French. He did not want Freddy to sign terms yet; thought he was too young and that he needed to grow up at home with his father and his three half-sisters. The negotiations took months and the key to getting Patrick onside was the club's willingness to let Freddy grow up in Senegal until he was ready. Other suitors wanted him to move to Europe; this was the clincher for Arsenal. Negotiations ended with an agreement to pay Freddy a retainer until he turned seventeen, at which point he would move to London. The scout was on the point of agreeing this deal when an even richer club came along – since Freddy Kamo was now one of football's least well-kept secrets – and offered the same deal except for two and a half times more money, at which point the biggest triumph of the scout's professional life turned into the biggest disappointment he had ever had, as Freddy signed terms for the other team.

And now Freddy Kamo had turned seventeen and was coming to London – specifically, to 27 Pepys Road. His father had chosen the house from the three alternatives offered by the club, in the person of Mickey Lipton Miller. Patrick thought living in town would suit Freddy better than the country and he thought there would be more black people there. He thought that might be an issue in England. The club had brought the two of them to England to look around three months before, in a sensible attempt to let them get a feel of the place. It had been the first time either Kamo had been out of Senegal, the first time either of them had been on an aeroplane, and several other firsts too – their first time in a lift, in a restaurant, in a taxi, in a hotel. Patrick had found the experience overwhelming, but hadn't wanted to let this feeling show to his son, so he had kept a straight policeman's face on for the whole trip. Freddy had been smiling and cheerful throughout all the extraordinary sights and experiences, the size and noise and richness and the meetings and the medical tests and the people, and Patrick had not wanted to betray his own anxieties by asking too many questions about what

Freddy really felt. The end result was that now, on their second trip to England, this time to move there permanently for the sake of Freddy's football career, he had no reliable idea about Freddy's state of mind. He might be panicking, just as Patrick was. Or he might be as blankly cheerful as he seemed.

But Freddy didn't look like he was panicking. He had slept, sprawled across the first-class bed-seat, all the way from Dakar to Paris, and then spent the short flight to London looking out the window and laughing at shapes he claimed to see in the clouds.

'That one looks like Uncle Kama,' he said to his father, about a cloud which did indeed look like a short fat man with very well-developed buttocks.

'Wrong colour,' said Patrick. Freddy reached across and very softly punched him on the upper arm.

Patrick was rigid with tension, ready to bristle and flare up, in the immigration hall, but although the queue had moved very slowly, the middle-aged woman looking at their passports and visas had let them through with no questions, indeed without speaking at all. Now they were in the arrivals hall.

'Are you ready?' Patrick asked Freddy as they stood beside the trolley on which they had put their suitcases. They were both wearing their best suits. Patrick had refused to employ an agent for Freddy, but he had taken legal and business advice. From this day, the club were paying Freddy £20,000 a week, with a complex series of escalators and option clauses taking account of what would happen when his career took off. In other words, from this moment on, they were rich. It was a hard thought to keep hold of; mainly Patrick was worrying about what would happen if they came through the arrivals door and Mickey Lipton-Miller and the others weren't there to meet them. Mickey had offered to fly someone to Dakar just to fly back with them, but Patrick was a proud man and that seemed too much; he was not a child who needed his hand held. But the chaos and rushing and sheer in-difference of Heathrow – the sense that every single person there was familiar with what they were doing and where they were go-ing, and none of them would spare a thought for the Kamos – were close to overwhelming.

'I am fine,' said Freddy.

'*D'accord*,' said Patrick. 'Let's go and start this new life. Do you want to drive?'

Freddy nodded and took charge of the luggage trolley. They went through the deserted customs hall and out before a wall of faces, two of whom, Patrick was pleased to see, were Mickey Lipton-Miller and the club translator.

17

Zbigniew and Piotr leaned against the wall of Uprising, their favourite bar, and watched the midweek crowd jostling and flirting and drinking and shouting. Piotr was going home early for Christmas, so they wouldn't see each other until the new year; Zbigniew was going to stay in London. He was on standby for any small plumbing or electrical jobs that came up at any of Piotr's sites. It was a good time to get work because British builders were all on holiday. For that very reason Zbigniew had a couple of jobs which he had promised to finish over the holidays, while the owners of 33 Pepys Road and 17 Grove Crescent were in Mauritius and Dubai, respectively. They would be staying in expensive hotels and doing whatever it was people did when they went to expensive places – sit by the pool with expensive drinks, eat expensive food, talk about other expensive holidays they might go on and how nice it was to have so much money.

Zbigniew was planning to go home in early January and had already booked a Ryanair flight for 99p plus tax. His mother would make a fuss over him and his father would take a day or two off work. It would be good to be home; Zbigniew hadn't been to Warsaw since the previous spring. He would see some friends and dandle some babies on his knees and dream about the time he would be able to come back as a wealthy man.

'That one,' said Piotr. The pub had no Polish beers so both

men were drinking Budvar, in their view the only good thing to come out of the former Czechoslovakia.

'The blonde? Too short. Almost a dwarf.'

'No, not the blonde, the one next to her. With dark hair. I am in love.'

'You are always in love.'

'Love is what makes the earth go around the sun.'

'No, that's gravity,' said Zbigniew. This was an old debate between them and they barely listened to each other. Piotr fell in lust very easily and made no distinction between that and falling in love. He would conceive a crush on a girl, go and talk to her, fall madly in love, undergo a passionate and violently see-sawing affair, experience extremes of elation undreamt of by most mortals, have his heart broken, go through bitter depression, and recover to await the next encounter, all in about forty-five minutes. When he did actually go out with a girl it was the same cycle, but spread out over a longer time. At the moment Piotr was between love affairs and so coming to the pub with him was, Zbigniew felt, an act of conscious kindness – it would involve listening to him fall in love with girls at least twice in the course of a typical evening. He was not shy, either. If he saw a girl he liked he never failed to ask her out, the first time he spoke to her. It wasn't that Piotr didn't mind rejection; he hated it. It was just that he recovered very quickly.

Zbigniew took a different approach. Women were a practical issue, a real-world problem, and like other problems were best solved with a methodical and pragmatic approach. Zbigniew had, not rules, but maxims. He would chase a girl only if he had good reason to think she was already interested. He had never been in love. He said he didn't believe in it. His philosophy was that if you were clean and financially solvent and not ugly you were already in the top 30 per cent of men. If in addition you listened to what women said to you, or were able to fake doing so convincingly, you were in the top 10 or even 5 per cent. Then all it took was to apply common sense: don't seem desperate, don't get drunk, do let the girl get drunk, and harness the power of texting. And then other things, like going out midweek when there was less competition. It was all to do with improving your percentages.

A man in a three-quarter-length dark coat came into the pub, looked around, and went over to the dark-haired girl Piotr liked. They kissed and she reached round behind him to squeeze his bottom.

'My life is over,' said Piotr, finishing his beer.

'Not necessarily,' said Zbigniew. On the other side of the unused fireplace where they were standing, two young women were looking round the room, flicking their hair, and holding huge 250 ml glasses of white wine. Zbigniew had already twice made eye contact with the girl who was facing him. She had blonde highlights and had taken out a pack of cigarettes and put it on the mantelpiece. Her coat looked expensive and she had a big handbag of the type that was in fashion. Her friend was doing most of the talking. There was something about the blonde girl that Zbigniew liked. Perhaps it was the cigarettes – which were disgusting, for their smell and everything else, but also, when attached to a woman, inexplicably sexy, because of the hint of recklessness that went with them; the hint of not-caring. She was a little untidy with it, her coat open at an odd angle. Zbigniew gestured with his bottle to Piotr and then finished his drink. Piotr took a look.

'Time to improve our English,' said Zbigniew. This was code. It was well known that the best way to improve your English was to have an English girlfriend. This was not easy but got much easier once you had a bit of money and spoke good English yourself – but then it was hard to really get good at English without an English girlfriend – so it was not easy. Zbigniew had learned most of his English from a girl called Sam whom he had met when he changed a car tyre for her on King's Avenue during a rainstorm. He had seen her for six months and it had done wonders for his English. She had been cheating on her boyfriend, but that didn't seem to bother her and so it didn't bother Zbigniew either, and they only split up a week before her wedding.

'I'm going home tomorrow,' Piotr said.

'I thought I was supposed to be the practical one.'

'Yes, but I'm going home tomorrow.'

'Just get her number then. You're only away for two weeks. She can be something to look forward to when you get back.'

'I just told you, my life is over.'

'And yet it goes on.'

Piotr sighed. 'Oh, all right.'

Zbigniew was a quiet man, but like his friend Piotr he was not shy. He leaned across to where the handbag girl was standing and said,

'It's terrible, isn't it? The ban.'

She smiled, looked away, looked back. Her friend turned to look. She had very dark hair, black, and wore dramatic red eye make-up. Zbigniew thought her movements were off-puttingly quick, but then she wasn't his type to start with. The two women looked at each other and some female communication passed between them, and they both turned to face Zbigniew and Piotr. And then it went on from there.

18

Patrick Kamo didn't like the card which had come to their door on the second morning, the one with a photograph of their house and the caption 'We Want What You Have'. Patrick found it sinister; he thought it disturbing that Mickey had no explanation for it and didn't know what it meant. To Freddy, on the other hand, it was obvious. Who in the world wouldn't want what he had?

Freddy's first two days in London slid past in a series of meetings and tests and measurements, the most prolonged of which was the medical for his insurance. He was taken to a room in a private hospital that was the cleanest, brightest, whitest place he'd ever seen, where a team of three brisk doctors, working through his interpreter, saw him prodded and weighed and assessed. His teeth and eyes were looked at, his knees tapped with a hammer, his fingernails and tongue and gums inspected. He was covered in wires and made to run on a treadmill. He was made to stretch and hop and jump. Freddy could feel his father beginning to bristle at all this, at seeing his son so comprehensively treated as a piece of meat, but Freddy didn't mind. Football was real, but most other things were not real; most things were just games people played. It was simplest to smile and go along. He was here to play football and the time for that would come soon.

The Wednesday before Christmas, Freddy's third day in London, was his first day at training. He had been out to the training ground in Surrey before, on his acclimatisation visits, but this was the first time he was going for real, and all the way there he couldn't stop smiling – so much so that his father, who was beside him in the back of the Range Rover, looking solemn and serious and worried in his aeroplane-best suit, would himself lose his game face and start grinning as he looked across and saw Freddy's expression cracking like an idiot. Mickey was driving and the translator sat in the front beside him, giving a running commentary on where they were as they headed out of town.

Freddy was impressed by how green everything was, even under the dark grey sky, which was almost the same colour as the roofs on the houses. There were many, many trees; and then they were out of London driving across a heath, which seemed unexpectedly wild and bare to Freddy.

'Did you see that film *The War of the Worlds*, starring Tom Cruise? The original story was set here. It is by Wells, a less intelligent English version of Jules Verne. This is where the Martians landed,' said the translator.

'The fight scenes were good,' said Freddy.

Then they were in woodland again, and then in small windy roads over small but steep hills, and then they were at the training ground, and Freddy began his first day of work as a professional footballer.

There was one bad thing about that morning: Freddy realised that he was going to have to learn English much more quickly than he'd thought. Patrick spoke a basic level of English, and he had gone on and on about how Freddy needed to learn the language, but Freddy had privately thought his father was making too much of this – he could read a team-sheet as well as anyone and knew how many different nationalities were in the squad, they must be very used to people not speaking English. But he now saw this worked the other way, and precisely because players came from everywhere they needed to communicate with a shared tongue. The manager was very nice about it but also firm: 'How are the language lessons going?' was the first thing he said. The star striker, who was francophone, had been incredibly friendly but he had said, 'We won't speak French at work after this week.' So Freddy was going to have to concentrate and work hard. But – he knew this in advance but it was still hard to believe – since the players only trained in the mornings, up until lunch, there was plenty of time left to get on with his lessons, and the sooner he did that the quicker the time would be free for fun things. So, English.

Apart from that, his first day at training was the best day of his seventeen years and four days on the planet. They had begun with stretches and then a game in which two players stood in the middle of the circle of five others, who tried to keep the ball away from them by passing. It was fun and good technical practice too, but the real buzz for Freddy came when he was sent for his turn in the middle at the same time as the £20 million midfielder, and the two of them set out to intercept the ball. The exciting thing was simply looking across and seeing this world-famous player and seeing that he was human, real, right there next to him, and that this was now to be Freddy's world from here on.

After the two-in-the-middle game, there was an hour and a half of fitness training: a warm-up run, then some interval running, then shuttle sprints. Freddy had spent the last two years working to the personalised diet and fitness programme sent to him by the club, so it was fine. He was used to being the quickest player anywhere he ran, so it was startling to be in the middle of the pack or a little behind – but in any case he was still growing, and Freddy knew very well that one of the bases of his game was that he could run as quickly with the ball as he could without it.

Once they'd finished the running they did some skills work,

and then they finished off with a game whose name was so odd that Freddy had to ask the translator to tell him it three times: *cochon au milieu*, he kept saying: pig in the middle. Freddy took his turn running around trying to tag the others and they took their turn in the middle too, grown men running and skipping and dodging and laughing, the oldest of them in his early thirties putting as much gusto into it as the youngest, Freddy himself, panting and giggling at the same time. And then the coach blew his whistle and training was over. The players headed for the changing room, and for their busy afternoons of shopping and gambling and meeting their agents and sex.

19

Petunia sat waiting to see the doctor – no, not just the doctor, but the consultant. She was on the eighteenth floor of a tower block in South-East London and so far no aspect of her day had gone well. She was feeling weak and dizzy most of the time, and there was also a new and horrible symptom – horrible because so disconcerting – that her vision was somehow being affected, as if a shadow or blur were intruding on the left side of her eyesight. It was such a strange sensation that at times she thought she might be imagining it and at other times she was sure she wasn't. Going out of the house at all was something of a challenge, so getting all the way across here hadn't been possible without taking a minicab, which was not something she liked to do – it was one of the subjects about which she agreed with Albert, he who had never, not once in his life, taken a taxi. Part of the trouble was that she would have to take a minicab back and although there would be a freephone in the hospital from which she could order one Petunia knew that this was certain to involve quite a lot of anxious waiting, wondering if the cab had been stolen by someone else, struggling to find somewhere to sit, and all while she was dreading the thought of another bad turn.

When she got there, having tried to be stoical, it was much worse than she had imagined, because the skyscraper forecourt of the hospital suffered from a wind-tunnel effect. There was a genuine gale-force wind raging across the piazza, carrying near-horizontal rain into the chaos of ambulances and taxis and patients and visitors and wheelchairs. Every other person seemed to have a clear idea of where they were going and of how to get there and a keen sense of their own rightness about the need to get there in a hurry, which was daunting for Petunia who had none of those things except an awareness that she needed to find the lifts and get to the eighteenth floor.

The first lift had a huge crowd outside it. Petunia couldn't get in. For the second lift, she was closer to the front of the queue, but some people overtook and got in first and then a man with a wheelchair and a leg in plaster said 'Excuse me' and went in front of her and then there was no more room. She did manage to get in the third lift, because a nurse took pity on her and created a space by holding her arm in front of the door so Petunia could slip past. The nurse smiled at Petunia as the lift began to go up, while four very tall young male doctors talked about a rugby game they had coming up that weekend.

She got out at the eighteenth floor and queued for five minutes to tell the woman on the desk that she had arrived. The woman asked her name and then typed it into a computer and then without saying anything wrote on a card and gave it to Petunia, who gathered from that that she was supposed to sit and wait until her name was called. So Petunia went and sat on a plastic chair in the waiting room. The chair was bright orange with a hole in the back and its seat was canted forward so that Petunia was constantly having to shuffle her bottom and adjust her position in order not to slip off. On the five seats next to Petunia, an Asian family of five sat waiting, a grandmother and her daughter and son-in-law and her two grandchildren. They had brought books, video game thingies for the children, magazines, and a plastic bag of snacks; their equipment for the wait and their obvious experience at waiting made Petunia feel very amateurish.

After about an hour, Petunia summoned up the nerve to go and ask if she had been forgotten. No one ever admitted that they had actually forgotten you, but the fact was that reminding people of your existence did sometimes have an effect. The woman at the counter looked up from her computer very briefly and looked down again before answering.

'There's a queuing system,' she said.

'Only my appointment was for one thirty and it's now a quarter to three.'

'All Dr Watson's clinic appointments are for one thirty,' said the woman.

'Oh well, that's all right then,' said Petunia. The woman looked up at her briefly again, and Petunia went and sat back down with her heart beating harder and more quickly.

Forty-five minutes later the woman called out, 'Miss Hoo, er, Miss Howe.' Petunia went in to see the consultant. A young woman doctor in a white coat – Petunia could see she was a doctor because of her stethoscope – smiled and said hello while in the corner of the room a man in his fifties sat at a computer screen typing. There was a lot of complicated-looking equipment in the room, machines with wires and screens, a couch with a drawn-back screen and a shiny metal device on a stand hanging over it, which instantly made Petunia think of something on a television nature programme, but gone wrong, like a huge steel insect.

The woman doctor indicated a chair and said, 'He won't be a minute.' The older doctor sat and typed for five minutes and then said,

'Yes, hello. You are?'

'Mrs Howe.'

The doctor looked at the notes.

'Symptoms worse?'

'I'm sorry?'

Raising his voice, as if the fact that she had not immediately understood the doctor's question meant that she was deaf, he said:

'Have the symptoms you reported got any worse? The things that you felt were wrong with you, are they worse? Are they different? Are there any new things?'

Petunia described her symptoms. When she came to the one about the vision in her left eye, she had the feeling that the doctor was listening to her with more attention. He had brown hair of the shade which in youth was probably red, and his face was reddish too; he looked like a drinker and he also looked like a man who was often angry, and who used anger to get his way. An effective man. He had the air of an over-quick listener, someone who makes up his mind about what is being said to him very quickly, and then doesn't entirely listen to the rest of what is being said. Petunia, perhaps because she had spent so much of her own life in what felt like passive states, attendant on other people who were better at expressing their wishes and needs, had always been very conscious of people's ways of waiting while other people were talking or doing things. This doctor was truly terrible at that. He was vibrating with impatience.

'Right,' he said. 'And the tiredness and balance? Feel tired, dizzy?'

Petunia described the ways in which that was true. As she spoke she felt herself becoming more anxious. Something about describing her own symptoms made her wonder, for the first time, if she might truly be ill; if she might be going to die. The thought had flitted through her mind before but now it seemed to be settling in. It was embarrassing, to have got to the age of eighty-two without having these thoughts before, but Petunia was now beginning for the first time to imagine what it would be like to die. It was talking to this doctor which was making her do so. Perhaps because he was so bored and so impersonal, he brought to mind the final impersonality of death – the way in which it was the same for everybody. An intimate event which was identical for all and could not be escaped.

'There are a few things we need to eliminate,' the doctor said. 'A brain tumour is the first of them.'

'I have a brain tumour?' asked Petunia. She saw a tiny flicker in the man which showed that he did in fact think it possible that was what she had; it might even have been the thing he thought likeliest. But he didn't admit that, what he said, in a patient, irritated way, was:

'No. When we talk about "eliminating" something we mean ruling it out as the cause of an illness. So we go through the list of possible causes, and we eliminate them one by one and the one we're left with is what's wrong with you, you understand? It's not to do with curing the tumour; it's about finding out whether you have one. Is that clear?'

He was so much more important than her, Petunia felt, perhaps that was all that it came down to. He was important, his time was important, and she wasn't – not that she wasn't important in her own eyes, necessarily, just that it was clear that she was much less important than him. His lateness, his haste, his impatience, everything about him was calculated to show that he mattered more than whoever it was he was talking to.

Petunia had always been prone to seeing things from the other person's point of view. This was supposed to be a virtue but Petunia herself sometimes wondered if it had in her become a fault; like her quietness and modesty, her reluctance to draw attention to herself or get above herself, it was a positive quality which she had taken too far. She had a glimpse of how she must seem to this confident, cross man: a small old mousy woman who needed to have things said twice, who took up very little space; she was just one of the dozens of people with whom he'd have dealings today.

'I understand. Do you think I have a tumour?' said Petunia.

The doctor looked at her, his red face immobile, and was clearly giving her some credit for understanding what was at stake, as well as for her directness. Petunia felt, with a twinge of self-dislike, that she liked the fact that the doctor was taking more notice of her.

'I think you may. I wouldn't say that it is probable, but it is possible and it is something which we can eliminate fairly quickly. You will have to have a CAT scan, and that'll tell us.'

'Is that the one where you go into a sort of tunnel?'

The doctor did not smile but his expression lightened a little.

'Yes. I hope you don't have claustrophobia?'

She could tell he'd asked the question before.

'I've seen it on television,' said Petunia.

The doctor began doing things on his computer. He gave Petunia a date for the scan, ten days away. Now that he was well on the way to getting rid of her, he became more friendly. He asked for her appointment card and wrote the date on it.

'Now you won't forget, will you?' said the doctor. He was trying to be nice; for him this was flirtatious. Petunia, who had spent so much of her life appeasing, managing, a difficult man, couldn't find it in herself to do anything other than play along.

She rode downstairs in the lift and spent forty minutes waiting before a minicab came and took her home.

20

Usman came into the shop at quarter past four on Friday, a little out of breath. Shahid was waiting for him behind the counter. Even though he was late, Usman paused for a moment inside the door. He could never quite get used to how much sheer stuff there was in the shop: piled and stacked and arrayed. There was something offensive and impure about this sheer amount of stuffness.

'Salaam, dickhead,' Shahid said to his brother. 'You're late.'

'Sorry. Traffic. They're digging up every street in South London.'

'And because you're late,' Shahid said, picking up his coat and lifting the counter flap to let himself out and his brother in, 'I'm going to be late, and if I'm late for prayers, it being Friday afternoon, I'm well on the way to not being a Muslim, and it's your fault.'

'You'd have to miss two more Friday prayers.'

'With an unreliable idiot like you to rely on, that's all too possible.'

'I said I was sorry,' said Usman, taking his place behind the counter. Usman spoke with some ill grace, since he was by no means sure that Shahid was actually going to mosque: they attended different mosques and he didn't know for sure how regularly his brother went to prayers. But since he and Shahid basically got on, unlike he and Ahmed, he didn't want to make too big a thing of it.

'Laters,' said Shahid in the high girly voice he used for saying that word to his younger brother. He held the door open for a mother with an enormous three-wheel pram. Then Shahid was gone; as it happened, to mosque, for Friday prayers.

Brixton Mosque had acquired a bad reputation thanks to a few idiots. There had always been an anger to the rhetoric, more outside the mosque than inside, often, but inside too, and there was no point denying it: the imam was not everyone's cup of tea. These things drew attention that you didn't want and Shahid couldn't help wondering, at times, just how many of his fellow worshippers were MI5 or Special Branch, operatives or informers or provocateurs or plants. And some of this had been self-inflicted by the community. Having a former worshipper plot to blow up a transatlantic jetliner via an exploding shoe – even if you believed only one word of every ten in the kafr media, this was bad PR. But Shahid had been going to Brixton Mosque for almost fifteen years, and was not about to stop now. He unlocked his bike – on dry days he chained it to the railings in front, where he could see it from behind the shop counter – and rode the first twenty yards along the pavement, then swerved into the road at the zebra crossing.

The traffic was strangely light, given that London in general was mad at the moment, everyone running around shopping as if their lives depended on it: the next three days were going to be insane, on every high street in the country, spending running up to however many billion it was. About half the people on the street were carrying shopping bags. The idea that the Christians thought this was a religious festival was hilarious; it was the most openly pagan thing Shahid had ever seen. Ahmed had been unable to prevent Fatima joining in the hoopla, so although the Kamals didn't celebrate Christmas the children still got presents.

Little Mohammed would grow up to enjoy the bounty created by his demanding sister. No doubt she wouldn't be shy about telling him so. Shahid weaved through the traffic, skipping two red lights and having only one near-death experience, when a car came out of a side street on Acre Lane without seeing him or stopping. He cut up the one-way street on the pavement to Gresham Road and was in good time for ablutions before prayers.

Standing next to him at the basins was a Caribbean bus driver whose name Shahid didn't know but who he'd seen on and off at the mosque for more than a decade. The man had a meditative, half-a-beat-slow way of wringing his hands under the taps. Shahid had noticed it before, the bus driver slowing himself down with the cleaning ritual before prayers. That was what he liked about Friday prayers: the sense of continuity within his own life, the ritual stretching into the past and into the future, and the familiar faces and the friendliness. Some of the rhetoric and especially the anger no longer felt quite right to him, was no longer the good fit with his mood and temper that it had once been; but the other things mattered more. He'd never been an especially good listener. But he loved praying, the physical act of prostration. Not five times a day, obviously, not any more – who had time for that? But when he was praying, it was one of the only times in his life when he felt fully *there*. It was not a sense of transcendence: he didn't go out of himself and he had no intuitions of other orders of reality. Some said that the self could be left behind; that Paradise could be glimpsed in the raptures of the most fervent, devout prayer. That wasn't Shahid's experience. But while he was praying, he was praying, fully given over to his own presence in the words and motions and the ritual. It was the best he could do, and for him it was enough.

The reading was from the Thunder sura, Al-Ra'ad, and Shahid could more or less follow it in his sort-of-OK Arabic.

'Allah is the One who raised the heavens without pillars that you can see, then assumed all authority. He committed the sun and the moon, each running for a predetermined period. He controls all things, and explains the revelations, that you may attain certainty about meeting your Lord.

'He is the One who constructed the earth and placed on it mountains and rivers. And from the different kinds of fruits, He made them into pairs – males and females. The night overtakes the day. These are solid proofs for people who think.'

'Solid proofs for people who think.' That was an idea Shahid liked. Who could possibly say that the Holy Qur'an was anti-scientific?

The imam said some things about Israel and the West and some other things about the evident political realities of the world, to which Shahid paid semi-attention. He had heard too much of it before and it was no longer the reason he came to the mosque. Then prayers were over, and the congregation spilled out onto the street outside the mosque for Shahid's second-favourite part of the ritual, the milling and chatting afterwards. During the service it had become night: this was after all the shortest day of the year, December the 21st. It was clear, and looking straight up Shahid could just see a star or planet, he didn't know which, and a winking, moving light which must be a plane at cruising height.

'How's your fat brother?' asked Ali, who'd been a loud but friendly contemporary of Ahmed at school, a pack leader. He now owned a chain of electronics shops through Croydon, Mitcham, Eltham and points beyond, and was said to be minted. He had recently given up smoking and it showed in his new soft podginess and also in the way he couldn't stop fidgeting, jangling his car keys in his pockets and looking round the crowd as he talked.

'No thinner,' said Shahid. 'Your lot all well?'

'Another baby on the way,' said Ali. 'Gave up the fags just in time.'

Shahid slapped him on the arm and turned to some faces he knew. 'Wasim! Kamran! Ali's gone and done it again! A seventh on the way!'

The men came and began joshing Ali, who looked pleased. Ali used to joke that he wasn't going to stop until he had enough for a five-a-side football team. But that was a few years ago. Was he trying for eleven a side? What was the view of Mrs Ali, whom Shahid had never met? Was she having any say in this? If you have seven children, Shahid wondered, does that mean you're keen on sex, keen on your wife, or keen on children? Or just shit at contraception? Or all four of those things?

'Excuse me,' said a voice with a European accent, 'Shahid Kamal?'

Shahid turned and found himself talking to a North African man, about his age, with a narrow intent face and a well-trimmed beard. He wore a leather jacket and jeans and was looking expectant.

'That's me,' said Shahid.

'Iqbal,' said the man, with a salesman's air, 'Iqbal Rashid. From Brussels to Chechnya? With the Udeen brothers? 1993?'

It came back to Shahid: this was one of the Belgian guys with whom he had gone on his great adventure. Shahid would not have been able to put a name to him for a million pounds, but now that he was standing here in front of him it came back. That's right. The two Algerians, Iqbal and Tariq. Iqbal had been both cooler and angrier than Tariq, hipper in his personal style, a big rap music fan, and also very very steamed up about the condition of Muslims everywhere. Well, they all were, they talked the talk and they were all walking the walk by virtue of going to fight for Chechnya, and Iqbal was the same only more so; there had been a personal edge to his anger. And now here he was, and Shahid had a flash of how he had aged himself by looking at him, because the guy he remembered as a skinny twenty-year-old kid was now unmistakably an only-just-young man, with a few streaks of grey in his beard and hair. Did he look that much older himself? That was a scary thought.

'Of course, of course,' said Shahid. 'Wow. What are you doing here? That's quite a memory for faces you have.'

'I often think of those days,' said Iqbal. 'Some events in one's life seem a long time ago, and yet as close as yesterday, don't you find?'

That's right: when Iqbal wasn't ranting, he was always taking the direct route to some general philosophical point. It was the same Iqbal for sure.

'How's Tariq? You still see each other?'

'People lose touch,' said Iqbal, making it quickly clear that that particular old friend was not his favourite subject, and then brightening to add: 'But then they sometimes find each other again! Listen, let's swap numbers. I'm in town, it would be good to see you, talk about old times, talk about new times.' He had taken a mobile out of his pocket and was standing with it open, ready to take down Shahid's number. It was important to live without too many barriers, Shahid felt. Go with the flow. What will happen will happen. You're only young once. Let things be as Allah wills. And so on. You had to go with what came to you. So Shahid, despite a feeling that something was slightly off about his old companion in jihad, his too-intent face perhaps, his not entirely casual attempt at casualness, gave him the number. The Belgian nodded and said his farewells and was gone.

Shahid thought: what was that all about?

He drifted back to where Ali and the other guys were discussing the Premiership, the usual Chelsea–Arsenal–Man United circular babble. They were like Sufis, if they kept it up for long enough they'd be able to levitate. Then someone said something so out of order, so libellous and grotesque, about Ashley Cole that Shahid had no choice but to enter the debate.

21

On Friday the 21st at five o'clock, Quentina Mkfesi BSc MSc picked up her pay cheque from the offices of Control Services Limited. The cheque was for £227 and it was payable to Kwama Lyons. Quentina put it in her inside jacket pocket and set off on foot towards Tooting. It took about half an hour to walk there. London was full of pre-Christmas bustle, which Quentina approved of: in a place where there was so little natural brightness and colour, it was good to create it through neon and optic fibre and shop windows and Christmas trees.

Quentina was still wearing her uniform; she was in a hurry and didn't want to change. As it was dark, she didn't trust the trip straight across the Common, and so stuck to the pavement on the side. The pub on the Common was already busy, people knocking off early to have a couple of pre-Christmas drinks. With Christmas on Tuesday, plenty of people would be starting the holiday today, and getting a full two weeks off. Quentina felt no resentment. She envied people's work, not their leisure. It was cold but she had a T-shirt, a shirt and a sweater under her ridiculous Ruritanian army jacket, and Quentina had learned long ago that the secret to keeping warm in the English winter was to keep moving. Once she got past Balham, she cut left-right-left through domestic streets, Christmas wreaths on the doors and lights on, trees lit up too, this domestic version of London looking warmer and more welcoming than the city actually was. It looked cosy, like TV Dickens, whereas the real place was cold and disconnected. Quentina found that she liked the softening illusion.

She came to the house she was looking for, a mid-terrace property with the multiple bins that signalled multiple occupancy. She rang the third buzzer up and was buzzed in without a word spoken. The hallway was narrow and smelt damp. A small table by the side of the door bore a stack of miscellaneous post and junk mail. Every time she came here the piece of paper on top of this pile was always a flyer advertising pizza. The English obviously ate an extraordinary amount of pizza.

Quentina jogged up the first flight of stairs, paused to get her breath back and then went up to the second floor. The door opposite was propped open so she went into the flat, which as she knew from previous visits was bigger than it looked, L-shaped, with a sitting room at the front and two bedrooms plus a kitchen round the corner. The front room was decorated with film posters, one for *Battleship Potemkin* – Quentina didn't read Russian but she had asked – and another for *Mandingo*. That presumably was a joke. At a desk opposite the door, his back to Quentina, a large African man sat at a computer screen with a mobile phone held to his right ear, and his left hand in the air, in a gesture which very eloquently asked Quentina not to make a sound while he finished his conversation.

Remarkable: this man had one of the loudest voices Quentina knew. Yet standing across the room from him, she couldn't hear what he was saying into the phone. She was glad of that, because everything Quentina thought and felt about this man could be very simply summed up: the less Quentina knew about this man who claimed to be Kwame Lyons, or 'Kwama Lyons', as his name appeared on her pay cheques, the better.

The man snapped his phone shut and swung around in his

chair. He was fortyish and wore an Adidas tracksuit. He opened his arms expansively and smiled with his mouth but not his eyes.

'Beautiful,' he said.

'I have your cheque,' said Quentina, matching her actions to her words as she took the piece of paper out and stretched across. The man nodded, took the cheque, read it carefully, then reached behind him for his wallet, opened it, and counted out £150 in ten-pound notes. Then he counted the money again. Then he handed it to Quentina.

'I am happy to be able to take this risk for you,' he said in his rich baritone.

'I am happy also,' said Quentina, which was a flat lie, but this exchange, or something similar to it, had become a sort of ritual. It was a dismissal too.

'Happy Christmas,' said the man, turning back to his screen.

'The same to you,' said Quentina, as she left the room, pulling the door behind her, and as always getting out of there with a mixed sense of shame and relief. She had succeeded in not learning anything new or in any way getting further involved, which was an unmixed positive. She ran down the stairs and was out of there. Quentina couldn't have been in the building for more than ninety seconds. That was a good thing.

Quentina's situation was this. In Harare in the summer of 2003 she had been arrested, interrogated, beaten, released by the police, snatched by goons on her way home, taken to a house, told that she had seventy-two hours to leave the country, then beaten and left by the roadside. After being treated in hospital she had been smuggled out of the country by missionaries, and came to England on a student visa which she had always intended to overstay. To make a long story short, she had overstayed on purpose, applied for asylum, been rejected, been arrested and sentenced to deportation, but the judge at the final appeal had ruled that she could not be sent back to Zimbabwe because there were grounds for thinking that if she was she would be killed. At that point Quentina had entered a legal state of semi-existence. She had no right to work and could claim only subsistence-level benefits, but she couldn't be imprisoned and deported. She was not a citizen of the UK but she could not go anywhere else. She was a non-person.

The limbo state in which she was supposed to live did not correspond with reality: she had no right to do the things she needed to do to stay sane and solvent. Fortunately, Quentina's lawyer knew of a charity that took in people like her, the Refuge. This was a group that addressed the needs of stateless people and owned a series of properties around the country. It was in this way that Quentina had come to be living in a terraced house in Tooting with six other stateless women and a house manager. The charity split nationalities up because it didn't like the idea of national cliques developing in the different houses and it thought that refugees learned English more quickly if they weren't with their own language group. That was a mistake in Quentina's view, but it was their charity, not hers, so she shared the house with a Sudanese woman, a Kurd, a Chinese woman who had arrived the day before and so far had not spoken, an Algerian, and two Eastern European women whose precise nationalities Quentina did not know.

Living in the Refuge house with these people was not straightforward. Work was even less so. The charity supplied food to its 'clients' – that was the word – but could not, legally, pay them. Quentina found she had no ability to do nothing all day and that sitting around the house, and not having any disposable income of her own, gave her acute claustrophobia – a sense of being trapped, powerless, inside her own head. This was made worse by the fact that she was, in actuality, genuinely powerless, with no ability to affect her own destiny in any of the relevant important ways. So she decided that she would have to do something with her days, would have to work, in order not to go insane.

There was a kind of grapevine among the refugees on exactly this issue, and that was how she came to encounter 'Kwame Lyons'. He was known as someone who knew someone who could get identity papers for you and therefore through whom you could find work, as long as you were willing to pay him his cut. Quentina had no idea for how many people he provided this service, but she knew there was no way she was Lyons's only – that word again – 'client'. She didn't know and didn't want to know how many 'clients' Lyons had, how he got hold of the identity papers, whether he used the identity 'Kwame Lyons' with all his clients, how much money he was making, or his real name.

Quentina had been told that one of the best places to go and work was a minicab company known to hire drivers with dodgy paperwork, but she also heard that a. they didn't employ women and b. the company was owned by one of the big South London crime families, as a way of laundering cash. The fake ID papers were enough illegality for Quentina, who was temperamentally law-abiding and who also thought that staying on the right side of the law was good practical policy. There was a certain irony that her entire existence was lawless and stateless, but never mind. So she acted on advice from a traffic warden she met in the street, a man from Zambia, who told her about Control Services and the fact that they hired a high proportion of West and Southern Africans. She had taken her fake ID, filled out a form, filled out another form as part of a test, and got the job, and here she was eighteen months later with the lowest rate of upheld appeals of any Control Services employee.

Quentina began to feel tired as she got closer to the hostel. She had been on her feet all day, and though she was used to it, they still ached. With luck there would be some hot water left; she was the only one of the 'clients' with a regular job and therefore the only one who arrived at home after five wanting a bath or shower. Quentina had always been clean and fastidious, but she had never really understood baths until coming to this cold country. Now a soak in steaming water was a significant physical pleasure. Tomorrow would be a day off; one of the blessings of work was that it made free time feel like a treat. She would watch a movie on the DVD player, have a drink, maybe go out dancing and look for a party. Quentina knew that she should probably call her lawyer to hear if there was any news, being as it was the Friday before Christmas and things would slow to a halt over the holidays, but she couldn't quite face it. If there was good news she would hear it and if there was bad it would not be made any worse by being delayed. And the overwhelming probability was that there would be no news, that her state of not-ness would continue. If you are lukewarm I will spit you out of my mouth. That's what the Bible said. Quentina did not think of herself as lukewarm, but it was hard to deny that she had been spat out.

At the end of the road where she lived an African woman with a gigantic bag of what looked like yams, maybe from Brixton Market, was pausing for a breather. The woman looked at Quentina assessingly as she walked past. I wouldn't mind some of whatever she's going to cook tonight, thought Quentina. Never mind, nearly home. Well, not home, but where she lived. She turned the corner, still in her traffic warden's uniform, still the most unpopular woman in the street, still spreading fear and confusion wherever she went.

22

When Roger had something important on at work, he did something that he never told people about because it was so feminine-sounding: he made a huge deal of his washing and grooming in the morning. He showered and shaved as usual, shampooed and conditioned his hair; then he moisturised with a face mask which he left on for ten minutes, trimmed any stray nose or ear hair, rubbed some oil into his legs and chest, took some vitamins, took some artichoke pills for his liver, did some stretches, went downstairs in his dressing gown and ate a bowl of microwaved porridge. Then he dressed in his best clothes: his softest, lushest Savile Row shirt and its matching tie, a pocket square, antique cufflinks Arabella had found on eBay, the suit he'd had made bespoke after a bonus, the handmade shoes and underneath it all, the slinkiest secret of them all, his special lucky silk underpants, brought back by Arabella from a shopping junket to Antwerp. The paradoxical effect of all this pampering was to make him feel fortified, defended, ready for trouble.

It was thus armoured that, on Friday 21 December, Roger went into the conference room at Pinker Lloyd ready to open the envelope that would tell him what he would be getting for his bonus. Going into the room, with its white noise switched on so that it was scientifically impossible to eavesdrop, and with the walls turned opaque for the meeting, Roger felt confident, fit and healthy, braced for whatever would come.

In the room was Max, the head of the compensation committee. Junior employees receiving their bonuses would tend to have
more than one person in the room, in case they flipped out in a
bad year, which meant that they had to have more than one person in the room in good years too, so that the number of people
in the room didn't become an immediate give-away as to the size
of the bonus. Heads of department got more credit than that, so
Roger knew he'd be talking to one person only and guessed that
it would probably be Max. The protocol for this meeting was that
direct line managers didn't usually come to it.

Max was one of those men who were summed up by their
glasses. As contact lenses and corrective eye surgery became
increasingly ubiquitous, glasses were turning into a deliberate
statement – not just the type of glasses but the whole fact of
wearing them. They were a way of being above vanity (popular
with nerds and certain kinds of actor or musician), or of trying
to look more intelligent (popular with off-duty models), or of
expressing intellectual disdain for disguise in a form-follows-
function way (architects, designers), or of being too poor or too
not-bothered. In Max's case, the glasses were a form of defence
mechanism or camouflage. They helped hide his face. At the
same time they tried to look cool: but this was an each-way bet
and as so often with each-way bets, it didn't come off. Max's
specs had narrow wire frames and were technocratic in a way
that tried to express personality but did not.

When Roger had been more junior, by this point he would
already have known the tenor of the bonus meetings – what kind
of mood music was being sent out about bonuses in general. So
you would be braced for a downer or psyched about a good year.
Now, as a head of department, he had no warning. No point trying to pick up cues in body language from Max; he did deadpan
for a living. His form of deadpan was smiley and let's-be-friends.
Although it was famously true that nothing you said in the room

had any effect on your compensation, people sometimes liked to have their say anyway, and it was no bad thing to let people blow off some steam at someone other than their boss. Roger's own assessments would have a direct effect on the bonus packets of his subordinates, and they would know that, and some of them would not be happy bunnies, and that was just the way things went.

'Roger!' Max said, pointing at the seat opposite.

'Max,' said Roger. 'Petra well? Toby and Isabella?'

'All good,' said Max. 'Arabella? Conrad?' – and then there was a half-a-beat or quarter-of-a-beat pause while he stretched for the name; which meant that Roger had won this exchange. 'Joshua?'

'Fit as fleas,' said Roger. 'You know what they're like about Christmas. They go mad, can't get enough presents, impossible demands. And of course the children are excited about it too.'

The two men shared a smile. Max reached into the leather folder in front of him and took out an envelope. Roger, who had been feeling cool and even-tempered in his silk knickers, felt his heart rate and blood pressure shoot up. A pound sign followed by a one with six zeros, one with six zeros, one with six zeros. Two with six zeros? No, that was greedy. One with six zeros.

'Good year for the department,' said Max.

Yesssssss!

'The figures speak for themselves.'

Yesssssss!

'As you know, it isn't always straightforward to, ah, parse the relevant figures from our competitors, so the comparison can't be exact, but we are confident that your department's performance is in the top quartile for the sector.'

Roger knew that, or strongly suspected it, but it was still good to hear.

'Your personal evaluations are strong. The compensation committee is of the view that your performance overall is strong.'

Yesssssss! This wasn't million-quid talk. This was two million, maybe more. Could he be heading for two and a half? A quarter of the way to ten million pounds. He and Arabella might even have sex!

'There is of course a context for all this,' Max went on. Now, for a smaller man than Roger, a man with less steady nerves, this might have been a warning note, an incitement to panic; maybe, even, an invitation to think about missed mortgage payments, promised but unbought diamond necklaces, the deferment of holiday plans; because to a lesser man than Roger, Max's words might have sounded awfully like a 'But'. Roger, however, was a veteran of Pinker Lloyd assessments. This was getting on for his twentieth. He knew that, just as a judge delivering a summing-up likes to make both sides in court shit themselves before reaching his conclusion, a member of the compensation committee likes to have you thinking about bread and water before he gives you a villa in Poggibonsi with a line of cypresses down the drive, a small vineyard, and a heated swimming pool.

Actually there was something to think about there. Minchinhampton was fine but, as previously noted, could be seen as dowdy, and it only took one wet summer to put you permanently off the whole holidays-in-England thing. A bonus of £2.5 million would, once he'd paid for all the things he had to pay for, salted some away in the pension and VCTs and all that, leave him with a fair few quid left over. It was said you could get somewhere pretty habitable on Ibiza for a million quid. Worth thinking about.

Roger's attention had only wavered for a moment, but when he got his focus back, Max was saying,

'. . . and of course the context for this is not just the wider problems in the industry, the cloud no larger than a man's hand

and all that, and the repricing of insurance and swaps. That's just the general weather. In addition, there has been the difficulty we have been having with our Swiss subsidiary.'

And all of a sudden, just like that, Roger felt his bonus beginning to shrink. This was not mood music, this was an actual, genuine, no-bones-about-it 'But'. That weaselly little fucker Max was giving him bad news from behind his glinting Nazi metal specs.

'. . . goes beyond routine volatility into areas of genuine loss. Once the extent of our subsidiary vehicle's exposure to the US market in insecure securitisations was fully known, in particular the fact that those losses are still not precisely assessed, though known as reaching into the ten figures in euros . . .'

Max was telling him that the bank had lost a couple of hundred million euros this year. This was through their Swiss subsidiary's exposure to subprimes. Well whoop de flipping doo. Roger stopped listening. He was getting it in the arse, and didn't need to know the details. Max talked on for a bit more and then the moment came when he slid the envelope across the table. It was clear that his bonus was going to be minute, could even be as little as his annual pay of £150,000. In practical terms, that would be the same as being dragged out the back of the office and finished off with a bullet in the back of the neck.

Roger opened the envelope. It was stuck down, and for a moment he felt a flash of irritation at the prats who ran the bank, the kind of people who didn't know the convention about hand-delivered letters, that they were never stuck down, on the basis that it was an implied insult to third parties handling the letter; the convention was that among gentlemen you could rest assured that private correspondence would go unread. But these nouveau twats had no idea about anything like that. He took out the piece of paper. His bonus for the year was £30,000.

He knew that there was no point saying anything; that it

would do no good to cough and splutter and remonstrate. He had been the person on the other side of the desk and was fully informed of the futility of saying or doing anything in protest. And yet he found himself saying:

'But . . . what . . . it isn't . . . contribution, billions . . . fundamentally not fair . . . when I think of what I've done . . . basic pay . . . not a question of greed but of necessary . . .'

Max just sat there wearing his glasses at him. What was the point? There was no point. Roger stopped talking. The white noise began to seem loud; then it went quiet; then it got louder again. Roger felt his stomach twitch, and then churn, and then he had a strange sensation in his oesophagus, accompanied by a gust of something that was like nausea. Then he realised that it was, in fact, nausea. He felt sick. Actually, he more than felt sick, he was going to be sick. Roger slowly rose to a crouching position and leaned forward over the table. He nodded at Max. He turned and left the room. There might have been people in the corridor; he didn't notice and didn't care. The lavatory was ten paces away. Roger just made it to a cubicle and then he threw up, three times, so hard that it made his stomach muscles ache.

When Roger finished, he lowered the lid of the toilet and just stayed where he was, kneeling on the floor. Wasn't this great? Wasn't this perfect? It was funny to think of all the occasions in a man's life, all the different contexts, when he was sick. It must add up to hundreds of pukings. Yes, thought Roger. I've been sick hundreds of times. There's a whole thesaurus to describe it. Talking to the great white telephone. Parking a tiger on the pavement. Blowing chunks. But this was different from all the other times he'd thrown up, because on all those other occasions, once he'd been sick, he felt better.

23

On Christmas Eve, the DVDs began arriving at houses in Pepys Road. Except it's misleading to say DVDs, plural, because in truth they were all the same DVD. The case had a printed label saying 'We Want What You Have' but inside the DVD had nothing written on it.

The footage was taken by a hand-held camera and began at the south end of the street, in front of the Kamals' shop. From the fact that the street was entirely quiet, but that it was daylight, it was possible to deduce that the film had been shot very early in the morning on a summer's day. At moments the low morning sun dazzled the camera and the picture went white.

From the technical point of view, the film was a mess. The camera-work was jerky and not always focused. The colours were blurry. It was like an early film, from the time before film had been properly invented. Whoever was holding the camera had wandered from side to side in the street. Combined with the wobbliness and the movement and the low quality of the digital film, the effect was to produce a faint sensation of motion sickness. Sometimes the person with the camera had gone up close to specific houses; he (though of course there was no reason to think that it was a 'he') had gone right up to Petunia Howe's front door, for instance, and held his focus on the door number. On other occasions he seemed to be standing in the middle of the road, and panning the camera from side to side, as when he stood outside number 27, the house belonging to Mickey Lipton-Miller. Or he would occasionally zoom right in on someone's car, and look through the windscreen, like a thief on the prowl for a satnav to steal. He lingered, with extra lasciviousness, on the Younts' Lexus S400, as if the camera wanted to be inside the car, running its hands over the leather upholstery. At other moments the cameraperson seemed to be taking a special interest in architectural details. No two houses in the street were identical, so the camera took a look at the pointing on number 36, and then later on the subtly different pointing five doors down at number 46. Or it showed the bay window at number 62, and then the differently shaped bow window at 55, which was polygonal. He or she seemed to take a particular interest in the big expensive double-fronted properties.

Although there was nothing sinister in the content of the DVD, its effect was sinister – something about the idea of somebody watching the street, noticing it so closely. It could not be taken for anything to do with an estate agent or viral marketing. And there was an air of yearning about the film. It was like watching a child looking in the window of a toyshop. Not everybody watched the DVD, but those who did were left with the feeling that somebody somewhere did indeed want what they had.

The DVDs came in jiffy bags. The postmarks on the bags were from all around London.

24

Quentina was not a devout Christian, just as she was no longer a believing Marxist, but she did like going to church. She liked the language and the precious sensation of warmth, she liked the Zimbabwean curate at St Michael's, the African Anglican church she went to in Balham, and most of all she liked the choirmaster, a beautifully firm-looking Botswanan called Mashinko Wilson, a teaching assistant (she'd discovered) with a voice so smoky and so sexy that it was made for singing hymns. The effect was not as noticeable with the African and African-influenced songs, but at Christmas, when he led the choir and congregation through the English Christmas hymns, it was mesmerising: 'O Come All Ye Faithful' sung in this warm voice, clear and sensual and so evidently linked to his healthy, muscular body. Quentina had discovered the Mashinko–Christmas carol effect a week before the previous Christmas, and she'd been looking forward to it all year since. Advent and now Christmas Eve were fulfilling all expectations. Today, after the service, she was going to go up to Mashinko Wilson and declare an interest.

As for the church itself, Quentina liked that too. It was built in a grey stone, not the same as the houses around – granite, maybe. The church had a narrow central aisle and high windows at the end, very traditional, but a section at the back had been glassed in to make a kind of sitting room and crêche, from which wailing and thumping sounds could often be heard during prayers and sermons. It was difficult for the preacher to compete.

Back home, Quentina had gone to the Christmas Eve service at St Mary's Cathedral in Harare every year, with her mother. Mama was the family Christian: Quentina's father used to say that she believed enough for the rest of them added together. She would take one child, Quentina or her brother or sister, to church with her on Sunday, and didn't seem to mind which, as long as it was one of them. She preferred but did not insist that they all come for Easter Sunday and Christmas. Quentina's father she left alone, by peaceable mutual consent. Quentina liked it, because it was one of the only times she got to be on her own with her mother, and she liked the high-flown language of the old Bible, and the exotic imagery of the distant dark cold Northern Christmas; there was an irony in the fact that now she was in the cold north, the thing she liked most about Christmas was the sense of warmth, the lights, the colour, the cosiness.

The baby as the most powerful person in the world. This idea had a deep resonance for Quentina, because she had experienced it first-hand, twice. Quentina herself was a child of the revolution, born in the year Zimbabwe gained its independence, 1980. Her brother Robert was born five years later, and she could still recall the sense of sheer injustice at her own displacement, and at the same time the magic sense of life being rearranged around this new arrival. Robert had had a squashed angry face and the inside of his mouth, which was often visible because he spent so much time howling, was the pinkest thing anyone had ever seen; and his mother and father's gentleness and devotedness were extraordinary to see. Much later Quentina realised that that was how they would have been with her too. At the time she only felt the injustice and envy and resentment of her displacement by this horribly powerful interloper.

She hadn't minded her sister's birth so much. It was hard to resent Sarah, who seemed sweet and placid when she was born and still seemed sweet and placid twenty years later. Robert had been furious, which Quentina at the time had thought was great. Let him get a taste of how it feels. The terrible power of the newborn baby. The defenceless child who rules the world. The bundle in the crib who is President of the World. Deal with that, little brother!

It was no doubt because Quentina felt Robert's terrible, unforgivable youngerness so strongly that his death hit her so hard. His first symptom was a cough that simply would not go away, followed by a cascade of other symptoms, none of which seemed big at the start, none of which ever resolved or improved, until he was, within a year, covered in sores, blind, breathless, visibly dying, and within another three months, dead. Aids, of course. What else? The young man who had once been the baby at the centre of the world, the Christ-child in his crib.

Perhaps that in and of itself would not have been enough to change Quentina's direction of life. His death made her philosophically angry, angry with life, but that wasn't the same thing as specific anger, the kind of anger that brought not just a wish for change but the will to act on the wish. That didn't come until Quentina broke her ankle in a fall and was taken to hospital. She was treated by a doctor who told her she hadn't broken it, just strained it.

'The best treatment is rest,' said the doctor. 'Will you go out with me?'

'No.'

Quentina spent the next six weeks pretending to evade his attentions, with steadily less zeal. He was called John Zimbela and was, Quentina gradually came to realise, the most admirable person she had ever known, and also just about the angriest, ecstatic with rage at the Mugabe government's Aids policy, or antipolicy, since its principal pillars were evasion and falsehood.

With several friends he belonged to an underground network which illegally printed and distributed leaflets about HIV, safe sex, infection rates, the course of the illness, and the treatment regimes which were available in the rich countries. He was risking his livelihood and perhaps his life, and though when she had met him Quentina had known about Aids, she had thought that her brother's death was a kind of accident, a too common accident perhaps, but basically an act of God, whereas she now realised it was the result of a set of policies that amounted to institutionalised manslaughter – not murder, you couldn't quite call it that, but manslaughter. And then she had got angry too, and had joined John and his network, and had begun to work against Mugabe, to stop just studying politics and start living them.

Quentina's father had fought in the bush during the revolution: he hadn't been a paper revolutionary but the real thing, living off mealies and carrying a gun for five years. Now he was a fairly senior member of Zanu-PF with a good job at the education ministry, education having been a priority and a pride for the young country of Zimbabwe. Quentina did not grow up in the back seat of a Mercedes, and there was no sense of entitlement anywhere about her family's life, but she was in her way secure, comfortable, a member of the established order. Now that changed. She became a kind of secret outlaw, and was risking her family's status in the process, and it was that which caused her deepest worries about what she was doing: she could admire her courage on her own behalf, but on the part of her family she felt at times it was almost an indulgence. She occasionally asked herself what Robert would have wanted, but came up with no answer. All she could really remember about her brother was his birth and his death. She felt she had no real recollection of what Robert had actually been like. It was as if

Robert's death had taken not just Robert but all memories of him too.

A month after she began distributing leaflets and going to secret meetings, her father died of lung cancer. He wasn't diagnosed, he just died of it. They found out about the disease through the autopsy.

Quentina's political career lasted for nine months. It began with Aids, then spread into a campaign against arrests and beatings and all the other human rights abuses. Quentina thought it would be a race between getting caught and Zanu-PF turning against Mugabe, with the odds fairly equal, but she was wrong. At her final beating, she was told that the only thing preventing her from being raped to death was the status her father had once had; the protection offered by that was now void. So here she was, three years later, in a church in London listening to the descant singers trying to compete with Mashinko Wilson's melody line in 'O Come All Ye Faithful'.

The service came to an end and the congregation slowly drifted out of the church. People milled about, shaking hands, chatting. Quentina knew a few of her fellow worshippers but kept her greetings brief. She was on a mission. Mashinko as usual had a small fan club around him, chatting and praising. As usual he was glowing, warm, his rich skin alight. She could wait for the group to thin out, but that would involve so much loitering that it would be difficult not to look weak, dithering: unworthy. Humans make their own history, but not under circumstances of their choosing. Quentina went straight up to Mashinko, who was being held by the arm by a short woman of about sixty and was smiling indulgently. Quentina stood in front of him and did something she knew very well how to do: she got his full attention.

'I just wanted to say, I thought that was beautiful,' said Quentina. Mashinko's face, which had already been shining, grew even more radiant. That was all she needed. He would remember her next time. 'Goodbye. Happy Christmas,' she said, and turned and left. Quentina went out into the cold dark of Christmas Eve in London.

Memory could not compete against hope. It was no contest. Even a small amount of hope would do.

25

'cn i c u?'

the text had read. Shahid had no idea whose mobile this message was from, so he texted back:

'ok bt hu r u?'

Shahid had to admit, he thought it might be a girl, a forgotten girl he had tried to pick up somewhere, or an old flame, who must be a bit keen on him because why otherwise would she have kept his number? There was a girl at Clapham South once, she'd dropped a whole bunch of papers on the platform as she got off the train, the rude commuters had just shoved past, of course, Shahid had picked them up, they'd got chatting, she was a law student, they'd gone for a coffee right there across the road, they'd swapped numbers, then about a week later he'd lost his mobile and he'd always wondered if she might have been the one . . . that was six months or so ago now. It might be her, it just might. He'd put a thing in 'Lost Connections' in *Metro* but had come up blank. But even if it wasn't the law student, basically, if it was a girl, it was good news.

The reply was disappointing.

'Iqbal hr When?'

Great. Just what I need, thought Shahid. Reminiscences about Chechnya from a Belgian-Algerian semi-weirdo jihadi I haven't seen for over a decade. He texted back:

'Tuesday at 6 ok 13 Pelham Rd'

Which was where he now was, on Christmas Eve, watching *The Simpsons* with one eye while trying to work out just how it was Iqbal seemed to have manoeuvred him into agreeing to put him up for a few days.

'I mean I've been let down,' Iqbal was saying. 'My friend let me down. If it were not for that I would not be having to turn to you.'

He was angry and ingratiating at the same time, and seemed keen to convince, as if his anger were something he was selling. Iqbal had come to London to stay with a friend, but the friend had kicked him out, offering a complicated alibi to do with relations who might be visiting and for whom he needed to keep the spare room free, plus he had a big work thing coming up, etc. etc. It was coming back to Shahid, a little too late: in Chechnya they hadn't got on all that well. Iqbal had been angry all the time about not just large issues and global injustices but about the fact that the hot water had run out or the only part of the bread left was the crust and he didn't like the crust. He was quick to connect the two, as well: if a petrol station in Austria had a lavatory that was closed because the flush didn't work, this was part of a planet-wide conspiracy to disrespect Muslims.

In Shahid's view, the best way through difficult times, as through life in general, was just to go along with things. It was a rare problem that couldn't be solved by being ignored. Iqbal would be difficult to ignore but if he put him up for a few days he would surely go away and things would return to normal.

'Brothers should not treat each other like that. And we are brothers, aren't we? Brothers should not behave in this way.' Iqbal was pacing.

'I've said you can stay,' said Shahid.

Iqbal seemed to collect himself.

'And I am grateful. I feel all appropriate gratitude. Forgive me if my anger got the better of me.'

'It's cool. I'm just going to watch the end of this and then I'll show you where stuff is, how to set up the sofa bed and all that.'

'You are a good man.'

'No, it's cool, really.'

Insistently, Iqbal said: 'You are a good man. Perhaps you have forgotten this truth about yourself. Perhaps it is something other people do not see or encourage you not to see. But you are a good man.'

Well, put like that, it was hard not to think there might be something in this Shahid-as-good-man theory. Shahid gave a modest aw-shucks shrug just as Mr Burns did his steepled-fingers thing and said 'Excellent.'

26

Hanging from a strap on the Jubilee line as he went home on Christmas Eve, Roger thought about when might be the best time to tell Arabella about his non-existent bonus. Arabella was good at making life seem easy, except when she suddenly and dramatically wasn't. Roger had an intuition this might be one of those times.

It would have been better to have done it already, obviously. But on Friday he had just been too numb, too freaked, too incredulous, too sick. He was in no condition to have a long talk about his missing million pounds . . . And anyway, by the end of the day the impulse to blurt everything out had long since faded. A lesser man, Roger felt, would have gone home straight after being sick. Roger was made of sterner stuff, and anyway what would he do if he went home? Sit there blubbing and moping and waiting for Arabella to get back from the shops? No, he sucked it up, took it like a man, and spent the day hiding in his office and pretending to work.

Not that much work got done on 21 December at Pinker Lloyd, as the compensation committee broke its news. Every now and then he would peek through the window and survey the scene in the trading room. The noise was about a quarter of its usual level. People were just sitting there. One or two of them had their heads in their hands. Some others were just standing around in a demoralised little group. They looked like refugees or something. Sad, so sad. It was like . . . Roger stretched to find some metaphor for the scale of the grief, the comprehensiveness of the disaster. Being in some shithole in Iraq or somewhere, where some Yank pilot has dropped a bomb on you by mistake. Everybody's blown into pieces, bits everywhere, limbs, blood, everything. And it's not your fault. That was the key thing – not your fault. He hadn't done anything wrong. But they went and dropped the bomb anyway. Those bloody Yanks . . .

Anyway: Friday had been too soon, and there hadn't really been an opportunity over the weekend. It was the sort of news you had to steel yourself to break, you had to create a pause around the moment, and there hadn't been an opportunity. Arabella had been out on Saturday, and he'd had a lie-in and then pottered about while the weekend nanny took Joshua and Conrad, then he'd gone to the gym in the afternoon and they'd had a takeaway after the kids were in bed, but things had by then felt too chilled out to spoil the mood, and then on Sunday they had a brunch date at the country club, and it had slid into the afternoon, and Roger had first been buzzed from a couple or even three Bloody Marys and then had been coming down from the buzz, and the day had somehow gone, and now it was Monday, Christmas Eve, and there was no way this could possibly be the right time, could it? To tell your wife you'd underperformed your own expectations – which Roger had mentioned to Arabella, one night a couple of months ago, a mistake he couldn't resist making to see the glint come into her eye, at some point when his marital stock had otherwise been rather low – but to tell your wife you'd underperformed by a cool £970,000, that wasn't the sort of gift you gave on Christmas Eve. Roger wasn't a monster.

What with all the whatever, he'd barely had time to think about its being Christmas. At least he had sorted out Arabella's present, some fancy sofa she'd had her eye on, which would be (this was the punchline) delivered *on Christmas Day itself*. The people at the furniture company, the delivery people anyway, worked on Christmas so you could have your present right there when you wanted it with none of that rubbish about waiting two weeks for the delivery. Fair enough, if you were spending ten grand on a sofa you could at least get the arsing thing delivered when you actually wanted it even if it was Christmas.

The thing was, to let Christmas be Christmas. Not to turn it into something out of a depressing film, *It's a Wonderful Life* without the happy ending. *It's a Shit Life and We're Suddenly Poor*. No. Don't tell her on Boxing Day, obviously. The plan was to go down to Minchinhampton on the 27th and stay into the new year, have a few chums down for a party and sleepover on New Year's Eve. That might be the time to do it, in Gloucestershire. Have a bit more perspective out of London. Arabella would be knackered from looking after the children – she'd already warned him that it would be 'just the two of them' doing childcare over the holiday – which would mean she would be grumpy but on the other hand she'd also be busy with the boys and that would keep her distracted. OK, that was the plan. Tell her on the 27th, in the country. Maybe go for a walk and tell her. He'd be carrying Joshua in a papoose on his back, which would make it hard for her to yell at him. As always when he'd made a plan, Roger felt better.

He trotted up the stairs at the Tube station and came out into the dark of Christmas Eve. The high street was mayhem: half the people there doing last-minute Christmas shopping, the other half determined to start the first evening of the holiday pissed. The bars were heaving. Roger dodged drunks and shoppers. Church bells were ringing: for a moment Roger thought about rounding everybody up and dragging them to the service of lessons and carols. But that wasn't really them, was it? Plus Josh would already be in bed. No: shower, change, glass of champagne. They might even have sex. When it was a holiday Arabella sometimes let him.

Roger was home. The front door bumped against Pilar's bag – that's right, she was off to whichever Latin country it was she was from, Colombia or something. At the other end of the open-plan ground floor the television was showing one of Conrad's Japanese-looking cartoon series. He would be sitting in front of the screen with his thumb in his mouth.

Pilar materialised by the door. She seemed in something of a rush.

'Mr Yount, thank you, I go now,' she said. 'Josh he upstairs. Already in bed.'

'Great, fabulous, thank you so much.'

'Happy Christmas,' said Pilar. 'Goodbye!' And she was gone. That was, as Roger's conversations with her went, on the long side: weeks went by without his seeing Pilar at all. Roger went through into the sitting room. Sure enough, Conrad was sucking his thumb and watching people fighting on rocket-power sky-cycles. Arabella wasn't with him so she must be upstairs, perhaps settling Josh or on the phone making plans for New Year's.

'Daddy's just going to have a quick shower,' said Roger. His son made no sign of having heard him. From the noise and the general sense of dramatic urgency, Roger gathered that it was a crucial moment in the story. He went upstairs, undressed, ran the shower until it was hot and the room was half-full of steam, and then got in. He felt his muscles unknot and some of the horror of the bonus question melt away. It was Christmas: family time: quality time: the thing was to enjoy it. Yes. Roger always felt better when he was completely clean so he shampooed his hair and shaved, both for the second time that day, then dressed in his non-going-out slouchy trousers and went downstairs. Conrad was now watching a different but extremely similar mock-Japanese cartoon. Time for a glass of Bollinger.

There was an envelope on the table in Arabella's large looping very feminine handwriting. Roger picked it up.

Dear Roger,

You stupid spoilt selfish shit, I have gone away for a few days. So that you get a glimpse of what it is like to be me, you spoilt lazy arrogant stuck-up typical male bastard. You have no idea at all what it's like to look after the children, and you have no idea at all what the last couple of years have been like, so this is now your chance to try it and see. Pilar has gone and the nanny agencies will be shut for the next few days at least. Congratulations, you are looking after your two boys on your own. As for where I've gone that's none of your fucking business but I will be back and when I am I'll expect to see some changes in your attitude and in what you actually do. None of that coming home from work acting like you're the one who has a difficult time of it. Welcome to my life, and if I ever get so much as a glimpse of competitive tiredness from you ever again I'll be leaving permanently – or rather you will and I leave you to guess who will get the house and the children.

Fuck off,
Arabella

27

It wouldn't be true to say that Roger saw the funny side, or had glimpses of perspective, or anything like that; but there were one or two moments on Christmas morning when he was able to remember that things hadn't always been like this. At about quarter to seven, for instance, he was downstairs on the sitting-room carpet trying to assemble a plastic robot which turned into a car and also into a gun and uttered set phrases through a speaker-box and could also be operated by remote control. The problem was that it was a very complicated toy: not only was it highly fiddly, with hundreds of small parts, but it came with instructions which seemed designed with the conscious intention to confuse and mislead. Beside and around and beneath Roger, the floor was covered in pieces of infant Lego from several different kits, which Conrad had torn open and thrown around the room while his back was turned. Joshua had upended the gigantic box of Brio he'd been given, so a substrate of wooden train tracks and engines lay mixed in with the plastic, paper, torn boxes, and various other toys which had been briefly experimented with and discarded. Conrad had already broken one of his main toys, a racing car with green stripes and a driver who was supposed to beep when you pressed down on his head, but who had been jammed down so firmly that he didn't stop ringing, like an alarm. Roger hadn't been able to find either an off switch or a battery hatch to open so he had smashed the toy with a hammer.

Conrad was still sniffling about that, while fiddling with one of his new lightsabers.

No, Roger had not seen the funny side. But there had been a moment when, after looking at his watch, he had thought: I can remember when Christmas morning would start at about half past ten with a glass of Buck's Fizz in bed. Now it begins at half past five, with a test of my fine motor skills and ability to read Korean.

There was no sense in which Roger had taken things lying down. The previous night, straight away on getting Arabella's note, he had bundled a protesting Conrad off to bed, then hit Google and looked up nanny agencies (not forbearing to try things like 'emergency nannies', 'last-minute nannies' and 'crisis nannies'). He had left messages on the answering machines of seven different agencies and knew that he was going to hire the very first person who was available. So help was at hand. But help being at hand was no help, not right in the here and now, with his wife away wherever the hell it was she was, and his parents a. in Majorca and b. useless.

After leaving the nanny messages, Roger had held the phone in his hand for a long time. The question was what message to leave on Arabella's mobile. He knew her well enough to know she wouldn't answer it, or even have it switched on; he also knew that she'd be checking her messages, desperate to know how her plan had gone. His first impulse was to ring her up and rant, de-nounce, deplore, ask her who she thought she was, tell her just how lazy she was, just how little a clue she had, and by the way they were £970,000 short of where they needed to be this hol-iday. To tell her not to bother coming back; to tell her that the locks would be changed; that all further contact between them would have to be through solicitors; that her children now hated her; and more of the same.

Roger also knew that she would be expecting and to some extent depending on a reaction along those lines. He had a simple maxim for all competitive or adversarial situations: work out what the other party least wants you to do, and then do it. Relieving your feelings was fun, but the best course of action was to make things as difficult as possible for the person trying to make things difficult for you. On that basis, the thing that would most freak out Arabella was for him to be cool, to act as if nothing could have disconcerted him less than having the kids on his own over Christmas. She would be relying on drama, on fuss; probably on an explosive row followed by lavish making-up, mainly engineered by him. OK, fine. He would give her the silent treatment. Knowing Arabella, she would have gone to some posh spa or hotel. Well, she could stew there. He'd be fine with the boys. How hard could it be?

Now it was Christmas morning, and as if to answer that question, Joshua, who had insisted on having his night-time nappy taken off, was making it clear that he needed to go to the toilet – which he did by pointing to the sitting-room door and roaring. Roger picked him up with his right hand, carried him up to the half-landing, and opened the loo door with his left. There should have been a potty, but there wasn't: the last thing Pilar did when she left on a weekend or holiday was disinfect all the potties with Dettol and leave them to dry in the boys' bathroom, but Roger didn't know that, so he tried to hold Joshua in place on the loo seat and stop him falling into the toilet bowl while his son did whatever he had to do. Joshua seemed to object to that procedure; he didn't like being held up with his bum in the air over the loo.

'There's nothing else for it,' said Roger. Joshua twisted his upper body round and tried to bite Roger on the arm. 'Would you rather I let you fall in?' asked Roger. The answer to that seemed to be in the affirmative. Joshua now began wriggling from side to side as hard as he could, with the full unrestrained strength of a three-year-old. He had the concentrated force of pure will and was also stocky, muscular, a tube of force and determination. He suddenly changed direction and bucked upwards, catching Roger right on the point of the chin with a ferocious upward head-butt.

'Fuck!' shouted Roger, his eyes stinging with tears. As his grip weakened, he felt Joshua slip. The little boy fell forward off the loo seat, seeming to be in tears before he landed on the floor. At that point, with no warning, he began to shit. A spray of excrement, not entirely liquid in texture but not solid either, came out of Joshua's bum and as if it were a form of propellant he began crawling at amazing speed out of the loo, heading for the landing. Roger, head ringing, one hand on his mouth and jaw, lunged after him but he was too slow and Joshua made it onto the cream carpet before his father could catch him. Excrement was still coming out of Josh's bottom and he was still crying. Roger was crying too thanks to the head-butt, which had made his eyes fill with tears. He lunged again and grabbed Josh with his right arm before he could make it down the stairs. Roger, wrestling with his son, noticed something that it was not helpful to notice: that the colour of the fresh shit-swirls on the carpet was exactly the shade of a perfectly made cappuccino. Then Joshua shat again, this time down the arm of Roger's dressing gown. The shit was liquid and hot. It smelt very bad. Then the front door rang.

'Fuck!' said Roger, under his breath, but not sufficiently under his breath, because Joshua, smiling now that he had relieved himself, also said 'Fuck!' Roger decided that whoever it was at the door could sod off. He took Joshua back into the loo and put him standing up in the sink. Then he shrugged his dressing gown off, thinking: that's for the bin. Then he ran the taps and washed Joshua, who was clean from the waist up but below that was about 70 per cent covered in shit. While he was doing this the doorbell rang twice more, each time for longer. Roger put Joshua down and looked in the cupboard under the sink, where there were about seven or eight different kinds of cleaner, none of them self-evidently the one to use to get shit off a carpet. There was something called carpet shampoo, Roger knew that. That would be the stuff. But none of these things admitted to being carpet shampoo. While Roger was looking at the various aerosol sprays, Joshua picked up the bleach and tried to get the top off, then when his father took it away from him made a lunge for the air-freshener, knocked the top off before Roger could react, sprayed himself in the face at a range of three inches, and burst into tears again. Then the doorbell rang for about the fifth time. Who rang the bell like that on Christmas Day, for God's sake? Roger put his dressing gown back on, trying to avoid handling the stripes of shit on the left arm, picked up his naked son and went downstairs to open the door.

Three large men, all of them at least Roger's height, stood there with a huge package, wrapped in cardboard.

'Happy Christmas,' the largest of the large men said in a South African accent. 'We have a delivery for Mrs Yount.' He lowered his voice to a loud whisper. 'It's the sofa.'

'Fuck!' said Joshua.

28

If asked, Arabella would have told anyone that she had a fabulous time over Christmas, never better; that she'd never enjoyed a Christmas more. That was what Saskia and Arabella told each other, as they met in the relaxation room between treatments, or had their goes side by side on the treadmill, or ate their special luxury light lunch (maguro tuna sushi, carpaccio of monkfish and prosciutto, Earl Grey sorbet, Krug to wash it down). That was what Arabella told herself, many times, when she woke in the morning on Christmas Day, when she took her first sip of champagne at breakfast, and when she and Saskia unwrapped the presents they had bought each other (a MacBook for Saskia, who was at last definitely going to get to grips with that screenplay; a lovely Indian necklace for Arabella), and at the other times she felt a wave of something she could not exactly name. It was not a doubt that she was doing the right thing, because she knew that she was: her rationalisations were in perfect order. This experience was sure to make Roger a better, more attentive parent and spouse, and that would be a good thing for every member of the Yount family.

Despite that, there were momentary wobbles. It was as if the ground was slightly unfirm under her feet; not for long, and only when she thought about Joshua and Conrad and whether or not they were missing her – how, exactly, they were missing her. She sat tight and waited for the uncertainties to pass, and so they did.

At dinner, she and Saskia got chatting to a couple at the next table, a South African lawyer and his wife whose twin daughters were gap-yearing around Latin America. Saskia was a little tiddly by this point and kept giggling and making goo-goo eyes at the husband, who had done that madly unfair thing of keeping his looks while the wife had aged much faster. Under other circumstances it would have been funny but Saskia was so blatant, there was something a little sad about it . . .

Saskia and her new friends – the wife looking like she was making the best of an evening she knew would be over soon – went through to the drawing room for liqueurs. Arabella knew that if she drank any more she would have a hangover and part of the point of being in this luxury spa was to go home looking and feeling fabulous, so she went to her room and read a novel set in Afghanistan until she realised she had fallen asleep twice already, and so she put the book down and turned out the light.

29

Boxing Day was Freddy Kamo's first day on the bench at his new club. He knew he had been doing well in training but he was still surprised to be picked. The game was against the team who were bottom of the Premiership. The manager's explanation had been very clear.

'You won't get on for long if you get on at all,' he said through the interpreter. 'But it will help you to get a feel of things here. This is our easiest game over the holiday and I'll be rotating the squad. And also,' smiling, 'don't forget to enjoy it.'

That was advice Freddy intended to take – but it wasn't easy. The warm-up was OK, but when he came out of the tunnel and ran to the dugout before kick-off, everything felt completely different. The noise and drama of the ground couldn't be prepared for: this was the real thing. He had been to the stadium many times before, but it was not the same from the bench. The sensation of being in front of the crowd, the sheer volume of it, the emotional intensity, was a physical thing, almost an assault. Freddy could feel his heart rate was up; he tried to resist the temptation to look around for his father, who he knew would be sitting in the stands beside Mickey Lipton-Miller. Then he did look round and saw Patrick, who looked back at him, not smiling, completely serious. That helped to settle Freddy. Seeing his father on edge gave him permission to relax. The translator came and sat beside Freddy, squeezing in on the bench. Freddy could smell that he had had a glass of wine with his lunch.

The referee blew for the kick-off and Freddy's team were two goals up within twenty minutes. There wasn't much pattern to the match that Freddy could see, but his side were generating chances more or less at will, and the striker took two of them with ease. It didn't seem likely to stay 2–0 for long, but they relaxed a little and stopped pressing so hard. Half-time seemed to come very quickly. The manager didn't say much, just told them to keep playing as they had been. As they were going out at the end of half-time, he tapped Freddy on the shoulder.

'I may give you a run at the end of the half,' he said, through the translator. 'Just a couple of minutes.'

Freddy nodded. He wished the manager hadn't told him; now he'd be nervous all half. It didn't occur to him that that was part of the point, to give him a taste of expectation and pressure. Back on the bench, Freddy began to concentrate on the left-back, who would be marking him. He seemed on the slow side; Freddy was confident, and more confident still when the £20 million midfielder scored from a free kick to put them three goals ahead.

With five minutes to go, the manager told him to warm up. With two minutes to go, the manager summoned him, and waved to the linesman, who checked his studs, then waved to the referee, and then he was on. Freddy ran to the far wing. His instructions were simple: be available for the ball, and get a cross in if possible or hold it up for the midfield if not.

In the stands, Patrick had a rush of sensations he couldn't explain to himself: frantic, scared, suddenly full of conflicting memories and emotions to do with his son's youth, the first moment he'd held him, the day Freddy's mother died, kicking a ball about in the dirt outside their house, watching Freddy play in his school team and score his first goals for them, holding his forehead when he was sick, taking him to games and picking him up after them and standing and watching him play hundreds, maybe even thousands of times, putting mercurochrome on his cuts, calming him when he had night terrors, his first-born child, his only son. Patrick felt his stomach turn over as he watched Freddy trot out onto the field, his awkward too-long legs looking skinnier and more elongated than ever in the huge crowded stadium, on the field with men fifteen years older than him. Patrick felt something wrong with his face. He reached up; his cheeks were soaked with tears.

The crowd roared. Most of them knew who Freddy was, though they'd never seen him play. The ball was down at the other team's end as the opposition passed sideways and backwards looking for an opening that wasn't there. Then the central defender and captain won a 50-50 and knocked it to the £20 million midfielder near the centre circle. He looked around and played a short ball to the holding midfielder, who hit a first-touch pass to Freddy. It was all happening very quickly, but Freddy expected that. He'd experienced this before. When a player in any sport goes up a level, the first, overwhelming impression he gets is that of increased speed. It's not that they're doing things he's never seen before, it's just that they're doing them faster and better and more often.

The opposition left-back, whose name Freddy didn't know, was about two metres away. At home, there was a move Freddy had done so often that, playing a kick-about game in front of his house in Linguère, it no longer worked, because all his friends, everyone in Linguère, had seen it a million times. Nobody here had seen it though, and it was a closer thing to Freddy than his own reflection in the mirror, as easy as getting out of bed. He lunged towards the ball with his left foot, but then, dummying, let it roll past and took it on his right foot instead. His weight was transferred, his direction switched, all in a second, and he was off. It was a dummy, a jink, and a burst out of the starting blocks, all in the same movement.

There had been rain that morning. The pitch was not completely dry; that probably had an effect. The left-back had no real idea who Freddy was. It was the ninetieth minute and his concentration was wavering. The result of Freddy's move was that the defender sold himself to Freddy's leftward jink and when he tried to adjust his balance to follow him, he lost his footing and slipped over on his backside, but slowly, windmilling his arms to try and keep himself upright as he went inexorably over. By the time he was actually on his behind, Freddy was ten metres away. One centre-back came over to close him down, Freddy hit a cross to the far post, the striker got above the other centre-back and headed it against the crossbar with a noise Freddy never forgot, a smack like an axe hitting wood. The goalie collected the rebound and booted it upfield, and then the referee blew for full time.

By midnight that night, a clip called 'Freddy's first touch' was one of the ten most-viewed items on YouTube.

30

People sometimes said that stressful or dramatic or unusual circumstances caused time to 'pass in a blur'. Roger wished that he had found that to be true. The forty-eight hours over Christmas were the most exhausting of his life. After the sofa was wrestled into position and signed for – he couldn't face having it unwrapped, so it spent the day in its assigned corner of the larger drawing room, still reproachfully in its cardboard container – he made the mistake of turning on the television and letting the boys sit in front of it while they played with their new presents. They both had made spectacular hauls. Conrad had his robot, as well as huge boxes of Transformers, Bionicles, Lego, Action Men, and two lightsabers. Joshua did not understand Christmas yet so the sight of his colossal new Brio train set did not seem to exert much grip; it was as if he did not realise that it now belonged to him. Arabella had also bought him a giant bright orange teddy bear, almost five feet tall – too tall to drag around after him, though he might be able to sit on it. Joshua looked at it carefully, thoughtfully, for about thirty seconds, then burst into tears, and wouldn't stop crying until the bear had been taken out of the room and hidden and Roger had promised that he would never ever ever see it again ever, not once.

'Nevertobeseenagain,' said Josh, when he had calmed down, repeating a phrase he liked from a story Pilar had read him.

'Never to be seen again,' agreed Roger. They were now sitting in front of the television watching a children's programme with shouting presenters. Roger knew that there were scandals involving children's TV presenters taking cocaine. To be that lively that early in the morning, it would in Roger's view have been much more shocking if they hadn't been taking cocaine. In fact, thinking about it, maybe coke could be the secret of a whole new parenting strategy . . .

But the television was a terrible mistake. He used it up too soon. Roger didn't know that his boys eventually tired of television, especially when they were allowed to watch it first thing in the morning; they became febrile and listless. In that condition it was as if they'd had too much sugar, and became unbiddable, unmalleable, prone to tantrums, both manic and exhausted at the same time. Roger should have used TV as a strategy of last resort. After no more than a couple of hours, he was knackered (also panicking, and full of rage, and self-pity); Joshua and Conrad were tired too, and bored, and bouncing on the old sofa, with each boy desperate for their father to play a strenuous game with him alone. With two sons and one father that was impossible, which made it all the more necessary, until Joshua trumped his older brother by flinging himself off the sofa-side table while Roger was distracted, and bumping his head, so Conrad retaliated by smashing his biggest new Transformer – Optimus Prime, his favourite – against a table leg, so hard that it didn't just break-for-effect (he knew they came apart into pieces and could be reassembled, and this was the outcome he was looking for) but broke-for-real, at which point his tears and tantrum became real too: genuine, inconsolable grief.

At that point, with both his sons screaming and crying, Roger, feeling as tired as he could ever remember feeling – feeling weepy with tiredness, gritty-eyed, furious, heavy, as if lying down on the bed would make him sleep for a month – looked at his watch. As he did so, he framed a wish about what the time might be; half past eleven, perhaps, with Joshua's nap, which he knew took place at some point in the afternoon, now in sight? Then he could stick Conrad in front of the telly, again, or lock him in his room, or something, and go back to bed himself for a little precious sleep. Sleep – he had never really valued it before. He had taken it for granted. That was not right, because you should not take sleep for granted, because sleep was the best thing in the world. By far. Much, much better than sex. Much. And he could be having some, soon, oh so very soon, if only the outcome when he looked at his watch was that the time was say eleven, which was likely, or eleven thirty, which was possible, or twelve, or, who knew? time could fly past – or even twelve fifteen?

It was ten. Roger felt his eyes fill with tears. His eyes lit on the card on the mantelpiece, the one which said somebody wanted what he had. Well, what he wanted at that moment, more than anything else, was a cyanide pill.

That established a pattern. A stretch of time would go past, and Roger would know that it was going past, while he, say, lay on the floor pretending to be a baddy Power Ranger, or pushed a train round the Brio track making chuffing noises, or ran very slowly away from the advancing Roboraptor pretending to be a plant-eating dinosaur in the grip of fear. He would do this for some time then expect that time had fulfilled its part of the bargain, and had, somehow, passed: that having been twenty past eleven the last time he looked at his watch it would now be significantly later. Instead it would be twenty-five past eleven.

Lunch was interesting. It was demanding to prepare – Conrad couldn't remember which kind of eggs he liked, so Roger had to fry an egg and throw it away and boil an egg and throw it away and poach an egg and throw it away, before it was found by trial and error that scrambled eggs were the ones Conrad would eat. The confusion came about because he had said he liked the one which was eggy. Even allowing for that, Conrad was much less tricky than Joshua. He angrily refused everything Roger suggested before eventually deigning to eat a single narrow slice of crustless white bread with a thin smear of smooth peanut butter, and that was at the fourth attempt: the first slice was too thick, the second was defiled by the use of crunchy peanut butter, and the third by the use of too much peanut butter. Scraping the spread off and re-serving the slice with a thinner smear was by no means acceptable. There was something about the texture of Joshua's tantrum, the way he thumped the table with his plastic plate while shouting 'no! no Daddy no!': the impersonal severity of his rage made it clear that this was a question of standards. A smear of peanut butter with some peanut butter taken off the top was not the same thing as a fresh smear of peanut butter.

For dinner they had the identical menu. This was two-thirds laziness, or exhaustion, on Roger's part, and one-third practicality, since there wasn't much else to cook: most of the fridge was occupied by a goose, bought by Arabella 'to eat on Christmas Day', and delivered on Christmas Eve. Her plan was obviously in place by the time she did this, so the whole goose thing was part of her strategy to first deceive her husband, then taunt him. It was one thing to be abandoned by your wife over Christmas, another to have the enormous American-style, almost walk-in fridge two-thirds-full of goose. Besides, as Arabella knew perfectly well, Roger hated goose. So for Christmas dinner he ate the boys' leftover eggs and peanut butter, followed by a cheese sandwich, followed by two packets of crisps, and washed down with a bottle of Veuve Clicquot La Grande Dame 1990, which was supposed to be the pre-Christmas-lunch aperitif. That, too, turned out to be a mistake, because Roger then had to cope with the last few hours of the day half-cut. Christmas Day spent alone with his children was, in Roger's considered view, the longest, hardest, most boring day of his life. The one good thing was that the boys had only once or twice asked after Arabella. It was as if, in the general mayhem of Christmas, they had barely noticed she wasn't there. Hah! Roger was very much looking forward to telling her that.

Boxing Day was slightly better. It began later, for a start: Josh didn't come thudding down the stairs until seven o'clock. Roger woke before he came into the room, and felt as if he had been awake already, but still, seven was better than six. Better still, Joshua, instead of immediately launching into demands and complaints, got into bed with Roger and snuggled up against him for a full fifteen minutes. That was a good feeling; it was a long time since Roger had felt himself still against the extraordinary density and heat of his son's small warm body. Then Joshua began jabbing him with his finger and saying 'bokfas, bokfas', which meant breakfast, and they came downstairs for chocolate cereal and the day's first burst of television.

The children's TV presenters still seemed to be coked out of their brains. Roger still envied them. Conrad came down at about eight, and his second day in full solo charge of his boys was in full swing. They went to Starbucks to get a triple-shot espresso (Roger), a cream-based java chip Frappuccino (Conrad) and a steamed-milk babycino (Joshua). Conrad managed to knock the fire extinguisher off the wall outside the disabled toilet while Joshua had distracted Roger by trying to climb up and/ or push over a stool, but the extinguisher didn't go off, which was another good omen for the day. They went for a walk on the Common, which was as empty as Roger had ever seen it. At one point, on their way to the dog-free zone to kick a football about, he walked past a young woman pushing a pram – middle-class, she was, as Roger registered without bothering to examine how he decoded that fact: something about her scarf, or her pram, or her hair – and she gave him a look of unqualified approval. Roger thought for a moment how he must look: dad shoving along a pushchair with one small boy in it, wrapped up in a coat and hugging a football; second small boy trotting alongside. The likely diagnosis would be, thoughtful father taking his sons for a Boxing Day walk while Mum has a well-deserved lie-in. Well, bollocks to that, thought Roger, and before he'd realised it the thought made him scowl at the nice, and distinctly fit-looking, middle-class mum.

It was windy on the bare Common, and colder than Roger had expected. There were no other children out today; only one or two addicted joggers. They gave up after about ten minutes and headed for home.

'Hot chocolate?' said Roger, realising, as he spoke the words, that he didn't in fact know how to make hot chocolate. How hard could it be? And maybe the tin would have instructions. But the boys had decided they were too cold to make that sort of decision. Joshua got back in his pushchair and made a token attempt at doing up the buckle before Roger helped him out. Conrad zipped up his own coat and pulled the hood over his head, then put his hands deep in his coat pockets with his shoulders hunched. He looked like a very small mugger.

Walking back across the Common, all three of them now crouching into themselves to keep warm, Conrad said:

'Witches' knickers.'

Roger thought he must have misheard.

'What?'

Conrad pointed towards some trees, twitching in the stiff December wind.

'Witches' knickers.'

Roger looked. The clump of trees had three white plastic bin bags in them, thrashing and dervishing in the black branches. Witches' knickers. He laughed for the first time in two days. Later they all became tired and cross with each other – a typical Boxing Day. But at least it wasn't as bad as Christmas.

Help arrived the next day. It came as more than a pleasant surprise when the Hungarian nanny, promised by the agency when Roger finally got through at nine, rang on the doorbell at quarter to eleven, and turned out to be a tall, pretty, well-spoken dark-haired girl in her mid-twenties. Matya. According to the agency, she had OK English and good references and a strong rapport with small children. As soon as he looked at her Roger felt ill with relief. He also did what he unconsciously did whenever he was attracted to a woman, and stretched to his full height.

When Matya came in the sitting room, the first thing she did, Roger noticed (after also noticing her startlingly good bum in tight jeans, once she'd taken her coat off), was look for the children. It was interesting, because most people coming in the room looked at the fancy decor and fancy stuff. Joshua and Conrad were having one of their infrequent five-minute episodes of getting on well, while the younger boy passed bits of Duplo to the elder, who was building what seemed to be a zoo.

'Let me brief you,' said Roger firmly. He introduced Conrad and Joshua, but Matya barely seemed to need the introduction; she was down on her knees beside the boys, discussing in her soft Hungarian accent the best way of getting the gorilla to stand on the back of the crocodile. All in all, for Roger it was like the moment in an action movie when the helicopter rescue crew gets to the special forces team deep behind enemy lines, and the viewer finally gets the feeling that, just possibly, and against all odds, everything is going to turn out all right for the good guy.

Part Two

April 2008

31

Spring was coming. At number 42, the crocuses Petunia Howe had planted the previous autumn, before she began to feel peculiar, had come and gone. The hollyhocks and delphiniums which she had planted to come up in the summer weren't visible yet, so the garden was less colourful than she liked it to be; the lawn was looking scruffy, too. She didn't like to ask her daughter to mow the lawn and there was no one else to do it. Even so, there was a sense that spring was here: when it was warm enough to have the window open – which at the sheltered back of the house it already was, some of the time – she could feel the distinctive texture of the new season's air, its fructifying softness. Petunia had always loved that feeling. She didn't think that you had to divide the world into spring or autumn people, because she loved them both, but if you had to pin her down she would have said she was a spring person. By May or certainly June, the cranesbill would be out, the Queen Anne's lace would be beginning, and the irises would be in full flower; the lily of the valley would be everywhere; the garden would be vivid and intimate with colour and growth, the way she liked it – with a sense of profusion, generosity, so many different things going on that it verged on being untidy. She liked to sit in her chair by the window in her bedroom and look down into the garden and imagine how it was going to be. It was hard to accept – it was impossible to get her head around – the fact that she was dying and would be dead by high summer. Her consultant had told her so.

He had done so the way he did everything else, awkwardly. It was as if he was remembering to try not to be brusque but not quite managing it. The brain tumour he had said needed 'eliminating' as a possible illness turned out to be what she actually had. The business about 'elimination' was, she now realised, doctor-speak for 'this is probably what you've got'. She had a large tumour, one which had, he said, grown surprisingly quickly for someone her age.

'I've got cancer,' Petunia had said, with a sensation that she had bumped into something. People talked about the floor opening up beneath you, or the ground falling from beneath your feet, and things like that, but that wasn't how Petunia felt; she felt as if she had walked into something invisible. Something which had always been there but which she hadn't been able, and still wasn't able, to see.

'Not strictly,' the doctor said, having visibly had a small struggle over whether or not he should factually correct a dying woman over a point of terminology, before giving in to the impulse to do so. 'Brain tumour is not a form of cancer. But you do have a tumour and I am sorry to say there is evidence that it is growing.'

Evidence – a heavy word.

The doctor said that the tumour was too big to operate on but that they could treat it with chemotherapy. Or rather that they could 'perhaps' treat it with chemotherapy. Many years ago, after watching her friend Margerie Talbot – who had lived at 51, where the Younts now lived – suffer horribly with the treatment for cancer and then die anyway, Petunia had resolved never to have chemotherapy. Now, sitting in the doctor's consulting office on the eighteenth floor of the hospital tower block, she was interested to notice that the practice was no different from the theory: she felt no temptation to accept the offer of treatment. Not that it was an especially tempting offer. It was something like six weeks' treatment for six extra months of life – Petunia couldn't now remember the exact details of the calculation but she could remember at the time thinking how strangely similar it was to the extended warranty offers, £5.99 a month for three years' extra coverage, which had used to make Albert so reliably furious.

'No,' said Petunia. 'Thank you, but no.'

'You don't have to decide here and now,' the doctor had said.

'Well, I have decided, and it's no,' said Petunia. The consultant looked, for the first and only time, a little taken aback. And that was the last time she had seen him.

The doctor's verdict was a shock. But at some level it was not a surprise. Things had suddenly got much worse in February. At the core of it was a feeling that this illness was different from any other she had ever had. Every other time she had been ill, there had always been a distance between her and what was wrong with her; she was over here, her illness was over there, and even when she had been deeply ill, delirious with flu and fever, say, she had known that the illness was not her. Her being and its being were separate. That was different this time. The symptoms were not spectacular, but Petunia knew that the sickness was very intimate, it was entwined with her thoughts and perceptions and deepest self. The shadow on her sight spread and grew darker, and then Petunia was dizzy and weak and at times couldn't do anything much: walk, or even get out of bed. She was taken into hospital. At times she could barely see. For a short period there she had uncontrollable hiccups, so much so that the other patients on the ward complained.

After two weeks things stabilised slightly and she was sent home to die. Her daughter Mary moved down from Maldon to look after her. The alternative would have been moving to Essex to stay with Mary and her family while she died, but there was something creepy about Mary's house (though of course Petunia didn't admit that this was the reason), something cold and sterile and unwelcoming and not-right. Mary spent most of her time cleaning and putting things away – she always had – and this habit was harder to bear on foreign territory. At Pepys Road, Mary spent most of the day doing things somewhere else in the house, but came when Petunia called her. That was shamefully often. She sometimes could manage to get to the loo in the night, but sometimes could not, and when that happened she had to call for Mary, who was sleeping in the single bed in an adjacent room which had once been Albert's den and now was nothing much, except the room which had once been Albert's den. But Mary was a deep sleeper and even though mother and daughter both left their doors open she often didn't hear her mother call until Petunia was almost losing her voice with shouting for her. And then they had the trip to the bathroom to negotiate. Petunia hated this, and Mary hated it too.

There was palliative care available, either at home or in a hospice, when Petunia was actually dying. But she wasn't quite there yet. The rate at which she was dying seemed to have slowed down sharply since her daughter had come home.

Petunia could hear a rattling from the kitchen downstairs. Mary had a very low tolerance for mess but a high one for noise, or at least a high one for the noise she generated herself. She banged and crashed, she left the radio on turned up loud wherever she went; even the Hoover seemed to make more noise when she was using it. Now she was, Petunia knew because it was eleven o'clock, slamming cupboard doors, rattling saucers, banging a tray down on the table, and thumping the kettle down on the worktop, all by way of making herself and her mother a cup of tea. So she would be coming upstairs in about five minutes. Petunia was glad of it. She and Mary didn't have much to say to each other but the way in which her daughter's routines broke up the day was welcome.

The specific manner in which the tumour had affected her brain meant that Petunia could not read. She did not want to watch television and she only intermittently wanted to talk; and when she did, Mary tended not to be there. So she spent the day in a state of pure being, a state closer to infancy than any she had experienced since. There were moments when she was afraid, and moments when she felt actual panic, terror, at the thought of dying. At other times when she thought of her death she felt a generalised sense of loss, strangely non-specific: not about the things she would no longer experience, because so many of these things had already faded. Her sense of taste and smell had gone funny, so coffee and tea and bacon and flowers were no longer themselves; or if they were themselves, the sense-impressions were no longer accurately recorded by her brain; they were lost in synaptic translation. But it wasn't anything specific she felt she was losing: it wasn't that she was losing this day, this light, this breeze, this spring. It was a general sense of loss connected to nothing and everything. She was simply losing, losing it all. She was on a boat drifting away from the dock. There were moments when it wasn't even an unpleasant sensation, when she felt safe with herself. At other moments she felt suffocated with a sadness that made her feel choked up and short of breath and so came to seem another symptom of her final illness.

32

Shit flows downhill. This basic principle of institutional life had landed a fat folder labelled 'Investigation: We Want What You Have' on the desk of Detective Inspector Mill of the Metropolitan Police. It had gone like this: half a dozen residents of Pepys Road had first complained to the local council and, to no one's surprise, had come up blank, so then they had written to their MP; the MP wrote to the Commissioner of the Metropolitan Police; the Commissioner sent a note to the divisional commander; the divisional commander had forwarded it to the nearest station commander, based at Clapham South; and the station commander had dumped the issue onto Mill. That was why he was now sitting looking at this folder. A cup of revolting percolated coffee was cooling on the desk next to the file, with a stack of report forms on the other side next to his charging mobile and a copy of yesterday's *Metro*.

A person who wasn't used to it would have found it impossible to work in that room. Not a single other body in it was in a state of silence and rest. Two dozen Met officers were in constant motion, most of them also talking, joshing, making off-colour jokes, often while simultaneously keying data into computers, or flicking through files, or dialling phone numbers, or eating muffins, or lobbing crumpled paper into the bin, or carrying piles of forms from one end of the office to the other. It was mayhem. Mill liked that about it.

He found himself asking the first thing he always asked about any piece of work: why me? It wasn't an idle question. Mill was not, demographically or psychologically, a typical policeman. He was a Classics graduate from Oxford, both the town and the university, the son of two teachers, who had joined the police as an experiment on himself, for reasons which he often speculated about – observing himself as from a distance – but still didn't understand. He wanted to scratch an itch to do with authority, his need for it, his desire to have it, his liking of hierarchy and order. It was that thing the centurion says to Jesus: 'For I also am a man set under authority, having under me soldiers, and I say unto one, Go, and he goeth; and to another, Come, and he cometh; and to my servant, Do this, and he doeth it.' Yes. That felt right to him. Five years out of university, on the graduate fast track up through the ranks, he was very aware of the ways in which his colleagues thought he might be a wanker; not that he was a wanker all the time, but that, through the cocktail of class and education, he had the kind of perspectives and opportunities which meant that he might at any moment say or do something wanky. As if being in the police was for him a lifestyle choice, rather than a fundamental expression of who he was. He resented that they saw him like that, while admitting, deep down, that it was also fair enough. So he learned to be careful.

Mill wanted to make a difference, whatever that meant – it was a phrase he thought about a lot. He was a Christian – had never stopped being one, had been one since childhood – and wanted to lead a good life. But you had to think about what that meant. To make a difference presumably meant either to do something that other people couldn't or wouldn't do, or to do their jobs in a way which was better than the way they did it. So it was a marginal difference. It was the difference between the kind of policeman he was and the kind someone else would have been. If he was, say, 15 per cent better than the other person who would have been Detective Inspector at his station, then that was the difference he was making, that 15 per cent. That was his marginal utility. Was it enough? There were days when he felt it was and days when he felt it wasn't. His girlfriend Janie thought he was mad to have wanted to go into the police, and was only now, four years in, beginning to accept the idea that it might in some bizarre way suit him.

That didn't mean he didn't think about giving it up and doing something else. He did, almost every day. The thought was a safety valve; the idea that he could quit whenever he liked was one of the things which kept him in the job. The exit was always in his line of sight. The idea of it helped him to stay put and to cope with the rough parts of his job and his day.

One of those rough parts, in the form of Constable Dawks, was heading towards his desk at that precise moment. Dawks was a decade older than Mill and would never be anything other than a constable. Mill had spent two years on the beat and then been promoted to inspector as part of the accelerated-promotion scheme, invented in the eighties as a way of attracting more graduates into the force. It worked, but not without attracting resentment at the gilded generation who slid effortlessly into jobs which ordinary coppers would never have a chance of getting. Added to this was the fact that Mill – as a slightly built, well-groomed 26-year-old non-smoking teetotaller can sometimes do – looked roughly half his age. As a detective there were times when that was an asset. In the station house, not so much. One of the reasons that was true was because of men like Dawks, a physically imposing, not very bright 35-year-old whose attitudes were less about law and much more about enforcement. Dawks was a natural bully, who over the nine months they had known each other had made a number of attempts at picking on Mill, like a shark circling potential prey; Mill had fended him off, but it was clear that Dawks would return for another go whenever he felt like it. The idea was to look for a weak spot, something he could find that Mill minded, and that he could then exploit to turning the Inspector into a figure of ridicule. Once that was done it was hard to undo. People liked Mill well enough but he was sufficiently different to make a good target, once the beachhead had been established.

Today, though, there was a reprieve. Just as Dawks was about five feet from his desk and opening his mouth to say something, he was called to the other end of the room by one of the custody sergeants. The constable stopped and turned away, not without giving a last look at Mill. So that was unfinished business. Back to work. Mill picked up the folder and began flicking through it again and returned again to the question, Why me? Mill's boss, Superintendent Wilson, was a dark-haired, trim, smooth-mannered woman in her middle forties, another product of the accelerated-promotion scheme. She was the most talented natural politician he had ever seen, especially when it came to sniffing out trouble in advance, spotting pitfalls, and knowing what things would look bad if they went wrong. It made her a cautious police officer but not necessarily a bad one. Her use of Mill, he noticed, implied that he was cut from a similar mould. She often sicked him onto problems with a political angle, real or potential. That was half a compliment, because it implied that she trusted him, and half an insult, because it implied that he resembled her.

In this case, her brief has been explicit. 'Find out what's happening, then make it go away.'

So the first question was, what was happening? The material on his desk had been accumulated by aggrieved householders in a local street called Pepys Road. They had been subjected to what they called 'a campaign of sustained harassment'. They had written a classic middle-class complaint letter, carefully phrased to press the maximum number of official buttons. According to them, the campaign had begun with postcards of their own front doors, then with videos of their street, and there was also an anonymous blog with photos of the houses, shot at a variety of hours and over a period of time. All of this material, without exception, bore the slogan or motto or injunction or threat 'We Want What You Have'.

Mill took his desktop PC out of sleep and navigated to the web page. He spent about half an hour browsing through it and another twenty minutes looking at the material which had come through the letter boxes. The postmarks were from all around London and the handwriting was the same on all of the addresses: block capitals in black ink. There was no other writing, indeed no other words of any kind except the same five, over and over again. As he did this, Mill began to get an answer to his question and to realise why the task had landed on his desk. There was something disturbing about the material. It was hard to know what it was after and it was hard not to feel there was something creepy about it. Somebody was taking too much interest in this street, in these houses and in the people who lived in them. It felt wrong. That wasn't the same thing as saying that a crime had been committed, though. Perhaps whoever was doing this had thought about that – about not breaking the law. On his notepad, Mill jotted down:

> *harassment*
>
> *trespass?*
>
> *privacy angle?*
>
> *antisocial behaviour*

Then he put a selection of the postcards and DVDs in an evidence envelope and did the paperwork to have them checked for fingerprints. He wasn't too optimistic about that, but it had to be done. As for the main issue, which was what this whole thing was, Mill's conclusion for the moment was that he didn't have a clue.

33

Mary, Mary, quite contrary . . . Mary loathed that poem but all her life there were times when she found it hard to get out of her head. Her father had recited it to her, often, and always with amusement. For him, so very contrary himself, up to and far beyond the point of total unreasonableness, contrariness was a positive quality. But Mary didn't think of contrariness as a positive quality, and didn't think it was one she had; though the lines did sometimes run through her mind, often when there was something she was subliminally cross at. Mary, Mary, quite contrary . . .

She put the pot of tea, which had now steeped for four minutes, onto the tray, then picked up the tray, then put it down again. Better just to take up a mug; the fewer things there were for her mother to drop or spill the better. And at the same time Mary was trying to defend against the slippage in her mother's condition by pretending it wasn't happening, and by setting small rigged tests for her to pass: look, she can still cope with a cup and saucer; look, she's still OK with a knife and fork. Though in fact Petunia wasn't, not any more. Her motor skills on her left side had sharply declined and though she could use a fork in her right hand she no longer could with her left. Mary was cooking and serving food designed to be eaten single-handedly, with a fork or a spoon, because it was important to preserve a feeling of normality, even as that normality was giving way to the fact that her mother was dying and there was nothing she could do about it. Mary was trying to postpone her mother's death by keeping up appearances. Because that was impossible, and also because it is easier being angry than being sad, Mary most of the time felt a low-grade irritation with her mother, with the fact that she was having to stay with her, with London, with the condition of 42 Pepys Road, with the kitchen fittings, with the kettle which did not cut out when it boiled but kept boiling so that you had to watch over it, with the traffic noise which made it hard to get to sleep, with the small-hours wakings she was having to endure to help her mother get to the toilet, with the fact that her husband Alan kept saying she must stay there as long as she had to stay there, as if that were not completely obvious and as if there were anything else she could do.

Clumping up the stairs with the tray, Mary went. Her mother was sitting in her usual chair, as usual looking out the window at the garden, as usual saying 'Thank you, dear' before Mary had fully come through the door. Even Petunia's gaze had somehow faded, was not fully there; it wasn't that she looked straight past you, it was more that when she looked at you it was as if she were looking halfway towards you and then conking out. Her attention didn't reach the whole way.

'That's nice, dear,' said Petunia. 'Tea. Thank you.'

'I'll just put it here on the side,' said Mary. She noticed that her mother, having briefly looked at her, was now looking away again.

'I've let it sit already,' said Mary. 'I'll pour it out now.' She poured tea into the mug. 'I'll take the tray back down to keep the space clear,' she said. Her mother was less likely to spill the mug if she had a whole uncluttered table to land it on. Also, this gave her an excuse to get out of the room. She had been in for less than a minute. When she went downstairs, the post had come. There was something that looked like a bill, and another of those bloody postcards of the front door with the menacing slogan on it. How dare you say you want this? Mary thought.

Mary liked change, movement, colour, walking, sex (with her husband), Ikea, going out to the pub with friends for Sunday lunch, being well-off in a pretty part of the country, being married to a man who had done well for himself (he owned a string of garages). She had always been depressed by her mother. Petunia was one of those people who stay in character, and whose character sets limits around them like metal bars. She wasn't a depressive, in her daughter's view, but she acted like one, constantly finding reasons for not doing things, for not acting, not changing, not breaking out. Parents are often a disappointment to their children, and Petunia was a severe disappointment to Mary. While her father had been alive, Mary had thought that he had been the difficult one, the person who set all the limits and restrictions on her parents' lives; after he died she saw that it was more complicated than that. Petunia never did anything that she didn't want to do, and what she wanted to do was what she had done the day before. She was a gentle and loving person but a very, very restricted one; restricted by herself. Mary found that lowering.

The punchline was that she was now dying. Petunia's story was an example of life's capacity to go on being one thing, to be it more than it was possible to imagine, and then to be more of the same, only more intensely so. It was unbearable. And like so many unbearable things, it had to be borne.

Mary opened the sliding patio door into the garden – which her husband had installed for Petunia after Albert's death, before they gave up on trying to change her life or improve it for her – and lit a cigarette. After a ten-year gap she had started smoking again while looking after her dying mother. The cravings had begun as soon as she moved in, and with no husband to nag her, she had given in to them. After Petunia died, and before she

190

went home, she would have to give up, because Alan would kill her if she took smoking up again. After giving up himself, he had become a fanatical anti. So she smoked because she needed a fag, and also to have something to think about, something that was about her life and not about her mother's, a future task to be accomplished – no small task, either, since giving up the first time had been one of the hardest things she'd ever done; it was something to be done in the future, after this other extraordinarily difficult thing was over, her mother's death.

Mary took a last puff on her cigarette, then stubbed it out on the patio floor. She set off back upstairs to tidy up.

34

Middle-class mediocrity.

Suburban mediocrity.

A culture that openly worships the average.

A society which allows the idea of the elite to exist only in relation to sport.

A culture of fat people, lazy people, people who watch reality television, people who aren't interested in anything except celebrity, people who eat in the street, people who betray their ordinariness every time they open their mouths.

The City of London is one of the few places in which this tyranny of the mediocre, the mean, the average, the banal, the ordinary, the complacent, is challenged. The City is one of the few places in which you are allowed to be extraordinary. No – it was better than that. The City is one of the only places in which you are invited to demonstrate that you are extraordinary. It did not matter what you claimed; claiming to be this or that meant nothing. Claiming has no effect. You have to show it.

This is what Roger's deputy was thinking about as he rode the train, clunketa clunketa, out to his parents' house in Godalming. The early spring sun was out and it was airless and warm inside the carriage. Mark sat in first class; he didn't have a first-class ticket, but knew from experience that on this fifty-minute journey on a Sunday, no one would check. His BlackBerry was on the table in front of him; the heath landscape of Surrey, its deceptive wildness and bleakness, was passing the window. It was Sunday, and he was going home for that immersion in mediocrity, convention, and stifling bourgeois horror known as 'Sunday lunch'. This was something he 'had to' do once a month. On these occasions Mark would either dress down or dress up. Last time he had worn ripped jeans and a T-shirt with what he was qualified to know was a semen stain on the lower left side. Today he wore a £1,500 suit with a very expensive shirt and even more expensive trainers. If he was very, very lucky, this might prompt his mother to say 'You look nice, dear' in her wavering, uncertain voice.

There was a tumult in Mark; there always had been. There was a panic or emptiness inside him, a too-weak sense of who he actually was. His parents were mild people, not strong, and his father had gone broke in the Tory recession of the early nineties, just as Mark was hitting puberty. His mother had just had another child, a daughter, which did not help. He lost confidence in his parents just as they lost confidence in themselves; he became angry and grew full of the certainty that his mother and father were frauds, were pathetic, were imitating people they were not; were not fully alive, not authentic. So he saw through them just as he was starting to wonder who he was himself, and the net result was that he grew up a typical angry suburban teenager. But with Mark, the confusions and uncertainties of adolescence had never really gone away. He did not let go of his fury at his parents for being nothing-special, and his reaction to that was to cling very firmly on to the idea that he was a special being, cut off from other people. He was so frightened of being ordinary that he had convinced himself he was not the same as anyone else. Mark had never told anyone else this, but Mark knew that he was extraordinary; he felt this knowledge deep within himself.

This for Mark was a certainty: his being had a quality in it which other people did not have in theirs. And he worked in one of the only places in modern Britain in which it was acceptable to demonstrate your superiority; one of the few areas in which doing better than other people was the whole point. Everything should be perfect. And yet – Mark prided himself on never lying to himself – everything was not perfect. He was stuck in a job in which his abilities were not acknowledged, working for a boss who, in Mark's considered view, was a throwback or hangover from how things used to be, a pointlessly tall, contentlessly smooth public-school twat, a bluffer and chancer and lightweight, doing a job which Mark could do a thousand times better. Roger was good at managing upwards – he must be, because he was head of department, and he hadn't been sacked, which had to mean that something was going on out of sight. The only aspect of this Mark saw directly was that Roger could kiss Lothar's arse as if he had a genuine taste for it. Apart from that he was a waste of space, and it was clear to Mark that Roger had only the sketchiest understanding of how the detailed mathematics of their trading worked. He was technically blank in a job that was all about technical things. That was unforgivable.

Mark should not lie to himself – a great man did not lie to himself. Roger was a dickhead and he, Mark, was a genius. He was rotting away as Roger's deputy, because Roger would not give him full credit, and the reason Roger wouldn't give him full credit was because if he did, he, Roger, would be exposed, and sacked or demoted. The system was this: Mark did the work, Roger got the credit.

It was time to do something about that.

The train got to Godalming and he got off. His father was waiting for him in the car park. It was typical of his father not to come into the station to greet Mark, but to wait outside, standing beside the brown Volvo in his brown trousers. He had caught a touch of sun, or had been outside a lot, which gave his face a trace of brown also; to Mark this made him look blurry, faded. Again he thought of mediocrity, of all the things he had had to work so hard to get away from.

'Mark!' said his father, who always started strongly and then faded. 'Hello, it's, um, nice to see you.' He bounced his arms against his sides, the gesture of a much younger man, as if he would have offered to carry a bag if Mark had one, which of course, since he was only coming down for lunch, he didn't.

Mark got in the car and sat there for the twenty-minute drive while his father made excruciating attempts at small talk. They got home to the 'chalet-bungalow' – a phrase which made him feel ill every time he heard either of his parents use it – where he had grown up. His father pulled up outside the garage and his sister, eleven years younger than him at eighteen, jumped up out of the front-garden deckchair where she'd been sitting reading *Heat* and ran up to him. Clare had the fairest hair of anyone in the family and had the kind of puppy fat which might well turn out to be the other kind of fat, unless she started to do something about it soon. She put her arms round his neck, which he suffered without making a counter-movement, kissed him several times, and then ruffled his hair, hard, which she knew perfectly well he hated.

'Marky Marky Marky,' she said. 'Have you got a girlfriend yet?'

He began smoothing his hair back down.

'Stop acting twelve,' he said.

'You make me feel twelve, big brother,' said Clare, pivoting her leg on tiptoe while pretending to simper and twiddle a non-existent ponytail. She had always had a talent for knowing how to irritate him, and to establish, completely, the fact that part of him was still an irritated teenager. That was part of what he hated about going home and being home: how stuck it made him feel. In Godalming, everyone, including himself, acted as if he was still fifteen.

His mother came to the door. He was braced for it; he knew it was going to happen; he had rehearsed it in his head; and yet all of that was no help. As with his father, as always, she started big and then faded.

'Mark!' she said. 'You look . . .' – eyes sliding, certainty level ebbing – '. . . nice?' she finished, as if it were a question, with her eyes flickering. He told himself that with every second that passed, this experience, like everything else, was getting closer to being over. Tomorrow he would begin to make his move. As Andrew Carnegie wrote, 'The rising man must do something exceptional and beyond the range of his special department. HE MUST ATTRACT ATTENTION.'

35

'I've got a new system to organise the Islamic calendar,' said Shahid to the table at large: Ahmed and Usman, Rohinka, Fatima and Mohammed. 'Instead of dating things from the hegira, we begin to date things from when that moron Iqbal moved into my flat. So instead of being the year 1428 it's actually the day 95. It makes sense. He's so boring that he can cause a fundamental disruption of the space-time continuum. He's so boring he's a one-man walking injustice. He leaves a deep sense of grievance everywhere he goes just because the people he's been with realise they've just spent time that they're never going to get back. He's a nightmare. And he's in my flat! He's stinking up the place with his smelly feet and his I-already-had-a-shower-this-month!'

Ahmed, good older brother, lost no time in saying, 'It's your fault for inviting him.'

'I didn't invite him, he invited himself.'

'Then it's your fault for allowing him to invite himself.'

'I didn't allow him to invite himself, he just invited himself.'

'I don't see a difference.'

'That's because you're a plonker too.'

Usman snorted a reluctant laugh through his unkempt, I'm-more-devout-than-you beard. Rohinka said, 'Boys, boys.' Fatima chanted, 'Fight, fight!'

It was Saturday and the Kamals were having lunch together,

something they didn't often do. Ahmed's friend Hashim was looking after the shop downstairs, and Ahmed found that he could, with an effort of will, put out of his mind for as much as five minutes at a time the thought of Hashim running up incorrect amounts on the till, taking orders for expensive part-works without getting the customer's full details, selling alcohol to fifteen-year-olds, and forgetting how to operate the lottery machine and the Oyster top-ups, while the queue backed out the door and regular customers vowed never to come to the shop again . . .

'Iqbal seems all right to me,' said Usman. 'He takes things more seriously than you do, that's all. It doesn't seem to me such a bad characteristic.'

'Get a shave,' said Shahid.

Rohinka brought another casserole over from the stove and put it on the table. There was barely space for it: the table already carried two oven-hot dishes, one of chicken in cumin and the other of stewed aubergines, both of them resting on heatproof mats; a platter of naan wrapped in a kitchen cloth to keep them warm; and a bowl of dal, one of Rohinka's specialities, something she cooked almost every day and never twice to exactly the same recipe. She lifted the lid of the new dish and a beautifully complex smell of lamb and spices, her recipe for achari gosht, floated above the table in a cloud of fragrant steam. The men made varying murmurs and groans of appreciation. The achari gosht was intended to change the topic of conversation, but it didn't work.

'That smells great but if I eat a single thing more I'll explode,' said Shahid. 'Look, the thing about Iqbal is the way he's just so oblivious. I come in, I hear the television upstairs, I know it's going to be tuned in to one of the news channels, him watching some latest atrocity or other, or ranting to himself about the kafr media, or he's going to be on the internet muttering and typing and he shuts the screen as soon as I get in, as if I care about his stupid life and his stupid MSN chats with his stupid friends in stupid Belgium or stupid Algeria or stupid wherever. He just acts like he thinks everything he says and does is a big deal and he's this man of mystery; meanwhile he's sitting with his feet on the sofa, and leaving dishes in the sink, and he's like this child who hasn't grown up yet and doesn't even realise it.'

Rohinka and Ahmed exchanged a look. Both of them were thinking that this would not be an entirely inaccurate description of Shahid himself. Shahid saw the look and knew perfectly well what it meant, but didn't care, because he knew he was right.

'Do you think he is, maybe, I don't know quite how to put it, up to something?' asked Rohinka.

Shahid didn't want to think about that. It touched too directly on the things he had done when he was younger and had been, not exactly a jihadi, but a fellow traveller in jihad, and the companion of people who were certainly up to things then, and were probably still up to them now, if they were still alive. Iqbal was a blast from that particular past. For Shahid, he was therefore both a reminder of it and a reminder of how much he didn't want to go there in his head. So he found himself not really asking too closely about who Iqbal really was and what his motives really were.

'I hope not,' was all Shahid said.

'Would it be such a bad thing if he were' – Usman waggled his fingers in contemptuous inverted commas – '"up to something"? Would it be so bad if somebody were doing something? Rather than just passively accepting a state of injustice and oppression?'

'You are a child,' said Ahmed, instantly very angry. 'You don't have any real opinions, you just strike attitudes to try and create an effect. It would be a boring enough habit in a teenager but in a man your age it's pathetic.'

'You were never a teenager, though, were you, Ahmed?' said

Usman, now just as angry. 'You were always half-dead. Injustice? Oppression? Not your problem. As long as there was enough on your plate. Why care about anyone else? Why care about your fellow Muslims suffering as long as you've got enough food to stuff into your stomach?'

'If you had ever cared for or looked after anyone in your life, you might know something about the responsibility of providing food,' said Ahmed.

Rohinka, loudly and deliberately, gave a cough. They looked at her, and she looked at the two children. The brothers recollected themselves and decided to calm down.

'This is very good,' said Usman, glancing down at his plate and then up from it, and declaring peace. There was an air of reluctance in the way he said it, as if he were making an unwilling concession to the existence of a physical pleasure. Rohinka smiled and they began talking about cooking, which had been one of Usman's interests before he went all super-religious.

Shahid grew quiet. He was irritated by Iqbal, more irritated than he could easily say, and that was against the grain of his character, because he prided himself on being the least easily annoyed member of the Kamal family. All the Kamals were fluent in irritation. They loved each other but were almost always annoyed by each other, in ways that were both generalised and existential (why is he like that?) and also highly specific (how hard is it to remember to put the top back on the yoghurt?). Shahid had been very angry indeed in his late teens, angry with everything and everyone, and especially angry about the state of the world, but when he came back from his travels he had, he discovered, been able to let that feeling go. It was part of growing up – which was one of the reasons Shahid knew that Ahmed was wrong about his not having grown up. He didn't want to be tied down, not quite yet, but that wasn't the same thing as still being a child. Ahmed himself was irritating, and yet Shahid didn't feel irritated. That was how grown-up he was.

Which was why Iqbal was such an issue. Shahid couldn't remember the last time he had felt so annoyed by anyone; and the secret at the heart of his irritation, which he couldn't quite bring himself to say to his brothers and sister-in-law, was that there was something he didn't trust about Iqbal. There was something not right about him; not sinister or nefarious, not necessarily, but not quite right. Iqbal liked to have an aura of mystery about him, which was irritating in itself, and he did it in a way that left Shahid feeling uncomfortable. What made this all the more irritating was that if he told his family about it they would blame him: say it was his fault for having travelled in the first place, ask him what did he expect if he came back from Chechnya dragging jihadi mates behind him and letting them crash on his sofa? Just enough of him acknowledged just enough truth in this to make it infuriating to hear; so, because the conversation would turn out to be infuriating, he couldn't even begin it. And nothing is more annoying than the thing you can't say.

Fatima seemed to feel that enough time had passed without her getting any attention. She pointed a plastic spoon at her father and said, 'Daddy! You promised sweeties!'

Mohammed was always much calmer than his sister, more self-contained. He spent enormous amounts of time pottering about and entertaining himself. But he knew a call to arms when he heard one.

'Seeties,' he said. 'Seeties!'

'You didn't,' said Rohinka warningly to her husband, hands on hips, the position Ahmed remembered from his cricketing days as the 'double teapot'.

'He's in trouble now,' Shahid said cheerfully to Usman.

'Only after they'd eaten,' said Ahmed. To the children: 'After! Not now. After!'

His wife, daughter and son all looked at him with suspicion.

'After!' he said again. They all slowly chose to believe him and order was restored. Fatima went back to swinging her legs and semi-eating, semi-playing with her curry, and Mohammed, who had finished a while ago and had his bowl taken away, went back to shuffling stray pieces of rice around on the tray table of his high chair. Rohinka made offering gestures with a serving spoon, to which the brothers variously groaned and patted their stomachs. Seeing the children distracted, Ahmed lowered his voice and leaned forward.

'There is the question of our mother to discuss.'

This was the real reason for the lunch. An air of seriousness came over the proceedings. Shahid pursed his lips. He said:

'Have you spoken about a visit to' – and then suddenly switching to an exaggerated Bollywood accent and widening his eyes so that the whites flashed – 'mamaji?'

'No, but she's expecting an invitation.'

'So invite her,' said Usman. He was only partly bluffing: Mrs Kamal was at her easiest, not all that easy but her easiest, with her last-born son. Shahid, who was next in line to get married, would have it much worse, and so would Ahmed, who while safe on the marriage front, would be the brother who had to put their mother up, and who therefore would be open to multiple bases for advice, criticism, fault-finding, factual correction and silent disapproval: the way he ran his business, the way he ate and how much he ate, the way he brought up his children, his conduct as a husband, as a Muslim, as a son. Mrs Kamal visited roughly once every two years, and no one looked forward to it. This would be her first visit since the immediate aftermath of Mohammed's birth.

'It'll be nice to see Mrs Kamal,' said Rohinka, sweetly. Ahmed swivelled around and glared at her. But Rohinka – it was part of what made her sexy – was a genius at mock-innocence. She fluttered and dimpled at Ahmed from her place by the sink. He gave a snort.

Shahid realised that he was sitting with his head in his hands. His mother would without question be on at him about getting married, an arranged marriage at that – she might well have a candidate in mind. If she didn't have a specific person she would certainly have a plan. She would bully him into agreeing to come to Lahore to assess suitable candidates. He had done this once before, two years ago, and it was excruciating, like a sustained assault on his sense of himself, on everything he wanted to be as a man, a free spirit, a traveller, a citizen of the world, a man who had seen and done things but was still young; sitting in a series of Lahore rooms with a series of variously embarrassed Pakistani women, some of them as reluctant as him, some (and this was much worse) evidently quite keen on the idea. At this point, it would be hard to find anything he more exactly didn't want to do than go to Pakistan and leave Iqbal in his flat with his smelly feet and his opinions . . . Then Shahid had an idea. Maybe he could use the fact that he had to go to Lahore as a way of getting Iqbal out of his flat . . .

'She'll be on at me. What have I done to deserve this?' said Shahid. He would like to say more – would like to say much more – but it was hard to, because Rohinka and Ahmed had had an arranged marriage, so it would be grossly insulting to go into his objections. And there was also the difficult-to-ignore fact that their marriage was a self-evident roaring success. Ahmed loved Rohinka and she (less explicably in Shahid's view) loved him back; and she was also seriously foxy. So arranged marriages were outdated, wrong in principle, demeaning, no better than a form of licensed prostitution (but then so was Western marriage), patriarchal, sexist, and yet on the other hand if you ended up with someone like Rohinka . . .

'Aren't you going to denounce arranged marriages?' asked

Ahmed, guessing what Shahid was thinking, since Mrs Kamal plus Shahid meant a guaranteed row on exactly this subject. Shahid thought about saying, not everybody is as lucky as you – but he didn't, because it was true, and would give Ahmed too much pleasure.

'Ahmed, how much weight would you say you've put on since you got married?' said Shahid. 'It must be at least ten kilos, wouldn't you say? Usman, don't you think our brother is about twenty-five pounds fatter?'

Rohinka returned from clattering around at the far end of the room with a tray of Indian sweets – kulfi, gulab jamun. Mohammed slapped the sides of his high chair to make sure his interest in this new development was generally known. 'Boys, boys,' said Rohinka, in a voice which made it clear that she hadn't been really listening, and beneath that, implied that male conversation never really advanced the state of knowledge much anyway, but should be tolerated all the same, as long as it didn't get in the way of important things.

'I'll go through and get some Häagen-Dazs from the shop,' said Ahmed. He wanted some ice cream, and he was also giving in to the need to check on Hashim. Fatima got down from the table and came over to take his hand. She had strong opinions about ice cream.

36

The Refuge was a double-fronted late Victorian house in a Tooting side street. It was near the Common, near the Tube, not too
far from the Lido, and handy for shops and amenities. There
was a kitchen and two communal areas, one of them dominated
by a large old cathode-ray television, the other furnished with
battered sofas. The garden was untidy but functioning; it was
possible to sit out there, but hardly anyone ever did. There were
eight bedrooms, with eight people staying in them, including a
house manager who was a paid employee of the charity. If it had
been a domestic residence it would have been worth upwards
of a million pounds. Instead it was a hostel for stateless failed
asylum-seekers, and locals felt, bitterly, that it had a suppressing
effect on house prices.

By now, Quentina had lived there for the best part of two
years, and she had a good acquaintance with the range of types
who came into contact with the charity. All of them were dam-
aged by their experiences, some grievously, and many of them
could barely function. Some were too angry: their rage was on
a hair-trigger. These were the likeliest to get into real trouble.
A Sudanese woman from the Refuge who kept getting into
fights over perceived insults – proper fist fights, like a man –
had gone to jail for three months for assault, after she punched
a woman who she thought had jostled her while they were
both sheltering from the rain under a butcher shop's awning.

She would normally have been deported at the end of her sentence, but thanks to the Human Rights Act she couldn't be because it wasn't safe for her to go back to Sudan, so when she came out of prison she had been taken in by another branch of the Refuge, this time in North London. Quentina did not foresee a happy ending for her. Other 'clients' were defeated by the burden of their own grievances and could think of very little else. The symptoms of this condition were silence, and then, in the face of kindness or interest or understanding, torrential unburdening. Ragah, the Kurd, was like that. She had no mode in between brooding on her losses and telling all about them, at length, in English which as she got more excited Quentina found impossible to understand, and which in any case she would often drop to lapse into Kurdish, apparently without realising that she was doing so. Ragah had lost her family, Quentina gathered, but that was all she knew, because beyond that she lost the thread of the story. By now she could hardly ask.

Silence was hard to diagnose because it was such a common symptom. In their heads, some of the refugees were still in whichever country they had left; they hadn't yet caught up with their own lives. Others were culture-shocked and had no idea what to make of London; they were blank. That was usually OK because it usually wore off with time. Others still were silent because they were depressed. There had been only one suicide recently in the South London refuge, an Afghan who had hung herself in the bathroom. That was the week after Quentina arrived. One suicide in two years was good going. Others were simply possessed by a feeling that they had made a catastrophic mistake. They had made an irreversible error in coming to England, and their lives would never recover – their lives would never again be their lives, but the story of this huge mistake that they had made.

Quentina didn't fit any of these categories. Perhaps what was decisive was that she was fully resolved to take part in her new life in London. She was determined to make a go of it. At the same time she was not planning to be in London for ever. Mugabe could not live for ever. Chinese peasants might once have thought Chairman Mao was immortal, but no one except the tyrant himself believed that Mugabe was. If he died the whole system might collapse overnight, or there might be a transition period, but Quentina felt sure that anyone who had had to flee him would be welcome back. So Quentina, however hard things currently were, felt sure that she had a future, and consequently she was the client of the Refuge who functioned best, a fact which was openly acknowledged by the charity workers and the other clients. She was not angry, she was not insane, she had a job (albeit an illegal one), she spoke good English, people could talk to her. As a result she had an informal but real role as a liaison and go-between for the refugees and the charity that was helping them. Quentina liked that: it appealed to the side of her that enjoyed administering and running things, getting involved. When the small committee of the charity had its weekly meeting to talk things over, she would be present as the clients' representative. Martin, the house manager, a shy Northerner with a bossy streak, would chair the meetings. New clients didn't often arrive at the Refuge – because to do so someone would have to leave, which they only did when they won a judgment allowing them leave to legally stay, which never happened, or they were forcibly deported, which had happened twice in two years. When new clients did arrive, they would be given a case worker to look after them, and then Quentina too would be asked to keep an eye on them. So Quentina was unofficially the leader of the Refuge, or anyway of its clients.

In that capacity, her current problem was Cho. She had arrived in the winter, when a client called Hajidi was deported back to Somalia – politically and ethically a sad thing, but on a personal level something Quentina found hard to lament too much simply because Hajidi had been such an awful person, a liar and bully and thief and all-round magnet for trouble. Start to finish, her battle with the legal system had lasted five years, but she had lost and been taken to Heathrow in manacles. In her place had come Cho. She was a Chinese woman in her mid-twenties, the only survivor of a group of Fukienese immigrants who had been smuggled into Britain in the container of a lorry. The lorry had developed a hairline crack in its exhaust system which leaked carbon monoxide fumes into the space where the seven would-be refugees were hidden. Customs at Dover inspected the lorry; when they opened the back they found six people dead, and Cho. She recovered in hospital and entered the legal system for deportation, but she couldn't physically be sent back to China because the Chinese, in accordance with their policy on people who had fled overseas, wouldn't take her.

Cho understood some English but would not speak it. She had had a shared room for the first few weeks, as was standard practice at the Refuge, but her room-mate had cracked under the strain of the silence and begged to be moved in with someone, anyone, else – so now Cho had the room to herself, at the top of the house where heat accumulated, in what would once have been the loft. The room's ceilings sloped and it was a difficult space for tall women, but Cho was about four feet eleven. She did not go out of the house, or even, willingly, out of her room. The one exception was when there was football on the television, and she was noticeably snobbish about that – Premiership or Champions League only, no FA Cup or England games. She could be angry, or depressed, or culture-shocked, or so consumed with regret she found it impossible to think about anything else. There was no way of knowing.

Today, football was Quentina's excuse to engage Cho in conversation. Quentina had no interest at all in the game, but Arsenal were playing Chelsea and it gave her a reason to knock on Cho's door. The response was a grunt – not a grunted 'Yes' or a grunted 'Come in' or a grunted 'What is it?', just a grunt. Quentina opened the door. Cho looked at her for a moment, and then blinked. It was as if she were making a tremendous physical effort to drag her attention back to this present moment, right here, right now. Then she grunted again, meaning, it seemed, something along the lines of 'Yes?'

'Just wanted to check you knew about the game on tonight. The "derby"' – Quentina loved that word. 'Arsenal–Chelsea.'

Cho looked at her for a moment and then nodded. The nod meant she knew about the game. Quentina had various gambits planned for dragging her out conversationally; nothing too fancy, more along the lines of who did she think would win? But there was no leeway for that here. Cho was as immobile as a lizard sunbathing on a rock. Not for the first time, Quentina found herself entertaining the thought that Cho's difficulties, or difficultness, might be partly a race thing. The Chinese had a reputation for racism, especially about Africans. Perhaps she was just speechless with loathing at having to share this space with a black woman. Well, if that was the case, then she could go boil her head. Quentina nodded back and began closing the door. Just as it was clicking shut, Quentina heard Cho grunt again. This time it could almost be mistaken for 'Thank you.'

37

Quentina's system for life was to always have something to look forward to. That was just as well, because that morning, after checking in on Cho and before going to work to put on her 1905 Ruritanian customs colonel's uniform, she had a call on the Refuge's communal phone from her lawyer. The Kurd took it and summoned her.

'Hello, I'm in a rush,' her lawyer began, as he often did, 'but there's some news I wanted you to have and it's not good news I'm afraid: there's a rumour the high court is going to rule that it's legal to deport failed asylum-seekers back to Zimbabwe. It's because of the election there. They're reversing the ruling that was made in July 2005. Letters will be sent out to the relevant people. That means you. I'm sorry.'

With five minutes' warning, Quentina might have had a few questions. With none, she had none. Her lawyer hung up. It didn't sound as if there was anything much she could do about it, so rather than spend her day worrying about what was going to happen, she instead decided to spend it thinking about the date she was going on that evening with Mashinko Wilson from the church choir, he of the voice and the shoulders, the defined muscles . . . The Black Eyed Peas had a song which Quentina thought was hilarious: 'My Humps'. There was a line in it about 'my humps, my humps, my lovely lady lumps'. It made Quentina smile and it made her think of her date with Mashinko. He was going to take her to the African bar in Stockwell to listen to a band from South Africa called the Go-To Boys. Life was sweet. In her heart she didn't think she would be returning to Zimbabwe until the tyrant was dead. Something told her that. In the mean time, my humps, my humps . . . my lovely lady lumps . . .

'Kwama Lyons' clocked in five minutes late at the office of Control Services and headed out for her shift. Quentina would be working until 8.30 p.m. today, a profitable time because many of the residents' parking streets had only recently shifted over from 5.30 to 8.30 as the time for parking limits to end, and many, many visitors hadn't yet realised the change. It was not especially fair, in Quentina's view, but then, if there was one thing about life which was unequivocally clear to Quentina, clearer by the day, it was that she didn't make the rules. If she did, she would make sure that life was fair. She would see to it. At the top of the to-do list if she was in charge of the world would be the item: Make Life Fair. But she wasn't and it wasn't.

The weather, very important to a warden on the beat, wouldn't settle. One moment, the sky was clear, the sun was out, and Quentina was sweating inside her ridiculous uniform. Summer was around the corner! Not real summer of course, but its British imitation. Then the sun would go in, the wind would rise, and all would be dark and grim, wintry, another British imitation, not snow and ice and wolves and drama but just grey dark cold.

At about eleven, Quentina found a ten-year-old Land Rover, a diesel, in a loading bay outside an electronics shop around the corner from the high street. The back of the vehicle was open; Quentina could see a jumble of cardboard boxes. This was a place where many tickets could be issued for people parking, which wasn't permitted, as opposed to loading, which was. From the licence plate Quentina could see that the car had been bought at a garage in Cirencester. That made sense because no

Londoner would leave a car boot open and unattended for as long as this. She stood there for a minute and then a man in a green waxed jacket came out at speed. A younger woman, his daughter perhaps, came after.

'Sorry sorry,' said the man. 'Got to drop some stuff off. Clearing out for my daughter. Two more loads. Hope that's all right?'

Loading was taking place.

'OK,' said Quentina. 'You have an honest face.'

The man was good enough to smile about that. He and his daughter picked up another couple of boxes. Quentina walked off, or tried to, because ten yards away a woman in a tracksuit blocked her. She had flushed indoor skin and crinkly, angry hair.

'That's right,' she said, 'that's right. Let those snobs park anywhere they like. Ordinary people, you stick a ticket on them without looking twice, don't care if they're in the bay they belong in or not, stick a ticket on them, meet your quota, let them appeal if you're wrong, you don't care, yeah, just meet your quota, all it is, only got your job in the first place because of positive discrimination, ordinary working people pay the price, pay the fines, but get snobs in their big car and you let them do what they like.'

Quentina felt that she had some experience of the world, and of people other than at their best, but she had never known a subject on which people became irrational as quickly and completely as that of parking in this absurdly rich, absurdly comfortable country. When you gave people a ticket they were angry, always and inevitably. And the anger could spread, and become catching, as it had with this plainly mad woman, crazed with resentments. There were times when she wanted to say: Get down on your knees! Be grateful! A billion people living on a dollar a day, as many who can't find clean drinking water, you live in a country where there is a promise to feed, clothe, shelter and doctor you, from the moment of your birth to the moment of your

death, for free, where the state won't come and beat or impris-
on you or conscript you, where the life expectancy is one of the
longest in the world, where the government does not lie to you
about Aids, where the music is not bad and the only bad thing is
the climate, and you find it in yourself to complain about parking? Woe, woe! Down on your knees in gratitude that you can
even notice this minor irritation! Praise God for the fact that you
resent getting this ticket, instead of rending your clothes with
grief because you lost another child to dysentery or malaria!
Sing hosannas when you fill out the little green form in the envelope stuck to your windshield! For you, you of the deservedly
punished five-minute overstay, you of the misinterpreted residents' bay area, you of the ignored Loading Only sign, are of all
people who have lived the most fortunate!

Instead Quentina said,

'Loading is taking place.' She held out her hand and as in a
dumbshow, the countryman and his daughter came out of the
electrician's struggling with a visibly heavy object wrapped in
cardboard, which from its shape and dimensions was probably a
fridge. With great effort they dropped this on the backboard of
the Land Rover and began pushing it in.

'Why don't you just fuck off back to nig-nog land, go eat your
fucking bananas in a tree and die of Aids, you nigger bastard?
Eh? What the fuck are you doing here anyway?'

'Have a nice day, madam,' said Quentina. She walked away,
angry and sick but not surprised, and then did the thing experience had taught her to do: she turned, photographed the car and
the loading bay (and as it happened the man and his daughter,
who were now extracting another large package from the car,
with difficulty, because it was partly wedged in by the fridge –
they really weren't very good at what they were doing). Then she
took out her notebook and wrote down what the woman had
said, and the time and place. Then she went about her business

for the rest of the day, a day on which she had something to look forward to. So while there was no denying that the things which happened happened, there was always that other more important thing in the future. Mashinko . . . my humps . . .

38

Zbigniew woke up and for a moment felt good. It was six, which was early, and a crack of light had come though a gap in the curtains and hit his face where it lay on the pillow – which was fine by Zbigniew, an early riser, a getter-up. His initial feeling on coming awake was a happy sense of busyness, with a day to be conquered, things to be done, tasks to be ticked off, progress to be made. He had three or four projects on the go. His stock portfolio was doing well. There was an English expression Zbigniew loved, a saying which was so good it could almost qualify as Polish: it's a good life if you don't weaken. So when he woke, while he was coming to full consciousness, Zbigniew had several seconds of being completely happy.

Then he felt that he was not alone in the bed. His body sensed it before his mind, that there was another body in the bed; he knew this as an animal knows it; and then he realised that he was not in his own bed; and then he knew who it was and where he was and what was happening, and he was immersed in a disconnection which had started out being a small thing, a joke, a quirk, but had escalated to the point where it was the bane of his day, the thing which was wrong with his life, the black sun overhead. His body was happy. He was in bed with Davina, the girl whom he had met in Uprising before Christmas. He had taken her out twice over the holiday, they had had sex for the first time in January, they had been seeing each other ever since. It was a disaster. A disaster of a complicated type, and one which Zbigniew had never experienced before, because from one point of view, and one point of view only, he was ecstatically happy: his body liked what was happening. Right from the first time, when Davina had come screaming at exactly the moment he came into her, they had had amazing sex; the best sex of Zbigniew's life. This was not a question of tricks or specific acts; it wasn't any single thing Davina did that no other girl had ever done; it was just that they somehow worked together. It was hard not to reach for engineering metaphors. The mechanism simply worked. Perfectly. And repeatedly. Every time. It was, considered purely as sex, the best sex of his life: the most inventive, the dirtiest, the most satisfying, the noisiest. His body was crazy about what was happening.

The trouble was that his mind, his spirit, his soul, his feelings, were in convulsions. The thing was – he couldn't stand Davina. He had noticed this at an early point, a very early point, indeed during their first conversation; if it came to that, he had noticed it before he even spoke to her, since she smoked and he couldn't stand smoking, even if it did look sexy. He had mentioned this to her after a few weeks and – she had given up! There and then! That was how bad the situation was!

It wasn't that Davina was overtly clingy. But she was completely, irrevocably dependent. He was her world; he knew that because she told him so. 'You are my world.' That made no sense to Zbigniew, as a thing to say, because it could never be true. People were people, one by one, individuals, and the world was the world. That was the whole point of it, that it was everything else. A person could not be your world. That was the whole point of what people and the world were.

The dependency, which appeared only after they had slept together for the first time, was a big issue. Every time they met – which if it had been up to her would be every day, in fact

if it were up to her they would already have moved in together, in fact if it were up to her they would already be married –
she would ask what he had been doing and wait on the answer
with her eyes large, her mouth slightly parted, as if ready to be
thrilled, amazed, aghast. There was a note of paranoia and jeal-
ousy there right from the start. She was jealous of his work, his
friends, his stock portfolio, Piotr, everything. She tried not to
show it, or tried to show it in a way that looked like a convincing
attempt not to show it.

All this, while obviously not all right, might have been bearable, if it were not for two other traits which interacted with and
magnified each other. The first was her theatrical way of acting
everything out. She did everything with a consciousness of being watched. She exaggerated everything she said or felt, often
by pretending to underplay her reactions; this was a particularly epic phenomenon when she was pretending not to be hurt
or upset. When Zbigniew had through pressure of work to can-
cel a 'drink', i.e. a bottle of wine followed by sex followed by a
bitter contest over whether he stayed the night at her flat, the
next time they met she would act like a cat greeting an owner
who had gone on holiday: looking away, shrugging and saying
'Nothing' when he asked what was wrong, saying 'Whatever' to
any suggestions or plans of any sort. ('Shall I ask for the bill?'
'Whatever.') Then there would be strenuous, tumultuous recon-
ciliation sex.

The second trait, the one which finally meant that Zbigniew
found his girlfriend impossible to be with for any time without
wishing he were somewhere else, was her gloominess, what she
called her 'black dog'. (Even the way she said that, theatrically,
looking down or away, as if the subject was too difficult, too
painful, as if the very words themselves were a burden which a
man as coarsely at ease with himself as Zbigniew would have difficulty imagining . . .) Once every three or four meetings, she

would be lost in herself, barely able to speak – or that was how she acted. But her histrionic side meant that it was impossible to tell. She might not have had anything much on her mind at all, but just been wanting a little more attention – this is what he often thought was the case. Or she might have been a bit down and needing cheering up, but instead of just asking for cheering up, she had decided to exaggerate how down she was on the basis that it was a more effective way of getting his attention, only to find that instead it had the effect of making him shut down, switch off, and turn away; which was what it did. Depressed people bored and annoyed Zbigniew; back home he knew too many of them, and their charms had long since worn off. Or she might have been genuinely, but briefly, depressed – except that to be as depressed as she seemed, she would have to be clinically depressed, in which case what she needed was a doctor and some pills, not a Polish boyfriend to sit across the table and be unhappy at.

Last night, for instance. They had gone to see a film. The time before, she chose, so this time, he did. *Iron Man*. It was OK – not great but OK. Afterwards, in the pub, she did not speak. He made small talk for a while then gave up. After a couple of minutes, with Davina sitting there looking at the table, she looked up and said,

'You're very quiet.'

'You are quieter than I am.'

Pause.

'Am I?'

'Yes.'

Pause.

'Well . . . I just don't feel there's much to say.'

At which point Zbigniew might have taken the opportunity to say, I agree, it's over. But instead he fell into the trap.

'Why not?'

She shrugged – expressively, tragically, as if being forced to give a preference between death by hanging or shooting.

'Is there?'

'Isn't there?'

Another shrug.

'You like films like that . . . Violent films.'

So that was it.

'It wasn't that violent.'

She shuddered.

'By your standards, maybe not.'

'What does that mean?'

'You're a man, you're entertained by violence.'

'No I'm not. I like action films. That's not the same thing.'

'When you have seen violence, though . . .'

So that would be the way it would go. Davina sometimes implied that she was a victim of violence in some private way linked to her childhood (maybe) or to past boyfriends (maybe) or both. She never said anything explicit but would often drop hints and then fight off Zbigniew's attempts to follow up and find out more. She preferred it when he made an effort to ask, so he said, while wondering just how he had been manoeuvred into asking a question when he didn't want to hear the answer and wouldn't necessarily believe it when it came,

'What do you mean?'

That was when she went into her black dog mode. And guess what? – it ended up with them having sex: after he had walked her home, she had burst into tears and invited him in, and about thirty seconds later they were, to use an expression Zbigniew had picked up from an Irish electrician, 'banging away like armed policemen'. The sex was great, of course. It was epic. It was the best it could be. Sex wasn't the problem. Or rather, sex was exactly the problem, because it was so great.

Zbigniew got out of bed as carefully as he could manage. The ideal thing would be to get out of Davina's flat without waking her, leaving behind a note expressing . . . expressing something. In his underpants, he made it to the en suite bathroom, where he splashed water on his face and brushed his teeth using the toothbrush she had bought for him. He pissed and – this was risky from the noise-making point of view but he was fastidious – flushed.

Back in the bedroom, he had a moment of not much liking himself. The room was bright pink – a stylish bright pink, Zbigniew had to admit – and had a large Ikea bed. Davina had a collection of teddy bears which, in the haste to have sex last night, had been thrown off onto the floor. They were in a variety of positions, legs akimbo, upside down, piled on top of each other, and the way they were strewn around, combined with what Zbigniew and Davina had done last night, made, for a jarring moment, Zbigniew think there was something sexual about their air of abandon. The bears looked forgotten and unloved, and also as if they were in the middle of a bear orgy. It looked wrong.

His clothes, also removed in a hurry, were on the heavy, ornate, very non-Ikea chair opposite the foot of the bed. He slipped on his T-shirt and sweatshirt, but one of his jeans legs was trapped under the leg of the chair. He lifted the chair with one hand and pulled out the jeans with the other, and heard from behind him,

'Oooh, muscles.'

He grimaced, then turned and smiled.

'I was hoping I wouldn't wake you.'

'I like being woken by you,' she said in a sleepy-sexy voice, which he couldn't help finding, despite himself, made him feel a twinge in his cock.

'Last night was nice,' said Zbigniew. She said nothing, only made a sleepy murmur. This was the best side of her and showed that she could indeed find the right tone. Davina hadn't yet lifted her head and her streaked blonde hair was splayed out on the pillow. She was looking half-awake and thoroughly ready for more sex.

'You're hard to resist,' said Zbigniew, saying in this light way a complicated true thing. Davina again said nothing, just pulled up the bottom of the duvet a little way so he could see her leg all the way up to mid-thigh, her swelling leg, her long leg, her warm leg, her leg which was so skinny at the ankle but which ripened so towards the thigh, her honey-coloured leg which Zbigniew knew from experience went all the way up . . .

He stepped towards the bed. Davina said mmmm.

39

Smitty's assistant was called Parker French, though that wasn't how Smitty thought of him. As was his practice, Smitty thought of his assistant as his assistant. What they did mattered much more than who they were. In fact who they were was barely relevant; in so far as it was relevant, it was, in direct proportion, annoying. The more he had to notice his assistants as people, the less well they were doing their job. If he could have got away with it, he would have quite liked to do that thing of calling all his assistants by the same name. Nigel, say. His assistant would always be called Nigel. Every year or so there would be a new Nigel. Short Nigels, tall Nigels, hairy Nigels, skinhead Nigels, Rasta Nigels – but always, in the final analysis, Nigels. That would be funny.

Smitty's assistant, however, didn't think of himself as Smitty's assistant. He thought of himself as Parker French. If Parker had known what Smitty thought of him, he would have been shocked and upset, but he would have nonetheless found out that he and his employer were in full agreement about one thing: Parker wouldn't be Smitty's assistant for ever.

A job like today's was one reason for that. Smitty was going to a party, an art-world party. It was in a warehouse in Clapton, and was given by a gallery owner who had been one of the first and most alert about tracking the London art world's relocation eastward. They had been onto Hoxton, onto Shoreditch, right as they were happening, and now they were onto Clapton. The stuff on display was by one of their new clients, an up-and-coming pair of brothers who specialised in smashing things and then incorrectly gluing them back together. It wasn't a question of whether they were going to be big. That was a given. It was only a question of just how big. For this first high-profile show, there were about ten small pieces and two big central works. The small pieces included a mound of four bicycles, some sofas, a fridge (that was quite funny because the doors had been glued on backwards), and some sets of golf clubs (also funny). In the middle stood one of their most controversial works, a number of paintings and artworks which they'd been given by other artists and which they'd chopped up and glued back together and given a one-word name three hundred and forty-four characters long which was all the individual titles of the artworks run together. *Hareonagreenshutteraftersoutineperformanceonesketchesincharco alıbaconwaswrongileftmymuminthecarparkpartsevenwinterdrea mpicturemehavingsexdoesmymumlookbiginthis(canisterofherash es)knickerpaintingifyouwantmybodyinspiredbyphilipkdicknumber twoselfportraitselfportraitselfportraitbyphotoshopspunkingupyogh urtpotbymoonlightshortfilmsstilllifewithfish* was one big central piece, which had already been bought by a collector. Smitty quite liked it and quite liked the idea too. It was funny to think of how pissed off all the other artists must have been to have their work chopped up, while having to pretend to be cool about it. But that wasn't his favourite piece in the show. The brothers had smashed a Ford Focus – or rather had found a chop shop to cut it apart – and glued it back together. The result was memorable, truly. It looked like a child's idea of how you might assemble a car, executed by a giant whose hands were too big to make the necessary fine movements. Because bits of it stuck out and were added on at the last moment – bits that the brothers couldn't fit in anywhere else – it also had something a little hedgehog-like about it.

Everyone agreed that it was a very strong piece. It was called *Can There Ever Be a Politics of the Dream?* That was where the party had got its theme. The party was called Politics of the Dream, which was why there were sword-swallowers and fire-eaters by the warehouse door as people came in, and also why the waiters were dwarfs.

Smitty had been sent an invitation via his dealer – his dealer in the old sense, as it happened, who was now his dealer in the new sense – and he felt like coming, so he did. He wanted to have a look around, not just to see the brothers' work, which he already knew about, but to get the feeling of the room, of the vibe, of what was happening and what might be about to happen. Art was a business, which might not be your favourite fact about it but was a fact you were unwise to ignore. It was good to sniff around, to look at the players. Because of that, going to art parties was something Smitty loved to do. There wasn't too much chance he would be recognised, even among an art-world crowd, because among that crowd there was a rumour – a rumour started by Smitty, as it happened, via a hint he'd got his dealer to drop – that Smitty was black. The existence of that rumour was Smitty's single favourite thing in the whole entire world.

So his identity was protected here. At the same time, he was careful not to do the party thing too often, because if he did do it too often, people might start to wonder who he was; might start to wonder properly, not just to be faintly, briefly, idly curious. Smitty liked to play games with his anonymity, but he preferred to be the person who was playing the game; liked it to be a private game with one player, Smitty himself. So he always dressed up in a suit and tie, a not-too-smart formal suit, not a wide-boy-at-play suit, and if anyone asked him what he did, he said he was an accountant who worked for the artists' insurers. That shut people up and made them go away pretty fast. If they didn't, well, Smitty had an economics GCSE and was confident he could bluff his way through. Plus he always took an assistant as hanger-on and as cover. Even a useless Nigel like this one could be good cover, because Smitty looked as if he was standing talking to him while in fact he was checking out the talent in the room – the talent in all senses.

Smitty recognised about a third of the people in the room; that was about average. There were some dealers who were mainly drinking champagne, a few artists who were mainly drinking Special Brew (nice touch) and a few civilians who were either on champagne or London tap water; that was being served out of magnums with 'London Tap' printed on the side (another nice touch). The dealers were for the most part wearing expensive versions of smart casual, the artists were carefully super-scruffy, and the civilians wore suits. Hence his disguise. There were more foreigners than usual, which was interesting; mainly Germans, Smitty thought. The word about these guys had got out quite far quite fast. Germany was a good market, as Smitty well knew. About a third of his book's earnings had been in Germany. That was really all there was to see here. Another glass of bubbles and Smitty would be off.

All this made Parker very unhappy. Smitty was right to think that his assistant wasn't exactly convulsed with respect for him. In Parker's opinion, Smitty's entire oeuvre was based on a mistake. Once you ignored the particulars of what Smitty did – which, in Parker's view, you could easily do, without missing too much – what Smitty's work was really about was anonymity. He was all about being anonymous, about the idea of, and consequences of, being anonymous. Warhol only had one idea, about the commodification of the art image; and he got that idea in all its implications, from every possible angle. Smitty too only had one idea, about the possibilities and consequences of anonymity. But his idea was, in Parker's opinion, a load of bollocks. People did not want to be anonymous. More: anonymity was one of the things that they liked least about life in the modern world. They wanted to be known, they wanted to be named, they wanted their fifteen minutes.

'It's not about being invisible,' Parker would say to his girl-friend Daisy when he talked about what was wrong with Smitty; which was fairly often. 'He's got it backwards. Art should be about making people visible. Making things visible. It's about attention.'

She knew well enough not to say anything, just to stroke the nearest available body part.

Parker knew just how being unknown, unacknowledged, unseen, presses on people; he knew because he felt the pressure inside himself. He felt it as an aspect of the city, of the crowds and the blankness and the attention always going elsewhere, up and out towards dreams of celebrity and fame, down and into the reveries of the self; and never where it belonged, some small but loud and passionate part of him secretly felt: towards him, Parker French.

'Yeah, we've done this,' said Smitty, draining his glass and handing it to one of the dwarfs. Parker knew what that meant: we are leaving immediately. Smitty's absolute indifference to most other people could seem a form of geniality, the affability of an older man, but Parker knew that Smitty wasn't at all genial, not even a little bit. Parker put his half-full glass on the same tray and the two men headed unnoticed for the warehouse exit.

40

Patrick Kamo had a secret. It was a secret he kept from everyone, but especially from his son, and the secret was this: Patrick hated London. He hated England, he hated the life he was living while he kept Freddy company. He hated the weather, he hated the English language, he hated the year-round cold and rain and the way it made him feel old, he hated the extra layers of clothing he had to wear to fight the weather, and he hated the way central heating made him feel sweaty and cold and dried out all at the same time. He had looked forward to the spring, to the time when, he was told, everything would start getting warmer, but the English spring was ridiculous, grey and not just cold but damply cold. He hated people's unfriendliness, and he hated the way he had gone from being a respected and important man in his own right to being an accessory of his son's life. He hated the way he was invisible in the streets. He hated the fact that nobody knew who he was; he had never been a man with many close friends, he was too guarded for that, but he had many acquaintances, people who looked at him with regard; in London, he had none, except the people who were paid to be polite to him because he was Freddy's father. He hated the house in Pepys Road, its horrible narrowness, its unexpansive tallness, the expensive toys which he found he couldn't operate properly. He was a man who had always worked, but here his job was Being Freddy's Father, which wasn't a job at all. A man should be a father, but a man should be a worker too. Here, because his job was nothing but to be with Freddy, he felt as if both things were being taken away from him. More than he would have thought possible, he hated being away from his wife and daughters. He expected to miss them in a way he could manage, a small pain, like a muscle ache. Instead he thought about them all the time. The agreement was that they wouldn't be coming to visit until the autumn, but Patrick had no idea how he was going to wait that long for the smell of Adede's hair, for the feel of his youngest daughters Malé and Tina crushed and squealing with laughter in his arms. In London, of course, all they would want to do was shop – but that would be good to see. It would sink in with his daughters what their half-brother had done, what he now was. And maybe Patrick would even get some pleasure from showing them this horrible city, this place he hated so much. Whenever the cursed postcards and DVDs arrived, the ones talking about how people wanted what he had, he wanted to scream and shout and swear and hit somebody. There was nothing in his new life that he liked.

He kept all these feelings to himself. It was a point of honour and principle for Patrick not to complain about things, that was one reason; the other was because it would be unfair to Freddy. To fulfil his dream, to live his talent to the full, to be paid more than anyone could imagine, to be a hero, to do the thing he loved and wanted more than any other – and to be greeted by his father with all this whining negativity: that would be crushing. Freddy was a good boy whose strongest motivation in life, apart from his love of football, was his wish to please his father. He should not have to deal with the fact that his happiness was bringing his father misery. So Patrick kept his misery to himself. Perhaps he could have talked to Mickey, who had become so fond of Freddy that Patrick had started to trust him; but there again, Patrick felt that telling him about his unhappiness would have been unmanly. He liked Mickey but he did not want to show him any weakness.

This week was particularly difficult because Freddy had gone to the Azores for a training break with the club. Patrick had talked things over with Mickey – when the matter touched on Freddy's interests, Mickey was a good person to talk to – and had decided not to go to the training camp with him. For one thing, they had been in London for five months now, and it would be good for Freddy to travel on his own for the first time – given that 'on his own' meant that he would be going in a party of fifty people, all of whom he already knew. For another, there was nothing at all to do at the camp except train, watch the training, then eat and take baths and watch training films and maybe a DVD in the evening. There were no temptations for Freddy to give in to (not that he was that kind of boy) and there was by the same token nothing for Patrick to do. So he chose to stay in London. He could be miserable on his own for a change. They were so rich now that he could have flown home to see his wife and daughters for a week, but that, again, felt unmanly to Patrick. It would be too like a child running to its mother to seek comfort.

So Patrick had the best part of a week on his own. The housekeeper prepared meals and left instructions on how to reheat them; the meals were in plastic containers in the fridge, the instructions, in printed handwriting, were on a notepad next to the cooker. Patrick followed the instructions, then added extra chilli sauce to make the food palatable. For the first two days, Mickey called him up to ask how he was doing. Patrick was grateful for his concern, but hid his gratitude behind a gruff manner because he didn't want to seem gushing. He did that so effectively that Mickey thought he was annoying Patrick by fussing over him, and so stopped ringing. Freddy rang in the evenings, usually with music playing or someone laughing in the background. Freddy was happy. He liked having lots of people around him.

Patrick Kamo, on his own in the London house in the rainy non-existent English summer, was as lonely and as bored and as underemployed as he had ever been in his life.

He took to going for walks. Up to now, most of the city he had seen had been out of a car window, and usually while travelling to or from somewhere with Freddy and Mickey. He had occasionally taken walks around the block, to the shops or just to get out of the house for a few minutes, but since it was hard for Freddy to go out in public now without being recognised, his time was mainly spent in cars or buildings. Patrick, left to his own devices, decided to change that. On Tuesday he went across the Common to the south, down past Balham and Tooting, and understood for the first time the alternation between the clusters of shops in old high streets followed by long stretches, block after block after street after street, of identical houses, all tightly squeezed in, and then the open stretches of the various commons. On that walk, he began to head eastwards towards Streatham, then tired and looped back and found his own way home after hitting the South Circular and following it around. The traffic had come to a complete halt, and he must have overtaken hundreds, perhaps thousands, of cars at his easy strolling pace. When he got to King's Avenue he discovered the reason: a helicopter was parked in the middle of the road, with two police cars to either side of it, lights flashing. He had heard of this but never seen it, the Air Ambulance. An Asian police officer stood behind a cordon and allowed pedestrians past. There was a white van, askew across two lanes of the road, and a glimpse of something wedged under its front wheels; from the stoops and frowns of the men around it, something was caught up in something else. A bicycle. Its rider could not have survived. Patrick felt pity but also incomprehension: this was a rich country, why would anyone choose to ride a bicycle?

The next day he went north-east, towards Stockwell, past

people speaking a language he took time to realise was Portuguese, past busy roads and housing estates which looked like places he would not want to live, all the way to the river and a sudden, unexpected view of the Houses of Parliament. He stopped to look at the broad grey river and the handsome old buildings, and as he did so a woman came up to ask him to take a photograph of her and her friend. It was the first time anyone had spoken to him since Mickey had stopped ringing him. He blinked to clear his sight, looked through the viewfinder, and took a photograph of the two middle-aged women in anoraks with their arms linked together, and the Houses of Parliament out of focus in the background behind them. Then he walked home.

The effect of his long solo foot trips through the city wasn't to make him suddenly love London, but he began to feel that he understood it a little better – understood where things were, understood the rhythm of the city. Patrick realised that what was disconcerting for him was the impression of everybody being busy all the time. People always seemed to be doing things. Even when they weren't doing anything, they were walking dogs, or going to betting shops, or reading newspapers at bus stops, or listening to music through headphones, or skateboarding along the pavement, or eating fast food as they walked along the street – so even when they weren't doing things, they were doing things.

On the third morning Patrick woke late; the building noises which were never absent on a Pepys Road morning had for some reason not broken through into his sleep. He ate toast and an entirely flavourless banana and instead of struggling with the coffee-maker – which had a French-language instruction manual but was still impossible to work out – brewed strong stewed coffee in a jug. He shuffled around the house a little bit, dressed, and left when the housekeeper arrived at about half past ten.

Patrick's third walk took him north, towards the river. He went down a local street which he'd never visited even though it was just around the corner: it had, it turned out, a delicatessen, a shoe shop, and a gym where an outstandingly fat man was fighting his own shortness of breath as he tried to chain up a bicycle. A minicab office, a pub, a pizza restaurant which might not yet be open for the day, or which might have gone out of business, it was hard to tell. Down the hill, past a greengrocer's shop with a sign in the window saying 'African Vegetables'. Under a railway bridge, past a huge poster with a close-up photo of a man's crotch dressed in Y-fronts. Past a bus stop with the usual cast of Londoners smoking, playing electronic games, listening to music, staring into space, all as if those activities were jobs in themselves. Past the gasholder, through the park, past joggers and cyclists, down to the river, along the riverside walk. The Thames was different colours depending on its different moods and today, with a rare glimpse of blue in the sky, it was lighter, happier, blue-reflecting. Unlike an African river, it seemed to have no smell. Patrick walked over the pretty, delicate, white-painted ironwork bridge. Again he was overtaking stationary cars, in which people posed and fumed as if they too were working at it. A couple in a low-slung car, a Mini, the girl also wearing a miniskirt, were using the time stuck in traffic to kiss and fondle each other. They were going hard at it. Patrick felt a pang of something, loneliness or lust or both. Maybe he should have taken this week to go home after all.

Over the bridge there was a pub, with a sign saying 'Cat and Racket'. The pub had tinted, mottled-glass windows, and electric lights designed to look like old gas lamps. Patrick looked at it and wished that he could go in. He had heard about pubs and had a fantasy image of what they were like: warm, brown, convivial. Not everything in London was people on their own, and pubs were proof of that. But Patrick had never been in one. He was too concerned about not embarrassing himself to go on his own, and too proud to ask Mickey to take him. That didn't stop him dreaming, and he briefly dreamed now, about how he might cross the road, and find men inside watching football on television, or arguing about some aspect of the game, and they would ask his opinion, ask him if he knew anything, and he would say, quietly, 'I am Freddy Kamo's father,' and they would be astonished, amazed, and they would be thrilled to meet him, and they would compete to buy him a beer, and to put an arm round him and tell him how great they thought Freddy was and how much they hoped things would work out. That is what he dreamed it would be like.

Patrick cut across the King's Road, which was a place Freddy had liked to come to and walk along, before he got so famous that it had become difficult. Freddy's distinctive walk was part of the problem: he could change his profile with a hat and baggy clothes, but no one had an athletically ungainly walk quite like Freddy, bouncing high on his toes, looking as if he might trip over himself but never missing a step. His son, who had been breathed on by the gods. No similar grace had ever rained down on Patrick – or rather, his son was that grace – and he had to accept that he was an accessory to that grace, that luck, that blessing. But Patrick, being honest with himself, had to admit that he didn't find it easy. He walked along this famous road, looking in the windows of the expensive shops selling things which he could not imagine anyone wanting or needing or using: lamps which did not look as if they would emit any light, shoes no woman could stand in, coats which would not keep anyone warm, chairs which had no obvious way to sit on them. People wanted these things, they must do, or the shops wouldn't be selling them – and yet Patrick was so far from wanting any of them for himself that he felt that it wasn't the things for sale which were useless, but he himself. Either the things or the person looking at them were in the wrong place;

233

but the things so clearly belonged here that it must be the person who was lost and redundant. The trim middle-aged African man whose hair was beginning to grey, smartly but inconspicuously dressed in a camel-hair coat and scarf and shined shoes, upright – he was the thing which was in the wrong place.

41

'You make me feel so young . . . you make me feel as though spring has sprung,' sang Roger, to himself, in the privacy of his own head. It would not have been appropriate to sing it out loud, because he was sitting in a meeting with his deputy Mark and some guy from accounts whose name he had already forgotten once, then got Mark to remind him of when the man stepped out of the room to take a call, then had forgotten again. The guy from accounts had a standard English name, but on the long side, Roger could remember that much. Jonathan was a possibility. Alexander also. Several syllables were involved. But for the moment Roger was having to stick to 'you'.

The purpose of the meeting: to prepare monthly figures matching the department's performance against budget – which was done daily and weekly too, but was done monthly for submission to Accounts. So Accounts helped prepare the figures which were then formally submitted to Accounts and then sent back to the department. Roger was barely listening, he was barely there. He felt so young, he felt that spring had sprung. In point of fact it was a grey day, with the low sky much in evidence from Roger's office, and a bleak and biting Easter wind moving the clouds along briskly, like an irritated policeman – but Roger didn't care about that. If pressed for the reason why he was in such good humour, he wouldn't have been able to give it.

He had been in a good mood more or less without interruption since the arrival of their new nanny on 27 December. With Matya downstairs, having apparently fallen in love with the boys at first sight and vice versa, Roger was free to go up to his study and work on his revenge. He put a Clash compilation CD in his fancy stereo and took out a notepad. At the top he wrote 'Economies'. Below that he wrote:

> *Reality: £1,000,000 shortfall.*

> *Necessity: cut outgoings.*

> *Actions: cut shopping bill by 70 per cent.*

(This meant that Arabella's spending would have to be dramatically, spectacularly curtailed. No more buying whatever she wanted whenever she wanted. In fact:)

> *All purchases, expenditure over specific figure*
> *to be mutually discussed and agreed. Suggest*
> *initial limit of £100.*

(Arabella loved spending money, but she hated, hated having to ask for it. The joint account, as currently constituted, meant that she never had to, and Roger couldn't be bothered to go through the bank statement every month. He would be bothering now, though. As for a £100 limit, Roger knew that Arabella would be incredulous.)

> *Either Minchinhampton or Ibiza/Verbier/*
> *Tuscany not both.*

(This was a definitive, below-the-waterline strike on Arabella's stated wish to have both a house in the country and two foreign holidays a year.)

> *No additional work on the house.*

(It was the 'additional' there that made it so good.)

No weekend/additional nannies.

(Here, Roger felt, Arabella had made her greatest tactical error. Now that Roger had had the children on his own over Christmas, he was a childcare expert. He knew what they needed and did not need. They needed their new nanny, Matya, but they didn't need any more help that Arabella couldn't provide herself.)

It was this last point that cheered Roger the most. She had inadvertently given him control over a piece of her territory; Roger had stepped in and taken charge of the nanny question. Arabella had never hired an attractive nanny, a fact about which he had heard her semi-joking with female friends; so now Roger had hired one for her. He would dig in on this issue.

Roger turned up the music – 'Guns of Brixton', one of his favourites – put his arms behind his head and leaned back in his chair. He began working on dialogue for when Arabella got home, which he assumed would be that evening or the following morning.

'Did you have a lovely time, darling? I hope so. We did. I hope you weren't too worried about the boys, they hardly seemed to notice you weren't there. They're so resilient, aren't they, children?'

It would be difficult to deliver that line with a straight face – without letting his rage and male hysteria show. But it would be worth the effort.

At lunchtime, Roger wandered downstairs to see Joshua in his high chair and Conrad next to him, both contentedly eating omelettes. A large drawing took up most of the rest of the table. It was in two very different styles and it was difficult to say what it depicted; given that there was a lot of red and orange, and given the identity of the artists, the likely subject was some sort of explosion.

'Wow!' said Roger, fully restored to his affable normal self. 'Great painting!'

'I did the top half,' said Conrad. 'It's Autobots fighting Decepticons.'

'Did bottub,' said Joshua.

'I like both halves!' said Roger.

'There is some more omelette, left over,' said Matya from the stove. Roger, who was very hungry indeed – as he now realised – felt that it would be bad tactics to say yes and risk being dragged back into having to be with the children again, just when the new nanny had ridden to the rescue. So he declined with regret.

'Think I'll just go stretch my legs,' said Roger. He took his keys, coat and phone and wandered out to get a sandwich, full of a delicious sense of freedom and moral superiority.

The brilliant thing about the moment when Arabella came home, at about four o'clock, was that the boys were so happily engaged in playing with the new love of their life. Roger, who was upstairs in his study reading the *Economist*, heard the door open and shut and felt his heart rate rise. Then he heard Arabella go down the corridor into the sitting room; then he heard her come out and walk slowly up the stairs. Arabella was carrying a bag, no doubt her suitcase. Something about the noises she was making had the tang of defeat. She turned past his study – she would be able to tell he was in there from the light under the door – and went into the bedroom. About ten minutes after that, she came out of the bedroom to his study and knocked on the door.

'Hi!' said Roger. 'Nice break?'

'Yes, thank you,' said Arabella. She was about to say something else, but Roger was able to cut her off with:

'You've met Matya. I've hired her.'

'Well—' said Arabella.

And then at that point, providentially, wonderfully, the telephone rang. It was one of Arabella's closest friends from university, now a big shot in publishing. Roger passed the phone handset to his wife and flipped the magazine back up over his face. He had a thrilling sense that a fundamental shift in his marriage had taken place. It was a destructive shift, and he knew that; but that was part of the thrill. There was a hole in their relationship which he was consciously and deliberately not going to make any attempt to repair. And that was why he now sat in his office, humming 'You Make Me Feel So Young' to himself, while his energetic but weird deputy ran through figures and reeled off management-speak, and Roger nodded and grunted and said 'Good point' and thought about other things. You make me feel so young, you make me feel as though spring has sprung . . .

42

Matya Balatu grew up in a Hungarian town called Kecskemét. Her father was a teacher and so was her mother, though she had given up work when Matya's little brother was born. They lived in a small house with a garden in which her father grew vegetables.

When Matya was ten, her father and brother were killed in a car accident. Her mother began drinking and her health declined quickly. She died two years later. Matya went to live with her grandparents, who had looked after her when she was a baby and her mother was working. She did well in school, and went to university to study mechanical engineering. After she graduated she worked as a secretary in a dentist's office while raising the money to come to London to pursue a dream of expansiveness, of a bigger life, a better-off life, a life not overshadowed by her own early losses. She wanted to be happy and loved and she also wanted to marry a rich man and she thought she would be more likely to find one in London than anywhere else.

Matya was prepared to do most kinds of work. She found a receptionist's job at minimum wage, but in order to do so had had to bluff about the level of her English, and as a result the work, which ought to have been so far beneath her abilities that it was relaxingly easy, was a constant strain. It made her worry, and because she was worrying her English did not improve as fast as it should. Then she found a job as a translator on a building site with Hungarian workers. It was black-economy work, but the pay was good, £500 a week cash. The difficulty was that the overseer and his employer spent a lot of time complaining and abusing the workers, and because the complaints were passed through her, they tended to be directed at her. 'Tell the stupid fucker I don't want to hear his excuses' – that counted as a pleasantry. Matya had been brought up strictly and carefully by her parents and then grandparents, and put a great emphasis on people behaving to each other with courtesy and restraint. At first she found the swearing, the bad temper, all that to be funny, and then it began to wear her down. She quit the job after three months.

By then she had some friends, Hungarian friends; she would see them only one night a week because it was bad for her English to speak too much Hungarian. But they were good friends and two of them had found work as nannies and childminders, and they knew an agency in South London, so Matya went for an interview. That was three years ago, and here she was, still a nanny.

Matya found the initial stretch working at the Younts' to be hard going. She liked the children very much, liked the house and the area. It was an OK commute over from Earlsfield, about half an hour by bus or fifteen minutes when she was in the mood to cycle. The money was good, not least because the Younts were her first employer for three years to pay her legally, including her National Insurance contributions. That might have been because it was the husband who hired her, and he didn't know that however rich English people were, they usually didn't bother paying their nannies legally.

What made the initial month or so difficult was that there was something going on between the husband and wife. It had been strange that Mrs Yount wasn't there on 27 December, and never fully explained, and Matya could sense the heavy atmospheric pressure around the subject of her absence. Also, the fact that the husband had hired her clearly made the wife feel uneasy, and she had been difficult at the start – watchful, resentful, and insisting on a four-week trial period, something he hadn't mentioned. The way she said it was a clear warning that if there were a reason to get rid of Matya, she would take it.

But more than three months had gone by, and all that was now in the past. Arabella did not object to the idea of holding a grudge, being difficult, giving people a hard time; but in practice, her fundamental laziness wouldn't let her. Anger and spikiness were, over a sustained period, just too tiring, not worth the effort. Matya, who had had a difficult childhood and had come to London to get away from things, and who was very good at holding grudges and keeping score, found this refreshing. She sensed that Arabella would have quite liked not to like her as a way of getting at her husband, but found that she did like her, so let the feeling go. Also, Matya made her life easier, by being so good with the children, and it was clear that Arabella felt a deep, sincere affection for anyone who made her life easier. When the delivery men carried boxes of groceries into the house, Arabella would tell them, 'You're an *angel*,' and in such a way that it seemed she really meant it – as indeed, in a small way, she did.

The great thing about Arabella was that she wanted things to be fun, to be easy, and acted as if they were – which went a long way to making them so. It was catching. One morning, handing over the boys to Matya when she arrived at nine o'clock and heading upstairs, as she said herself, for 'a long soak', she caught sight of Matya's shoes. They were a pair of flat tennis shoes with a grey and white check pattern.

'My God! They're fantastic! Must have! Where where where?! I can tell, you're going to tell me it's some mad little boutique tucked away in some souk in Budapest!'

'Tooting,' said Matya.

'More exotic still! Right – we're going there this minute.'

'This minute' was a flexible concept for Arabella. She still had to have her bath and do her face and make a few phone calls, but when that was done, by about eleven, sure enough she bundled Matya and Conrad and Joshua into her BMW and insisted on Matya's directing her to the shoe shop, with her energy and excitement about the outing carrying all four of them along, giggling and shrieking. Arabella had bought, as she herself put it, 'half the shop', and insisted on buying two pairs of shoes for Matya in the process, with generosity so unthinking and instinctive it was almost as if it were not generosity at all – it was as if it were something else, an overflow of energy; or as if there were no such thing as money, as if things did not cost anything, so it was perfectly natural to give them to other people, because they were free to start with. Matya had never met anyone like that; she had had a few employers who were rich, but they tended to be very careful about money, vigilantly checking change and receipts and making small mistakes always in their own favour when they totted up hours worked. It was hard not to like Arabella's open-handedness.

The best thing about the job, however, was Joshua. Conrad was back at school now, so she only saw him from 3.45 or on his holidays and days off. He was a good-hearted boy, though with a short temper and not used to being denied things, so he was not always easy to manage. At the moment Conrad was mainly interested in superpowers and his conversation tended to turn on them. He would announce that he could fly, or ask Matya whether she could shoot heat-vision rays out of her eyes, and if she couldn't, why not? Or he would announce that he had 'power of double-punch!' and shove both his fists out. He liked trying to say 'invincible' but was not clear on the difference between that and being invisible, so all three of them played games in which

243

invincibility and invisibility went together. So Conrad was fun. It was different, deeper with Joshua.

Joshua was hers every day. He and Matya were in love, and made no attempt to conceal the fact from each other. On some days he would be sitting on a chair by the window looking for her as she came in, like a dog waiting for its owner; that made her heart do a little flip. Then he would come running to the door and grab her hand and drag her behind him while she fought to take her coat off with her free arm before he had wrestled her into the sitting room and launched into whatever game, story, or demand was in the front of his mind. He was always, at the start of the day, in mid-thought; he had something he needed to get off his chest, or a plan that demanded immediate action. If Matya came in the room and Joshua was lying or sitting on the sofa, she knew that he was ill, and that it would be a 'floppy day', as Arabella called it.

Other things Josh liked included going to the pond on the far side of the Common to feed the ducks, and stopping for an ice cream at the café by the bandstand on the way back; standing by the edge of the skateboard park and watching the older boys zoom and swoop down the ramps (also up the ramps, on the edges of the ramps, backwards, sideways); riding the bus, anywhere, for any reason; going to the Aquarium, where he was fascinated by the idea of the sharks but also scared of them – in contrast to his attitude to the rays, which he was also a bit scared of but loved to reach into the tank to stroke, and afterwards was thrilled with himself (and with the rays), so the contrast between his attitudes to the two fish precisely drew the line between stimulating excitement and fear. As for food, that took a while for Matya to work out, and it was by no means a stable arrangement – he seemed to like baked potatoes, rice and chips, but not steamed potatoes; he sometimes did and sometimes did not like mash, he loved broccoli but hated cabbage, he liked cheese on some days but not on others, but always liked parmesan so long as it was grated, he liked meat but not burnt bits, dark bits, bits which had the appearance of potentially containing gristle even if they contained no gristle, bits which looked bloody or underdone; he disliked green flecks such as herbs, under all circumstances; he disliked the sight of dark spots which might be pepper; he disliked fizzy drinks but liked sweet ones; he liked fish fingers; he would not eat any kind of sausage except a hot dog; he liked pasta and pesto but not pasta with any other kind of sauce; it was impossible for anyone including Joshua to tell in advance of the food being put before him whether this would be one of the days on which he loved or hated bacon. A useful rule of thumb was that Joshua liked anything to which he could add tomato ketchup or soy sauce.

It was strange for Matya, finding herself so deeply in love. At the start of her time in London three years before, she had had fantasies of meeting a perfect man, and of finding children to look after who she really liked. Neither thing had happened. With her looks, attracting men had not been a problem; attracting men who she actually felt something in common with, who treated her respectfully, who were employed and responsible and good fun, was much less straightforward, and the one man who had seemed to be those things, and who she had begun to properly go out with, had turned out to be half-mad with control-freakery, much of it linked to the question of money. He wanted to treat her to things and then act as if she were his property. He had rages, he would go silent, then she would look out the window of her flat at four in the morning, woken by who knew what, and see him sitting outside in his car looking up at her, looking angry and lost, like a little boy trying to reclaim his dignity after recovering from a tantrum. When she finally, irrevocably broke with him – by putting it so plainly that he actually understood she didn't want to see him any more – he did something which, even by the standards of men and their irrationality and unreasonableness, was amazing. He sent her a bill for the holiday they had taken together, the holiday whose whole point, according to him, had been that he wanted to treat her to a week in Ayia Napa, clubbing and swimming and having sex. When she opened the letter she had laughed with rage – and also with delight, because this gave her the chance of definitively finishing things. She wrote him a cheque, which cleaned out her bank account, but left her feeling free of him, for good. She knew he would have one more go at getting back with her, as indeed he did, sitting in his car outside her flat one morning. But she had no difficulty in telling him to go away and leave her alone, and this time even he could tell that she meant it. Since that, six months ago, no men.

With children it hadn't been quite so bad, but still disappointing. She had had five jobs in her three years' childcare, the longest for ten months, with a family in Clerkenwell. Both the husband and the wife were lawyers. They had two girls and a boy, aged ten and eight and four, and as with quite a few of the people she had worked for, the children were angry all the time. Matya had no theories about children, she took them as she found them, but it seemed to her that many of the children she had looked after were both spoilt and neglected. It wasn't something she knew from Kecskemét in Hungary, so it took some time to figure this out. The other thing was that while they were used to being ignored, and to going to almost any lengths to get attention as a result, they were not at all used to hearing the word 'no', especially not when it meant what it said. So they would be angry to get attention, and then angry when they didn't get their way, and taken together, that was quite a lot of anger. It was tiring and also, even when she knew that the anger wasn't about her, it was demoralising. If anger is directed at you, it feels as if it is about you, even though another part of your brain knows that it isn't. The lawyers' children had been like that, so that although Matya had liked them (when they weren't raging) and had liked the parents (what little she saw of them) she had left, and had only short-stay jobs, a couple of weeks at a time, until she came to work for the Younts.

What it boiled down to was, the chemistry hadn't been right. But with Joshua, right from the start, it clicked. There was nothing she could explain about it, it was just that they fitted each other – and it was not that he was unlike the other spoilt-and-neglected rich children, and not that he didn't get angry. It was just that he was Josh, and she loved him and he loved her.

43

Mary was going for a night out in London. She didn't particularly want that night out, but Alan thought it would be good for her, and because Alan was good at keeping his advice and interference to a minimum, when he did suggest she do something, it had extra force. That was how, without ever feeling keen on the idea, Mary had found herself enlisted to go for a 'Big Night Out' with two friends who were coming down from Essex for the night. They were booked into a hotel near Leicester Square and seemed much more excited about the whole thing than Mary did on her own account. The plan was to go and have a drink at their hotel, then go and see a musical, then go and have dinner afterwards.

'We'll be starving,' said Mary. 'Our tummies will rumble, it'll be embarrassing.'

'If you eat before,' said Alan, 'you'll fall asleep. Have some nuts or something when you have a drink. Canapés. Whatever. Better that than snoring your head off.'

Alan, bless him, had done the booking and bought the tickets. Mary suspected he might even have paid for the hotel, but didn't want to ask. All she had to do was put on her frock, go out and enjoy herself – and perhaps because that was all she had to do, it felt oppressive. Mary had always had a problem with holidays, with the idea that it was compulsory to be having fun. On holiday, having fun became a job. As the children got older, then

Graham left home and Alice went to university, they had gradually stopped having a proper holiday, and Alan had just taken a run of days off at home in the summer. Mary preferred that; she found it less stressful.

So now she was standing in front of a full-length mirror in what had been her childhood bedroom and was now a sort of spare room, even though no visitor had ever stayed there. She hadn't brought any dressing-up clothes to London and was having to make do with the nicest floral dress she'd packed; it wasn't ideal, and it might not be warm enough, but she would take along a cashmere cardy and it would have to do. Alan had suggested she bought herself something new but she drew the line at that. The fact that her mother was dying was no reason to go on a spending spree.

The doorbell rang. This too was part of what Alan had arranged. He knew that Mary wouldn't go out unless someone she could trust was looking after Petunia, and knew too that there was no stranger who Mary would trust, so he had asked Graham to come and grandma-sit. Again, because Alan never asked anything of Graham – Mary was the one who did the worrying and fussing and checking-up and advice-giving – when he did, it was treated as a direct order. That was annoying, given what Graham was like with her. Anyway, here her son was. She went downstairs and opened the door.

It took a lot of effort and discipline not to exclaim in alarm at his clothes. Graham was wearing a no-longer-white white T-shirt with paint stains, a pair of torn, ragged, saggy jeans, and trainers. He could look so smart and handsome when he bothered to make an effort, Mary thought it was a real shame that three-quarters of the time he went around looking like a tramp.

'Hi, Mum,' said Smitty. 'Sorry, I've been sitting in the car for ten minutes waiting for it to be six o'clock so that the wardens didn't get me. One of those African ones was eyeing me up. Walking past pretending not to have seen me. I swear, it's like the nicer your car, the more likely you are to get a ticket. Is that capitalism?'

'Your grandmother's asleep. She might go straight through the night from here but she also might wake up. You know what to do, yes?'

Mary had gone over this, at length, twice. The instructions were simple, since all Graham had to do was go and help his grandmother if she called for him. They had now installed a baby monitor so that the person downstairs could hear Petunia if she called out.

'Sure I do, Mum. Chuck in a grenade and shoot the first one who comes running out. Off you go, off off. Dad said to tell you to take a black cab from the rank.'

'Right,' said Mary, who had no intention of doing any such thing. And then, since she couldn't stop herself, since she was the one who did the family's caring and worrying and asking and noticing and minding, and since Graham was looking so rough and so ragged – was looking a lot like someone who had lost their job, or didn't have a job, and was in no hurry to get another one, she said:

'Work . . . everything, everything OK at work?'

'Never better, Mum. Off you go. Have a good time. I'll keep away from the drinks cabinet.' He held up his car keys and waved them as he said that. 'Shoo. Hoick it. Scram. Vamoose. It's your Big Night Out.' So Mary had no choice except to pick up her clutch bag and go out into the evening.

When the door closed behind her, Smitty clenched his fist and made an arm-pumping gesture. Yes! Ker-ching! He had bet himself ten million pounds that however short their interaction on the doorstep, his mother wouldn't be able to stop herself asking about his work, or how things were going, or something.

He actually said it aloud, 'I bet myself ten million quid.' It was nice to be proved right. That was something you never got tired of. Making a joke of his mum's way of carrying on made it less of a mind-fuck. From his dealings with his mother, Smitty had learned the following truth: the person doing the worrying experiences it as a form of love; the person being worried about experiences it as a form of control.

Smitty took a wander round the ground floor to see that everything was in order. It was – of course it was. If anything his mum was even tidier than his nan – though having said that, now that he was looking around the kitchen, there was clear evidence that she had taken up smoking again: a washed-up ashtray on the draining board, and the sort of tobacco smell you get when someone is trying to be careful about smoking near the window but doesn't realise non-smokers will pick up odour any way. Ha! Well, sort of ha. His mum taking up smoking would have been funny if the circumstances had been different. Her taking up smoking because she was sad and stressed about Nan dying wasn't something to laugh about. He withdrew his mental ha.

The kitchen was the same as always. It had been funny to see it as a form of time travel to 1955 when his nan was just being his nan, as permanent and unchangeable as a piece of sculpture. From a certain perspective, his nan's kitchen was a genius piece of camp. But it looked a little different now that she was dying and would probably, no, certainly, never use it again: never open the world's oldest fridge, never stand by the stove waiting for the ultra-retro kettle to sing. The objects had Nan in them, her care and attention and her wanting them to be this way. She had chosen them (or more likely her husband had chosen them and then she had chosen to put up with them). While she was dying, it was as if they were dying too, the care and the wanting-them-this-way draining out of them. Now she'd never be in this room again.

Never was a hard word. Smitty's art didn't take much interest in never, and he found that it wasn't something he wanted to spend much time thinking about.

From the sitting room, he could hear a faint echoing noise which he took a moment to figure out; it was the baby monitor. You could set it to go both ways, presumably so people could talk back to their babies – yes darling, ga-ga-goo-goo, or whatever it was people said to babies – but Mary had disabled the feature so she didn't have to worry about making noise downstairs. He'd best go check on his nan. Taking the stairs two at a time, Smitty went up to her bedroom. She was lying on her back, propped up against the pillows, and her eyes were open.

'Graham,' she said. 'Your mother said you'd be here. I didn't mean to bring you up.' Her speech, Smitty noticed, had a faint slur, like that of someone who's had a few drinks and doesn't yet realise they're becoming pissed.

'Yeah, Mum's gone out. She's on a large one,' said Smitty, sitting down on the chair beside the bed. 'You all right?' And then he realised as soon as he'd said it how stupid that was. His nan just smiled at him, as if she hadn't heard, but it was a sad smile, which meant that she probably had. He didn't say anything else; there wasn't any need to. His nan looked at him for a bit, then closed her eyes. Not long after that, her breathing changed, and Smitty saw that she'd fallen asleep.

Smitty went back downstairs, wandered out into the garden, which was looking good, as far as he could tell, which wasn't very far, since as he liked to joke, 'I'm not competitive enough to be interested in gardening.' He went back inside and turned the TV on, but everything was shite and his nan (of course) didn't have Sky, so there wasn't much choice, so he went back into the kitchen again and there on the table, along with some junk mail which his mother hadn't yet chucked, he saw one of those cards saying 'We Want What You Have'. It was another photo of the front door. Smitty picked it up and stared at it, and couldn't tell whether what he was feeling was foreboding or sadness.

44

At the Polish club in Balham, Zbigniew sat with a bison-grass vodka and a bottle of Żywiec beer, waiting for Piotr. Zbigniew did not repress things, he believed in letting complaints out to give them some air. So he was going to tell Piotr what was going on with Davina. Zbigniew felt that he was going to have to tell Piotr what was happening, because if he didn't his head was going to explode, but the cost of doing that would be to suffer Piotr's amusement. He knew that Piotr would think what had happened in his love life, or his sex life, was hilarious; he would think it was a punishment for his pragmatic and deliberately unromantic approach to women.

This was made very much worse by the fact that a tiny part of Zbigniew thought there might be some truth in Piotr's view. But knowing that you had gone wrong, and knowing how you had gone wrong, were not the same thing as knowing how to put it right.

The bar was half-full. It was a popular spot with the older generation of London Poles, the ones who had come over during the war – there were even people here who remembered that time first-hand. Favourite fact: one-third of all the planes shot down during the Battle of Britain were shot down by Polish pilots. So it was a place for old men to play cards and watch the Polish TV and generally carry on as if they were still back in the old country. The younger generation hadn't yet colonised the club, which was one of the things Zbigniew liked about it. Without really examining the feeling, Zbigniew was aware that the club reminded him of his parents, of the evenings when his father had his friends over for Zechcyk and his mother pottered about in the kitchen, pretending to complain about how late they would keep her awake.

Piotr came in, looked over, saw what he was drinking, made a sign with two fingers pointing up in curls at the sides of his head – their private gesture for bison, therefore for bison-grass vodka – and came over from the bar with two more vodkas and two more Żywiecs. They touched glasses and downed the vodkas and then took a shot of beer.

In Polish, Piotr said, 'This Chelsea job stinks. It's like that job we did in Notting Hill where Andrzej wanted to leave a dead rat in the cavity wall. Remember them, the fat music producer with the skinny blonde wife? These ones are the same. They're the kind of rich people who fight you over every penny and because he's a crook he thinks everyone else is too. She acts as if she has the authority to make decisions, then he comes the next day and reverses everything she said and claims that we shouldn't have acted on her authority so we should carry the costs. It's like watching a divorce in slow motion and being expected to pay for the privilege. I was a moron to take the job.'

'Good money though.'

Piotr gave a sharp shrug which indicated that while this was true it was also obtuse since it wasn't the point at issue. Zbigniew found it important to have no feeling about his clients one way or another, and was about to say this to Piotr, with some smugness, and for about the hundredth time; but since he was also going to be spending a significant part of the evening complaining about his predicament with Davina, he didn't feel this was a good moment to point out a philosophical error on Piotr's part.

There was a burst of noise from one of the card tables; two

of the middle-aged men sitting at it had their arms above their heads, in victory or horror. The other two were looking at each other and the noise mixed laughter from one side, protest from the other, and general incredulity. One of the men with his arms in the air lowered them to the table and began raking in money. The man to his left, shaking his head and muttering, began to shuffle the cards. Money, money. Sometimes Zbigniew had to remind himself that that was the whole reason he was here in London, earning more in a month than his father had ever earned in a whole year. His real life was back home in Poland. This was a place he was in order to make money. That thought often brought Zbigniew some ease, when he was fed up with some aspect of his immigrant life; today, it didn't help. Woman trouble was what it was.

Piotr knew that Zbigniew had been seeing Davina – he could hardly not know – but he was tactful, as he always was; it was one of the things Zbigniew loved about him. He was waiting to be told. So Zbigniew took a deep swig of his new beer and told him the details. It took quite a bit of time.

He had been expecting Piotr to laugh. Perhaps that was even what he was needing to hear from his friend – that the whole thing was ridiculous, and that he'd brought it on himself, and that it served him right, and so on. Piotr did indeed smile a bit, and Zbigniew did the best he could to try and make the story sound funny, the determined non-romantic trapped by great sex in a terrible relationship. But his smile faded as Zbigniew talked on. Then Zbigniew finished and went back to the bar to get another four drinks for the two of them. If nothing else, he'd get drunk tonight.

When he got back to the table Piotr was flipping the beer mat over with his large fingers. Zbigniew raised his glass of vodka and downed it in one. Neither man said anything. Perhaps this confession was going to be received in silence.

'I suppose you thought I'd think it was funny,' said Piotr, and from his tone, which didn't resemble anything Zbigniew was expecting to hear from his old friend, he knew that this was not going to be the comic, consoling, making-light talk he had hoped to have. 'But I don't. You know I love you like a brother and always have. But you have a grave fault in your character. You see people not as people but in terms of how useful they are to you. You say I am a romantic, always falling in love, and all that. It's a joke between us, a set piece. Very well, it's true enough. But at least I can fall in love. With you, I'm not so sure. You use women. You use them partly for company, when you need it, but you mainly use them for sex. I've always known this would cause trouble one day and now it has. You've trapped this vulnerable English woman into falling in love with you, and you are going to hurt her very badly; you are doing her real damage. I hear it in the way you talk about her.'

Zbigniew, because he had not been expecting this, and because so much of it was right, felt himself become very angry. His head filled up with blood; he was exalted and exhilarated by rage.

'You say this because you are a priest? A priest hearing my confession, or giving a denunciation from the pulpit?'

Piotr got up and walked out. And that was that. Zbigniew sat there and drank his beer and vodka, then another round, then another, and went home drunker than he had been for a long time.

45

On Friday evening, after doing a shift in the shop, Usman set out across the Common on his bike, to go to the mosque for evening prayers. This is what he saw.

An advertising poster with a woman lying naked on purple sheets, her hindquarters on full display, with the slogan 'Does my bum look big in this?' A poster with a woman eating a chocolate as if she were fellating it. A poster on the side of a bus with an advertisement for a horror film, with a stamp across it saying 'Banned! To See Full Trailer Go Online'. A poster with a woman bending over and looking back at the camera through her legs, advertising tampons.

Two lesbians holding hands while out walking their dogs.

A young woman with her trousers so low that more than half of her bottom was exposed to the air, bending, while smoking a cigarette, over a pram, and saying as she did so, 'Where have you hidden it, you little sod?'

Many women whose breasts were almost fully visible under, over or through their thin summer clothes.

A newspaper headline saying 'Muslim terror cell loose in capital says Met chief'.

Many people outside the public house on the Common, openly drinking alcohol.

As Usman stopped to cross at a red light, he found himself looking at a man standing at a bus stop reading a newspaper. On the page facing out toward Usman was a picture of a completely naked woman, above an advertisement for a car-leasing company. The ad promised a BMW 3 series for a payment of £299 a month.

Usman carried on. Many people were drinking alcohol in the bars beside the Common, women smoking, women and men kissing. Alcohol everywhere. Because it was only six o'clock, most of the people drinking were not yet drunk; it wasn't the way it would be at ten or afterwards, when, especially at weekends, the whole area would be like a combat zone, a contest between man and alcohol which alcohol won, every time. No, alcohol didn't just win, alcohol reigned: it presided over weekend evenings like a king, like a malign archangel. And although there was grumbling about this, the occasional complaint, it was the very British kind of complaint that was more like moaning, and expressed a deep accommodation with the thing being complained about; it contained no rage, no outrage, no desire for change. Whereas to Usman, this looked like a society that was turning itself into a version of hell, in the interest of people who made money through selling alcohol.

The imam at Usman's mosque was an angry man, but he was not stupid, and society had given him one overwhelmingly powerful advantage: the first thing he said on most subjects was true. He railed against capitalism and the cheapening of sex and the degradation of women through the pornographic imagery which was, in this country at this time, now, everywhere. He spoke about things that had become so taken for granted it was as if people literally did not see them any more. But Usman, who had after all grown up in this country, who was no alien – he saw them.

Usman had come to believe that the imam was right: these were symptoms of decadence. Sex being used to sell things, the corruption of the fundamental human impulse to love, sex being turned into a vehicle of yet more capitalist debasement – sex was everywhere. It was never real sex, as Usman understood it to be, an ecstatic state such as that enjoyed in paradise, a transcendent experience; instead it was naked women, coupled with an attempt to sell something. Sex was fundamentally linked with money. And then the imam would start in on the subject of an intoxicated society. Here, too, he was saying something that everyone knew to be truthful. Usman had done holiday jobs as a hospital porter, and had seen with his own eyes that any A&E unit on a Saturday night was like an encyclopedia of all the different things you could do to yourself when drunk. Men and women fighting, puking, men hitting each other, men hitting their women or being hit by them, men raping and women being raped, both sexes contracting diseases, hurting their children, crashing vehicles, killing themselves, killing themselves with drink. And why did this society have such a deep need for intoxication? Because it knew it was lost, it was on the wrong path, and it had to blot out that knowledge with all the means at its disposal.

And then the imam, having said these true things, would move on to some other truths. He didn't care about the spies who would certainly be listening, the spies in the pay of the kafr government of Britain; he was above that. The imam simply told the truth. He was too intelligent to say that there was a global war against Islam. In Usman's opinion, actually, there was, you could prove that there was, from Palestine to Kosovo to Afghanistan to Iraq, and then through the subtler examples of suppression in Egypt and Pakistan and Indonesia and everywhere else that Islam was not allowed to express itself democratically and fully – but you didn't need to prove that. All you needed to do was ask a simple question. Was a Muslim life worth the same as a Christian or Jewish life? In the order of the world, did a dead

Muslim child count for as much as a dead Jew? Was a Muslim death worth as much attention as a Christian death?

The answer was so obvious, it barely needed to be spoken. In the scales of the West – which meant according to the value system that ran the world – a Muslim life was worth a fraction of other people's. A war on Islam – you could argue about that. The manifest truth that Muslims counted for less – that was not possible to challenge. Much followed from this.

Usman came to the mosque, pulled over onto the pavement and dismounted before his bike could ride up on it, because that would be discourteous. He chained his wheels to a rack – this was a high-risk spot, he realised, because a thief seeing a bicycle locked up outside a mosque would guess where the owner was and how long he would be likely to be in for, but inshallah, either it would be stolen or it wouldn't – and he joined the men heading into the building for the ablutions before prayer.

46

Smitty liked to go against the grain, so where he might have been expected to have no desk, or something very modern – a workstation, with a sloped surface to sketch on and a laptop stand – instead he had a huge old Victorian partners' desk made out of oak. He had no partner, of course, so both sides of the desk were his, and both were dominated by his filing system, which consisted of stacks of paper arranged by theme. On one side of the studio there was also a blackboard with curtains, so that whatever was being worked on could be hidden from casual view. There was also a £5,000 music system and a sixty-inch plasma flat-screen TV. Smitty was no Luddite. His assistant, his Nigel – who was always a 'he', because Smitty believed in a strict absence of sexual tension at work; he had no trouble pulling and didn't need the extra hassle – had a corner of the office with a desk and phone and PC; he was allowed to roam around in the course of doing his business, but he wasn't encouraged to allow his stuff to spread out and colonise Smitty's space.

Sometimes the desk had ten or twelve huge mountains of paper, to do with either pieces Smitty was thinking about or what he called 'admin crap', a category which covered more or less anything that did not directly involve making art. At other times there was only a single pile. Today there were two stacks of paper on the desk, and both of them had been there for two weeks. One of them was the stuff he had taken from his nan's house, the We

Want What You Have postcards and DVD. He had been flicking through these on and off all day since he got back from Pepys Road. The cards were a little like an installation, an artwork. The DVD, which was still in the player underneath the TV, was sort of the same thing as the cards, only in moving pictures. It consisted of lingering close-ups of houses in Pepys Road, shots of particular details of houses, tracking shots moving up and down the street. It looked as if it had been filmed in the early summer morning over two or three occasions. The DVD was about forty minutes long.

When he'd seen that, he Googled 42 Pepys Road and after a bit of clicking around found himself looking at a picture of his nan's front door. The blog was, of course, called We Want What You Have. It had a list of numbers and when you clicked on the numbers you were taken to a photo of the house – sometimes the front door, sometimes a detail from the door such as a close-up of the number, or of the letter box, or the steps, or the doorbell. Some of the photos were taken from across the road, to frame the whole house; some of them were colour, indeed some of them were in heightened, super-real colour; others were black and white and amateurish. One or two of them seemed to have been taken with a pinhole camera held at waist height. In those photographs, the spy-like ones, you could just catch a glimpse of part of a person – a leg disappearing out of show, somebody's shadow falling across a front gate. Other than that there were no people to be seen. Whoever was behind We Want What You Have was going to some trouble to leave the people out of it.

So that was part of what was on Smitty's mind. The other thing was more immediately troubling, because the other thing was not a thing at all but a person. Smitty's assistant. Smitty's about-to-be-ex-assistant, who had been his about-to-be-ex-assistant in Smitty's head for many weeks now, but who was no closer to being simply Smitty's ex-assistant because Smitty hadn't got round to firing him.

Smitty's art was all about confrontation. It was about shocking people, jolting them out of their well-grooved perceptions. Parodies, defacements, obscenities, spray-painted graffiti of Picasso being sucked off by an octopus – that was what Smitty was all about. Right up in your face. No prisoners. In person, though, Smitty did not like confrontation. He was a peacemaker, an accommodator, a finder of the common ground. It was a yin-and-yang thing. Balance was the key.

His art was about extremes, his life was about balance. The ideal thing for Smitty would have been if he could get an assistant to sack his assistant. Get a new Nigel to get rid of the old Nigel. That would be perfect. No point dreaming about that, though. This had been going on for long enough, and Smitty had decided that today was the day. On his desk, to the right of the pile of stuff from his nan's, was a Post-it note with 'GET IT DONE' written on it. That note had been there for a week; which was too long. In his head, he had given the assistant a second and then a third chance, both of which he had blown. Now it was over. The decisive factor was his assistant's way of making it clear that in his judgement, he and not Smitty was the person who should be treated as the famous artist. The fact that he hadn't actually made any art since leaving St Martin's, the fact that all he did was chores for Smitty, seemed in his mind to be a minor, disregardable detail. It was only a question of time before the world realised its mistake in being interested in Smitty rather than in him, and it was tiresome of Smitty to insist on the current hierarchical order of their relationship, which was so soon and so inevitably to be reversed. That was how he acted. Well, thought Smitty, he can piss right off with that. He thinks it should be about him. Today is the day when he learns that right here, right now, it is all about me.

That was how Smitty talked to himself to try and get into the right frame of mind.

He had a plan. The first step was to begin with a small gesture that today was not an ordinary day. He had tried to prime things by saying to his assistant that the two of them needed to have a chat about some stuff in the morning. Since that was not the kind of thing Smitty ever said, and since having a chat about some stuff was also not the kind of thing Smitty ever did, that was warning sign number one. The second gesture – the second thing he never, ever did – was to buy himself and his assistant a cappuccino each at the Italian café on the corner, on his way in to the studio. He was late on purpose so that the assistant would already be there. Seeing the cappuccino bought for him by his employer, the assistant would know that something was wrong. That was the plan.

It didn't work. Parker French came in with his earphones on and his bag and jacket both swinging over his right arm. He made a little performance of hanging them up, all without turning off his iPod, which was in his jeans pocket, or taking off his earphones, which were in his ears. So when Smitty crossed the room to offer him the cappuccino, he took it while still listening to his music and still in his oblivious, entitled, irritating bubble. If Smitty was having second thoughts, the fact that the little shit couldn't even be bothered to say 'thank you' would have dispelled them. He stood there waiting for Parker to sort himself out and put his stuff away. That took a while. Then he sacked him.

It was pretty horrible – worse than he had expected. It occurred to Smitty about five minutes in that he had been an idiot not to do this at night, when the snotface was going home, rather than when he had just come in to work. But what really made it bad was the way his now-properly-ex-assistant had been so slow on the uptake.

'We're having a bit of a problem,' Smitty had begun. 'This is one of those it's-not-you, it's-me conversations.' Every single person in the world knows that if someone uses those words a. it is you and b. you are being dumped. But Parker showed no sign of knowing this, this thing that every single person in the world knows. His face settled into a not quite sarcastic, but not sincerely deferential, pretending-to-listen-to-a-bollocking face. Authority figures had had words with him before, it was clear: parents, teachers, tutors. His manner implied that his charm and looks and brains (none of which in Smitty's view was at all evident) had always got him through in the past, and would do so again. He would half-heartedly pretend to care for the duration of the bollocking, then he would go back to doing whatever he wanted – that was what his manner said.

About halfway through, Parker's demeanour suddenly changed. He realised that this was not a could-do-better, untapped-potential, not-angry-just-disappointed, hate-to-see-you-wasting-your-talents talk of the type he was used to. Smitty's words and tone were gentle because his conclusions were final. What was going on here was something Smitty had seen before: a young person's first real farewell to the world of school and college, where even if they are rebelling and faffing about and getting in trouble, the truth is that the whole experience is about them. They think that the whole world revolves around their needs, for the good reason that the institutions and authority figures in their world do, in fact, put them first. They're not wrong to think they're the centre of the universe. They're just wrong to think it will stay that way. Then you get to the adult world, and at some point the penny drops. No one cares about you and most of the time they don't even notice you're there. It was this revelation that was now taking place in Smitty's studio.

Parker's expression began to crumple and darken. He looked much younger, like a rebuked schoolboy. It seemed as if he might even cry. He switched from looking cocky to looking numb and devastated. Smitty was aghast – he hadn't wanted the kid to go skipping out the door, but he didn't want to feel as if he'd just shot the little bastard's puppy. He sped through the last part of his prepared speech, about maybe we'll work together again one day, and handed him his envelope with a month's pay and his P45. By now, no question, there were tears in the boy's eyes. He collected his jacket and his bag and his iPod in a lot less time than he had taken to get them off, and was out the door without a further word.

Smitty thought, thank fuck that's over.

47

At 42 Pepys Road, Petunia Howe was dying. Her condition was worse in every way. Her level of consciousness varied: at times she knew where she was and what was happening; at other times she was living through a delirium. Memories swam through her like dreams. Albert was alive and beside her, or she was already dead and in some place where he had gone before to wait for her. At other times, all she could feel was pain, pain so general and at the same time so intimate – as dental pain or earache is intimate – that there was no point at which the pain stopped and she began. Petunia spoke only in fragments and could only move with assistance. Her daughter had to help her to use a bedpan.

Mary tried not to think about what was happening. She kept herself as immersed as possible in the daily detail of her mother's illness. Every now and then she would pull back and get a glimpse of things in the round, an overall look at the reality of these terrible days, and she would think: this is the worst experience of my life. My mother is dying horribly, I'm more tired than I've ever been, more tired than I was when the children were small, she is in pain, she doesn't know who or where she is, and there's no end in sight, because it's dragging on and on, and the only release is for Mum to die, so I want Mum to die, which is a terrible thing to want, and it will happen to me too, one day, I will die too, and I'm stuck here in London and I'm lonely and frightened and I have to lift my mum to the bedpan to have a shit and then have to wipe her bottom and put her back in bed and go to the toilet to empty her shit down it and then flush it and wash my hands and go back to bed and sit there staring at the ceiling waiting for sleep which I know will never come, and it won't end until my mum dies, and then I'll have to sell the house and it'll be worth a million pounds and it will come to me and everything will be different, but if I think about that I'm a bad person so I mustn't think about anything other than today, right now, the things I have to do right here and right now. And so Mary would return to the daily, immediate demands of the house, the sickroom, her mother's death; and she would feel easier.

Her contact with home was through phone calls. She had to ration these because otherwise she called Alan ten times a day, mainly just to hear his voice. Ben, who was seventeen, was too grumpy to have a proper conversation with, and Alice was away at college, and Graham was off at his London life, so with all three of them she confined herself to a daily exchange of texts. ('u ok?' 'yes k.') Alan knew well what she was going through – he was good like that – but in the end there wasn't much that could usefully be said.

'I'm worried about you, Maggie.' He was the only person who had ever called her that.

'Sometimes I feel I can't cope. Then I think: I've got no choice, I've got to cope. It's one of those. It's a cope.'

At which point Alan, being Alan, started singing, or pretending to sing, 'Did you ever know that you're my hero?' Which made Mary laugh, which in turn made her feel, when they had both rung off, much more lonely. Her mother was dying and she felt lonely. Mary told herself: they're only in Essex. It's only an hour and a bit away, it's not like they're in bloody Peru. But still she felt very much on her own.

She also felt she had been here long enough. It was time for her mother to die; it was time for her to be able to go home. She'd thought she would be here for a week or two, and now it was the best part of two months later, and here she still was. But that was a terrible thing to think; it was terrible to be that person, the person who thought that. So she tried not to think it.

It was lucky she was so busy. Because 42 Pepys Road was not a modern house, it was not easy to keep tidy; it was a place of nooks and corners, hard to vacuum, harder to dust, harder still to wash. So tidying and cleaning took a lot of effort. Mary was aware that tidying was a trap, that it was her own version of her mother's limited horizons, her stuck-within-herselfness; but the fact was that knowing that made no difference, she still liked things tidy, it made her feel better, it calmed the sense of things sliding away from her that was brought by untidiness, chaos, disorder, dirt. It brought a sense of accomplishment. Today, there was an extra reason to get things in order, because two visitors would be coming from the hospice to assess Petunia's condition. There was a possibility that she might be taken in for respite care, to give Mary a break, or alternatively that she might be so ill she would be taken in to die. Or she might be fine as she was – but Mary didn't think so.

The drawing room, bedroom, and staircase were all fine, apart from the faint smell of sickness and disinfectant, which Mary only now noticed when she stepped back into the house from having a ciggie in the garden. Today's task would be the kitchen, which was a dream of modernity and convenience from the fifties. Dad had been too mean to ever change it and it was the kind of thing about which Mum was either oblivious or defeated. Either way, the floor might have been designed to look permanently dirty; it looked clean only in the immediate aftermath of being washed. So Mary set out to wash it. She got out the mops and brushes and ran a bucket of warm water and set to. The water turned grey and so did the linoleum, as it always did at first. It looked cleaner when it was wiped down and began to dry. If the people from the hospice were late there might also be a chance to give the downstairs a quick vacuuming.

Mary went out into the garden with her packet of Marlboro Lights and her shameful new plastic cigarette lighter (shameful because buying a lighter meant she had properly gone back to smoking). The spring warmth, combined with the wildness which her mother so surprisingly liked in her garden, combined with the fact that Mary hadn't touched a thing since she arrived in February, made the colour and sense of profusion seem riotous; everything was overgrowing, bursting, fertile. Mary was looking at the garden but could not see it; she had enough on her plate. If it became another thing she had to take care of it would be just too much. The greenness did not reach into her. She lit her fag, drew deeply, coughed, drew again. It was going to be a warm day, humid too, she could feel it.

The hospice people weren't late. The doorbell rang at ten on the dot. By now the kitchen floor was shiny – gleaming – perfect. Mary went and let in the two women, one wearing a nurse's uniform under an outdoor coat. The other one she had met before, when she took her mother to the hospital for an assessment. Mary poured tea and they made small talk. The woman she had met before said something nice about the garden, which Mary didn't quite take in. Then the nurse said:

'Might we go and see your mother?'

Mary took them upstairs. The nurse and the other woman approached Petunia where she lay in bed. Because she spent large periods without moving, Petunia had developed sores on her side and back, which the nurse, whose name Mary had to her embarrassment already forgotten, spotted straight away.

'Poor thing, she's having awful trouble with those bedsores. Are you getting any help with that?' she asked.

'There's the GP. I mean the GPs. It's difficult for them, they don't know me, I'm just some woman ringing up, the district nurses are nice, they say they'll come, they mean it when they say it, I don't know, it's just sometimes that you feel you've fallen down a crack, you're sort of invisible, they can attend to what's directly in front of them but . . .'

It wasn't the question but its kindly tone, and the sound of despair in her own voice, that affected Mary, who found as she spoke that she was crying so hard she had to sit down. The two women from the hospice looked at each other. My mother's dying and they have to give their attention to me, to worry about me, Mary thought, which made her cry harder. The truth was that Petunia's GP surgery had been useless. Mary had been slightly shocked to find that her mother didn't have a doctor as such – apparently that had changed since Mary was a child. Kindly, brisk Dr Mitchell had looked after her all her childhood. He had been one of those men who looked forty all his life, from his late twenties up until he retired, the year after she married Alan and moved to Essex. He had looked after her childhood sniffles, diagnosed her mumps, written her first prescription for the pill, been the witness for her first passport application. But it wasn't like that any more. It was hard to tell who regarded themselves as being in charge of her mother's care, and combined with the fact that the district nurses were clearly overwhelmed, this made it seem that there simply wasn't any help. When she did speak to the nurses they kept pointing out that there was no pain involved in a brain tumour 'because the brain doesn't feel pain', a fact which had been explained to Mary, she felt, twenty or thirty times too often. 'It's the bedsores I'm worried about,' she said, but it was as if they weren't hearing her; it was like talking to one of those people on the phone, on helplines or complaints lines, who are following set scripts and won't listen to you unless you tick specific boxes in the dialogue. Mary's fatigue and disorientation made it all much harder to deal with. Petunia hadn't seen a nurse or doctor in nearly two weeks, and Mary was treating the bedsores by cleaning them and trying to get her mother to swallow the strongest ibuprofen-based painkillers she could find.

'I think you could do with a little bit of a break,' said the lady who she had met before, who was now squatting beside Mary on the floor and holding her hand. Mary started to cry again.

48

Freddy Kamo slid his cue back and forward, sent the white ball into the black ball, and the black ball into the pocket.

'Bollocks!' said Mickey Lipton-Miller. 'Arse! Double bollocks! Jammy sod!'

It was half past three in the afternoon. They were in Mickey's private club, in West London. Freddy was wearing a tracksuit, Mickey a three-piece suit minus the jacket. The snooker room had wooden-panelled walls; around the sides were leather arm-chairs beside low tables with lights that carried red lampshades; it smelled of cigar smoke; it was perfect. Two friends of Mickey's sat in chairs, nursing gigantic brandy snifters full of Hennessy X.O. He was parading his closeness to Freddy in front of them. In Mickey's view, life did not get much better than this.

Freddy put his cue back in the rack against the wall.

'You must be calm,' said Freddy. 'Breathe, like this.' He took a deep stage breath, then exhaled, slowly and theatrically. 'You must take your own good advice and become a patient man.'

Mickey lifted the cue again and pretended to swing it towards Freddy's head. Then he sighed and let it fall back to his side.

'Jammy sod,' he said again, more quietly – knowing perfectly well that luck was nothing to do with it. He had seen Freddy pick up a cue for the first time in this very room two months ago. As with everything else Freddy did, he had looked awkward, gangly. In his hands, however, the stick went where he wanted it to go, and so did the ball. Freddy could already beat Mickey at snooker – and Mickey was rather proud of his snooker.

'I must go home,' said Freddy. 'I have a lesson at four.'

'But what about my revenge? OK, I'll run you back. Adios, guys, be lucky,' said Mickey. He put his arm on Freddy's back and steered him towards the door; Freddy, being Freddy, wouldn't go without shaking hands with everybody. They got into the Aston Martin and set out back to Pepys Road. Mickey was fine to drive, he had had three units of alcohol at most.

Mickey's tone with Freddy was different when he wasn't showing off in front of his friends. He was less joshing and more paternal.

'You won't need these lessons much longer. It's amazing, I wouldn't have believed it. Four months. At this rate you'll be speaking better English than I am.'

'Same as snooker.'

Mickey faked a sideways swipe towards Freddy with his left elbow.

'Any word about Saturday?'

Freddy shrugged and briefly pursed his lips – which given that Mickey was driving wasn't the most helpful way of giving his opinion, but Mickey knew what he meant. Freddy had yet to start a game. The manager kept bringing him on in the second half, often when they were in control but had yet to score, or yet to open enough of a gap between them and their opponents. Freddy had been on the field nine times and had scored four goals and was becoming a favourite with the crowd – a 'cult figure' he was told, which sounded very strange to his ears but apparently meant something good. At the level of the Premiership, new players often have an impact that lasts only until opponents have them worked out: a winger who can cut in only in one direction, a striker with strong physical presence but a weak first touch, a disturbingly quick player who can be put off by being given a kicking early on. Opponents suss this out and a player's impact diminishes. Very good players learn new tricks, or learn to extract full value from the ones they have. Mickey thought that was the reason the manager was holding Freddy back for the latter stages of games – he wanted to prolong the honeymoon period for as long as possible. Freddy felt that the manager's reservations about him were to do with stamina or strength – he might not last ninety minutes, he might be shoved off the ball. Freddy didn't feel that was fair; not that it made him angry or resentful, not yet anyway. But he liked to play football, and this was the only time in his life he had ever spent any time on the bench.

Mickey liked hanging out with Freddy on his own. Most of the time they were together, Patrick was there too – and it was a little bit different, because while Mickey could still feel paternal, he had to mediate his paternalness through Patrick's presence; had to defer to the father's superior claim on his son. That was fine. Mickey had nothing against Patrick; but Patrick was a hard man to read. His slow and wary English made their exchanges slow and wary too. The more time Mickey spent with him the less surprising it seemed that Patrick was a cop; he had a cop's judgemental watchfulness, an on-duty lack of small talk. There was a strong sense that there were lines which should not be crossed, and you couldn't automatically tell where or what those lines were. It did not make Patrick relaxing company. Also, Mickey had the feeling that Patrick disapproved of him.

'It's only a matter of time,' said Mickey. 'You know it's only a matter of time. These things take time. Get the right balance. Time.'

'I like to play,' said Freddy. Meaning, I want to play for ninety minutes.

'Yes, OK.'

Freddy kept looking out the window. He had not come close

to losing his sense of the newness and wonder of London, and one of his favourite things was exactly this: looking out the window of the car as he was driven somewhere. One or two of the players teased him about not being able to drive yet – sometimes they would claim he wasn't yet old enough – and Freddy's official line was that he had enough to learn with the English language, and driving would come next. That wasn't strictly true, since Freddy was in no hurry to learn; he preferred being driven. London was so rich, and also so green, and somehow so detailed: full of stuff that had been made, and bought, and placed, and groomed, and shaped, and washed clean, and put on display as if the whole city was for sale. It seemed too as if many of the people were on display, behaving as if they were expecting to be looked at, as if they were on show: so many of them seemed to be wearing costumes, not just policemen and firemen and waiters and shop assistants, but people in their going-to-work costumes, their I'm-a-mother-pushing a-pram costumes, babies and children in outfits that were like costumes; workers digging holes in their costume-bright orange vests; joggers in jogging costume; even the drinkers in the streets and parks, even the beggars, seemed to be wearing costumes, uniforms. Freddy thought it was delightful, every bit of it.

They were stopped at a traffic light near Wandsworth Common. Freddy had what he thought was a vision: a parrot, no two parrots, no a whole small flock of parrots, in one of the thick dark green English trees, the parrots bright electric green shining against the foliage. Then the lights changed and Mickey's Aston roared very slowly into movement. Freddy blinked.

'Mickey, I think I just saw some parrots.'

'The Wandsworth parrots. There are about twenty thousand of them. Some dimwit set some breeding pairs loose, and here we are. Global warming helps. But they must be tough little buggers to get through the winters.'

Freddy, who was in a good mood anyway, felt his heart lift even further. Parrots!

49

Roger hated those creepy cards he'd been getting, the ones with 'We Want What You Have' written on them; they were starting to seriously get into his head and mess with it. He felt surveilled, watched over with ill intent. He felt envied, but not in the reassuring, warming way in which he quite liked being envied. The thought of other people wishing they had your level of material affluence was an idea you could sit in front of, like a hearth fire. But this wasn't like that. This was more like having someone keeping an eye on you and secretly wishing you ill.

Still, it wasn't all bad. There were times when he managed to put the whole thing entirely out of his mind, and tonight was one of those times. It was the night when, because Roger was the head of his department, he was supposed to take the people who worked for him on a 'team-building exercise'.

Part of Roger thought this was ridiculous – both the phrase and the idea. If you didn't have a team you couldn't build one by going paintballing, white-water rafting, or 'any other bullshit that they make you do if you're a dickhead in the East Midlands who wants to get into Al Qaeda', as Roger put it, privately, to his peers. What was wrong with going to the pub? And yet, this was how it was done. Roger did not invent modern management culture, and he knew it too well not to go along with it. He knew Pinker Lloyd well enough to know the areas in which it paid to be iconoclastic and vociferous, and the areas in which it didn't.

As current management fashions went, this one wasn't worth fighting.

The part of Roger that went with the corporate flow, that quite enjoyed implementing the policies he was told to implement, was proud of his team-building exercises. Because his people were traders, and because traders were supposed to be competitive, acquisitive, and aggressive – a trader who wasn't those things would be shit at his job – he made them do things which went with the grain. Nothing co-operative or consciousness-raising, no Buddhist meditation retreats. Roger's usual method was to pick a competitive activity and use the whole budget for his exercise as the prize, winner takes all. He had done it with go-karting and clay pigeon shooting, with great success. Today's contest was poker. It was Friday night. The £5,000 budget had gone into the kitty, they had booked a room at a poker club in Clerkenwell, and they wouldn't be leaving until someone had won it all. Now his crew were in the bar, warming up for the main event. The mood in the City was a little anxious since the collapse of Bear Stearns a few weeks before, and though that didn't have much to do with Roger's department at Pinker Lloyd, it was still a good moment to let people get together, blow off a little steam and get trashed.

Roger had played some poker, usually with clients who insisted on taking him to some casino or other. He had once watched Eric the barbarian win £100,000 on a single hand of Hold 'em with a full house, aces over jacks. So he knew a little bit; enough to know that any serious poker players would not be drinking alcohol tonight. He was taking a good look to see who was and who wasn't already at the booze. Most of his boys and all three girls were already on champagne, which was a good sign. A couple of people had clear fizzy drinks which might have been vodka-tonics but which could also be fizzy water. Surprise, surprise, his deputy Mark was one of them. One or two of the better traders were already half-cut. Jez, the best of them all, was three-quarters cut, which wasn't surprising, since he was drinking Jägerbombs. Good, all good.

At about eight they went into the separate room that Roger had booked. It was dark, with a low ceiling and a hard-to-define catering smell of old or stale or ignored food. There were two oval tables, each with a dealer sitting at the end wearing a red waistcoat; nine seats for players; nine stacks of chips. Some jostling for position took place, as people chose where they wanted to sit. That was always one of the informative things about team-building exercises, who ganged up with whom, and who was left out. It was like the moments at school when the boys were allowed to pick their own teams – it was useful information to see who was left for last.

His crew were who they were: they wouldn't respect Roger if he didn't try to win; in fact the thought of doing anything else never occurred to him. So who was at his table was an issue. Roger ended up at the same table as Mark, which wasn't what he would have chosen. Nothing specific, just that slight awkwardness which hovered around his deputy and his too-willingness, his too eagerness, his unctuous body language. Nobody ever seemed to dislike Mark, but he was too whatever-it-was for anyone to actively like him. Roger, with a large Talisker inside him, thought: just another mystery not worth solving. More of a problem was that he was sitting to the right of Slim Tony, called thus to distinguish him from Big Tony, who had in fact left Pinker Lloyd before Slim Tony arrived, but whose nickname lingered in the collective memory, not least because of his habit of always eating at his desk, and never one of anything – three Pret a Manger sandwiches, four Big Macs. Slim Tony was a pointy-faced 'Essex boy', in reality from High Wycombe, who had paid his way through university by playing poker online. Roger knew that, because that was the reason he had hired him. The place you didn't want to be seated in poker was to the right of the strongest player. So that wasn't good.

On his right was Michelle. Female traders, in Roger's experience, either went super-girly and manipulative, or were more like alpha males than the alpha males. Michelle was the second type. She was about thirty and came from Bristol. She had a uniform: pinstripe trouser suits, worn with lots of make-up and very short, almost cropped, hair. She was deliberately abrasive and swore conscientiously, painstakingly, as if she had taken a course in it. And yet there was a femininity to her too; her clothes were always slightly too tight, as if her womanliness wanted to burst out, to contradict the rest of her persona. When Roger wondered about it, which he quite often did, he would speculate about her weekend and holiday self, whether it was gentler and softer. To see her cursing and rowing at work was to wonder if she spent the weekend lying on a chaise longue, having her toenails done while eating Turkish delight and watching *Sex and the City*. He slightly fancied her, truth be told, but Roger was very careful at work, well aware of the ancient City motto, borrowed from the Italian restaurant trade: you fugga da staff, you fugga da business.

Their dealer explained the rules: blinds going up every thirty minutes, to keep it interesting. Roger knew that you had to keep your stack up at least to the level of the average, allowing for the fact that people had been knocked out. No rebuys allowed – when you were out, you were out. Eliminated players could go home or start playing at a separate table with their own money – which is what Roger felt sure they would do. Roger brought his attention to the table. He had played enough poker to have a clue, but not enough to be really good; who had the time for that?

After two hands, there was an all-in after the flop. Michelle, of course it would be her. It was hard to tell whether this was a clueless move or an astute one, making a point of establishing a reputation for crazy aggression right at the start – which would be very Michelle. The hand had been checked all the way round to her, so she could assume no one had anything. Based on what he knew of her, Roger was pretty sure she'd be setting up her table image with not much. If he had any hand at all he would call, but with 8-6 offsuit, that would just be stupid. Roger was in the small blind, Slim Tony in the big, so when Roger folded, the table's only semi-professional player was left thinking about what to do.

'You've got naff-all, I can tell,' said Slim Tony. Michelle said nothing, did nothing. 'Typical girl. They either fold every time you play back at them or they try and pretend to have a cock. Not just any cock, a really massive one. Big, big cock. Have you got a big, big cock, Michelle?'

Roger did a good job of pretending not to be shocked; one or two of the boys were smiling, one or two others frowning; Tony and Michelle knew each other pretty well so he must have a sense of whether or not he was crossing the line. At least Roger hoped so. Michelle, you had to give it to her (as it were), had no expression at all. She was just sitting there. It occurred to Roger that Tony was needling her the wrong way round – if Michelle did have nothing, and was being aggressive with nothing, this would be something she had rehearsed very deeply, so goading her about it would be pushing at a firmly closed door. If Michelle minded people accusing her of being phonily aggressive she would have caved in at work years ago. So Tony would get no information by teasing her about her imaginary cock. Roger had a sudden intuition: she has a good hand. Tony's got this wrong. Just as he thought that, Tony used his forearm to push all his chips into the middle of the table, and said, 'All in.'

Michelle flipped her cards over. Ace-king of hearts. Her reputation for acting aggressively had made him think she was pretending to be over-aggressive with a rubbish hand, where in fact she had a monster. Tony, to give him credit, laughed. 'Fuck!' He turned his cards over and stood up – he had nothing, king-jack offsuit. The dealer burnt a card and then flipped the three next cards in one move. There was nothing to help Slim Tony. The turn card came; it was an ace, and Tony was drawing dead – there was no way he could win. He put his hands above his head and said, 'I surrender!', to general laughter. But before he did that, Roger caught his expression as he looked at Michelle, and it was one of sincere and complete loathing.

Team-building – oh, the wonder of it.

Michelle was nice about it though; she didn't do more than the minimum necessary gloating. Tony signed to the waiter and ordered a bottle of champagne, which he then drank in about forty minutes. By then three other players had been knocked out; the traders, being traders, were for the most part crazily macho, and seemed to prize themselves on their avidity for going all-in. One or two more knockouts and they could start a cash game of their own. Roger made it to the final table, which had been his minimum goal; but his stack had been eaten away by the increasingly large blinds, and he had to go all-in with a marginal hand, a pair of fives. He had given in to the need for a couple more whiskies and had a pleasant sense of how the alcohol was mixing with the adrenalin inside him so that he was sharp/blurred, tired/elated, eager for victory but quite keen to go home and sleep. His bet was called by Mark, with ace-jack suited; Mark hit his jack and Roger was knocked out. He pushed back from the table; it was one in the morning but he'd gone too far to leave without finding out who won.

The winner turned out, greatly to his surprise, to be Mark, who knocked Michelle out at quarter to four in the morning. Mark was so fidgety and shifty and twitchy that he was very hard to read; he touched himself constantly, his wrist, his ear, his sleeve, his chest; it was a kind of St Vitus' dance. He appeared to be equally nervous all the time, which made him hard to decode; in fact it was hard to sit across the table from him. His nervousness made other people start to feel nervous. But it was no bar to his winning the £5,000. The crew, most of them drunk and loud, were shouting, joshing, leaning on each other. Tony was asleep on a sofa. There were plans made for shared taxis, or alternatively to head for a place in Spitalfields that stayed open all night and began serving full English breakfasts at four.

The dealer had already left. The waiter, a Filipino, lingered a while for tips. He wasn't paid – tips were his whole income. They were variable; some mornings he went home with nothing, but his record was a thousand pounds. On this occasion, Roger slipped him two hundred quid as he and two others half-carried Mark out into the street. From the waiter's point of view, it was a happy ending.

50

Piotr was still not speaking to Zbigniew. So Zbigniew was no longer speaking to Piotr. But they still lived together. It was awkward sharing a room with someone and not talking to him. In the moments when he was not angry with Piotr, he thought it was going to be something they would one day find very funny. For now, most of the time, he was simply furious. Piotr's Catholic moralising streak, which had always been the worst part of him, had for the moment ended their friendship.

This was a problem, because if it weren't for the fact that they temporarily hated each other and weren't speaking, Zbigniew could have done with his old friend's advice. He realised that he was going to have to break up with Davina and he needed to do it soon, because the longer he left it the more entangled he felt and the more difficult it would be. It was easy to make bold plans to tell her in her absence; after leaving her flat, going home and all the next day, Zbigniew would have no difficulty crafting messages which perfectly expressed the sentiment: you're dumped, it's over, it's not you it's me, we mustn't see each other for a while, but we'll always be friends, only let's not call or see each other. He would possess a rocklike certainty about what he needed to do, and how to do it. At about the halfway point between the last time they met and the next time they were due to meet, the certainty would begin to fade, and then as the time to see Davina grew closer, he would get more and more nervous, and his sense of how things were likely to go would become darker and more realistic. He would mumble, he would say everything wrong, the message was stupidly mixed, it was impossible to dump someone and stay on good terms, besides Davina was hysterical, a mad-woman, she would go crazy, she would scream, she would beg, she would shout and throw things, she would weep, she would clutch his leg, it would be impossible, a disaster.

Then, when they met, the thing he always forgot to allow for would kick in. At her flat on the saggy sofa, in the pub, in the cinema bar, at the pizza place, he would sit opposite her, get a good look at her, and feel a surge of lust. He was thinking about ways of dumping her at the same time as he was wanting to have sex with her; and in these circumstances it was always possible to postpone the break-up, while the sex would seem increasingly urgent – after all, it would be the last time! The very last! Then things would take their course, and the sex would be over, and there Davina and Zbigniew would be, on the sofa, or the floor, or the bed, and Zbigniew would be filled with a tormenting mix of complete physical well-being and utter emotional misery. He felt weak, and a coward, and it was worse because in those moments Zbigniew also felt a warmth towards Davina, a sense of emotion-al closeness and gratitude, which made him feel even more of a shit and weakling. Zbigniew disliked disliking himself.

Texting – there was always that. He could dump her by text. This was so unthinkable that Zbigniew enjoyed thinking about it.

Sometimes, the only way of doing something is to do it. Zbig-niew knew that. He was working on a house in Clapham which the wife was redecorating because the husband had run off with his secretary. She was painting the walls purple – an angry purple. People did break up with people. It was difficult but it happened all the time. People had final, definitive arguments, and said things which could not be unsaid; people woke up in the morning and realised that they could not go on with their lives, as they were currently constituted. People decided that they were no longer in love, so they left. And it was amicable, sometimes, too. The person being broken up with often turned out to be thinking about breaking up, too. It was often surprisingly easy. For the best – people agreed that breaking up would be for the best. It happened all the time!

This was therefore, for all these reasons, the day. Zbigniew had decided the day before that today was the day, and his first thought when he had got up in the morning was that today was still the day. He had woken, ignored Piotr, gone to the loo, got dressed, ignored Piotr a little more, eaten some cereal, set out for work, been let into the house by the crazy divorced lady, painted the hallway purple, had a break for lunch, checked his share portfolio, painted some more walls purple, talked a little bit with the crazy lady about how long the rest of the job would take and pretended to ignore her while she had a fifteen-minute conversation on the phone with someone about how much she hated her ex-husband and how she didn't blame 'that whore', only him; then he had gone home to change out of his work clothes, ignored Piotr again, and gone out to the bar by the edge of the Common, the one where they'd met for the first time, to meet Davina, to dump her. All this time he had been possessed by the certainty that today was the day for the break-up, and had been working on how to say it. From experience, Zbigniew knew that the information needed to be conveyed clearly and at the start of the conversation; after that, he could say nice things, if she were amenable to being spoken to, and if she wasn't, it wouldn't matter, he would just run away. The worst would be over.

'My grandmother is dying. I must go home to Poland. We can never see each other again.'

'I am gay.'

'I have Aids.'

'I am gay and I have Aids.'

'I am gay and I have Aids and my grandmother is dying in Poland, also of Aids, and I have to go back to Poland and my mobile contract is about to lapse so you can't call me.'

That might be too much.

Zbigniew arrived in the bar fifteen minutes early. The choice of venue was the product of a great deal of thought about whether to have the talk in public or in private. This boiled down to whether she was more or less likely to explode if there were other people around. He had decided that a public place was better; and had then realised that this was probably a mistake, but it was too late to change his mind now, because if he did that would be a good reason to postpone the split-up, and he wouldn't do that.

He bought himself a glass of sparkling water. If he had alcohol it would increase the chance he would end the evening by having sex with Davina.

The bar was crowded for a Tuesday night – but then it was always crowded, like everywhere else around this part of town. If Zbigniew had to sum up London in a single image, there would be a number of candidates: a group of young Poles sitting in a flat watching television in their socks; two dustbins outside a house, with a plank of wood balanced between them, to reserve a parking space for a builder's van; the Common on a sunny weekend day, with exposed white skin stretching to the horizon. But the winner would be the high street on a busy evening, full of young people bent on getting drunk – the frenzy of it, the particular pitch of the noise, the sex and anger and hysteria. Zbigniew had once had a sense of the British as a moderate, restrained nation. It was funny to think of that now. It wasn't true at all. They drank like mad people. They drank to make themselves happy, and because alcohol was an end in itself. It was a good thing and people want good things, want more and more of them. So, because alcohol was good, the British wanted more and more of it. With drink, they were like Buzz Lightyear: to infinity and beyond!

It would be good to go home soon and see some Polish drinking, in its natural habitat. He should see his father and reassure his mother that he was eating properly and had not caught tuberculosis.

Then Davina came in. She looked around, as always with an element of theatricality: standing slightly on tiptoe, turning her whole head, her expression seeking, expectant. She had a faint frown which was ready to turn into a smile when she saw him. It was like a one-woman performance called 'searching for my boyfriend in a crowded bar'. In the few seconds between him seeing her and her seeing him, Zbigniew was struck yet again, yet again, by her prettiness, her blondeness, her faint but sexy dishevelment – she was wearing a patterned black and white scarf which had slipped on one shoulder, so it was trailing much lower on one side than on the other, indeed was on the point of slipping off. Zbigniew, for the billionth time, felt the uncomplicated wish to have sex with her and the complicated reservations and aversions that went with the wish, but told himself, firmly, that tonight was not for having sex with Davina but for dumping her. He phrased it like that to himself, words he wouldn't use out loud, to brace his intentions. Dumping, not sex. This was the plan.

Davina saw him. Her face lit up like someone acting out the phrase 'her face lit up'. She began to walk towards him with her quick stride, swerving to avoid a man who without looking where he was going lurched back from the bar carrying three pints.

'Darling!' she said. Davina was in a good mood. And then, dropping into one of her stage voices, she repeated a line she often used, from some film Zbigniew had never seen, and which she always seemed to find inexhaustibly funny: she said, 'You came.'

Zbigniew cleared his throat and said, 'Glass of white wine?'

51

That went well, Zbigniew thought, on his way to work the next morning. In fact he could hardly believe how well it had gone.

The thing about breaking up with someone, Zbigniew now realised, was that it was a type of job, a specific task, and like other specific tasks was best accomplished by being broken down into its component parts, analysed, and then put back together in the correct sequence, accompanied by a plan of action. That was what he had done. So the break-up needed to be 1. unequivocal, 2. as gentle as possible while still consistent with 1, and 3. executed with the minimum possibility of public disruption and fuss.

It was not that different from plastering a wall or rewiring a socket. A practical-minded man did not flinch from such tasks. Piotr was an idiot.

He had told her that he could not see her any more; that she was a lovely girl but that he knew she deserved more; that he was not ready to settle down, it was not the reason he had come to London, that his real life was in Poland and that he would be going back there one day (he implied that it would be soon) and that he could not act on the basis of a lie, and that he felt he was lying to her by acting as if he was ready to be in a stable relationship. Zbigniew was proud of that line, the implicit claim that the reason he was breaking up with her was that he thought so highly of her. She was so important to him that he was chucking her. What woman could resist that?

Not Davina, evidently. She had been quiet, head down, not saying much, no tears, no rage, no public explosion. She had been as untheatrical and self-contained as Zbigniew had ever seen her. He had run through his reasons and she had listened to them and accepted them.

'So that's it, then,' she said. Her tone was sad and resigned and in no way crazy.

'I am sorry,' said Zbigniew, reaching the climax of his talk. 'It's not you, it's me.'

'I'm going to go now,' Davina had said. And she had got up and left. It was starting to become a pattern, Zbigniew thought, people getting up and leaving him in bars. He had stayed for a beer and gone home and had been in such a good mood that he had come close to speaking to Piotr.

Zbigniew let himself into the crazy divorced lady's house – she had given him a key the previous day, explaining that she might be out with her personal trainer when he arrived. He went to get the papers to cover the patch of floor where he was working. One thing he had learned to do, part of the way in which he distinguished himself from British workmen, was to be meticulous about cleaning up at the end of the day, so there were no traces of work-in progress, apart from the work itself. It was a common complaint about British workmen that they behaved as if they were the owners of the property. Zbigniew knew not to make this mistake. It took more time at the beginning and the end of the day, but it was worth it.

He would finish the painting today, he thought. The divorced lady had mentioned 'one or two other little jobs' that there might be for him to do, without being specific, so there either would or would not be extra work. He didn't mind; he had another job back in Mackell Road, around the corner from

Pepys Road, fixing up a kitchen, and work in general was not a problem. If he had nothing lined up immediately after that he would go home to Poland for a few days.

Painting was one of Zbigniew's favourite jobs. He liked that it was repetitive but also demanded care; the mix of detailed work on which you had to concentrate, with periods where you could charge ahead and get a lot done quickly. He liked the way new paint could completely transform a space, change even its shape, as in this case, where the purple was making the hallway close in on itself, and he also liked the smell of paint. As jobs to do on your own went, it was one of the best.

After about half an hour he heard the divorced lady come in and go into the kitchen. About five minutes later she started coming slowly up the stairs. Zbigniew stopped painting and stood up to let her get past. She was wearing a saggy grey track-suit, had a headband keeping her hair back, and was carrying a pink iPod nano.

'That man is going to kill me one day,' she said.

'Maybe you should kill him first,' said Zbigniew. She thought that was very funny.

He went back to painting and as he did so began to make a plan about how to speak to Piotr again. It was clear from his experience with Davina that he was now a master of communicating with other people. Piotr was a Catholic bigot and a fool and a hypocrite, given his own history of failed and broken relationships, and a moralising know-all, but he was also his oldest friend and this had gone on long enough. So perhaps the simplest and best thing would be just to approach him and say 'this has gone on long enough', and then they could move on. He did not need a complex plan.

To celebrate last night's successful dumping – though now that it had happened Zbigniew in his mind was more gentle and named it 'the break-up' – he took himself to the café round the corner for lunch. It was what the British called a 'greasy spoon' but in fact the food was not greasy at all, since it served salads and pastas as well as the large plates of fried food that British labourers ate. Zbigniew had acquired this taste and ordered a full English number 2, consisting of bacon, a herbed sausage which was not as good as Polish sausage but was still not bad, blood sausage, chips, fried bread, fried egg, mushrooms, tomatoes, and baked beans, a British speciality which Zbigniew had initially disliked but through repetition – they were often included as a standard ingredient – had come to like. As with many foods the British liked their secret was that they were much sweeter than they pretended to be. There was also a large mug of not very good coffee. This meal cost £6 but on a special occasion was worth it. If Zbigniew finished the job today, as he fully intended to do, he would be half a day ahead of his work schedule (the real one, which he carried in his head, rather than the estimates he gave to customers) so he could move on to other work, which meant he could move on to earning more money, which was almost as good as money in the bank, so he was already up on the day.

He got back to the house and to his brushes. He had two more hours of painting to do, then about three hours of filling, then he was done, unless the crazy divorced lady had more work for him. At about three o'clock, just as he was preparing to go round filling and touching up and finishing, the doorbell rang. A delivery, Zbigniew assumed, as the woman of the house went downstairs and stayed there for a few minutes; then Zbigniew heard her footsteps coming all the way back up to the top of the house.

'It's for you,' she said, her expression tight with something he could not read. Zbigniew wiped his hands and went downstairs.

His first thought when he saw Davina was that she had been caught in the rain. Her head drooped, her hair was lank, her expression sagged, her shoulders were sloped, her clothes seemed to hang off her. But it was not raining, had not rained all day. Davina's skin had lost all its colour and with her blonde hair she looked like a ghost. Zbigniew felt a lurch, a physical sensation in his chest and stomach, rather than any emotion he could name.

'Hello,' said Davina. 'I wanted to talk to you.'

Zbigniew had seen her acting miserable before, theatrically miserable, but there was something truly frightening about the flatness with which she now spoke.

'How did you know where I was?' he asked. As he put the question, he found himself posing it to himself with much more energy: yeah, how exactly? He was sure he had never told her where he worked. So it was creepy and strange that she knew. This was wrong; felt deeply, lurchingly wrong, with the sensation of dangerous weightlessness and loss of control that came when a car went into a skid.

'Piotr,' she said.

'We can't talk here,' he said; though the crazy lady had gone upstairs and so if he wanted to, he could. But it did not feel right. He came out and half-thought about taking her arm before deciding not to and going in front of her, making a decision as he did: a park bench on the Common. It would be a good compromise between a public and a private place. She did not speak as they walked. One or two people looked at them as they passed. They must be giving off a strange atmosphere, the distinct microclimate generated by a couple in the middle of an argument. Zbigniew had the momentary sensation that he was being taken hostage, and wanted to appeal to passers-by to help him: Save me! She's taking me against my will! Help!

They sat on the bench. About twenty yards away a middle-aged man about to go jogging was doing stretching exercises against a tree.

'Those things you said were so awful,' said Davina. 'You can't say things like that. You must think I'm stupid. "It's not you it's me." How dare you? It's not a rhetorical question, I really mean it – how dare you? To talk to me as if I was your idiot whore who you could just walk away from, skipping away into the Polish sunset with whoever it is you're going off with.'

'There is no one else,' said Zbigniew, 'I have left you with the wrong idea if you feel that—'

'Don't insult my intelligence, there's always someone else, that's what people say when—'

'I'm not lying to you, there really is no person who could—'

Zbigniew for a moment saw a glimpse of opportunity, a potential escape route. If she kept on like this, angry and getting angrier, he could get angry too, and then they would have a shouting argument, which would leave them very broken up, even more broken up than they had been at the start of the conversation. He might yet get away from this . . . But even as he was formulating the thought, her tone changed.

'I don't want you to leave me. I can't live without you. I won't live without you. Do you understand me? I won't live without you.'

She said many more things, all of them along the same lines. Zbigniew saw that there was no getting out of this. She was as upset as Zbigniew had ever seen anybody, and one sign of it was that she did not seem in any way to be acting, or presenting, her feeling. Davina was genuinely distraught. Zbigniew knew that this had gone disastrously wrong; that he could not leave her in this condition. He felt the pressure of something he had known about, but not quite acknowledged to himself: her isolation, her friendlessness. That first night, drinking with the girl beside her, had been misleading. That had been a new girl at work, and that was the first and only time they socialised together. She was cut off; she didn't like people enough, or trust them enough, to have friends. And that made everything much worse. She would have a breakdown, or kill herself, and he would be to blame. Everything Piotr had said was true. He was trapped. He felt a cloud settle on his spirit. This was something he had done to her, and because of that it was something he had done to himself, and from which he could not get away. He put out his arm and touched her hand where it lay in her lap. She did not react. Out there in the open air, on the park bench with joggers and walkers and London going about its business all around, he felt the walls close in.

52

The purpose of respite care is to give the carer a break. Mary wanted a break; more, she needed a break. But she couldn't take a break. When she went home to Alan in Essex, to her own house and what should have been her familiar routine, she found she could not settle. Her mind was on her dying mother back in London and although she wished that it were not so, Mary found that she couldn't resume her own life, even for a week or two. It wasn't that she kept thinking about her mother; on the contrary, Mary found it unbearable to think about her mother, who was by now lost to her, closed off and unspeaking. Petunia had turned her face to the wall. But Mary, who couldn't bear to think about that, also couldn't think about anything else. Having been absent because she was away, she felt just as absent now that she was at home. Alan would have to say something to her four or five times before she heard it, and when she went for a coffee with two of her girlfriends – which would normally have been a riotous catching-up session ending with her having to take a cab home after they switched to white wine – she found herself having to dig deep to summon up the energy to talk at all. She could feel her friends noticing the change in her and deciding not to comment on it; she knew they'd talk about it between themselves afterwards. She's just not herself. She's all over the place. She's taking it hard. Poor Mary. And all that.

Part of what made it difficult was Mary's feeling that she was much more like her mother than she had ever realised. Mary had always seen her mother as someone who was stuck, trapped within limits she imposed on herself, and living only a fraction of the life she could have been living. Mary had blamed her father, but when he died it turned out that it was just what Petunia was like, or had become like. She was always someone who was worried about being 'too' something, too noisy, too bold, too conspicuous, too careful, too fussy, too worried, too whatever. Back in her own life, cleaning her own house, tidying and fussing around her own sitting room, Mary was being forced to ask herself whether she was really any different. What have I ever done that's so big, so expansive? If my mother lived in too small a way, where's the larger scale in my life?

Since she couldn't get away in her head, Mary decided that she would do better not to be away in the flesh. After three days at home, she told Alan that she was going to go back to London.

'I'm sorry, love,' she said. 'I just feel I have to be there.'

'Poor baby,' said Alan. She knew him so well, she knew that the expression which flickered off his face was something like relief – which in turn made her realise how difficult she had been to live with. Being human, she resented Alan for thinking that, at the same time as realising it was probably justified. So she went back to London on the train, the fifty-minute journey which always seemed so much longer: countryside, the hills and fields and sparse villages of Essex, then the low spreading outer suburbs of London, then the taller blocks and the East End and the sense of old London, of working-class London, the places where you could, still, see the memory of the Blitz in the gaps between buildings, and then just at the end the sudden shocking wealth of the City, and then Liverpool Street. Ever since she had moved out of town this had been for Mary the longest short journey in the world. This would be the last time she took this journey while her mother was alive; the last time her mother's house, the house she herself had grown up in, was there as the other place she could go to if she had to. A row with Alan, a night in the city to see a show, a visit for Petunia's birthday – although there hadn't been many of these occasions, there had been enough of them to keep Pepys Road as a somewhere else for Mary, a place of potential refuge, a toehold in her old life. That was all going to end soon. Soon her mother would be dead and there would be no somewhere else. It was like the comforting feeling you had as a child of sitting in the back of the car, with your parents in the front; and then one day that feeling is gone for ever.

This late spring had days, or parts of days, on which it had flipped over into summer. The day Mary went back to Pepys Road was properly hot, and humid, with a faint haze about the deep green that the Common always had at this stage of the year, before it had been dried out and trampled on by the summer crowds. Mary walked to 42 Pepys Road from the Tube station, dropped off her bag, had a pee, and set off for the hospice. It wasn't far. She could walk there in five minutes or so. She walked as slowly as she could and spent the whole walk wishing that time would stretch out, slow down, that the hospice would turn out to be further than she remembered it to be, further than she knew it was.

'Hello, you're back early,' said the woman in the reception at the hospice. One of the things Mary liked about it was that you never had to explain who you were or why you were there; they always remembered. It made things much easier.

'Couldn't stay away,' said Mary. In her head those words had a light tone, but when she said them they came out as a plain and desperate statement of fact. The woman's eyes registered that.

Mary could have gone straight to her mother's room, but she decided to go out into the garden first. It was one of those unexpectedly large hidden London gardens, with a conservatory, an area of wild grasses, a lawn that was tidy but not over-trimmed, a patch of fruit trees at the far end, and a path around the edge with formally planted borders to one side. Petunia had come to the garden several times on the hospice's summer open day; she had admired it very much and often expressed admiration for whoever was the person in charge of its keeping. Now she was in the hospice, and too ill to take any pleasure from any aspect of it. Mary sat on a bench for ten minutes, in the shade of an apple tree. She could feel the heat of the day radiating off her.

Then she went up to her mother's room. The hospice was a well-established respectable charity, and it had the feel of someone's country house in an earlier time, the mid-fifties say, deposited in the middle of the city. It felt calm and ordered and some of that feeling seeped into Mary while she was there.

Petunia was in a room at the front of the building, whose window looked towards the Church and the Common. There was some traffic noise, but she didn't seem to notice that, or anything else. Mary opened the door carefully in case she startled her mother, and almost jumped back in shock to see that there was another visitor in the room. There was her son Graham, sitting in the sagging leather armchair pecking away at his iPhone.

He looked up.

'Wotcher, Mum,' said Smitty. 'She's asleep.'

'Graham!' said Mary. 'What . . . er . . . what are you doing?'

'I was over this way. Just dropped in to see Nan. She was already asleep then, so . . . well, so nothing really. I hadn't seen her since your big night out.'

'That's . . . nice,' said Mary, entirely failing to conceal her surprise. Her son was getting to his feet.

'I've got a thing,' said Smitty. 'My parking ticket's about to end. If she wakes up, tell her I popped in to say hello.' He gave Mary a kiss on her cheek and went off to his mysterious life, leaving Mary, not for the first time, thinking how little she knew him. She looked after him for a moment and then turned to her mother. Petunia was lying on her side with her face towards the window and her eyes closed.

'Mum?' said Mary. 'Mother? Petunia?'

No response. Mary sat in the chair beside the bed. On the table next to her there was a jug of water, a glass and cut flowers. Mary felt the pressure of being in the room, an agonising sense of her loss, of her mother's death occurring in slow motion. At the same time, nothing was happening. Time seemed not to pass. Her mother, in approaching so close to death, had moved to a state of pure being. Mary found it hard just to be.

She thought: I'm tired of this. My mother is going to die, and if she is going to die, I need it to be soon. It doesn't matter what she needs, any more; what matters is what I need. A voice in her head said: Mum, please leave soon.

A nurse was standing in the doorway. Mary couldn't remember if she had met her before, but it didn't seem to matter, because the woman knew who she was. They talked about Petunia for a bit.

'She could come home,' said the nurse. Mary understood that to complete that thought she would have to add the words 'to die'. And the alternative was for her mother to die in the hospice.

'How long?'

'Not long. A week.'

53

Parker rolled over in bed and muttered something in his sleep. The hotel bedroom had been full of light since before six in the morning, because the blinds were flimsy and in any case let in sunshine around their edges and at the bottom. That had woken Daisy, Parker's girlfriend, hours ago. She lay there feeling irritated by the blinds. The bow window had huge heavy ruched curtains in deep scarlet, but they were only pretend-curtains, which you couldn't actually pull all the way across. That was in keeping with what was wrong with the hotel. It was pretending to be some olde-worlde haven of calm and order and how-life-should-be, while being full of small modern bits of crapness. The daylight showed no signs of waking Parker, who occasionally shifted and gave little snuffling noises but otherwise seemed dead to the world. Sleeping had always been one of the things Parker was very good at. Daisy, a tad tetchy and underslept, allowed herself a bad thought: maybe it would be good if Parker was as talented at some other stuff as he was at sleeping. But as soon as she let that into her mind, another part of her was telling herself that that wasn't really fair. Parker had plenty of talents, he really did. He just hadn't had much luck yet.

Daisy had offered to take Parker away for the weekend to cheer him up after he had lost his job; so here they were in a fluffed-up little Cotswold hotel with a view out of the window of hills and sheep and stone walls and an annoying fan noise from the kitchen which mercifully cut out at half past eleven. It was Daisy's idea, her treat for Parker, and she was happy to do it: Daisy was a solicitor and was already earning money. She and Parker had been girlfriend and boyfriend since the last year of sixth form, five years ago now.

A weekend like this felt like a very grown-up thing to be doing, and to be paying for with your own money. It was exciting. It should be exciting, anyway. It should also feature lots of giggling and getting tipsy in the bar and going for long walks and sex. Instead, what it featured was lots of watching Parker look depressed, and listening to him talk about how unfair everything was, and how much of a bastard his former boss had been for sacking him. Daisy knew that Parker had signed all sorts of confidentiality agreements with his old boss and that there were limits to what he could say; limits which, she noticed, Parker was careful not to cross, so that although she knew that his boss had been a bastard and had sacked him for no reason, and was a total bastard, a bastarding bastard of bastardness, who had sacked him for no reason whatsoever at all, the bastard – although she knew that, she didn't know much more. Except that it was the very worst thing that had ever happened to anyone, ever.

Well – there was no denying that it was hard. Daisy knew that Parker had always wanted to be an artist. He had wanted it from the age when other boys wanted to be racing car drivers or astronauts or pop stars. He couldn't remember any time when that hadn't been his main, his only, ambition. His idea about being an artist had been a dream of autonomy, of the freedom to dream and think however he liked, and to turn that dreaming and thinking into making, into – well, not things in the crude sense, because that could easily be a debased and commodified form of art, but into thoughts, into provocations that made other people think and dream too. And that would make him acknowledged; that would make people see him, see him for himself. He wouldn't be anonymous any more. He would make things and he would be known and that would be his life. Instead, what he was was some other artist's now-sacked former assistant. So it was hard for him, Daisy could see that.

Abruptly and without warning, Parker swung his legs over the side of the bed and sat up. This was the other side of his co-matose sleeping, and it was something Daisy had never got used to, even though she must have seen it a thousand times: when Parker woke, he immediately came to full consciousness and began to be physically active. There was no transition period; it was as if he had an off/on switch. He stood up stark naked, stretched his arms over his head, and headed for the en suite loo. Already, merely seconds after getting up, his body language was slouchy and downbeat and depressed. His trim, narrow-shouldered, compact body didn't look like its usual self. Daisy felt rays of gloom emanating off him. Oh, yes, that was another thing Parker was good at: projecting his negative moods.

Daisy, as she had done many times before, listened to the noise of Parker's extraordinarily powerful and lavish weeing – that was another part of his skill set, he had a bladder like a carthorse – and then to the noise of his electric toothbrush. When he came back into the room she had sat up slightly in bed with the top sheet pulled up just over her tits, in the faint hope that this might give him ideas.

'What shall we do today?' she asked.

But Parker was still doing Nobody Knows The Trouble I've Seen. He shrugged.

'Don't mind.'

'We could go and walk to that village with that church that has the dirty statue you told me about. The pagan one where she's opening her legs and showing her vulva, the old pre-Christian artefact. What's it called, a Sheela-na-gig?' This, Daisy knew, was right up Parker's street: he had spoken about it before, more

306

than once. Her idea was the equivalent of offering a child an ice cream.

'Could do,' he said. And these two words were almost a declaration of war. Parker and Daisy had both grown up in Norfolk, where the most boring people she had ever known would use this phrase as a way of sucking the oxygen out of any conversation, discussion or plan. 'Could do': it was, as it was intended to be, an intellectual passion-killer. Parker knew how much she hated it, and knew how it summed up the safe, stale, provincial childhood world they'd both tried so hard to get away from. 'Could do': right.

'Look,' said Daisy, pulling more covers up over her. 'I'm sorry you lost your job, I really am. It's not fair. I'm sure you did everything you were asked to very well. But there are other things which aren't fair too, and one of them is acting as if I've done something wrong, when I'm trying to be nice to you and get you out of yourself and give us a nice time for a weekend. That's all I'm trying to do – something nice. You don't have to treat me as if I'm your aunt forcing you to do the washing-up.'

Parker sat on the bed. There was a merciful, welcome glimpse of him turning back into normal, non-convulsed-by-grief Parker.

'Sorry. I don't mean to be such a downer.'

Daisy immediately felt herself melt.

'Oh baby, I know, and you're not a downer, you're never a downer.'

'No, I am, I have been, I know. It's that I didn't see it coming, you know? I wasn't braced for it. Out of nowhere. One minute it's all, you know, London' – and this was an important word for both of them, a code for Escape, for the World, for the Big Life and the open road and the possibilities of things that were larger than home – 'and the next it's just, I don't know, it's like I'm suddenly on the rubbish heap. I'm nobody. I'm back to being nobody again.'

'You're not nobody to me.'

'No, I know,' said Parker, and for the first time in a few days gave a version of his real smile, a small but cheeky smile which was one of the things Daisy did genuinely love about him. 'I'm not nobody to you. I'm not nobody. He can't take that away from me.'

Daisy patted the bed. Parker, still in his birthday suit, sat beside her and took her hand.

'Unreachable and blank with misery,' she said, 'not good. Able to talk about it, much better.'

'I just don't want to get boring, and there's loads I can't say.'

'I know. But this other way of doing it is much, much more boring.'

'OK. I'll do my best,' said Parker, giving her hand a squeeze of the type which was a form of farewell, so that he could let it go and cross the room and start putting his clothes on.

'Come on, fatso, I want to get some of this breakfast that we've paid for.'

Daisy pulled down the covers and got out of bed.

'You seem much jollier all of a sudden,' she said.

'Yeah, I am,' said Parker, pulling on his jeans. She had noticed the night before that he was the only man in the hotel wearing jeans, but never mind. 'When I was in the loo I remembered an idea I had in the night.'

'An idea?'

'Well, more like a plan, really. A sort of plan. Anyway, let's go and get some breakfast and then go and see that old bint's tumpsy.'

Daisy threw a pillow at him. She missed.

54

Freddy Kamo had been told on the Wednesday that he would be playing in the first team on Saturday. It was going to be his first start. He had wanted this moment, longed for it, pined for it, dreamed about it, and been angry that it hadn't come yet. He was ready. Patrick, who had always tried to take a calm, philosophical long view about when Freddy's first full game would come, found himself just as excited as his son. He's going to play a whole game! In the Premiership! My little boy! Help!

To Freddy, Patrick said, 'I am pleased for you. You will make us all very proud.'

Patrick sometimes resented Mickey's relationship with his son. He knew perfectly well that Mickey was indispensable, and that he genuinely cared about Freddy; but he was only human, and couldn't help feeling, however faintly, displaced by him. It was a little as if Freddy had acquired another father. Today though, with the news, he knew there was only one person in the world who would be as giddy as he was, and that was Mickey, so once Freddy came back from training, and headed up to the games room to play with one of his consoles, Patrick was straight on the phone to the fixer.

'Do you think he's ready? Really ready?' asked Patrick. That morning they had had another one of the cards which he disliked so much, the ones which said people wanted what they had. Normally they made him feel full of apprehension, but today was different. Patrick knew that plain envy was an appropriate thing to feel about what was going to happen to Freddy.

'He's going to eat them alive,' said Mickey. He was even more excited than the two Kamo men: he couldn't stop smiling, his legs were jiggling at twice their usual rate, and he kept making little jerking movements with his head, as if he were competing for the ball in the air in an imaginary game of football. Tucking one in at the near post, or flicking the ball on for his striking partner. 'He's more than ready. He's super-ready. He's not just ready, he's red-hot.' As if he now owned the idea of Freddy's readiness, and was trying to sell it back to Patrick.

With some reluctance, Patrick said, 'I don't worry about his body, but about his mind.' He didn't much want to share this confidence, but he had no one else to say it to. He didn't like to let Mickey in to his feelings, and this was the first real time he had ever done so; and Mickey, who was a delicate man under his noisiness, recognised this, and took what Patrick said completely seriously.

'If I thought he knew what a big deal it is, I'd be worried too,' said Mickey. 'But he's seventeen. He can't know. For him it's just another game – a big game, the biggest he's ever had, but just another game. We're the ones it's hard on. He's going to be fine. In ten years' time, he'll look back on it and be amazed at how he just took it as the natural next thing.'

'Yes, yes,' said Patrick. But for all that, Freddy seemed excited all week – he hadn't slept properly or been able to sit still since he heard the news. He was bouncing around, terrified, thrilled, nervous. It was hard not to catch both his happiness and his nerves, and by Saturday morning at the hotel the team stayed in for home games, Patrick felt as ragged and stressed as he could remember. When Freddy went down for the post-breakfast team meeting, he lay on his double bed changing channels and playing with the minibar's bottle opener. He made the electrically operated curtains close and then open again. He turned on the radio, which was tuned to a sports phone-in programme, and then turned it off again. He looked to see if the room had a Bible, but couldn't find it. He hadn't been able to eat.

Freddy seemed calmer after the team meeting. Patrick noticed and resisted the temptation to ask him what had been said. They pottered around a bit, then headed downstairs to get in the coach. Because Freddy was the team's only legal minor, Patrick was the only relative to travel to games with the team on match days; this often felt like a privilege, but today it was a form of torture. One or two of the older players made a point of coming over and saying hello, asking him if he was all right. The £20 million midfielder put his arm on Patrick's back and said, 'It's a bit like having a baby. When my wife went into labour, you know what the midwife said? She said, "Don't look so nervous, when it comes to husbands, we haven't lost one yet."'

It was kindly meant, but Patrick had a sudden memory of Freddy's mother, and of how she wasn't here, or was here only through Freddy, since his gawky grace had been hers too; and all the things she had missed pressed on him for a moment. The midfielder squeezed his shoulder.

'He'll be all right, big fella,' he said. He squeezed harder and then let go and moved on. Patrick felt a prick of tears, not from the shoulder-squeeze; he had to pull himself together. He couldn't possibly be carried onto the coach crying his eyes out on the day of Freddy's full-game debut. At just that moment, with perfect timing, the man in charge of the kitbags, who always made a tremendous fuss about everything, even on home games when the kit was already at the stadium, came past shouting, 'Anyone seen the Adidas bags? Anyone seen the Adidas bags? I need the Adidas bags!' – which was the perfect opportunity for everyone to look at each other, roll their eyes, and let go of some of their nervousness. Patrick saw Freddy nudging one of his teammates in the ribs, and his weepy moment passed. There was only the present to think about. Let the dead bury their dead. Even the dearest of them.

The coach ride to home games was always strange. Coach travel in general is slow, not comfortable, anonymous, and takes place over distances which always feel too long. But the team coach felt more spacious than the Kamos' home back in Linguère, and certainly had better facilities, with on-board entertainment, a lavishly stocked fridge, and personalised climate control. The engine felt muted and distant. And their travel was the opposite of anonymous. As soon as the coach left the hotel, people began to wave at it, honk their horns, brandish their team scarves, or – because this was a match day, which meant there were always plenty of opposing fans around – shout abuse, flick V-signs, call out player-specific insults (poof, black bastard, arse bandit, sheep-shagger, fat yid, paedo goatfucker, shit-eating towelhead, Catholic nonce, French poof, black French queer bastard, etc. etc.) and, once, take down their trousers and moon the coach. Patrick had heard stories of wilder days in the past, when angry fans would rush the coach and begin to rock it on its wheels, a genuinely frightening thing. But this wasn't frightening. The hate was real, and disconcerting, but it was theatrical too. Patrick understood it without being able to explain it, even to himself. It was real but not-real.

Mickey almost never came on the coach – on match days he had usually gone ahead to the ground, if there wasn't some specific problem that needed his attention. Today, though, he came with them, sitting in the seat behind Patrick and Freddy, leaning into the gap between their seats, rubbing his hands with nerves and excitement.

'Feeling all right?' he asked Freddy for the tenth time, as they pulled into the road in front of a group of fans who were bowing in unison and doing a 'we are not worthy' thing. Freddy, for the tenth time, nodded. 'Hope the traffic's not too bad. All-time worst for this journey, barely a mile, guess what? An hour and a half. Last year that was. Burst water main, two roads closed, gridlock. Would have been quicker to crawl there blindfold. Bloody nearly late for kick-off, imagine that for a home game. Gets worse every year. Government needs to sort it out. Will they, though? Bollocks. No intention, too anti-car for that.'

This, by Mickey's standards, was nervous wittering. He was barely listening to himself, and anyway, as if in ironic counterpoint, the traffic today was moving with complete fluidity. The lights were green, other vehicles let them change lanes, pedestrians stood back from zebra crossings until there was a natural gap in the traffic. Patrick looked across the aisle. The team captain was chewing gum and staring straight in front of him; three seats in front the manager was talking to the coach and holding his hands apart in a cat's-cradle shape and then moving them sideways. And then they were turning off the road, the club's main iron gates were opening, and they were at the ground. Freddy's first start! This was it!

55

They separated after getting off the coach. Patrick went upstairs to the directors' box with Mickey. Freddy was pleased to see them go. On match day, in the last hour or two before games, he liked to get ready inside his own head, and that was harder with his two paternal figures in attendance. The manager was good about things like that. All the preparation was done in advance. Freddy had been briefed on what to do and there would be no last-minute surprises, no rousing speech in the changing room. Everyone was there to do a job, and everyone knew his job. Before they went out on the pitch for the pre-game warm-up and stretch there was a little time. Some liked to sit and think, some walked around, some listened to music. Freddy liked to change as soon as he could, and then just be quiet. Freddy had heard that at some clubs they had rituals, listened to loud music, had specific lucky songs they sang along to. It wasn't like that here. This was man's work.

Freddy sat and thought about what he had to do today. Essentially, he had forced his way into the team. The manager liked to play a narrow formation up front, with one striker advanced and one lying behind him, making late runs, connecting with midfield, giving the central defenders a difficult choice between tracking him one-on-one, and therefore being pulled out of position all round the pitch, or leaving him to roam free with all the space and time he needed. It was a formation with which the manager had won national championships in three countries, as well as the European title. But Freddy was a born winger, a young man made to skin defenders on the outside; to suck them in to tackles and skip past them and then cross the ball; to cut inside and shoot; to lay the ball back for a midfielder coming forward at pace; and then do it all again and again, full of running and full of trouble, and gifted with the one thing which every defender in the world most hates to play against: startling, authentic speed. The speed meant that for an opponent there was no chance to recover from a mistake, and no forgiveness for a lapse of concentration. Blink, and Freddy was gone. His ungainliness, his deceptive air of being about to trip over his own feet, helped too. He would run towards a defender, looking as if the ball were about to get away from him at any moment, and simply kick the ball past. It would, to the defender, be completely obvious that the ball was now his: no way Freddy could get there first. He would turn and chase – and then Freddy would be beside him, past him, his leg would flick out, and he'd be gone. Once he was half a metre past, it was over.

When Freddy first arrived it was clear he needed to put on a few kilos in his upper body, otherwise the bigger and older men would be able, if and when they caught him, to muscle him off the ball; and maybe the extra weight would mean he lost a yard of speed. That had happened before with many other young footballers. But it didn't with Freddy. Not that he put on the bulk; it turned out that he didn't need it. His running style was so odd, so unpredictable and awkward and elusive, it was as if it short-circuited something in defenders' brains. He was like an eel. They just couldn't get a proper hold on him. The manager was very reluctant to believe this, but he finally accepted the evidence of his eyes, gathered over many fractions of games, leading up to entire second halves. OK, he eventually conceded.

Freddy was ready. Or even if he wasn't ready, he was still going to play.

Freddy, in his match-day strip and tracksuit, sat on the bench by his locker and did up his boots. On Mickey's advice, they hadn't yet signed a contract for the boots, so he was wearing a pair of Predators with the logos blacked out. If today went well, and there were other days like today, his shoe contract would be worth many millions. Freddy couldn't care less about that, because he already had all the money and all the stuff he would ever need, but it mattered to Mickey and to his father, so he did what he was told. The only thing that mattered for Freddy was football. Everything else was to some degree fake.

A pair of shiny brown shoes appeared in front of him. Freddy looked up. It was the manager with the owner of the club behind him. The owner did not often come to the dressing room and this was, in nine months at the club, only the fourth time Freddy had met him: the others were when he'd first arrived, at an end-of-season club event, and once in the dressing room when Freddy had come on with fifteen minutes to go against Blackburn, and scored the winning goal. The owner smiled down at Freddy in his uneasy way, his eyes moving about as they always did, his air as always that of a man who wished to be somewhere else. Freddy caught a look in the manager's eyes, and stood up. The owner waved him back down again but Freddy stayed standing.

'Good luck today,' the owner said in his slow, clear English. 'Be fast!'

'Yes sir. Thank you. I will try my best.'

'More than try!' said the owner. 'Do!' He was laughing; this was a great joke. He turned to the manager. 'Do!' The manager joined in his employer's laughter. Still laughing and nodding, the owner moved on. Freddy sat back down. Across the room he caught the eye of the club's longest-serving player, a central defender who had come up through the club's youth system nearly twenty years ago, and never left. He winked at Freddy.

Then they were into the pre-match ritual: the walk on the pitch, the stretch and warm-up, the last words from the manager, who said what he always said, a saying that was partly a good-luck charm, partly a mantra, and partly a piece of good advice: 'We are better than they are. The only way they win is if they work harder than us. So if we work harder than them, we win. So that's what we'll do.' And then they were in the tunnel, the noise level changing as the crowd sounds filtered back into the enclosed space, the other team there too, jogging on the spot, their shoes scratching loudly on the cement flooring, the mascots in front holding hands with the captains, the referee looking back to check that they were all there, and then they were running out onto the pitch, the adrenalin and the exertion and the noise and the sudden emergence into daylight blending into each other so that they were all one thing. Freddy felt as excited and nervous as he could ever remember. He was carrying a ball: as he came onto the pitch he kicked it ahead of him, hard, and put on a burst to get to it, and the crowd shouted and gave the chant they had started to give for him: Fredd-y, Fredd-y. He pretended not to notice, not to be pleased, but his heart was glowing. Then he and the striker passed the ball between them. He flicked it up onto his head and nodded it off the pitch. He was ready. Freddy knew that his father was there, in the directors' box, and knew also that he wouldn't be able to see him if he looked for him – which was perfect.

He had his first touch within a minute of the kick-off. They knew he would be nervous so the holding midfielder, who was the player who made the team run – who covered and tackled, who got up and down the pitch, who broke up the opposition's moves and did the short-passing to keep his own side in constant motion, who never seemed to do anything particularly noteworthy but never made a mistake and never had a bad game – knocked a short ball to him with his defender a couple of metres away. Freddy came to it, took it and turned in one move, and saw that the defender had dropped off him; he hadn't tried to match Freddy's speed to the ball. That meant he knew about him and was being careful. They were nervous of him: a good sign. He took two strides and knocked a pass at forty-five degrees to the striker, who tried to flick it back to him but was blocked by his close marker. The ball ricocheted back and went into touch off the striker.

They were playing well today. They had most of the ball but no chances in the first ten minutes. There were days with this club, these players, when the momentum felt irresistible. The opponents were just there because they had to be there, but they were only there to provide a game so that Freddy's team could turn out the winners. This felt like one of those days. The home team were quicker, more fluid; it was as the manager had said, they were just plain better. Ten minutes into the game, the central midfielder was carrying the ball forward, and Freddy decided to try something. His defender was going to hang off him if he could; he'd been warned not to get too close, where Freddy could turn-and-burn him. OK. Freddy had no theories about anything, as far as he was aware, but he had an instinctive understanding of one strategy in particular: do the thing your opponent doesn't want. So Freddy, instead of looking for space away from the defender, drifted closer to him, forcing the man to back off even further – basically, he had to run away from him, back-pedalling, or he had to accept that he'd be caught in no man's land, and step closer, exactly where he didn't want to be. So the full-back stepped in to Freddy, just as the midfielder shaped his bandy right leg to pass him the ball. Perfect. Freddy took a half-pace towards the ball, then checked, and with the defender lunging towards him, switched his weight onto his left leg and as the pass got to him, dummied and pivoted his body in one movement, and that was it, he was gone. Just as he was thinking, I've beaten him, the big man, who had dived in late with his right leg fully extended and with all his mass behind his lunge, a slightly reckless tackle but without ill intent, connected with the place where the ball had been less than a tenth of a second before, a point that was now occupied by Freddy's fully extended left leg. The defender's leg hit Freddy's ten inches above the ankle, and spectators sitting as far as fifteen rows back heard the bone crack. Even people who didn't hear that could see Freddy screaming and rolling his upper body from side to side, and the fans right at the back who couldn't hear could see that the lower part of his leg was bent back under his knee at an angle that was not possible.

56

On a warm morning in May, two weeks after his failed attempt to break up with Davina, Zbigniew went to the front door of 42 Pepys Road. He had heard on the street's grapevine that the owner needed some redecoration work done, so had called to make an appointment and give a quote. Work, thank God for work. While he was at work he didn't have to think about Davina and about the dead end, the impasse, the stuck-with-his-leg-in-a-bear-trap disaster he had made of his own life; he managed not to think about those things for ten or fifteen minutes at a time. They were a good ten or fifteen minutes, the best of his day.

Zbigniew assessed the house professionally as he stood there: he knew these buildings well. Decent condition, ugly but sound. A kind of job he'd done many times: make it less unfashionable, less out of date, fix up the wiring, bit of plumbing. A decent-size job. Quote in the high single figures.

The woman he'd spoken to over the phone opened the door; she looked tired and older than she had sounded. Mrs Mary Leatherby. She had the air of someone not giving the matter immediately in front of her her full attention. Zbigniew knew how that felt. It was fine with him. He had no interest in her either. She showed him round the downstairs. It was as he thought. Linoleum. Strip and repaint, take out the kitchen, put in a new one from a kit. Check the wiring. Zbigniew guessed that it would be OK; it didn't look as if the place was broken, just tired. The toilet under the stairs was horrible and she wanted to take it out. He'd have to get help with that, which wouldn't be a problem. Quote in the low teens. He scribbled in his notebook.

The sitting room was also straightforward. From the choices she was making it was obvious that Mrs Leatherby wanted to sell the house. Everything was going to be neutral, cream and white. Modern fittings. No problem; Zbigniew knew how to do that. More scribbling. Quote heading toward the middle teens. They continued going around the house. There was a bathroom upstairs, in more or less the same condition as the one downstairs, except this was for renovation rather than removal. More work for subcontractors, no problem. New bath and shower and basin and cupboards and fittings, good margin on all that, subs would be happy. Quote in the middle teens.

'There's another bedroom but we can't go in there,' said Mrs Leatherby. She showed him into a little study bedroom where she had been sleeping on a sofa bed. There was an opened, unpacked suitcase on the table and a photograph of a man and three children beside it. They went upstairs. The linoleum here would be going also, maybe to be replaced by carpet. That was a specialist job he could not do but he wouldn't tell her that yet, he could put something in the figures and outsource it later, besides she had so little idea of what she wanted it would be premature to be too clear. The client not sure of what they want – every builder's nightmare, every builder's dream. Upstairs, two more bedrooms, both dark and poky, a small bathroom, ditto, a loft which had not been converted. He went up there and took a look: it was the usual – unlagged, warm and humid, with low exposed wooden beams and a centimetre-thick layer of dust. He could get in a crew to do this but it would be a step bigger than any job he had taken on for himself.

'We might do it up, or might leave it for the buyer. A rough quote is all we're asking for. But then there's the hassle, the permissions . . . the council . . .'

Mrs Leatherby seemed to fade in and out. She was not always listening to herself. Zbigniew wondered what it was . . . wondered about the room he wasn't supposed to be going into . . . wondered why it was she who was selling when it wasn't her house. Then he got it. She was selling her mother's house, and her mother was still alive. Not for long, obviously, or she wouldn't be selling the house. But what it boiled down to, after all the rationalisations and justifications, was that she was getting builders' quotations to renovate her mother's house, in order to sell it after her mother's death, while her mother was still in the house, dying. A feeling of wrongness grew in Zbigniew; a feeling that he was, by participating in this, doing something that he should not be doing.

'I'm getting a few other people in,' she said. 'A few quotes. You were recommended . . . I told you that. Rough figures to start with then something more specific. I'll have more idea later when . . . Well, anyway, thank you for coming. Look around a bit more if you like. I'll be in the kitchen.'

Moving much quicker than before, she half-ran downstairs. Her heels made a skidding, skittering noise over the floor. It was too much for her, Zbigniew saw; she wasn't a bad person doing a bad thing, she was just lost, didn't know what to do.

As he thought: she doesn't know what to do, Zbigniew came back from his holiday. It had been short but he had enjoyed it. Now he was thinking about Davina again; or not thinking about her, just remembering how it was. Her way of pretending that nothing had happened, while the fact of what had happened sat in the room between them like a rotting corpse. The complete lack of any way out, that he could see or imagine; her expression sometimes, when he caught her looking at him with a look that was like the look a dog gave its master, needy, abject, beaten, eager. The way all talk between them had taken on a falsity, so that even the smallest of small talk was like a perfumed fart.

Zbigniew, standing on the landing, heard Mrs Leatherby go all the way downstairs into the kitchen, then heard another door close. She had gone out into the garden. He was alone in the house, except for whatever or whoever was behind the bedroom door. It was like a horror film: the creature behind the door . . . And then for no reason he could name, Zbigniew went to the door and put his hand on the handle. It was wood, and warm to the touch. Very slightly loose, too; not fitted quite correctly; another piece of work. He took out his notebook, made a note, and then folded the book shut and slipped it into his jacket pocket. He turned the door handle for the moment, telling himself that he was checking the condition of the handle, seeing how smooth it was, how well the door had been fitted, but knowing that what he would do next was what he actually did do, turn the handle past the point of release, and then gently push the door so that it moved, with a faint creak. The door swung open. There was a smell of alcohol-based disinfectant.

An old woman was lying in the bed. She was lying against the wall with the wooden bedstead against the window, looking towards him. He was on the point of apologising, and then he realised that although the woman's eyes were open and she was apparently looking straight in his direction, she could not see him. It was as if he was invisible to her. Zbigniew had seen that look in the eyes of animals: a cow could look at you with a depth and intensity that was explained only by its absence of mind. That was the look in the old woman's eyes. The power of presence combined with the power of absence. He realised that she must be Mrs Leatherby's mother, and also that she must be dying.

She looked at Zbigniew – if she was really looking at him, and not just lying with her eyes open in his direction – for about a minute. Then she slowly closed her eyes. Zbigniew felt his breath catch: perhaps she had just died, right here, right now! What could he do? What should he do? What was his responsibility? But no; that wasn't what happened; dying people didn't close their eyes like that, as if they were going to sleep. She hadn't just died. She would soon, though, that was clear.

It was something Zbigniew was never to forget: the smell, the feeling of the close, over-warm air of the bedroom, the presence of the old woman who had already gone some distance over to the other side and was partly not-there, and with it the sense of another presence in the room. Zbigniew was no believer, not in anything; but he found himself believing, for the first time, in death. Death was not just an idea, or something that happened to other people. He would die one day, just as this woman was dying, and he would die, as she did, alone. Even if there were people who loved him all around, he would die alone. It is a thought, a realisation, that comes to many people for the first time in the small hours of the morning, but for Zbigniew it came right there in the middle of the afternoon, in the bedroom of 42 Pepys Road.

That night, Zbigniew broke up with Davina, definitively. He left no room for the possibility that they might get together again. He was as gentle as he could be, and also as final. It was over.

57

Mary wasn't sure what to make of the specialist cancer nurse who came to stay at the house when her mother was dying. It didn't help that she kept forgetting her name. She was called Joanna but Mary had some sort of mental block about it: she got the Jo but kept landing on Josephine, Joan, Jody, Jo, then realising the name wasn't quite right and bailing out part of the way through. Every day she told herself at least ten times that Joanna's name was Joanna, to no effect.

The nurse was a brisk woman of about forty-five. She had hair which had gone from blonde to white-grey and wore her uniform with conviction. The staff at the hospice had been warmer; this one was all business. She had a faintly Scottish accent which added to the sense of chill. No doubt she saw so many people falling apart so completely that she had to make clear boundaries. I, the nurse, am over here; you, the family of the dying person, are over there. At quiet moments, she would commune with her mobile phone, having very quiet conversations which could be seen but not overheard, and texting at length. When she texted she bent forward to look at the keys. She was old to be such a mad texter.

One thing you had to say about the nurse, though, was that she did everything. She knew what was happening, which was a big help to Mary, who was lost, especially so since her mother was now not reacting to anything and had all but passed over.

This made Mary feel, more than anything else, lonely. She was sad too, but that was beneath the surface; what she was mainly aware of feeling was her complete isolation. She had an overwhelming wish to help her mother, to ease her last moments, and at the same time knew that there was nothing she could do. Except smoking. Smoking seemed to help. She was back up to a pack a day; Alan would kill her, if the fags didn't. But she was sticking to her rule about not smoking indoors. To smoke indoors would be to have properly taken up smoking again, rather than to have adopted it temporarily as an emergency measure. Also it would stink the place out when they were showing buyers around.

Afterwards, she knew, there would be plenty to do. The funeral, the probate, the tax bill, selling the house, or more likely fixing up the house then selling it. All that would be a nightmare; but the business of it would be a relief too. For now there was nothing to do. The cancer charity were not shy about saying that their nurses only came during the final days, so she knew it was a matter of hours until her mother died, and yet the time still seemed to stretch.

In the evening Joanna, in her uniform, came into the sitting room where Mary was sitting in front of – watching would be too strong a word – *EastEnders*, and fighting the craving for a cigarette. Joanna's body language was different: she clasped her hands in front of her lap, like a child standing in front of Teacher for a telling-off.

'I think you should come up now,' she said, and her voice was different too. Mary went upstairs to the bedroom, wishing, as she did so, that the ten seconds it took would last for much longer. When she got to the opened door it was immediately apparent that her mother was breathing differently. It was a shallower noise but seemed to come from deeper in her chest; it had a note of rasp to it. Mary turned and looked for guidance from the nurse, who moved her head forwards in a gesture which Mary understood: it meant, go to your mother's bedside and take her hand. This she did.

Petunia's hand was warm. That surprised Mary. Her mother's breathing was unnatural, but it did not sound as if she were struggling for breath; this was some more profound shift than that. She tried to imagine what was happening inside her mother's mind, inside her being. Was it a succession of images, of recollections from childhood – glimpses of things which had happened to her in this very house, decades ago? Her father and mother, walking to school, the birth of her children, the thousands of meals cooked and eaten? Was it a kind of dream of those things? Or was she immersed in pure feeling, so that there was nothing but fear, or love, or loss, or some other pure state? Or was she given over to pure sensation, warmth or cold or pain or itching or thirst or some terrible combination of all of them? Or was she looking into the light, moving towards it, fading into it, becoming light herself? Or was her mother not there any more, so that this was just her body?

Petunia took a ragged, broken breath, then made a cracked, fragmented, deep exhalation. Mary felt a change in the way her mother's hand felt in hers; it did not go limp, because it already was limp, but it no longer felt the same. A charge of presence was no longer there. Her mother was no longer there. Petunia Howe was dead.

It was frightening and wrong to see her mother's eyes still open. The nurse, as if she realised – but then she probably did, she had done this many times before, you had to remember that this happened all the time – the nurse reached out and closed them. Strange, Mary had seen that gesture in films, it always looked hard to believe, as if the eyes had little levers in them so you could pull them down just like that, with the palm of your hand, but it must be true because that was just what the nurse had done. Maybe they taught you how to do it. The nurse put her hand on Mary's shoulder; the first time she had touched her. She didn't say anything, and nor did Mary, who more than anything else in the world, at this moment, wanted a cigarette. After a minute or two she got up and went downstairs, taking the packet of Marlboro Lights out of her cardigan pocket and opening the garden door. She thought: my poor old mum. Thank God. My poor old dad. One of them suddenly, one of them slowly, the first hard on the survivors, the second hard on everybody. Poor me, she thought also. Orphan Mary. Mary Mary quite contrary look at her parents go. If you had been a better daughter they would still be alive, a voice told her, as another voice immediately contradicted it: rubbish!

I suppose this is what they call denial, thought Mary. Except it didn't seem to her that she was denying anything; what she mainly felt was numb. Anaesthetised. She must call Alan. She finished the first cigarette then did something she hardly ever did and lit another from the stub.

If Mary had been looking outside herself, there still would have been just enough light to see the garden, which had kept growing and growing, untrimmed and unattended to, all through the spring. Now the hollyhocks and delphiniums were flowering, and the lupins had started to bloom. The clematis at the back wall had stretched into the neighbours' gardens on both sides, and reached over the wall into the flats which fronted onto Mackell Road. The unkempt patch of lawn was a deep, chaotic green. The garden was sheltered, and when the plants were in bloom their perfume hung in the air; today that smell, always more vivid at dusk, was also sharply green. Even through the cigarette smoke, Mary could detect the spearmint that had spread all through the left-hand flower bed like the weed it was. It was a time of day, a time of the year, that Petunia had loved. The honeysuckle which grew around the door had spread, and one or two tendrils of the plant had reached around the window into the kitchen itself. It was as if the garden Petunia had loved was trying to reach towards her, into the home where she had lived and died, as she set out on her final journey.

58

'I have to do another poo!' said Joshua. Matya wasn't sure whether to sigh or laugh, so did a little bit of both. They were in the sitting room downstairs, with the loo mercifully close. It was raining, so they were having an indoors day, though if the weather improved Matya had promised that they would go to the pond on the other side of the Common and feed the ducks. On the way, they would discuss superpowers, an interest Josh had now caught from his older brother: which were their favourite powers, which one they would have if they could only have one, which one they would have if they could make up a new one, and which superhero was best. Joshua's current favourite was Batman because he liked his cave.

'OK,' said Matya. She took his hand and steered him towards the toilet. Joshua preferred to go to the toilet on his own, but did not like the door to be closed – it made him feel lonely. He also liked to carry on a conversation while he was in there because he liked the feeling of having company.

'It's runny,' said Joshua.

'Poor darling, do you have diarrhoea?' said Matya.

'No it's not that runny. It's poo sauce,' said Joshua. He had been exposed to over-frank discussions of his own toilet habits, and since they were of great and legitimate interest to him, had acquired a complete confidence that anything which happened to him in the lavatory could and should be gone into in detail, with whoever he was talking to. Poo sauce was a term, invented by him and found very useful at 51 Pepys Road, for a stool which was neither liquid nor firm.

'Oh well, that's not so bad,' said Matya. 'Do you need me to wipe your bottom?'

'Not yet!' said Joshua. 'Hmm. I wonder.'

This was a new expression which he had picked up from who knew where, and which made Matya's heart do a little flip every time he used it. He went on:

'Matty, you know the ducks?'

'Yes?'

'What if there are no ducks? What if they've all gone away?'

'Well, then we won't be able to see them.'

'Yes, but what if they don't come back?'

'They always come back. They live there.'

But Matya was being deliberately obtuse, and Joshua started to become annoyed.

'Yes, but one day.'

'I don't think that could ever happen, Joshua. I don't think the ducks would ever go away for ever.'

That brought reassurance. It made sense that the ducks would not go away for ever if they had not gone away for ever before. 'Could you please wipe my bottom please?' said Joshua. It would have been untrue to say that this was Matya's favourite part of her job, but she did her duty. Joshua climbed down from the loo seat and then climbed up on the step by the sink to wash his hands. He liked washing his hands but needed to be supervised or he would use up the entire soap dispenser to make bubbles.

'All clean now,' he said, holding his hands up for inspection.

'All clean now,' agreed Matya. 'Shall we go up and see Mummy?'

'Hmm. I wonder. All right!' said Joshua. He held out his hand for Matya to help him get down from the step, and then kept holding her hand as they went upstairs together.

'Then we can go and feed the ducks,' she said.

'Afterwards.'

'Yes, afterwards.'

They knocked on the Younts' bedroom door and were greeted by a faint, brave call of 'Come in, darlings.' Matya pushed the door open. Arabella lay propped up on a throne of pillows, watching a black and white film; the sound went off but the picture stayed on.

'Hello, Mummy,' said Joshua. 'Are you better yet?'

'A little bit, I think, darling,' said Arabella. She had been out late the night before with her friend Saskia, and they had ended up at two in the morning at Saskia's club drinking what the man they ended up talking to insisted on calling 'post-ironic' Brandy Alexanders. The alcohol and late night had brought on a bug that Arabella had been fighting off for a few days, and now she was ill. It had to be admitted that she did not look well: she was pink-eyed and red-nosed and pale.

'How is my lovely boy?' she asked.

'I did poo sauce.'

'Oh.'

'Not very runny though. Not dia, dia, diary. Just poo sauce.'

'Good.'

'Now we're going to feed the ducks. As long as you're not going to die?'

'No, I don't think I will die, darling. It's just a little coldy thing.'

Joshua climbed onto the bed, gave his mother a brief powerful hug, then climbed back off it again and said 'Goodbye, Mummy!' as he headed for the door.

'Can I get you anything?' asked Matya.

'You are an angel. No, thank you.' And then, as she heard the front door being opened with a key, she said, 'What the hell's that?'

It was her husband. Roger made bag-and-coat noises down-stairs, then came bounding up to the bedroom, greeting his son with a 'What's up, matey?' on the way.

'I did poo sauce,' said Joshua.

'That'll show 'em,' said Roger. 'Hello, darling! How's the dreaded hangovirus?'

Arabella knew how tall her husband was; and yet about once every two weeks she was surprised by it. Here, as he filled the door frame while she lay in bed, was one of those moments.

'Bastard. I'm dying.'

'You said you weren't dying, Mummy,' Joshua said from the hallway.

'Not really, darling. I'm just saying so to Daddy. What about that lovely walk now, darling? The ducks?'

'They'll still be there,' said Joshua. 'Matya said.'

Arabella waited while her son and his nanny went out. There was a struggle with shoes and clothes and a paper bag of bread-crumbs, and then the door shut.

'What are you doing? Been sacked?'

'Don't be silly, it's that thing,' said Roger, who was taking his clothes off and heading for the shower.

'Thing? What thing? Oh fuck!' said Arabella, remembering that Roger had, in fact, told her some time in advance that there was a thing; had given it a follow-up mention a week or two ago; and had mentioned yesterday morning, when she had said that she was going out to see Saskia, that she shouldn't end up too hung-over because there was a thing. It was some bank do for one of the charities Pinker Lloyd supported to advance the social ambitions of its senior partners. Arabella couldn't quite remember which – it was Spina Bifida or Aids Orphans or the Soil Association. Something like that. It was a big thing too, she remembered, some sort of ball or banquet or ball-banquet. These occasions were, for Arabella, half fun and half ghastly, depending on the exact social mix much more than on the entertainment or venue. Now and then she would buy something for charity, a frock or cooking lesson or holiday week at somebody's house. That would be out of the question tonight, of course, for two reasons: one, since the Christmas bonus disaster, they were officially tightening their belts; two, with this hangover, it was out of the question for her to go to the thing. It would literally kill her.

Roger came out of the shower and Arabella broke her news.

'Well, that's great. A pair of tickets at two hundred quid each and I'll be sitting there on my own like a spare prick at a table of my senior colleagues. Still, it's fair enough, though, I suppose, given that I didn't give you any warning. Oh wait, hang on a minute – now that I think about it, I've been reminding you at regular intervals for three bloody months, up to and including yesterday.'

'Darling, I said I was sorry.'

'Actually no, in point of fact, you didn't. What you said was that you were too ill to come.'

'Well, I meant that I was sorry.'

'Oh, fine, so that's all right then. That's fantastic. Fabulous. And I only agreed to go in the first place because I knew you wanted to.'

Which wasn't true, and both of them knew it; Roger liked the firm's charity dos, where he could show off his good nature and his good manners and his gift for work-related socialising; but Arabella, under the circumstances, allowed it to pass.

'Take someone else, darling. Take—' and Arabella, who had been about to suggest Saskia, caught herself just in time, a. because Roger didn't like Saskia, b. because she didn't entirely trust her friend with her husband, and c. because Saskia would be just

334

as hung-over as she was, and if Roger called her and she turned him down he would be even more cross than he was already. 'Take Matya.'

Roger blinked and blushed slightly and stood a tiny bit straighter. Arabella, who was often oblivious to things, had not consciously registered that her husband fancied their nanny; but as she saw Roger's reaction to her suggestion, she realised that he did. Not to worry. Roger was not the kind of man to sleep with the nanny, he just wasn't the type; he was too lazy and too vain to make himself ridiculous in that specific way and Matya wasn't the type either, and besides, if she fancied Roger so much as a tiny bit it would have shown up on Arabella's radar. No, it was all fine. All it meant was that Roger would be more likely to go along with the suggestion, which was so much the better. Except – shit! – she herself would have to get the children ready for, and then into, bed. Shit. But that was still better than five hours or so given over to clean drinking water for Haitians or whatever it was.

To cover for the fact that he liked the idea, Roger began to make objections.

'She'll be bored out of her mind.'

'It'll be a nice change for her.'

'She'll be out of her depth.'

'With your colleagues? Don't be stupid. She won't have to talk much, just sit there looking pretty and silent and pretending to listen while they go wanking on about shooting and the congestion charge.'

And then finally something real:

'They'll laugh at me if they know I've taken the nanny.'

'So don't tell them. Just say she's a friend. We'll brief her to say the same thing.'

'They'll think she's an escort.'

'When you've got me at home to come back to, I don't think so.'

So Roger found himself in a good mood, and looking forward to his evening. He began humming show tunes as he opened the wardrobe and flicked through the racks, looking for his Armani dinner suit.

59

Matya had an ambivalent relationship with the currents of money on which much of London seemed to float. It was part of the reason she was here: she had come to this big city, this world city, to try her luck, and she would be lying if she said that the idea of making money was no part of that luck. She wasn't sure how to make money, exactly, but anyone with eyes could see that it was everywhere in London, in the cars, the clothes, the shops, the talk, the very air. People got it and spent it and thought about it and talked about it all the time. It was brash and horrible and vulgar, but also exciting and energetic and shameless and new and not like Kecskemét in Hungary which had seemed, as the place we grow up in always seems, timeless and static. On the other hand, none of the money sloshing around London belonged to her. Things were happening, but not to her. If the city was one huge shop window, she was outside on the pavement, looking in. Getting on for four years after moving to London, at the age of twenty-seven, she was still waiting for her life to begin.

She was in a receptive mood when Roger and Arabella asked if she would go to the charity do. She might not have been as amenable if she'd known that Roger was worried about her being taken for an escort; but the idea of playing an international woman of mystery was one that she immediately understood. There was no time to get home and back and changed, and in any case Matya had nothing she could confidently wear to a ball-banquet. This sort of thing brought out the best in Arabella. Once Matya had picked up Conrad from his play date, Roger was banished downstairs to look after the children for an hour. Arabella lay on her pillows and gave orders and a running commentary as Matya tried on various of her outfits. Though Matya was an inch taller, with smaller boobs and a bigger bum, they had established in the past that some clothes fitted both of them. 'It's proof that there is a God,' said Arabella. Now, as Matya tried on dresses, she lay propped up on the pillows and passed judgement.

'Not that, darling. You're going to have to wear something open-toed and with that it'll just look weird. Try the Dries van Noten. The one with the print . . . Twirl . . . No, makes you look a bit hippy. Try the black one again . . . No, you need the push-up bra. Damn . . . OK, try the green one.' And so on. Eventually they settled on a bias-cut emerald-coloured vintage dress Arabella had bought in Brighton, worn with a twenties necklace which had belonged to Roger's mother. Arabella did something to her hair with pins, then stood back and said, 'There.' Matya checked herself in the full-length mirror. She looked, even to herself, like a movie star.

Roger came galumphing up the stairs, knocked and called 'Are you decent?' and then crashed into the room. 'Time to be – wow,' he said.

Then they were off in the taxi. For Matya, black cabs, which she could not afford, were part of the glamour and romance of London. She had thought her employer would be heavy going, on his own – she had hardly spent any time with Roger, since their intense first thirty-six hours or so back at Christmas – so his ease and nice manners and ability to talk about not very much came as a happy surprise.

Heading into town, they were for the first part of the journey travelling against the flow of traffic. Matya realised that she didn't know exactly where they were going, and didn't care. Roger sprawled over the back seat of the cab like what he was, a man to whom a thirty-pound taxi fare was nothing. The day was fading so the headlights of cars and the interiors of buildings were beginning to shine more brightly; she felt both snug in the taxi, and a little bit on show. A cyclist at a traffic light, from the bag slung over his shoulder a messenger rider, gave her a long look. As well he might, thought Matya, as well he might . . .

The do was at Fishmongers' Hall. It was a spectacular old livery company building, high-ceilinged, deliberately imposing, with both the solidity of old London and the moneyed gloss of the new City. Outside was the sort of stone staircase up which visitors could sweep or trot or prance. There was a team of waiters holding flutes of champagne, and a reception line shaking hands, at which Matya momentarily panicked, but Roger, reading that, whispered, 'Just say your name,' which she did, and the man turned and announced:

'Matya Balatu'

at top volume, as if it were the name of a celebrity or aristocrat. And she went on Roger's arm into the main ballroom, lit with huge chandeliers, and full of dressed-up City types. Matya could see that this was a routine thing for many of the people present, a charity do like all the other charity dos they had been to and would go to again, nothing special. She also knew that she could decide what to make of it, so she decided that there was something magical about it, and that she would enjoy her evening; she decided to be an international woman of mystery and to like the strangers looking at her and wondering who she was, and to like the champagne, and the feeling that this life could with only one or two small accidents be happening to her. Because as Arabella said – one of her favourite pieces of life-wisdom – 'When it happens, it can happen very fast.'

'Want to take a moment?' said Roger, who while not her type, and off-limits for several reasons, did look tall and handsome in his black tie. 'I can see people I know. We can pitch in or take our time. I know it's all a bit much.'

Which it was; but Matya nodded and they moved across the room to the already-not-sober crowd of Pinker Lloyd employees and associates and wives and girlfriends, gathered under the room's central chandelier, the men arguing about football and cars while the women talked in the low fake-confidential tones of people who didn't much like each other but had to socialise together anyway. In darker moods, Roger would look around gatherings such as this and work out who the most important men in a group were, just from the body language. It was seldom difficult, and wasn't difficult here and now: Lothar, looking red-faced in his healthy outdoorsy way as usual, was demonstrating something with the side of his foot, as if showing how to balance or control a ball on it, while various men beneath him in the hierarchy of the bank gave him their full, devoted attention. But Roger didn't mind. A bank had to have a hierarchy, and a hierarchy had to have a boss, and as bosses went you could do much worse than Lothar. The only person apparently not joining in the general rivetedness was Mark. His weirdo deputy was looking down at his feet and scowling, as if he'd suddenly realised that he was wearing the wrong shoes. Roger thought nothing of it; he had long since given up any effort to work out what was going through Mark's mind. It was lucky that he didn't know, since a lot of what was on Mark's mind was very dark, and was focused on Roger.

'This is my friend Matya Balatu,' Roger said to the general company. The moment in which he might have offered an ex-planation of who she was passed without taking place, and Roger noticed it pass: ha ha, he thought. He could feel his male col-leagues rearranging their self-presentation, shifting from joshing-with-males mode to presence-of-unknown-attractive-female-with-potential-to-be-impressed mode.

'I don't think we've met,' Lothar began. Matya, looking demurely not-quite-at-him, said, 'I'm sure we haven't.'

Good girl, thought Roger. At the same time, the wives counter-attacked.

'Arabella well?' said Carmen, who was married to Peter in contracts. She was a dumpy woman in her middle forties, less like a Carmen than anyone Roger had ever met, though in fairness not as dumpy as her husband. She hated Arabella, so this was a win-win for her: she got to be bitchy about the presence of a pretty girl on Roger's arm, and for all she knew, perhaps Arabella was ill or had been dumped, so she could be unpleasant to him and celebrate Arabella's misfortune at the same time.

'In cracking form,' said Roger. Instinct told him that to offer an excuse, even a triumphant one – she had to go to an investiture, she had to stay in to show the *World of Interiors* people around – would be a tactical mistake, implying that an excuse was called for. Better to be on the offensive. He asked:

'How's Heathcote?'

This was Carmen and Peter's notoriously troublesome son; the previous week, he had been suspended from Rugby for putting what was supposed to be his headmaster's penis on sale on eBay. The listing was accompanied by a photo. The 'Buy Now' price was set at 50p. Roger knew all this because Peter had told a colleague and the colleague had immediately betrayed his confidence by telling Roger. Carmen must assume that Roger was very unlikely to have known that, so he was almost certainly making a genuinely friendly, well-meaning enquiry, which should be taken in good faith, but with the faintly perceptible possibility that he was indulging in an exquisitely calculated piece of malice. In the film *Conan*, the hero, played by Arnold Schwarzenegger, is asked what is the greatest happiness in life,

341

and he answers: 'To crush your enemies, see them driven before you, and to hear the lamentation of their women.' That was Roger's favourite line in all cinema.

'He's well,' she said, her eyes flicking sideways towards her husband. A waitress arrived with more Taittinger, and they all took refills. Then a gong was sounded, and someone called out, 'Ladies and gentlemen, dinner is served.'

After the main course, a few things were auctioned. One of the prizes was supposed to be given away by Freddy Kamo, the African footballer who lived in Pepys Road – the charity, it turned out, was to do with Africa and clean drinking water in villages. His club had had a certain amount of tabloid news-paper trouble over players' sex lives, and as part of a PR counter-offensive was encouraging its players to do token char-itable activities. Roger had been keen to see the African boy – his working hours were such that he'd never seen Freddy in the street. But Freddy had been injured a few days before and in-stead his prize was given away by a weaselly man called Michael Lipton-Miller, representing the club.

'That was a little disappointing,' said Lothar when Mickey sat down.

Looking back on the evening, Roger realised that there was no single definitive moment when he realised he had fallen in love with Matya. It was something to do with the way she looked in his colleagues' eyes and it was not just her looks – though it had to be admitted that her long, very dark, only just off-black hair, worn down tonight over her vivid jade gown, emphasising her height and her shapeliness and her slightly too large, meaning exactly perfect, bum – well, Roger would be the last person to say that her looks weren't an important factor. He would defend those looks to the end; he wouldn't hear a word against them. He would pick up the standard for those looks and charge towards the foe, axe swinging, ready to die, ready to kill, ready for . . .

Roger didn't follow through on the thought. Let the record show merely that he fancied Matya. But the thing which had made him fall for her, fall properly, was the way she seemed so calm and so quiet and so sad. Surrounded by noisy bankers showing off, and their variously pushy or beady or anxious or competitive wives, she seemed to be from somewhere else; a place where people carried their own burdens; a grander and realer and more honourable place. Roger didn't know that Matya spent a lot of that evening thinking about home, but he could tell that she was thinking about something, and it was that other thing which, for him, did it. She was like a countess; and that became his private, only-to-himself nickname for her, the countess. His countess.

Roger had taken the precaution of booking a taxi for half past midnight. He knew too well how a scrum of pissed City types could fight over late-night cabs. He had had enough to drink to spend the ride home thinking about how nice it would be to take her straight to bed and give her the seeing-to of her life, her hair spread over the pillow, face-up, then face-down, then face-up again . . . then roses and champagne in the morning, and start all over again the next day. Following this train of thought, he found himself with a huge erection as the car turned into the corner of their street, and had to fumble, pretending to look for his wallet, to give it a chance to subside, while he tried to think about things other than how good she would look in nothing but her knickers. So he thought about work for a few moments – something he found himself increasingly reluctant to do, these days, especially when he was actually at work, but a few seconds contemplating the prospect of collating the weekly figures to run past Lothar, and bingo, no erection.

Roger got out of the cab, handed the driver three twenty-pound notes, and gave him Matya's address. He didn't trust himself to kiss her goodnight.

'I hope you had a nice time,' he said through the open window as the cab rattled in the otherwise silent street.

'It was wonderful,' said Matya.

'See you tomorrow,' said Roger, who in fact probably wouldn't – he would be gone before she arrived and back after she had left. Then he went upstairs, got into bed beside his deeply sleeping wife, and lay awake for a long time.

60

Everyone at Pinker Lloyd was at work by eight in the morning. Many were already at their desks by seven. If you wanted to be on your own in the building, you had to get there well before six.

At half past five, when Mark came into the foyer, the night guards were still on duty. He had got home from the charity dinner at quarter to one, and slept for four hours; it was a sign of his strength of will that he had been able to train himself to not need much sleep. In the dark, the atrium looked warm and inviting, much more so than it did in daylight, when the vast expanses of glass made it seem overheated and airless. Today the security desk was occupied by an unspeaking, unsmiling Caribbean man in his fifties. He checked Mark's ID and signed him in. Mark went through into the lift. He looked at his reflection in the stainless steel. He said:

'I've come in to get a jump on the weekly figures, before the meeting with Lothar.' His voice, bouncing back off the metal walls, sounded sincere. It was good to practise; this was something he always did, when he had a lie he knew he was likely to have to tell: say it out loud, to check how it sounded. 'Got to get ready for the meeting,' he said. 'It's like they say in the SAS. The seven Ps: Proper Planning and Preparation Prevent Piss-Poor Performance.'

He was fine. There would in all probability be no one in before six o'clock or so. Certainly no one was in yet; he had checked the out-of-hours sign-in sheet when he came through security.

Mark liked being on his own in the trading room. There was something creepy about the empty space, the blank monitors and the dark outside, the uncanny stillness in a room designed for a crowd, for noise, for shouting and anxiety and action and looking at three screens while talking on two phones while juggling a dozen trades; but that unsettlingness was what he liked about it. Most people could not do this. They would be too freaked out. But he was not most people. That was the whole point.

He dropped his briefcase at his desk, took his jacket off, and stretched. Today's mission was passwords. About a year before, Pinker Lloyd had called in a team of outside consultants to assess its levels of risk in relation to computer fraud and hacking attacks. One of the main recommendations had been that the bank was too lax in the security level of its passwords, in particular because it allowed employees to set their own. In too many cases people used passwords that they used on other computers; in some of the most egregious cases, people even had the same password on all their accounts, for work and home. This was flagrantly unsafe: any third party getting hold of someone's private email password, or eBay account password, or any password set up on any internet shopping site, would have access straight into Pinker Lloyd's systems. Not acceptable. So the recommendation was for the company to adopt new protocols for anything that allowed access to its systems, unguessable chains of letters and numbers with rAndom caPItalisâtiᵒn. The new passwords would change weekly. The logic was impeccable. But it was also mistaken, because the new passwords had a flaw: they might be unguessable, but they were also unmemorisable. Since no one could keep the passwords in their heads, everybody wrote them down. So all you had to do to get access to someone's account was to find where they had written down their password.

Mark first went into Roger's office. His undeserved corner office, with the view of Canary Wharf and the river, the family photos on the desk; the office which was going to be his. He woke Roger's computer up from sleep, then navigated to the file called 'Passwords'. If he had to sum up his boss's stupidity in one detail, it would be the fact that he hid his passwords in a file marked 'Passwords'. The file was itself protected by a password, but Mark had seen Roger type the first few letters of it, and because Mark was not an ordinary man, with only a little thought he had been able to deduce the rest. The first letters typed were c o n so it had been easy to work out that the password was conradjoshua, his horrible children's names run together. He opened the file to see Roger's bank passwords. They were the usual strings of letters and numbers. Mark took a note of them in his little Moleskine book.

He went back on the trading floor. He began with the passwords whose hiding places he knew: on a piece of paper; in a locked drawer, whose key was in turn left in a jar of pencils; on the bottom slip of a set of Post-it notes (the bottom slip chucked away when a new password was set); on notepads left beside monitors. He collected five passwords in as many minutes. His dream was to find his way into another department, Compliance, and unlock some of their passwords. Compliance's job was to make sure that the bank was obeying all the idiotic legislation designed to make the City safe for the timid and the frightened and the conventional and the weak, all the pathetic little bits of string with which governments tried to tie down the giant. Access to Compliance's systems would be useful for the things he had under way. Root access and administrator privileges for the bank's mainframe would be even better; but that would not be easy, and it would be silly to focus on something likely to be un-achievable.

A few more passwords in this room, however, would be very easy to achieve. All he had done so far was gather the low-hanging fruit. Jez, the room's most successful trader, moved more money than anyone else, and dealt with more accounts, and so access to his systems would be very handy. Jez was someone Mark greatly disliked, not least because he could sense in him a real competitor, someone whose view of life was very similar to his own. Jez liked to win. Well, they would see who would win. Mark went to Jez's desk. He switched on the monitor and was greeted by a picture of Scarlett Johansson's arse in pink knickers, freeze-framed from the opening shot of *Lost in Translation*. Despite himself, Mark smiled for a moment. He ran a search for 'Password' but nothing came up. He hadn't expected it to. Then he stepped back and had a look around Jez's desktop. A rule of thumb was that things were always in the most obvious place. Arsenal mug, blank yellow legal pad, copy of *Mountain Bike Monthly*, Casio calculator in its plastic case. Mark peeked inside the mug, flicked through the magazine, riffled the legal pad, checked the underside of the keyboard, and opened the two desk drawers, both of which were empty apart from stationery and a Caffè Nero loyalty card. Jez might have been forceful and noisy but he kept nothing personal at work; interesting. As he was putting the office junk back, though, Mark felt something else, a piece of paper lying flat pressed against the back of the lower drawer – and had the secretive person's instinctive feeling for when he might have come across a secret. But the piece of paper was hard to get a good hold on, it seemed to have stuck to the metal at the end of the compartment, so Mark was stretch-ing and reaching and trying to get his fingers around the piece of paper to pull it out without crumpling it too much, which would give away that it had been taken out and looked at, when he heard a voice loudly say,

'What the fuck are you doing?'

Oh no. Jez. He stood at the entrance of the room, his hair wet from a shower, a bag of sports kit over his shoulder. This can't be, thought Mark – it's only two minutes past six – and then he thought, oh no, he must be here to get something done in Tokyo, and at the same time how useless that thought was since here he was up to the neck in shit and sinking fast. And then Mark realised he had a big problem: he had turned on Jez's computer monitor. There was no possible, no conceivable, innocent reason to do that. If Jez moved three or four steps into the room he would be graced with a look at Scarlett Johansson's bum-cheeks, and Mark would be out of a job. Even while the thoughts were running through his mind, Mark was moving: he jerked backwards from the drawer and pushed it shut. It would not be possible to look more like a man with a guilty conscience. He felt complicated, nauseating things happen in his stomach.

'Stationery. Legal pad . . . couldn't find mine. I know you used them, thought I'd take one, didn't think you'd mind.'

Jez just stared at him. He hadn't moved and he looked angry, suspicious, hostile.

'Been to the gym?' Mark said.

Jez started chewing gum. He must have had a piece on the go and then suddenly stopped when he came into the room and saw Mark. But other than that he didn't move or speak.

'Good habit,' said Mark. He moved slightly closer to the edge of the desk, where the monitor's off button was no more than nine inches away from his hand. But Jez had a perfect view of his upper body and there was no way he could just reach out and turn the thing off without Jez seeing.

'Here for Tokyo?' he said. Jez grunted, a sound which could have been yes or no or fuck off or none of your business. Then he took a step forward, so Mark had no choice but to contort his face and shout –

'Behind you!'

– and as Jez turned, reach out and turn off the monitor, which in his heightened sense of the moment seemed to take long seconds to fizz and flare and close to a point and go black. Then Jez turned back to him, now unmistakably furious.

'Made you look!' said Mark. Jez was walking towards him. 'Sorry,' he went on. 'Schoolboy joke. Silly.'

Jez stopped very close to him; too close. He was invading his space. But this wasn't, perhaps, the moment to complain. Jez was a big man, seen at close range; bigger than he looked. He smelled of shower gel.

'I don't see any legal pad,' said Jez in his estuary accent.

Mark didn't know what to say to that. He moved back and sideways to get away, but Jez closed the space between them again, and leaned in towards him. Then he put his face right up to Mark's, tilting his head sideways, and loudly, deliberately, sniffed. Then he did the same thing again. Jez straightened up.

'You don't smell right,' he said. And then he walked away.

61

DI Mill sat at his desk, head in his hands, pile of folders stacked up in front of him, and the rest of the room in its usual hubbub. He looked the picture of gloom. The files were those of the We Want What You Have inquiry, and they had now mounted up, because complaints from Pepys Road had kept stacking up. As a brief, it was a nightmare: a significant number of irritable, entitled upper-middle-class people were annoyed, and as a group they were horrible to deal with, not least because they could never get two sentences into any exchange without mentioning how much tax they paid. There were no clear leads, no clear suspects, no apparent motive, and no obvious directions for the inquiry. Up until recently, there was also no obvious crime. It wasn't clear in what way he/she/they, the person or persons behind the campaign, had broken the law. But then there had been some changes with We Want What You Have. First, some way into the new year, the cards and videos had stopped, and the blog was no longer being updated. It wasn't taken down but it no longer had any new content. Then, about a month later, the blog suddenly disappeared. When he saw that, Mill, who had the page bookmarked and checked it twice a day, punched the air. Fantastic! It was the best sort of problem, one which had gone away of its own right. The whole episode could be filed in that large, happy category of things you just ignored until they didn't matter any more.

Then, about a month after that, disaster. Every single person in the street got a fresh postcard of their own front door, with nothing written on the back except a short URL. Mill typed in the address and sure enough the blog was back up, hosted on a new platform and with all the content that had been there before – only now it was worse. The same photos were there, but they had been defaced by digital graffiti. Somebody had written swear words across the pictures; not all the pictures, just some of them; about one in three. The swear words focused on very simple, very direct abuse: 'Rich cunts', 'Wankers', 'Arsehole', 'Tory scum', 'Kill the rich', and so on.

So this should have been a nightmare for Mill. Having gone away, the problem had now un-gone away. That should have been a perfect formula to produce the gloom that Mill, with his head in his hands, looked as if he was feeling. But that wasn't what he really felt, not at all. What Mill mainly felt was curious. Most police work is routine. Mill didn't complain about that since the job was the job; also, when the work wasn't routine, and you didn't know exactly what had happened, you still in some sense knew what had happened. If some drug-dealing toerag bled to death on an estate stairwell, even if you didn't know who'd done it, you still knew who'd done it: some other drug-dealing toerag. Kosovan pimp shot outside a kebab shop, ditto. This case was not like that, and though the anthropology of the station prevented him from saying so, he was pleased it was up and running again. He had spent about forty-five minutes looking through the new material on the site, and his main feeling now was happy curiosity, with a twinge of something else. The new material felt, seemed, somehow different.

Taking the top folder down off the stack in front of him, Mill tried to focus on what it was about the new stuff that was hitting a fresh note. Talking it through with the DC who'd been helping him with the first wave of enquiries, Mill had reached a conclusion.

'It could be an arty thing,' said the DC. 'You know, a performance. Something people are supposed to look at. To make them think, you know, stuff.'

He gave Mill a glance which clearly said: you should know, more your sort of thing than mine.

'It doesn't seem like that, though, does it?' said Mill. 'The photos are a bit shit, as opposed to seeming a bit shit but then when you look at them they're actually quite good so it's sort of art. You know that Fatboy Slim video, "Praise You", where they're dancing in a mall, really rubbish dancing, then when you look closely, you can see they're really good dancers pretending to be crap ones? Well, not like that. This is bad photography which when you look closely looks more like bad photography.'

'But he's also done nothing violent. He doesn't seem to single out individuals. It's more about the houses.'

'Yes – the houses and the place. It's somewhere he knows well. And it feels like a he. A bloke. It's a bit obsessive. A tiny bit OCD or Asperger's. Going over the same thing over and over. He has feelings about the place, he knows it well. He walks or has walked past these houses over and over again. He's boiling over with what he wants to say to the people in the houses. So, yes, it's local. He's local.'

And that was where they had left it. But now there was a whole load of new material, much darker and more abusive. Mill rummaged through the pile of photos and found the list of Pepys Road inhabitants he and the DC had made when they'd been working on the case, a few weeks before.

His mobile rang. Janie. Mill was pleased and also annoyed – why did his girlfriend always, but always, ring when he was in the station house?

'I can't talk.'

'I know but I'm in Sainsbury's, I want to do that kale soup I was talking about, the one with chorizo and garlic, but it's got potato in it, are you still doing that low-carb thing?'

Janie was a serious cook and Mill, as he got closer to thirty, was starting to think about maintaining his weight. Being boyish was not always easy for a detective inspector, but it was better than being fat.

'That's correct.'

'Is this because you couldn't fit in those jeans? I told you, they're Japanese, and a Japanese thirty is like an English twenty-six. You're skinnier than you were when we met.'

They had been shopping at the weekend and Mill had had a denim crisis.

'I can't confirm that.'

'Well, I'm going to make it anyway, there's about a hundred grams of potato in the whole recipe. So long fatso, love you,' said Janie and hung up. Mill tried to keep his face straight while he broke the connection, and didn't quite succeed. Janie knew him too well.

Yes – and that was the thought. Whoever was behind We Want What You Have knew the street well or at least had strong feelings about it. He looked again at the list of names and opened up his web browser again to the new blog page. He scrolled through the list of names and cross-checked with the graffiti that had suddenly sprung up.

Mill's notes said:

'51 Pepys Road: Roger and Arabella Yount, two small children: banker and housewife, 40 and 37.'

Written across the top was 'Tory cunts'. It was a handy generic insult for well-off people who worked in the City, and so yes, that might have been written by someone who knew them. Or it might have been a lucky guess.

'42 Pepys Road: Petunia Howe, 82, widow, lives on her own.'

That had been defaced by 'Wanker'. And that seemed odd. It wasn't a word you'd use for a geriatric single woman, not if you were trying to be personally abusive. And if you weren't trying to be personally abusive, what was the point of personal insults?

'68 Pepys Road: Ahmed and Rohinka Kamal, 36 and 32, newsagent and his wife, two small children, shop downstairs living quarters upstairs.'

This had the word 'Bell-end'. Now that was a very good insult, one of Mill's favourites, but again, what had it to do with the Kamals? He had dropped into their shop to ask if they had been getting the cards – he had suspected that, since they lived in a shop and not a posh house, they might not. But they had, and had kept them, and were polite and helpful, so much so that he had only been able to get out of there after a cup of tea and two insanely sweet, highly transgressive gulab jamuns. No, the Kamals could not be described as a bell-end.

46 Pepys Road, Mrs Trimble and her son Alan, 58 and 30, divorced housewife and son an IT consultant. Single word 'Plonkers'. Not a perfect fit but not 100 per cent off.

Ah, here it was. 27 Pepys Road. Mickey Lipton-Miller, agent and factotum for a Premiership football club; Mill hadn't spoken to him but he knew he was the owner. The house was lived in by Patrick Kamo, 48, policeman from Senegal and his son Freddy, 17, a footballer. The graffito daubed over the picture of their front door said 'Fat tossers'.

Mill and the DC together had done that interview, for the unlofty motive that they both wanted to meet Freddy Kamo. He had been very nice, almost speechless with shy politeness, and his dad was obviously a copper of the old school. He'd fit right in at the station. It had been interesting. But no sane person could call Patrick or Freddy Kamo fat. Something had changed. Whoever was behind We Want What You Have either didn't know anything about the inhabitants of Pepys Road, or didn't care.

62

Even before her mother had died, Mary had been dreading the funeral. The last weeks of Petunia's life were the longest sustained period they had spent together since Mary's childhood. That now seemed a terrible fact, and one which bore down heavily on her, with the weight of the trips to London she could have made, the weekend visits her mother could have spent in Essex, the holidays they could have invited her to join. A time would come when Mary would see things more in balance, and would remember all the reasons, the good reasons, why none of that had happened; but at the moment what she mainly felt was guilt for all the things she hadn't done. Balancing that guilt was the time she had spent with her mother when she was dying, the long hard lonely days and longer lonelier harder nights. It had been a journey she had taken on her own. That was why she dreaded the funeral, a public acting out of her mother's death, which, deep inside, she felt belonged only to her. It was her loss alone. It wasn't really anything to do with all these other people.

And now here she was at Putney crematorium. Petunia's will had been surprisingly specific: no church burial, just a cremation at Putney, ashes to be interred with Albert's. Mary could remember her mother saying that Putney was the nicest of the London crematoria, but she hadn't thought it had any practical bearing. Now she knew it hadn't been a chance remark. Petunia must have been there a few times before. Mary would have preferred a church, where good things happened to people as well as bad, where weddings and christenings had soaked into the walls over the years to counteract the effects of all the funerals. There was none of that with a crematorium, which was only there for one reason. But her mother had been right, this was a calming place: a low red-brick building with a half-circular driveway and a well-tended garden beyond; much nicer than the place in Wimbledon where they had burned her father's body. You didn't notice the crematorium's chimney. The driveway was designed to let the cortèges come and go efficiently.

The late May afternoon was bright and clear, and it was warm, which was jarring; her father's funeral decades before had also been a nice day. You wanted rain and cold and gloom to match your mood, but Mary could feel herself growing flushed and sweaty as they stood outside under the portico, waiting to go in. Her mother would have wanted to be in the garden on a day like today.

It was interesting to notice the change in turn-out from her father's funeral. That time, half the population of Pepys Road had come. But most of those people had sold their houses and moved, and everyone had lost touch, so there were far fewer people here this time, twenty or so, over half in some way or another family. Petunia – another surprise – had wanted the service to be read from the Book of Common Prayer. They had recruited the parish vicar for Pepys Road, who was – yet another surprise – a young woman, much younger than Mary, who when they met had just got back from a run around the Common and was still wearing jogging clothes. Mary knew about woman priests in theory but had never met one. The Reverend was bright and nice and immediately agreed to read the service, tapping the time and place and Petunia's 'details', as she called them, into her smartphone, before looking up and smiling.

'I know it looks funny, but I can back it up to my computer,

357

so I'm less likely to lose it,' she said. 'I used to get through three paper diaries a year.' Mary could see that she liked being more modern than people thought she would be. This meeting with the trim, practical, kind-faced priest made Mary feel sad. It gave her a sudden sense that it was now her turn to grow old, to find the world changing, sliding away from the old ways of being and behaving, so that you were gradually a stranger to the place you lived in. The woman priest with jogging clothes and a Black-Berry gave Mary a glimpse of what life must have been like for her mother as she grew older.

But the priest read the service beautifully. Her speaking voice had been light and slightly breathy, perhaps from exercise, but her ceremony voice was richer and deeper.

I am the resurrection and the life, saith the Lord; he that believeth in me, though he were dead, yet shall he live; and who-soever liveth and believeth in me, shall never die.

I know that my redeemer liveth, and that he shall stand at the latter day upon the earth; and though this body be destroyed, yet shall I see God.

Petunia hadn't believed a word of that, to Mary's certain knowledge, but the language felt right, as a way of talking about the very last things. After all, it really was the end of the world, for Petunia anyway. Her father, a roaring, furious, militant athe-ist, would have been livid at the idea of the Prayer Book being read; so this was a final, a very final, very much overdue, form of insurrection on the part of her mother. For once she had done what she wanted instead of long-sufferingly keeping quiet. Mary smiled and sniffed and felt Alan squeeze her arm, right there be-side her, all flesh, all fifteen stone of him in his best black M&S suit, and felt reassured. On her other side, Ben was doing a hero-ic job of not being bored and fidgeting as much as he wanted to. Graham and Alice both looked pale and composed and she felt a moment's pride in them and herself for raising them. Mary said to herself: I haven't done so badly.

The vicar read some more in her strong voice, and said a prayer for Petunia Charlotte Howe. Then she pressed a button, the curtains parted, and the coffin with Mary's mother's corpse in it trundled through a hole in the wall to, presumably, the fires beyond. Mary had expected more melodrama, a glimpse of licking flames perhaps – wasn't that what happened in films? – but instead there was just that mix of the ceremonial and the municipal. She was glad of that; it could easily have been too much. Outside, people drifted about, some of them coming up to Mary and Alan and Graham and Alice and Ben and others chatting to each other in small groups. Alan, who had been brilliant, had booked a room over a pub for food afterwards, so they could all go for a drink to let off steam after the ceremony. This was a chance to tell people about that. 'Give them a drink and a sandwich,' he said. 'People expect it. Part of the ritual. Then they can piss off home.'

Home – that word had a different charge for Mary, now. Where was home? Maldon, of course. There was now nowhere else in her life, no bolt-hole, nowhere she could run away and hide, no mother to run to. This, the small-talky after-ceremony, was harder than the service itself had been. One of the men from the crematorium appeared in the entrance and disappeared back in again. Mary got the impression that lingering here was something of an inconvenience for the staff – maybe they had another cremation booked. In fact, thinking about it, they were bound to. But she could not find in herself any appetite for hurrying up, shooing people away, or any other form of being helpful. Not today.

'I'm so sorry' is what people mainly said, or sometimes 'I am sorry for your loss.' The Indian newsagent, whom Mary was surprised and pleased to see, said that; so did the man down the street whose name she didn't know, who'd been smiley and friendly; so did the two of Albert's old colleagues who came. Greatly to Mary's surprise, so did the Polish builder who had come to the house to give a quote for the renovations. It must be a Polish thing, she thought. Maybe they liked funerals. She would have to make up her mind what to do about the house, and she was strongly minded to take the Pole's quote, renovate, and then sell; the house would be worth, what, two million pounds? It was ridiculous, but it was also what it was. She caught herself having these thoughts and felt ashamed. 'With her mother not cold in the ground' – but in fact her mother had already gone into the flames.

Graham, looking very smart in a suit, was standing close by as if he was keeping an eye on her. He was also looking, as he often did, faintly knowing and ironic. Her son looked as if he thought he could tell what you were thinking. Well, what I'm thinking is, My mum's dead, and I'm rich.

63

It took two weeks for Mary to decide what to do with 42 Pepys Road. After the funeral, she had a small collapse. Nothing dramatic, just that she felt tired all the time, and found it impossible to make even the smallest decisions. Every choice that she could delegate to Alan, she did. When she couldn't, she boiled with indecision. One symptom was that she found she was unable to decide what to cook. She'd been looking forward to getting back to cooking, and because she had lived on ready meals while her mother was dying, being back in her own kitchen making proper food felt like a good thing to do. There was also the fact that Ben, though he obviously would not say so, because that would involve communicating in something other than a grunt, liked her cooking and greatly preferred it to his father's non-cooking.

Perhaps for that very reason, she couldn't muster the mental or physical energy to cook properly. The need to decide what to make for supper would leave her standing in front of the fridge for ten minutes, not feeling depressed or frustrated or angry or resentful about having to make the meal, not consciously feeling anything, just unable to choose between pasta and a ready-meal shepherd's pie. She could see her cookbooks on the shelf, Nigella and Nigel and Delia and Jamie, the unopened books standing there as if reproachfully, their arms folded. At Sainsbury's in Maldon she would stand in front of the frozen food cabinet, unable to discriminate between the Bird's Eye fish fingers, twenty-four for £4.98, and the Sainsbury's own-brand fish fingers, same-size box, in all probability made by the same people, for £4.49. But what if they weren't the same? But what if they were? She took to calling Alan at work and asking him what he wanted, so she didn't have to make up her mind. It was the same with watching TV, with deciding which radio station to have on in the background, with choosing what clothes to wear. Everything just seemed like a huge effort. Actual grief would hit her too, completely unpredictably, catching her as she heard 'Love Me Do' on an oldies station or as she was standing in a queue at the bank and saw a woman of about her mother's age, hunched over to fish something out of her handbag in exactly the way her mother had used to do – grief would come and lift her off her feet, like a wave; but the fatigue and demoralisation she felt were different from that. They were there all the time, like the weather.

There was no miracle, she didn't wake up one morning and suddenly feel different, but there were at first moments, then hours when the feeling lifted. The waves of grief still came but she didn't feel knackered and indecisive all the time. She made Jamie's guinea fowl with fresh oranges. It was revolting – the recipe didn't work, it was one of Jamie's duff ones – in fact it was an obviously stupid idea, chicken with oranges? – but she felt so much better because she had found the energy to make it. Gradually she found she could make small decisions, then bigger ones, then one evening she found she wasn't just ready to think about what to do about the house: she found that she had already decided. The Polish builder didn't have experience running a job quite this size; but he had done all the constituent parts, he had experienced contacts who could help, he had offered the lowest quote (by 30 per cent) and he had come to her mother's funeral.

She talked it through with Alan. 'I'm all in favour of buying British,' he said, 'but a third cheaper is a third cheaper.' Then she called the Pole on his mobile. He sounded pleased and surprised and a week later began work on number 42, starting by stripping down and redecorating the rooms at the top of the house. And now he was living there too, after a conversation he'd had with Mary when she came down to check on progress with the house – something they'd agreed she would do once every two to four weeks. Not minding about being checked up on was one of Zbigniew's ways of being different from English builders.

'I don't like it being unoccupied,' Mary said. She disliked the thought of this house, which had in her memory never not had her mother in it, now lying empty. The sense of someone missing was too big; it left too big a gap in the world.

'This is easy to fix,' said Zbigniew. 'I can stay here. Mattress on floor. I don't mind. That way, there's always someone in the building. It's more secure, it makes your insurance cheaper because the house is occupied' – Mary hadn't thought of that – 'and I can get to work earlier and finish later so the job is done more quickly.'

'Well, let me talk it over with my husband, but it seems like a good thought,' said Mary. And then two days later she had called back and said yes.

That was how Zbigniew came to be doing up, and living in, 42 Pepys Road. The work question was a little awkward for Zbigniew, because some of the work would require Piotr's crew, and he and Piotr's relationship had never fully recovered from Davina. But they agreed a schedule. It was good of Piotr, who did not take a cut, and in effect by doing this was taking the decisive step in letting Zbigniew set up on his own – in other words, they were getting ready to let their work go in separate directions. So be it. The crew weren't free until later, so Zbigniew would do the single-man jobs, the fiddly redecorating, at the start, and the manpower and specialist jobs in a couple of months' time.

There was a loft, but Mary and Alan had decided that they

wouldn't fix that up themselves – which was good news for Zbigniew, because although he had worked on lofts, he wasn't sure he could have run a conversion project as the man in charge. Ditto the basement: Zbigniew had done basements, had had the experience of sweating London clay out of his pores for weeks, and he wasn't at all sorry not to be doing it here. In both cases (though he didn't know this) the reason was that the inheritance tax bill after Petunia's death had been so big that they had no capital left to do up the house before selling it. Alan could have borrowed the money, but they both felt there was something surreal about inheriting a lot of cash and immediately going into debt as a result. Alan and Mary were old-fashioned like that. So Zbigniew was working on his own, beginning with the small rooms at the top of the house, stripping the wallpaper, taking out a strange plasterboard partition that had been there since Mary's childhood and that made one of the small bedrooms into two even smaller rooms, ripping out the wiring, and painting the walls with test colours for Mary to vet on her next visit to Pepys Road. Zbigniew's target was to finish the work in about four months.

For the first few days Zbigniew worked on number 42 Pepys Road, he was tense, without being able to understand why; and then it occurred to him that it was about Davina. As if he expected at any moment to hear the doorbell ring and find her on the step outside, or waiting for him when he got back to the flat. When his mobile rang, he thought it was her; when he saw a woman of the right age with the same hair colour, he had a flash of what he thought was recognition, until he had a better look and realised the truth. His nerves were juddering with the expected confrontation. This time, he had decided, he would not be calm and moderate. If she had another go at unbreaking up, he would be angry and rude. That should work.

He liked working alone, but it was strange to be on his own in an empty house all day. It was not precise or difficult work, and it was physically tiring in exactly the manner he found welcome. Most of the house had not been touched in a long time; the wallpaper must be close to fifty years old – Mary had said she never remembered a time before it. At points it crumbled in his hands as he tried to strip it off, sending a fine powder over him, the dry-damp smell of paper and old glue. The wiring was as old as any he had ever seen; again, half a century at least. It too brought smells with it, the ancient dust and brick residue from inside the walls. Coils of wiring, stacks of wallpaper were now mounded on the floor. Mary had ordered a skip and arranged three months' permission to park it outside the house; the skip was easy to arrange, the permission, from the council, was inevitably slower, so for now Zbigniew was on his own in the house with the rubble and rubbish. He took to playing the radio loudly for the sensation of company; because the wiring on his floor was out, he set the radio up on the downstairs landing, just outside the bedroom where Petunia had died. Every time he went past that doorway, he had a flash of memory of the old woman, dying in bed; an image of the irreversibility of life and time passing; of the truth that not everything we do can be undone.

He was back on speaking terms with Piotr, but their relationship hadn't really been repaired. His old friend seemed the same, looked the same, and sounded the same; but something in the balance of forces between them had shifted, and talking to him was not the same. When he allowed himself to think about it – which he did briefly and with reluctance, and out of the side of his mind, as if out of the side of his eye – he could feel his irritation with Piotr, still there from the night in the Polish club. It wasn't that Piotr had been wrong about him and Davina; it was the fact that his friend had obviously been nursing these angry feelings about him for some time. So although they had now made up, the idea lingered with him that the angry, judgemental Piotr was the real Piotr. He didn't want to be friends with that person. Perhaps, when they were back in Poland and all this was in the past – when the London interludes of their lives were over and they were back in their real Polish lives – they would be true friends again. Perhaps. But in the meantime he could not talk to Piotr about the Davina he saw hiding behind every wheelie bin, waiting to jump out at him.

And then something did jump out at him, a big surprise, but it wasn't the one for which Zbigniew had been bracing himself. There was a room at the top of the house which had obviously been unused for many years and which had once been a study or office. It contained a large old desk, well dusted but neglected, and both older and of better quality than it seemed at first glance; in fact, that desk might really be worth something. A set of shelves held old crime paperbacks whose spines had cracked and faded. There was a filing cabinet full of utility and council bills and not much else. The wallpaper in this room was in worse condition than anywhere else in the house, another sign that it hadn't been used much. Zbigniew decided to move the cabinet out of the room and strip the wallpaper and check the wiring.

As he ran his fingers around the loose edges where the paper was coming unstuck he noticed that there was something not quite right about the feel of the wall. He tested by tapping, and found that his first impression had been correct: at one point the wall made a hollow noise. Zbigniew tapped around the wall and found that there seemed to be a hollow space, about the size of a wardrobe, on one of the walls. Starting at that point, he tore the wallpaper off and saw that there was a thin film of a different type of plaster covering a hole in the brickwork. Zbigniew paused and thought for a moment. He could leave things as they were and cover the wall with paper and no one would ever know, or . . . Even as he asked himself the question, he knew what he was going to do. Zbigniew went downstairs to pick up his goggles and his sledgehammer. Then he planted his feet and swung at the wall.

The plastering had not been well done: it was dry, and the whole covering exploded into fragments. A battered suitcase, which had been flat against the hole in the brick, fell out onto the floor. Zbigniew puffed his cheeks and put down the hammer and sat down beside the suitcase. It had a small built-in lock and no evident key, but by now he was not in the mood to be slowed down or deterred. Zbigniew took a pick out of his tool kit and went at the lock, which was not a complex piece of work, a standard tumbler model. It took about five minutes to undo the lock and open the suitcase.

It was full of banknotes. More banknotes than Zbigniew had ever seen gathered together in one place. The notes were all worth £10 and Zbigniew, his mind zooming all over the place, found that he could make no sensible estimate of how much cash was in the case. Only one thing to do, count it. Best time to count it? Now. He sat down on the floor beside the suitcase and got started. The counting was much harder work than it might have been, because although the money had once been clamped together by rubber bands, there were two problems. For one thing, many of the bands had eroded, and the money was now loose. For another, the clumps of cash were irregular in size. They hadn't been counted and then put in bundles; the bundles were random. So there was no alternative except to flick through the dusty, chalky notes one by one and make a tally after every ten – after every hundred pounds. In this way Zbigniew found out that the suitcase contained £500,000. He also found out, because he emptied the case to count out the money, whom it had belonged to. On the bottom of the case there was a label saying it was the property of an Albert Howe, Esquire. The label and the handwriting looked old but not antique. Mrs Leatherby's mother had been, in Zbigniew's estimate, in her eighties when she died; so his best guess was that the suitcase and the money belonged to her husband, Mrs Leatherby's father.

Zbigniew threw the bundles of money into the case and leaned backwards so his head was against the door. He could see it: a cottage with a garden, his father tending roses, his mother in the kitchen, music coming through the window, the fading warmth of an early summer evening in Poland. The life his father had worked for all his life, bought for him by his son who had made good in London.

Part Three

August 2008

64

'They love it,' Shahid said to his brothers. 'All this fussing, running around, calling meetings—'

'There are no meetings, plural, this is the first,' said Ahmed.

'First of many – meetings, speeches, demands, fussing. It's that great British middle-class battle cry: "Something must be done!" Same as the war. "Something must be done!" That can lead anywhere, with people like this. They'll stop at nothing once they get their indignation going. "Something must be done!"'

'They didn't do much about the war, did they?' said Usman. 'It probably didn't have the same effect on property prices.'

'That's our neighbours and our customers you're talking about. Talking rubbish about,' said Ahmed.

All three Kamal brothers were hunched over against fat August raindrops as they swerved and slalomed around the commuters heading home from the Underground station. It was shaping up to be yet another lousy summer. Faced with the rain, Ahmed, typically, was trying to hurry, and Shahid, typically, was trying to take his time. Usman, also typically, was hanging a couple of steps behind and was trying to send signals that the other two men were nothing to do with him. Ahmed and Shahid had both separately been very surprised that Usman wanted to come to the meeting, but he seemed to be taking a special interest in what had been happening in the street. Normally he acted as if everything to do with the shop was so far beneath him it was barely visible.

The brothers were walking towards a special meeting convened by the local police Community Action team. The gathering was being held in the hall attached to the big church on the Common – a first for all three of them, since they had never been inside a Christian church. The meeting had been convened because the phenomenon of the postcards and videos and blog, all with the slogan 'We Want What You Have', had, for the residents of Pepys Road, gone past the tipping point. It had begun with abusive virtual graffiti on the blog, and had escalated through abusive postcards delivered to the houses. Then there were three incidents of graffiti in the street; 'cunt' and 'wanker' were spray-painted on the side walls of the houses at numbers 42 and 51 – a place on the buildings it was hard to spot from the street, so it wasn't clear how long the abuse had been there before it had been detected. Then envelopes containing truly disgusting things had begun to arrive at the houses: some residents were sent dog excrement in jiffy bags – reeking, horrible jiffy bags. And then, one night in late June, somebody or somebodies had run a set of keys down the cars parked on the even-numbered side of the street – every car, all along the street. The damage ran into many thousands of pounds. A number of residents had complained to the police, who had bounced the query back to the local Neighbourhood Watch to ask how many people had been affected. It was this criminal damage to the cars which really got the police's attention. When it turned out that everyone in the street had had some encounter or other with We Want What You Have, it had been decided, just as Shahid said, that Something Must Be Done. Hence this meeting.

'It makes them feel important,' said Shahid. 'This is a rare example of Usman being right about something. It gives them an excuse to talk about property prices. It's the only time they're ever allowed to talk openly about money, so it's no wonder it gets them excited.'

They came into the church grounds and could see the side door to the hall, held open by a man and a woman talking. As they walked past they could hear her saying,

'. . . that's if it doesn't drive prices down, which is a real worry, because . . .'

Shahid flicked his brother on the bum with a rolled-up copy of *Time Out*. Ahmed swatted him away.

The hall was a square room, decorated with posters of a Christian, charitable and ecological nature. One wall was dominated by a large stencilled painting of a white dove with a leafy green branch in its beak. There were a hundred chairs laid out in ten ranks of ten, and the room was about half-full with locals, some of them known to Ahmed by name and more or less all of them by sight. The woman who ran the Neighbourhood Watch stood at the end of the room on a low dais next to two uniformed policemen, one in his late twenties and the other at least two decades older. Ahmed smiled and nodded at everyone he recognised. People didn't seem keen to chat. They were eager for the meeting to begin.

Roger Yount came into the hall, direct from work, his pin-stripe suit emphasising his height and posture: the kind of figure to gladden any mother-in-law's heart. Looking at him, women would often find themselves wondering: tall, rich, well-dressed, clean: why isn't he sexy? Roger looked around the room, ignoring everyone until he saw Arabella, who was sitting with her head down composing a text message to her friend Saskia:

'Can't m8k libertys 2mrw, hws dy aftr? A x'

The two women had decided that they had a knicker crisis, and the plan was to go shopping for new ones. Arabella felt she had been so incredibly good since the non-appearing Christmas bonus horror, she deserved a little discretionary spending. She and Saskia would hit the shops, then a restaurant, then would accidentally drink a couple of glasses of champagne and then perhaps have a wander down Bond Street. Matya was looking after the boys. What was the point of living in London if you couldn't splash a bit of cash about every now and then?

Mary Leatherby had come down from Essex for the day. Her builder had started work on renovating number 42, so she wanted to have a look at how things were going. From peering around, she realised that she now didn't know a single soul in the entire room. Zbigniew had told her about the graffiti on the side of the house, and the jiffy bag of excrement which had lain unopened on the floor until it started to stink. He had thrown it away, but not without calling Mary to tell her what had happened. Mary had wanted to come to the meeting to find out if anyone knew what was going on. Her plan was to catch the train home afterwards, even if the old house was habitable; she felt she had moved on. She didn't plan to spend a single night there before the house sold.

Mickey Lipton-Miller was there, and not happy. The cards, the blog, the graffiti and nasty pranks, it was a wind-up, and somebody needed to get it sorted. Thanks be to God, his Aston hadn't been parked in the street when the cars were keyed . . . If there was time, he was planning to hit his club afterwards for a G and T and a game of snooker. But work came first. And he had a theory about the bastard who was responsible for all this.

The woman who ran the Neighbourhood Watch stood and put her hand to her mouth while making a harrumphing cough – evidently this was her way of calling the room to order. A pool of silence began in the seats closest to her and then spread until the church hall was quiet, broken only by a mobile phone playing the opening bars of 'The Girl from Ipanema' and then abruptly cutting out.

'Thank you so much for coming,' she said. 'I know you've all been concerned about this . . . this business. So I have invited our local bobbies to talk to us, and they've gone right to the top, so that Chief Superintendent Pollard, the divisional commander, has come to fill us in on the situation as it stands, and he's brought Detective Inspector Mill. And then afterwards they will take questions. So without further ado, Chief Superintendent Pollard.'

The policeman was one of those men it was difficult to imagine without his uniform: he seemed to wear it on the inside as well as on the outside. He had a rough London accent.

'I'm Chief Superintendent Pollard,' he said. He found it hard not to sound menacing, so even stating his own name came across, faintly but perceptibly, as a threat. 'I'm here about these occurrences. You've been getting postcards. You've been getting DVDs. There's stuff on the internet. Abuse. Vandalism. Harassment. Graffiti. Criminal damage. I don't need to tell you, that's why you're here. What's it all add up to? Who's behind it all? My colleague Detective Inspector Mill will fill you in on the details. He is going to be in charge of the inquiry, with me' – and here the older man made no attempt to restrain his air of threat – 'keeping an eye on him.'

The other policeman stood up at the lectern. He was a well-groomed young man and as soon as he began speaking it was clear that there was some strange class reversal taking place, since while the Chief Superintendent spoke in broad cockney, the Detective Inspector was impeccably middle-class, verging on outright posh. It was as if the enlisted man had mistakenly been put in charge of the officer. The impression of the Detective Inspector's poshness was enhanced by a gesture he made just before he began talking, when he brushed the hair off his forehead, as if he were worried it was going to get into his eyes. His hair wasn't in fact long enough to get in his eyes, but this gesture was like an atavistic survival of a period during which he had a long, floppy fringe. So for a moment everyone in the room glimpsed him with that languid public-school hair.

'Thank you, sir. Thank you all too, ladies and gentlemen. The question to which we'd all like an answer is, who is doing this? I imagine some of you at least will be thinking that the simplest way of finding out would be to trace the owners of the blog. We're going to get it taken down, but that's not the same thing as finding out who the person or persons responsible are.'

The inspector talked a little bit more about how clever they were going to have to be to find out who was behind the 'campaign' – that was his word. When he finished he asked if anyone had any questions. There was a little muttering and murmuring, and then Usman put his hand up. Beside him Ahmed went rigid with irritation and embarrassment. The senior policeman pointed at him. His extended finger looked as if it was making an accusation.

'The gentleman there.'

Usman, putting on his sweetest and most reasonable voice, the one he most liked to use when being deliberately irritating during family arguments, said, 'How do you know the damage to the cars was done by the same person who did the other stuff?'

From the stillness with which the Chief Superintendent and the Detective Inspector greeted Usman's query, and their failure to look at each other to decide who was to answer it, it was clear that they considered it an awkward question. The younger man spoke first.

'Yes. I see where you're coming from. The short answer is, there are indications which we can't go into here. These . . . incidents fit into a pattern and therefore our advice, our judgement, is that they are the work of the same person or persons.'

The way the policeman finished, his body language and the intonation, did not solicit a follow-up question, but Usman gave him one anyway.

'And harassment, that's just something in the head, isn't it? So it's just in the mind of the person who feels harassed? Like, if I feel harassed by you, that counts as harassment?'

Ahmed sat next to his brother in motionless horror. I wonder, Ahmed thought, if I killed Usman right now, just struck him down dead, I wonder a. if Allah would forgive me and b. if a British jury of my peers would acquit me.

'I think we're straying from the point,' the policeman said, smoothly. 'The majority of the people in this room are here because they feel upset and distressed by these things that have happened. It isn't fair to call it just "something in their heads". People feel stalked by the individual or individuals who are doing this. So we're going to find them and punish them, but we need your help.' Then the Detective Inspector talked for a while about how everyone in the street could be the police's eyes and ears, and how they wouldn't be able to solve the crimes without everybody's assistance. Ahmed could tell that his brother wasn't quite finished, so he pinched his leg, hard, to get him to shut up. Usman looked at him, annoyed, and Ahmed looked even more annoyed back.

'Will there be any compensation?' somebody asked 'Are we eligible for anything?'

'I fear that isn't a police matter,' said the Detective Inspector. He really was terribly smooth. There were a few more questions, and then the woman in charge of the Neighbourhood Watch stood up again, thanked the two policemen, and declared the meeting over. There was some more chat, people coming up to him and the Chief Superintendent and, basically, wittering on, and then he and his boss were able to get out into the fresh air on the Common for a quiet word between themselves.

'OK,' said the Chief Superintendent, lighting a cigarette as the two policemen headed back together across the open space. The rain and wind were such that he had to stoop over to do it. As a side effect of the weather, everyone around them was scuttling, heads down. A few yards away, two crows stood face to face, their luminous blackness seeming to absorb and reflect light. Mill thought, in his shiny uniform, the boss looks a little bit like a crow. 'That's the PR bullshit finished with. Keep checking the postmarks and the DVDs. See if forensics have anything on the cars. Then if something more happens, at least our arse isn't hanging out the back of our trousers.'

Detective Inspector Mill unwillingly found himself thinking about his superior officer's exposed behind. The image made him want to smile.

'Maybe that stroppy Asian guy was right,' said Mill. 'I'm not sure that we need harassment now that we've got criminal damage to the cars.'

'Yeah, well, let's just keep everything we have in the tool kit. We don't know what we might need.'

With that, and without a farewell, the Chief Superintendent was off in the other direction, trailing smoke – to a meeting? To the pub? To the bookies? To a mistress? He was the kind of man whom you couldn't ask. Mill was amused by his senior officer, and tried not to let it show, out of an intuition that he would dislike being thought of as a source of private entertainment.

'Can I trouble you for a moment?' said a voice. A sharp-featured middle-aged man in a light summer suit had come up to the DI while he was watching the Chief Superintendent disappear across the Common. Mill assessed the new arrival rapidly: good citizen, well-off, something he wants to confide or complain about. That was one thing he was still unsure about, in his job: the view of your fellow Britons it gave you, from the sheer amount of whining and complaining and lying you heard.

'Of course,' said Mill.

'Michael Lipton-Miller,' said Mickey Lipton-Miller, his manner confidential and blokey, that of a man well used to having a sidebar with the police. 'Just came out of that meeting you were in. Wanted to have a quiet word.' He had come close enough to the DI to cover him with his umbrella.

'Pleased to meet you,' said Detective Inspector Mill.

'I've got a theory about who might be responsible for this,' said Mickey. Oh, sweet Mary and Jesus and all the saints, he's a nutter after all, thought Mill. He said:

'How interesting.'

As he said this Mickey took out his wallet and took a card out and handed it to the DI, not easy to do while holding the umbrella above both their heads. DI Mill looked at the card, saw that Mickey was a solicitor, and became aware of the need to be professionally careful.

'I know what you're thinking. I'm not a nutter,' said Mickey. 'It's only this. Whoever's doing this knows the street well, yes? Has gone up and down Pepys Road lots of times. Practically lives there, if he or she doesn't actually live there. A fixture. Someone who fits in, part of the landscape. Not someone you notice. Comes and goes without a trace. Fits in. Yes? Like one of those detective stories, nobody notices the postman. Who does that sound like? Not the postman, obviously. You'd notice him going around with a bloody great camera filming everything. So, another angle. Who's got a camera? Comes and goes, nobody notices, has a camera. No idea, fine. Add something else. Comes and goes, one. Camera, two. Three, whoever it is has a grudge. Yes? Right? It's obvious. This isn't the work of Norman Normal, this is someone with a major beef. With society, with the world, with Pepys Road. Angry. Who's angry, in general? The kind of person everyone is angry at. It's one of those turnaround things. Right. So who's a. got a reason to be in the street, b. got a reason to have a camera, c. angry at everyone because everyone is angry at them? Once you see it like that, it's obvious: a traffic warden. Or wardens, plural.'

'So this is all the work of an angry traffic warden.'

'Or plural, wardens. Everybody hates them, so they hate everybody. It's clear enough once you spell it out.'

Mill had a talent for extricating himself from situations: he thanked Mickey and said goodbye at the same time, nodding energetically as he turned and headed back to the station. Mickey thought: that's a polite young detective. Mill thought: that man is a little bit mad, but it's not the worst idea I've ever heard, and it certainly falls under the category, the important category, of being seen to do something. Mill would open yet another file, talk to a few people at the Post Office, talk to somebody on the web side of things, talk to a traffic warden or two, and then go back to hoping the whole business went away.

65

Experience had taught Rohinka Kamal that the most useful way
to think about visits from her mother-in-law, Mrs Fatima Kamal,
was as a form of natural disaster. Just as you could take sensible
precautions against earthquakes, tsunamis, forest fires, floods,
but there was no real point in worrying about them, similarly,
there was no point dreading Mrs Kamal's biennial trip to London. You could take steps to mitigate the effect, maybe, but the
steps might not work, and either way it wasn't worth losing sleep
over.

This would be Mrs Kamal's fourth visit to London since Ro
hinka had married Ahmed, and although the focus had changed
from nagging, criticising and undermining them about when
they were going to have children, to nagging, criticising and undermining them about how the children were being brought up,
the emotional dynamic was as it had always been. Mrs Kamal
would start complaining and being difficult on the way back
from the airport – no, she would probably start at the airport;
she would have detailed, passionate grievances about the food
on the plane, or the in-flight entertainment, or turbulence, or
the state of Heathrow, or the rudeness of the immigration offi-
cials, or the traffic. Whatever had happened would be the fault
of whomever she was talking to – though there was often a tremendous subtlety to the way she did that, for instance in her
talent for complaining to Rohinka about Ahmed in a manner

which made it clear, while also leaving it entirely unspoken, that the reason he was such a useless man was that she was such a useless wife.

In advance of the visit, Rohinka and Ahmed had fallen into doing what they usually did, which was to make jokes about how awful it would be, as a means of reducing the strain on their relationship when Mrs Kamal ran through her repertoire. Her talent, her genius, was for what Rohinka called 'needles'. These were comments designed to be hurtful, but not so much so that the recipient felt he or she could draw attention to them.

The night before she was due to arrive, Rohinka lay on her side in bed facing Ahmed and, keeping her voice down so that it wouldn't wake light-sleeping Mohammed, said:

'It's like she thinks I'm just intelligent enough to notice, but not intelligent enough to say anything back to her. So she says, "Ahmed is looking very well-fed," or whatever – I don't have her gift, I can't get the perfect example, but it'll be something like that – no, I can remember one, from last time, she said, "Fatima looked so lovely yesterday in her dress." Of course she is stressing the "yesterday" because Fatima was wearing the same dress that day because the washing machine was broken. So what I am supposed to say is, "Thank you very much for telling me that my husband is fat and my daughter is filthy. What a fortunate daughter-in-law I am!" I'm supposed to be just enough aware to hear the sting in what she says, but not enough to say anything back to her. I'm supposed to collaborate in putting myself down! I lend her the use of my own brain to get the point of the barbs she sticks into me!'

Ahmed chuckled, which made the bed gently bounce.

'What do you mean, well-fed?' he said.

'Fat boy,' said Rohinka, poking him in the side with her finger. 'It's the way she can say ten critical or negative things in a row.

You can actually count them, add up the sequence. She's a machine for denigrating people.'

'She lives in Lahore.'

'Not for the next few weeks she doesn't,' said Rohinka, and rolled away to her other side.

The next morning there was a family summit meeting, prior to setting out for the airport. All three brothers, Rohinka, and the two children sat around the kitchen table while a friend of Shahid minded the counter. It had been decided that the whole family would turn out to meet Mrs Kamal. The last time, Ahmed had gone to meet the 8 a.m. flight on his own – which wasn't so unreasonable, he felt. He had to get up at six to make sure he was there on time, and he went on his own because Rohinka was fully engaged with Mohammed who had just been born, and because somebody was needed to look after the shop. Mrs Kamal was still referring to her 'unenthusiastic' reception when she set off back to Pakistan a month later. ('I'll make my own way to the airport, I know how inconvenient it is for all of you to make the effort.')

'Shock and awe,' said Shahid. He was in a good mood. He had been able to use the fact of his mother's arrival to get rid of the Belgian, Iqbal, whose ability to ignore hints and suggestions and open but polite requests to leave had gone from being annoying to borderline psychotic. Seven months!

'Moving on soon' was what he would say when Shahid brought it up. 'Moving on soon.'

But the imminent arrival of Mrs Kamal had done for him. Shahid was proud of his own brilliance here. He knew that Iqbal knew that the whole family was genuinely frightened of her – or maybe frightened was the wrong word; maybe they just dreaded her. Whichever it was, Iqbal knew that she was a living terror. Shahid didn't have to lie about that. All he had to do was lie about where she was going to stay when she came to London, and stick to the lie – and that's what he had done. As soon as Mrs Kamal had said she was coming to visit, Shahid had gone steaming straight to his flat, told Iqbal he had to get out, and given him the date. Iqbal, amazingly, had had the front to complain, and to act as if it wasn't fair. The Belgian had more front than Selfridges. With bad grace, he had eventually conceded that he had to go. And then, yesterday, most amazing thing of all – he had gone! Moved out! Vamoosed! Iqbal was out of there! Elvis had left the building! The fat lady had sung! Mandela had been freed! Shahid had his life back! He could lie on the sofa watching his own TV programmes, surfing his own websites, breathing the smell of only his own socks and farts! They think it's all over! It is now!

'We will overwhelm her with our love and devotion,' Shahid went on, to the family breakfast table. 'She won't know what hit her.'

'That doesn't sound like Mamaji,' said Usman. This was hypocritical, since he was Mrs Kamal's favourite, for no reasons the other brothers could understand except that he was the youngest – the bad-tempered, sulky, charmless, semi-fanatical youngest. Ahmed gave Usman a warning look: he and Rohinka were careful not to speak ill of Mrs Kamal in front of her grandchildren. They had a strict no-badmouthing policy about her. This was partly to set a good example for their old age, and partly because they were worried that Fatima would pass on anything they said.

'We'll love-bomb her,' said Shahid. 'It'll be like the Moonies.'

'Lub bob!' said Mohammed.

'Everybody ready?' asked Ahmed. Rohinka slid around the table, attending to their breakfast plates so briskly and efficiently she might have been a Hindu goddess with more than one set of arms, clearing and stacking and sweeping and racking, and then bumping the dishwasher door closed with her hip before setting it going. Fatima was in a bright green dress – a clean bright green dress – and Mohammed was wearing his smartest red jumpsuit. He was carrying his favourite Power Ranger. The two younger brothers were dressed as if for manual labour, and Ahmed was wearing pressed jeans and a smart leather jacket. They piled out into the people carrier, Ahmed's huge VW Sharan, and set off for Heathrow, the traffic predictably rubbish, the weather predictably rubbish.

As they crawled out through West London, Ahmed was reminded of how his world had contracted around work and the children. The shop, the kids – it felt at times as if that was all there was. Even though the big car was full of his family, he felt a sense of the bigger city around him as they struggled past the amazing size and variety of London, the feeling that everything had a history, and the press of the present too: roadworks, billboards, a small accident where a white van had driven into the back of a milk float and the police had closed a lane, as well as that good old favourite, 'sheer weight of traffic'. Sheer weight – how much of life was sheer weight of something? Then the traffic eased and they were out towards the elevated section of the M4, and the road rose and curved through office buildings that had once looked like someone's idea of the future. It was a different London from the one Ahmed knew, and he liked it.

Shahid decided to make his own entertainment.

'Let's have a bet on what she'll say first.'

Usman scowled: gambling was unIslamic.

'Not a real bet, dip—' and then remembering Mohammed and Fatima and cutting himself off before he could say 'dipshit', 'stick. Dipstick.' Ahmed tried to give a silencing glare via the rear-view mirror, but Rohinka spoiled everything by chuckling, which Shahid took as permission to go ahead. 'I'll go first. It'll be: "Ahmed, you are fatter than ever."'

'Daddy fatty!' said Mohammed.

'The flight was a horror,' said Rohinka, adding some Lahore

and deepening her voice half an octave and, it had to be said, sounding unsettlingly like Mrs Kamal.

'Hello!' said Fatima. 'She'll say hello!' There was applause, and it was agreed that she was a clever girl – and Shahid realised that he had better be careful what he said.

Heathrow, never a pleasure to visit, was even worse than usual, thanks to a combination of roadworks and increased security measures. Ahmed could feel his stress levels rising as they sat immobile, moved ten yards, then sat immobile again. The smells emanating from the very back of the car indicated that Mohammed, who seemed entirely content and was looking out the window from his child seat with a certain lordly calm, had nonetheless had an incident in his nappy.

'We're going to be late,' said Usman. The unhelpfulness of this observation was compounded by its truth. They had allowed two hours to get to Heathrow, but it wasn't going to be enough. Ahmed could feel their mother's visit sliding towards disaster before it had even begun – because if there was ever a person capable of spending four weeks punishing you for turning up late to meet her at the airport, that person was Mrs Ramesh Kamal of 29 Bandung Street, Lahore. Ahmed tried to imagine what he could do; but they weren't even through the Heathrow access tunnel yet – they weren't even at the roundabout where there used to be a model of Concorde, before the plane crashed and was withdrawn from service – and they'd never make it on time on foot, even if they were allowed through the tunnel on foot, which Ahmed didn't think people were. He could turn around and go home and pretend to have got the day wrong . . . no, what was he thinking?, the others would never keep that secret. And then suddenly, in its mysterious way, the traffic eased. The brake lights of the cars in front went out, the cars first bumbled, then crawled, then they were actually, genuinely moving. Allah be praised. The policemen with machine guns standing at a checkpoint were, for whatever policemen's reason, now letting all the traffic through. Ahmed turned into the short-stay car park, a little too briskly so the near front wheel rode up on the divider, took the ticket, parked, shooed his family out of the car, helped Rohinka unfold the pushchair and load it with Mohammed, who took all this fussing with great equanimity, and hurried everybody over the concrete walkway, following the signs, rushing, Ahmed pushing the pushchair, Rohinka pulling Fatima by the hand, the two younger brothers behind, Shahid laughing and Usman scowling, through the crowd and the professional drivers holding signs and the tearfully hugging silent couples, the tour party gathering around a raised umbrella, the family group all crouched by a wheelchair, rushing into position by the arrivals area, the oddly free-form Heathrow arrivals area where it's hard to tell arrivals from arrived, exit from concourse, and just as they arrived, just as they started to compose themselves, there was Mrs Kamal, frowning and pushing a trolley with three suitcases on it, her expression not changing as she caught sight of them and steered the heavy luggage towards them, all six of her family, three sons and two grandchildren and daughter-in-law, all with their greeting faces on. Mrs Kamal pulled the baggage trolley to a halt and said.

'So who is minding our shop?'

66

In a café in Brixton, holding himself as still as he could in front of his plate of bacon, eggs, sausages, beans, chips and toast, sat Smitty.

Smitty had a fabricator whom he employed to make the things he used in his pieces. He gave the man the designs, they had a conversation, the man knocked up some 3D images on the computer, then made a prototype, then he made the object for real. His factory was in Brixton, so when they had a piece on the go, Smitty would regularly be schlepping backwards and forwards on the Victoria line, if he was in a hurry, or in his Beemer, if he wasn't. At the moment the man was working on perfecting a nine-foot-high dildo in concrete treated to look as if it was plastic, or silicone, or whatever it was dildos were made out of. Smitty wasn't yet entirely sure what this was for. He just liked the idea of this thing which looked as if it had to be made out of one thing which was by definition lightweight and pleasant to the touch, which turned out to be this other thing which was immovably heavy and nastily abrasive. Dildos were private, statues were public. It would be a piece about, about, about . . . about something. The tricky thing would be moving the nine-foot concrete dildo into place, but that was a problem for another day. Smitty had two more immediate concerns.

The first was that he'd come to the factory and his man wasn't there. The building, a former warehouse a bit like Smitty's own studio, was chained and locked. No reply on the entryphone. There had been a cock-up. He'd have liked to blame the fabricator, but he couldn't, because this just wasn't the sort of thing his guy got wrong. So the cock-up was almost certainly at his end. Probably it was his new knob-head assistant, the replacement for his old knob-head assistant. To be fair, as knob-heads went, this new Nigel was much less of one than the last Nigel. Humanly, he wasn't a knob-head at all, and had the great virtue of showing a proper respect to his betters, i.e. to Smitty. But he did make knob-head-type mistakes, and the timing of this meeting looked like being one of them. So Smitty was going to give it another half-hour and then piss off back to Shoreditch.

The result was that Smitty was sitting in a café a hundred metres down the road from the warehouse, having a cup of tea and putting himself outside a Full English. That wasn't a typical breakfast for Smitty, he was more a slow-carb, bowl-of-microwaved-porridge person, but he was having this monster fry-up because of the second thing which was wrong with his day: his colossal, reeking, throbbing, ear-ringing, cloth-mouthed hangover. A mate had had a do the night before, there was an eighties theme, and it had been good fun. There were people dressed as New Romantic pirates and dandies, there was Duran Duran and Wham!, and as a further concession to the theme, there were tequila slammers. At some point early on in the evening, that had seemed like a good idea. Smitty was, as a rule – it really was a rule – as careful with drink as he was with drugs, but a tequila slammer and an eighties theme night was just something you had to go with. The result was the way he felt now.

Smitty made a point of never taking a day off when he'd overdone it. Part of the reason he was so careful about not overdoing it was because of this rule, so it was a win-win: he got off his face less often, and he got more work done. Because you could have lie-ins and free time whenever you wanted as an artist, the temptation was there to go it slightly too large, slightly too often. Smitty had mates who did that. So it was part of his samurai-style code that he had forced himself across town to this meeting, which was why it was doubly annoying that the whole thing was a cock-up.

Unfortunately, telling yourself you were adhering to a samurai-style code did not help you feel any less hung-over. From that point of view, things were touch and go. The fry-up had looked challenging when it arrived, generously coated with visible grease, but he had felt better after the first couple of mouthfuls. Then he had started to feel worse again. Now Smitty was taking a moment before returning to his plate.

Seemed like a good idea at the time. That would make a good name for the giant-concrete-dildo piece.

The café was rough, the kind of place Smitty liked. It had one of the things Smitty always thought a good sign in a café, restaurant or pub: a table of four men all wearing yellow high-visibility jackets. A radio was tuned to Heart FM. It would all have been perfect, if he wasn't having to concentrate so hard on not being sick. To take his mind off his waxing nausea, Smitty picked up the *South London Press*. The front page was about a stabbing at a bus stop, a black teenager. Smitty had long been of the view that if middle-aged white people were stabbed with the regularity of black teenagers, the army would be on the streets. Page two was objections to a new Tesco somewhere – no prizes for guessing who would win that one – page three was people getting their knickers in a twist about parking ('local residents say they are at breaking point'), page four was protests about a prospective library closure, and page five was, at the top of the page, a picture of a child sitting on a donkey at a fairground, and on the bottom, a short item about the road where his nan had lived and We Want What You Have. Apparently the cards and whatnot had kept coming, and there had been a Neighbourhood Watch meeting.

Smitty sat up. He had mentioned the cards to his mother, and she in turn had mentioned them back once or twice, but the house was being done up by a builder now and he had no idea there had been what the paper called 'a sustained campaign' or that it had included 'graffiti and obscene abuse' as well as 'criminal damage' and 'items sent through the post'. The paper said that a copper called Detective Inspector Mill had promised 'prompt investigation and decisive action', which sounded to Smitty like rozzer-speak for 'we haven't got a clue'. Smitty still had the folder of cards and the DVD back at his studio. He'd been interested in it, whatever it was. Graffiti, obscenity – it was his kind of thing.

As he had that thought, Smitty had another one. It came unbidden and he couldn't have said how exactly he knew what he knew, but even as he had the idea Smitty felt certain that he was right: that he knew who was the person behind We Want What You Have. That it was this person didn't make complete sense – there was something funny about the chronology – but at the same time he was sure. Yes: he knew. And he also knew that there wasn't a blind thing he could do about it. He could go to the cops, yes, but the cops would immediately want to know who Smitty was and how he knew, so there was no way he could do that without giving away the secret of his identity, the single most precious thing he had. Oh, it was clever. It was evil. Clever evil weaselly fucker. Part of the point, Smitty guessed, was that he would work out who it was, and how limited his options were. Well, that had happened. Smitty knew who it was, and he couldn't do a thing about it. He put down the newspaper, pushed away his fry-up, and picked up his car keys. He felt an overwhelming need to be somewhere else.

67

'Bogdan!' said Arabella, opening the door of number 51 to Zbig-niew, her mobile tucked under her ear. 'Darling! You don't need one of those parking thingies, do you? Five seconds, literally five seconds, OK?'

She showed him through to the drawing room and retreated back into the hall. Why would she think I need a parking permit? wondered Zbigniew, as he looked around the room, which seemed substantively unchanged from the last time he had done some work for the Younts. Today, Arabella had asked him in to see if he could 'chuck a few splashes of paint about', which he guessed meant repainting one or more of the bedrooms and per-haps the hall too. At a guess – since she liked him – he would be the only person tendering at this stage, so he would not have to give his most competitive quote. Well, he didn't need the work anyway, now that Mrs L had given him the job at number 42 and he had half a million pounds in cash hidden in a suitcase to worry about. He would have a look-see and politely turn it down. But there was no cost attaching to finding out the size and nature of the job, and if he passed it someone else's way he would accrue credit in somebody's favour-bank.

After a moment he realised that something about the room was different. Zbigniew had a strong visual memory and noticed these things. Perhaps there was a new sofa, or a new table, or something. No, it was a new mirror, antique and gilt, on the far side of the room. The mirror faced the door, and as Zbigniew was looking at it, a very small child, a small child, and a slim young woman with black hair came into the room. The small child and the woman stopped and the very small child came over to him and put one hand on his leg and said,

'You're It.'

Zbigniew, taken by surprise, didn't know what to say, so he didn't say anything. The slim young woman, who was Matya, gave him a moment and then came towards him to take charge of Joshua. A typical useless man, she thought. He can't be bothered. Zbigniew thought: that is the most attractive woman I have ever seen. I want to have sex with her.

'We were playing a game,' she said, not liking the fact that she felt herself wanting to explain, but managing at the same time to imply to Zbigniew that he was emotionally stunted, frozen, imbecilic, full of himself, and if it were up to her, he wouldn't be allowed in the house.

'Yes,' he said. 'I am here to see Mrs Yount. I—' he found that he had temporarily forgotten the English word for painting, so he made an up-and-down motion with an invisible roller brush. Joshua and Conrad were now clinging to Matya's legs, one to each of them, both of them with their thumbs in their mouths, both of them looking up at Zbigniew as if he were something entirely new.

Joshua took his thumb out of his mouth. 'I haven't done a poo today,' he said, kindly, to help break the ice.

Zbigniew grunted. It was supposed to indicate mild amusement, but came out sounding surly. Joshua put his thumb back in his mouth. Zbigniew wondered what to say. Well done? That's good? I too have been to the toilet, would you like me to tell you about it? What were you supposed to say to children? And also: I wonder what she thinks of me? If he had known what Matya was thinking he would have been mortified, because what she was thinking was: typical arrogant Pole, can't be bothered, thinks Warsaw is the capital of the universe, useless with children, vain, conceited, lazy about everything except work. Matya hadn't yet found what she was looking for in London, but since her evening out with Roger she had a clearer idea of what it was – something to do with money, and space, and a bigger perspective. Something to do with looking out the window of a black cab in the small hours of the morning, and a house with a garden with roses in it, and children of her own. It was not to do with Polish builders who hadn't grown up yet.

Zbigniew, if he had known, would have thought that very unfair. He thought he had changed a lot; he thought he was a much more mature person than six months ago. The old lady's death, the horrible thing with Davina, had marked him, he felt. Also, he was spending hours a day wondering what to do about his magic windfall. His thoughts began with the practical – how to launder the cash and get it paid into a bank account, how to put it to use – and then slowly, as if by their own volition, turned to the question of just how morally wrong it would be to take the money. He started with rationalisations for why it was all right: because the Leatherbys didn't know the money was there, it was in effect already lost, ownerless; because they had no need of it, given that the house was worth millions; because his father was a good man and deserved what the money would bring. But then his grip on the rationalisations would weaken, his self-justification would start to slip through his fingers, and he would, by an act of will, force himself to think about something else. He was struggling with this, every day. So Matya's thoughts would have seemed a terrible injustice, and even though he didn't know them, he could tell that first impressions weren't going well. In his experience with women, it was difficult to recover once things began to go wrong – once they had unreasonably decided that you were a person with whom they were not under any circumstances ever going to have sex.

Arabella came back in the room.

'Mi dispiace, darlings, I'm racked with guilt, do forgive me Bogdan, I'm now absolutely a hundred per cent all yours. Can I show you my little thingies?' With that, she ushered him out to the hall, and then up the stairs to the bathroom he had painted for her seven months before. She wanted to change the colour to 'one of those Swedish types of white, you know, they've got sixteen different ones, this is sort of warmish, clean but not antiseptic, like, I don't know, apple juice or something, only white'.

Zbigniew told Mrs Yount that he would think about it and give her a quote. It made no sense to take the job on, but he hated to turn work down, and a voice in the back of his mind told him that by coming to the house he would have another chance with the sexy nameless nanny.

68

On Sunday morning at his flat, Usman opened up his laptop and took out his 3G mobile to do a bit of net-surfing. This was his preferred way of getting news and entertainment. He did not like or trust the kafr media and for the most part avoided it. The two exceptions were football and *The X Factor*, which he had first watched when babysitting Fatima and Mohammed one Saturday night. Fatima had heard about the programme from her peers and was able to insist that everybody watched it. Usman wasn't sufficiently experienced as an uncle to see through the manoeuvre. So the first time he saw the programme was on the TV next to the counter, with Mohammed asleep upstairs and Fatima sitting on the floor, her chin on her fists, utterly rapt. It was rubbish, of course it was, but there had been one or two occasions since when he happened to be near a TV on Saturday night, and there didn't happen to be anything much else on, and he happened to find himself watching it, not in any concentrated way, obviously, but keeping an interest, staying in touch with the distractions of the masses . . . Know your enemy . . .

As for football, Usman loved the fact that Freddy Kamo lived a few houses away – well, a hundred yards away – in the very same street. The first time he'd heard of Freddy he had been incredibly excited for more than one reason, since Freddy was a brother Muslim, and there was something extra-cool about that, even though this was a fact that he'd never seen mentioned anywhere in the press, not once. Nobody seemed to know where Freddy went to mosque. It would be cool to go to the same mosque, to worship next to him at Friday prayers, maybe to fall into conversation afterwards, discover the Pepys Road connection, maybe even become mates . . . Freddy was Usman's favourite footballer and he had watched YouTube clips of him dozens, maybe even hundreds of times. He loved the way he looked as if he was crap but then you actually realised he was brilliant. He loved his youth too. As the youngest brother, Usman was always on the side of the youngest person or entity. Islam was the world's youngest major religion and the only one that told the truth – see?

It was desperately sad about what had happened to Freddy. The game had been televised and Usman had been watching at a mate's house; an old mate from school, whose lifestyle was un-Islamic because he drank alcohol, but he and Usman had known each other for so long that he was, in his mind, partially exempt from the rules. Besides, he had Sky Sports. The tackle which smashed Freddy's leg was shown, in the usual way, about ten times, and it was something that made you feel sick when you looked at it. Freddy had always seemed vulnerable; that was part of what was so thrilling about him, that he looked vulnerable but never got caught or hurt. Now that he had been, it all felt different.

Usman wouldn't have minded having a look at some clips of Freddy in his prime, but this particular technique for surfing the net was too slow for that. He had broadband, obviously, but there were some things he didn't like to do over his own internet connection. Usman was, always had been, careful about stuff like that. A neighbour had until recently had an unencrypted wireless connection which he used for his own surfing when he wanted to do something that couldn't be traced, but the neighbour – he didn't know who but he guessed it was the flat in the basement – had wised up and gone to WPA encryption about three months ago. So now Usman used a pay-as-you-go 3G mobile phone which he'd bought for cash and was therefore untraceable, and tethered it to his laptop. He ran the browser with all its privacy settings on, via an anonymising service. An electronic spy or eavesdropper would have no way of knowing who he was.

Not that Usman did anything against the law on the net – nothing illegal, not exactly. Looking at or downloading Al Qaeda training manuals, for instance, was a criminal offence. Usman had no wish to go that far, even in the privacy of his own head. As for whether the people who did go that far were all wrong, well, he would once have said that if you have no other way of getting attention for your grievances, then it may be regrettable but there was sometimes no other way than violence. But now, without fully adopting another position, he had gone a long way to abandoning that one. The bombings of 7/7 had been in large part responsible for that. Seen at close hand in the city where he lived, the violence was too stupid and too random to be a viable course of action. The engineer in him rebelled at the sight of something so ugly and wasteful and so – in his heart he could admit this – wrong.

He still had an appetite for the conversation, though. He still liked to know what the angry people were saying. A global conspiracy to destroy Islam was something he no longer believed in, but the idea that there was a fundamental anti-Muslim bias in the attitudes of the developed world was, in Usman's view, manifestly true. Mind you, if anything could put you off that idea, it was the kind of people you found contributing their rants to some of these websites. Usman had contributed a few times himself, but even when he was hiding behind a pseudonym and using a completely anonymised technique for accessing the net, it made him nervous. Too nervous to keep on doing it. A common theme, indeed a common obsession, on the sites was how thoroughly they were penetrated by spies and provocateurs and informers. No doubt that was true. Contributing to these forums when so many of the people on them were trying to find out who you were and get you in trouble, to trick you into saying things or giving things away – that was scary. And then there was the fact that the (by local standards) moderate and reasonable arguments he was making immediately generated flame wars in which people accused him of everything from being a stooge to a phoney Muslim to being himself a spy/provocateur/informer – that was too much. Usman stopped posting. Now he just lurked.

There wasn't much to read today. Iraq and Afghanistan and the global conspiracy and all the usual. A long rant about how Al Jazeera was a tool of Western oppression and how the Qataris who funded it weren't real Muslims. The connection over the 3G was slow today, and Usman found his taste for the debate just wasn't there. He logged off the site he was reading and went back to his Google home page. On impulse, just for old times' sake, he typed in 'We Want What You Have' and told Google that he was feeling lucky. To his amazement, there the blog was, hosted on a new platform, but with everything that had been on it before and a whole load of new stuff too. Usman was so surprised it was as if someone had jumped out of the computer and shouted Boo! He clicked on the links and looked through the pages that came up. More images, some of them now with virtual graffiti. Nasty stuff for the most part. Abuse was tagged onto most of the houses in the street. Even – sacrilege! – to the house where Freddy Kamo lived. An image of their own shop at number 68, the old image that had been on the site before, was defaced with the word 'Bell-end'.

That made Usman smile. His brother could certainly be a bit of a bell-end. But what had happened to the site was weird and disturbing, and Usman didn't understand it at all.

69

It would not be entirely fair, Rohinka realised, to blame Mrs Kamal for every single thing that was wrong with the Kamal family dynamics. But it would be a little bit fair. Taking in the deliveries at five o'clock in the morning, she found herself reflecting on the fact that she had been braced for irritation, had psychologically prepared herself to feel irritated, to breathe deeply, to rise above it – and yet here she was, unpacking cartons of milk, stripping the wrapping off newspapers with a Stanley knife, waiting for the grocery truck, irritated.

That was the main thing wrong with Mrs Kamal. She spent such an extraordinary amount of mental energy feeling irritated that it was impossible not to feel irritated in turn. It was oxygen to her, this low-grade dissatisfaction, shading into anger; this sense that things weren't being done correctly, that everything from the traffic noise at night to the temperature of the hot water in the morning to the progress of Mohammed's potty training to the fact that Fatima wasn't being taught to read Urdu, only English, to the fact that Rohinka served only two dishes at dinner the night of her arrival to the cost of the car insurance for the VW Sharan to the fact that Shahid didn't have a 'proper job' and seemed to have no intention of getting one, let alone a wife, to the unfriendliness of London, the fact that it was an 'impossible city', to the ostentatious way she complained about missing Lahore, especially at dinner time, giving meaningful, sad, reproachful looks at the food Rohinka had cooked. I should poison the bitch, that'll show her. In her head, Rohinka growled and muttered and seethed with – and she was well aware of the irony – irritation.

She could hear movement upstairs. There was no way this could be a good thing: either it was Mrs Kamal, preparing to announce that she had had no sleep, which was a declaration that she would be in an even filthier temper than usual, or it was Fatima, announcing that she was now awake, and required entertaining. The steps paused for a moment, as if in thought, and then headed towards the stairs: a small person making thumpy steps: Fatima. She came around the bottom of the stairwell.

'Mummy, I'm freezing.'

'It's quarter past five in the morning. You should be in bed.'

Fatima put her hands on her hips.

'I couldn't sleep.'

'I bet you could if you tried. Think how warm and cosy it is in bed. Under the duvet. With your toys.'

'I hate my toys!'

This was such a lie that Rohinka just looked at her. Fatima took a moment to listen to what she herself had just said.

'Not all of them,' Fatima admitted. 'I don't hate Pinky,' a doll she'd been given for her last birthday. 'I could get in bed with Daddy, I bet it's extra-warm.'

Inside Rohinka there was a violent but short pitched battle between her conscience, which told her she should wrestle her daughter back into bed, and her wish for a quiet life, which told her to let Fatima get into bed with Ahmed, and maybe, just maybe, they'd both sleep; knowing perfectly well that she was likely to wake him and try to make small talk for an hour or two. She looked at the piles of work she still had to do.

'Maybe you should try Daddy,' said Rohinka. I'll make it up

to him, she thought. Fatima rocked her weight from foot to foot while she considered the proposition.

'Don't want to,' she said. Rohinka sighed. She hated the feeling of being already tired from the day's events, right at its very start, before the real day had even begun, but she pointed to Fatima's favourite stool. 'Ten minutes, and back to bed,' Rohinka said. 'Or you'll be too tired to go to school.' Then, when her daughter hopped up and down, clapping with delight at being allowed to stay with her, she felt guilty.

Rohinka had wanted to be married, had wanted to have a husband and a family, and a family's life together, and as the middle of five children had a pretty good idea, she thought, of what family life meant; but nothing had prepared her for the sheer quantity of emotion involved, the charge of feeling. There could be wild mood swings, tantrums, exhilaration, giggling laughter, a sense of the complete futility of all effort, a grinding realisation that every hour of the day was hard, the knowledge that you were wholly trapped by your children, and moments of the purest love, the least earthbound feeling she had ever had – and all this before nine o'clock in the morning, on a typical day. It wasn't so much the intensity of the feelings as the sheer quantity of them for which she had been unprepared. Rohinka had a guilty secret: sometimes, out walking or shopping with Fatima and Mohammed, she would look around at people who didn't have children and think: you don't have the faintest idea what life is about. You haven't got a clue. Life with children is life in colour, and life without them is black and white. Even when it's hard – when Mohammed is sitting in the supermarket trolley breaking open yoghurt cartons, and Fatima is screaming at me because I won't let her stock up on sweets at the checkout, and I'm so tired my eyes are stinging and I've got my period and my back hurts from carrying the children and stacking shelves and everyone is looking at me thinking what a bad mum I am, even then, it's better than black and white.

And maybe that's what had happened to Mrs Kamal. Maybe it was the sheer quantity of feeling that had got to her; that had somehow mismatched with what she had expected life to be, what she had wanted for herself. Or maybe it was like a chemical reaction gone wrong. She was supposed to feel x but instead she felt y. The things that were supposed to mature her had instead curdled her, so instead of being older and wiser she had got older and more and more irritated, so that now she had become someone who carried irritation around with her like a smell. The irritation was catching in the way that yawning was catching. Rohinka could see, now, that this was why the Kamal boys were the way they were. All of them were, in most of their dealings, reasonable men (with the exception of Usman, who was in many respects still an adolescent). They were calm and sane and functioned well; men who could be talked to, reasoned with, who saw things in proportion. With each other, though, and with their mother, and in everything to do with the Kamal family, they were all irritated, all the time. It wasn't that they rubbed each other up the wrong way, it was that things always started up wrong and never improved. Ahmed, who was annoyed by very little – his disposition was so even, it verged on being a culpable passivity, a failure to get-up-and-go – was annoyed by his siblings and his mother. It was as if, in each other's company, the Kamals all went into their special irritation room, like the panic room in the Jodie Foster film.

Blame the mother – that's right, blame the mother. Since becoming a mother herself, Rohinka had been sensitised to just how many explanations for everything that happened boiled down to: blame the mother. It couldn't be the real answer for things nearly as often as people said it was. But on this occasion, she did think it was true that Mrs Kamal was to blame. Rohinka wouldn't be like that with her own children, definitely not. She looked around the room at the undone work, the papers still unwrapped, the shelves still unstacked, the first customers due before long, and sighed again.

'Are you cross, Mummy?' said Fatima.

'No, I'm not cross. Not with you. I was thinking about grown-up things.'

So now it was time for Fatima to give a big, theatrical sigh. Rohinka beckoned her onto her lap, and her daughter hopped up.

'I'm never cross with you, not deep down. Even when I'm cross I still love you.'

'I know that, Mummy,' said Fatima, who did. She bounced and wriggled on Rohinka's lap to get more comfortable, and it was from that position, in a moment of complete happiness, that Rohinka looked up to see the door opened, tentatively at first, and then very abruptly, and then shouting men dressed in black and blue came into the room, several of them, moving quickly and loudly and creating such an impression of violence and disorder that it took her a few seconds – it can only have been a few seconds, but at the time it felt much longer – to realise that the men were shouting 'Armed police!'

70

It would be impossible to list all the ways in which Shahid's quality of life had improved since Iqbal had moved out, but one of the particularly important changes, for Shahid, was that he was sleeping better. He had always been a champion sleeper, which was just as well since he needed his sleep to function properly; but the toxic Belgian, lounging around the flat, blocking the route to the bathroom, had got into his head enough for him to be aware of his movements at all times. That was bad, because Iqbal moved around a lot at night, using the kettle, running taps in the kitchen and the bathroom, putting on the television at a volume where it was too low to hear exactly what he was watching (usually – when Shahid went through to check – some rank action movie: Chuck Norris, Jean-Claude Van Damme, Steven Seagal). Or he would be on the computer. A faint light under the door, a silence that wasn't quite silence, all this at three or four in the morning – this meant that Iqbal was surfing the net. As for dawn prayers, forget about it. The problem wasn't that Iqbal got up to pray: if it had been that regular, Shahid would have learned to tune it out. The problem was that he got up to pray when he felt like it. Some weeks that was every day, other weeks it was no days, or it was day-on, day-off, or two-on one-off, or the other way around, or whatever. And this wasn't something you could complain about, especially as a non-dawn-prayer yourself.

Excuse me brother, but would you mind regularising your fajr schedule, because IT'S DRIVING ME INSANE.

All now a thing of the past. For the first four days after Iqbal left – which he only managed to get around to the day before Mrs Kamal arrived, stalling and digging in right to the end – Shahid slept the beautiful, untroubled sleep of the just. Then he'd wake and for a moment he would get ready for the first irritation of the day, the trip to the bathroom, with the unwanted Belgian jihadi sprawled on the sofa in his greying underpants – and then, joy! He would realise that Iqbal wasn't there! No one was there! It was his flat, his very own flat, peeling paint and creaking windows and semi-functioning stereo system and all, all his! He could go to the toilet naked! He could do a handstand in the sitting room! No one to stop him! It was the sensation of pure happiness that came from waking up and realising that a bad dream wasn't real. And Shahid had this sensation for four days in a row, and felt that he was enjoying some of the best sleep and the happiest wakings of his adult life.

The fifth morning was different. Shahid went to bed at about twelve, read a Stephen King for about fifteen minutes to help knock him out, then put out the light and slept like a baby until about half past four, when he began to have a dream, a dream which, even inside the world of the dream, felt strange and violent, a thriller gone wrong, something about armed men, about shouting, about people breaking into his flat, and then abruptly it wasn't a dream but it was real, there were shouting policemen in his room and two guns were pointed straight at his face from no more than two feet away. 'Armed police!' was what the men were shouting – it was quite hard to make that out because several of them were shouting it and they tended to overlap each other. There were crashing noises from elsewhere in the flat. Well, somebody certainly has screwed up, big time, Shahid thought, as one of the policemen reached forward and pulled the

duvet off him. He felt his consciousness split into several different parts, different voices, with one part of his brain crying out,
Please don't shoot me, while another said, I'm glad I put on clean
boxers last night, and another said, I wonder whose fault all this
is, and another said, It'll make a good story one day, and another
said, It would be much easier to understand them if they stopped
shouting. And then in addition to all these voices there were the
plain facts of the matter, which were that five armed policemen
were in his room pointing guns at his head.

'Turn over, turn the fuck over,' shouted the nearest policeman.
Behind and outside he could hear an extraordinary amount of
banging and crashing. Shahid had once, when he was in bed
with flu, seen a television programme in which a group of people
with ambitions to be builders had knocked down and torn out
everything inside a house except the supporting walls. The
noises they had made were similar to those now coming from
his sitting room and kitchen. That was part of what he said to
himself; while at the same time, and suddenly, he felt a surging,
physical fear. I might die here, right now, today. He turned over.
Something – with a man's full body weight behind it – pressed
down on the point between his shoulder blades, while his arms
were very roughly pulled behind his back. There was a touch of
cold plastic and a click as what must be handcuffs were put on
him. What they never showed you on television was how much
the position of being cuffed hurt, and how uncomfortable it was,
and how completely vulnerable it made you feel. Face-down and
cuffed, he was as immobile and trapped as a beetle on its back.

Two or more sets of hands pulled Shahid up and began shoving him out of the room. He could see six policemen in front of
him, and hear others behind, and knew that there were others
elsewhere in the flat. All of them were white and all of them
looked pinched and angry. As he collected himself a tiny bit,
Shahid could see that about half of them were firearms officers,

and the others were gloved and overalled for searching. One of them had already booted up his computer and was sitting at the keyboard. Whatever they were looking for, they were certainly looking for something. Through the bedroom door he could see that all the drawers in the kitchen had been turned out on the floor. He'd never realised just how much cutlery and crockery he had.

From behind, so he didn't see who did it, somebody put a waxy jacket over his shoulders and then another policeman stood in front of him holding up a pair of tracksuit bottoms. For a moment Shahid didn't understand. Then he realised that he was supposed to put the tracksuit bottoms on. From shouting at him, the police had now gone silent, as if they expected him to work out for himself what he was to do. The policeman held the trouser legs up and Shahid, like a child being helped to put on his pyjamas, stepped forward into them. Then his treatment abruptly became ungentle again as he was shoved forwards, out through the chaos, the flat full of police but looking as if it had been burgled, and then downstairs, this frightening as he was half pushed and half carried, never really in balance thanks to the handcuffs, skidding down the stairs, past the café's side door which he could see opening just as he was carried out the front of the house.

A police van was outside the building; it was stopped in the middle of the street with its back door open, facing the flat's front door. If it were a civilian piece of parking it would have been illegal. The man pushing Shahid, always keeping him at the limit of his balance so he felt he could fall at any moment, pushed him against the back of the van so that he barked his knees. Then another policeman banged on the back of the van three times, and another one opened it from the inside, and he was pushed, roughly but not violently, upwards, and hoicked into the back of the vehicle, where two policemen, not firearms officers, were sitting waiting for him. The van had benches along the sides, and a railing from which sets of handcuffs hung suspended. There was a thick glass wall between the passenger compartment and the front of the van, and there was also a separate compartment, a kind of cage with metal bars, in which a prisoner could be kept separate from other passengers. Shahid could not stop himself from thinking random, completely inappropriate thoughts, and one of them, looking at this cage, was: if I was Hannibal Lecter, they'd put me in there.

The two policemen who had shoved and pushed him into the van sat down on either side of him, so now there were four of them in the back. The door was slammed shut from the outside, and the van moved off. Both of the police across from him were staring at him, one of them smiling, the other scowling. The scowling policeman was chewing gum. No one had spoken to Shahid yet, and he began to feel, as well as confused and angry and frightened, a wave of stubbornness. Whatever this is, it's completely wrong, and I'm not going to play along with it.

The van was travelling at speed. Not much traffic at this time of the morning.

71

From all the police dramas Shahid had seen, he knew that what would happen next was that he would be read his rights, all that stuff about you don't have to say anything but if you don't it means you're guilty, then be taken up to a counter in a police station and booked, have his details taken, his personal belongings logged, then an interview room, and at some point he's allowed to call his lawyer, all that. If you were lucky the police person in charge of your case would be Helen Mirren, if you were unlucky it would be David Jason, but underneath they were the same hard but fair basically decent truth-seeker.

It didn't work like that. The van, noisy on the outside and silent within, drove for about twenty minutes, then pulled up in an underground garage. Shahid was pulled and manhandled out of the van, then shoved into a lift, the four policemen with him all the time. Then he was led down a corridor decorated in institutional green paint, and shoved into a brightly lit room, and left on his own. He still hadn't been spoken to, not once.

There was a toilet in one corner of the room, with no lid and, now that he studied it, no seat. Shahid looked at it for a moment. Rooms did not tend to have toilets in them. There were four strip lights, of which one had a slight flicker, giving the whole room the sense that it was vibrating, uneven, as if something had gone wrong with your head and you were about to have a stroke, an aneurysm, a freak-out. There was a single folding chair at a table with a plastic wipe-clean top, and a horizontal plank in the corner of the room – no, looking at it, it wasn't a plank. It was a small single bed whose sheet and blanket were folded so tightly they looked like a tablecloth. There was no pillow. The earliness of the morning and the horror of what was happening had slowed Shahid's brain, but now he realised: this was a cell. He was in a cell. Something had gone horribly, eerily, impossibly, grotesquely wrong. He had an intuition what it was, too. In fact it could really be only one thing. But now there was nothing to do but wait.

72

Detective Inspector Mill had a talent for distinguishing between what needed to be done and what didn't, between make-work and real work; he was good at asking people to do things and letting them get on with it. A clear brief and a free hand, that was the formula, and how he looked forward to being able to apply it all day long.

At the moment, though, there were times when he had to do a lot of his own shitwork. Routine legwork, routine paperwork, other people's idea of how his time should be spent. That was how it was. He didn't enjoy that so much, and a part of him couldn't help but feel, when he was doing routine repetitive work, that it was the equivalent of harnessing a racehorse to a plough. He was philosophical about it, and his police career would either take off or it wouldn't; for now he kept his head down and did what he was told. Today, that meant a. getting hold of a list of traffic wardens who served the area including Pepys Road, and b. going to talk to them.

Mill knew that being a traffic warden is a lousy job and as such is done by recent immigrants. They tend to cluster together – somebody from some part of the world gets a job, tells their family and their mates, they get jobs too. Same the world over. In this part of town, most of the traffic wardens were from West Africa, a fact which caused racial tensions, especially with indigenous blacks of Caribbean descent. Mill was braced for a wasted day talking to wary, uncommunicative West African traffic wardens whose skills in English wouldn't be great and who would be pretending they were even worse than they were. I could quit, he thought. I could quit right now . . . and that thought helped him to get out of bed and get on with it.

The morning's work began with a visit to the offices of Control Services, the company which supervised the borough's parking. The contract for parking had been enforced with such lack of sensitivity, such aggressive pursuit of the officially non-existent quotas and bonuses, such a festival of clamped and towed residents, such a bonanza of gotcha! tickets and removals, such an orgy of unjust, malicious, erroneous, and just plain wrong parking tickets, that in local elections it had cost the incumbent council control of the borough not once but twice. And there was nothing the borough could do, because the terms of the contract were set out by central government, so that there was no effective control, at local level, of this local service. It was a local government classic: it was a total cock-up, it was completely unfixable, and it was nobody's fault.

A sense of guilt or upset at this state of affairs was hard to discern at the head offices of Control Services; in fact it would be hard to imagine a more fully developed atmosphere of not noticing and not caring. Several bored men and women sat in front of computer monitors while two radios competed, the far end of the office favouring Magic FM while the end by the door preferred Heart. It was OK at either end of the room, but the crossfire in the middle was hard to take. A man with a narrow ratlike face came over to Mill and stood holding his hands clasped in front of him and Mill could tell that the man knew he was a policeman. Mill asked for and was given his list of names and addresses, and went out to wander around the beat and find traffic wardens.

It was a long morning. Mill spoke to a Ghanaian and four

Nigerians, none of whom gave any sign of knowing anything about Pepys Road or We Want What You Have. They were variously wary, sullen, and blank, but none of them, to his eyes, looked guilty, there were no clues and no tells. In Pepys Road itself he tried to interview a Kosovan warden who seemed not to speak any English at all, and barely to understand any either. Gradually this whole idea came to seem like a stupid mistake, a notion from another world – the fact that these people were so cut off from the area they worked in was part of the problem, rather than the key to the mystery.

There were four names outstanding on the list. One of the names was an -ic, which presumably meant another Kosovan. All of the other names were African. By about two o'clock, Mill had convinced himself that the idea of talking to traffic wardens was a dud; but he couldn't stop, since he couldn't write up the report in a convincingly arse-covering way until he'd spoken to every relevant warden. Then he could stick it in the file and forget about it. That, in this context, would be a result. Mill went into a sandwich bar on the high street, realised that it was more expensive and pretentious than he was in the mood for, but couldn't be bothered to abandon his place in the queue and go and find another one. He ended up with gouda and prosciutto and rocket on ciabatta, and a two-quid bottle of sparkling mineral water, which would make him burp during his afternoon's legwork, but the bubbles at least gave the illusion that you were drinking something more interesting. Sitting at a window seat with his five-quid sandwich, leaning carefully forward as he ate so as not to get food on his suit, Mill got out his notebook and checked the names and addresses. Three of them were local, the fourth, incredibly boringly, was in Croydon. He'd start with the nearest, a twenty-minute walk or so. Take advantage of the fact that it was one of the summer's few rainless days.

Actually it was a good sandwich. Mill didn't mind paying for things as long as he felt he was getting what he paid for. He wiped his mouth with a napkin and set out down the high street, along the stretch by the side of the Common where a crew of street robbers on bicycles were currently targeting anyone on a mobile phone. Mill had been working on that project until he was pulled off it to do this. The street robbers came from the estate a few streets away, and had all the rat-runs and pavements down pat, so they weren't an easy target, but the crew had slowed down in the long summer evenings.

A small cluster of school-age teenagers were hanging about by the fishing pond. Term hadn't finished yet, so they shouldn't be there. Mill clocked them but his day was already sufficiently pointless without wasting time hassling chav truants – anyway that was a job for uniform. Ah, the uniform. How he didn't miss it.

He had underestimated the length of the walk – by the time he got to Balham it had been about half an hour and his feet were starting to hurt. Well, at least he'd feel virtuously exercised after his wasted day. He checked the notebook, found the house, rang the buzzer for the second floor. A thick, wary male African accent came over the intercom:

'Yes.'

'Kwama Lyons?'

The pause was longer than it should have been and Mill immediately felt more alert.

'Yes?'

People who can immediately recognise a policeman are usually people who have reasons for immediately recognising a policeman. From its tone, the voice at the other end of the intercom had reasons for not wanting to talk to him.

'I'm Detective Inspector Mill. I'm looking for a Kwama Lyons, for a routine inquiry.'

'She is not here.'

'But this is her home address?'

'Her home address.'

'Would you like to check my identification before we go on?'

Legally, the man at the other end of the intercom was not obliged to let Mill into the house – a fact he perhaps knew. He must also know that acting odd would only make Mill more interested. So there was a pause now, during which Mill could hear the man weighing the choice. After about ten seconds he said,

'I will come down.'

Weighty footsteps approached down the stairs. A heavy-set African man in his thirties, his eyes rimmed with red, opened the door wearing, of all things, a grey cardigan. Mill put his foot over the threshold, good copper's trick, and stepped into the house while flipping open his warrant card. The man leaned closer to look at it, squinting slightly, and Mill raised the estimate of his age upwards: forty, say.

'How may I help you?' the man now formally asked.

'I'm looking for Kwama Lyons. She wasn't at her work so I came here. It's a routine inquiry.'

'She's out.'

'Might I ask who you are?'

'I am Kwame Lyons.'

'Are you related?'

A flicker before the man said, 'Yes.' Whatever he was lying about, he was certainly lying about something; hard to imagine that it was We Want What You Have, but something smelled wrong. Mill liked, indeed loved, this part of his job – the part when you could tell things were not as they seemed, and there was more to find out. For the first time he felt his full energies gather around this inquiry.

'What would be a good time to find Ms Lyons?'

'Tomorrow.'

'Does she have a mobile?'

'I'll tell her,' said the man, now moving to close the door, with Mill still half-inside the house hallway. House divided into flats, he noticed. This man not the owner.

'I'll be back,' said Mill, stepping backwards over the threshold.

He meant it, too, but the next day, when he did come back, another man, an Italian man in late middle age who identified himself as the landlord, opened the door. He told Mill that the man calling himself Lyons had moved out the previous night, leaving no forwarding address; that he always paid the rent a month in advance, in cash; that he had lived there for two years; that he was quiet; and that he knew nothing else about him, except that he had frequent brief visitors but lived alone – no wife, no female relation, therefore no Kwama Lyons at that address.

73

One of the things Quentina found strange about being a traffic warden was that despite being on her feet all day and walking what must surely be many miles, she didn't seem to lose any weight. She brought this up with Mashinko one evening, after they had had a drink at the African bar in Stockwell and were walking homewards. (She made Mashinko leave her at the end of her street; she wasn't letting him see the hostel, not yet. He lived with his mother, so they couldn't go there easily. The trials and troubles of young love.) It verged on flirting, this subject, and Mashinko was a very very correct Christian boy, yes with a cheeky side, but he didn't like anything too sexually joshing – and Quentina, to her surprise, found that she liked that about him, his touch of uptightness which suggested such strong feelings lurking beneath.

'Anyway, I walk ten miles a day, and don't lose an ounce.' Risking it: 'This is where you say I don't need to lose an ounce.'

Luckily, he laughed.

'Of course, of course. Not half an ounce! It is a mystery. We must seek an explanation. But tell me – tell me how fast you walk, when you are at work.'

They were strolling, a nice evening pace. The pavements were busy.

'About like this.'

'Like this!'

'Like this.'

Mashinko shook his head.

'Too slow. No aerobic effect. Not working hard enough!' Seeing Quentina's expression, he hurried to add, 'I don't mean, not working hard enough at your work. I mean, not working hard enough to burn fat and lose weight. Science! You must burn calories to lose weight. Like this –'

and he started walking at about twice the speed, swerving around a group of single women who had come out of a bar and were leaning on each other, screaming, laughing, smoking, and coughing. Quentina let him get away for a few yards, then realised that he wasn't going to slow down, and set off after him. He was fit, he did exercise – football, and although she hadn't asked, he must do some gym things or press ups or something too, because he had the upper body to show for it. Hard muscles, tight skin . . . She had to break into a trot to catch up and was annoyed by the time she did, but he stopped and his smile was so wide and so affectionate she felt her irritation fade.

'Like that,' he said.

'Like it's the Olympics.'

'No, just more intense than you are used to. That's what you need to do if you want to lose weight. Not that you need to!'

Quentina, the following morning, was acting on the advice. Not all day, naturally. When she first woke she was a slow and sleepy mover, not someone who hit the ground running, not quick out of the blocks – she liked to come awake gradually, over coffee and a bowl of the strange British cereal which someone had introduced into the refuge, the coarse meal-like dish known as – the word made her laugh – 'porridge'. All this in her dressing gown, yawning, shuffling, the other residents doing much the same, except the Albanian Mira, already outside on the landing halfway through the day's first pack of cigarettes, looking as if she had been up all night muttering to herself. Then back upstairs to dress slowly, the day beginning to take shape in her head, face and teeth to be cleaned, only a little make-up for a work day, pay day in two days' time and a visit to the hairdresser booked for the day after, another date with Mashinko that same night, things to look forward to. No, it was right now that the new exercise regime could start! A brisk walk to Control Services to pick up her uniform, and then she was away! No dawdling! She was a whole new Quentina!

Of course, when she had to stop to write a ticket, she had to stop to write a ticket, but in the passages in between, she moved like a racing mamba. How she moved! She was rocket-powered! Well, not really. But she did push herself a little faster, down Pepys Road, back up Mackell Road, up the side street Lindon Road, back down the other way, all at a much brisker rate. Or at least she tried to – except that Quentina found she couldn't stop herself breaking into this small, tight, irritating cough, every time she began to exert herself. I'm so unfit, she thought. I am an elephant. I started doing this just in time. Quentina didn't mind the idea of turning into a generously built African grandmama one day, and no doubt she would end up like her mother and her mother's mother, big womanly women, but not just yet. After children, after life settled. Mashinko Wilson would make a good husband, a man it was easy to imagine being good with children, good with money, good with a house, a good man to cook for and to have come home in the evening, a good man for a lie-in at the weekend . . .

In Mackell Road, Quentina found an Audi A8 with a one-day parking permit in the windscreen. The correct portions of the ticket had been scratched out, day and date and month and year, but the person using the permit had not written in their car licence-plate number. These were always difficult ones. On the one hand the Control Services policy was unambiguous: if the permit had not been filled out correctly and in full, issue a ticket.

On the other, the reality was that this was clearly someone visiting someone who lived in the street, who had been handed the permit to park for a few hours and who hadn't looked at it in sufficient detail. Quentina had a look in the car, and saw a dog-seat and a travel blanket. Someone had travelled some distance to get here. It didn't seem entirely fair to her, but rules were rules, and if she wrote the ticket she was contributing to her quota, whereas if she didn't write it, the next warden to come along would do so. Life was not fair. Also, on a lucky day, a fully specced three-litre Audi A8 had a chance of winning the contest for most expensive ticketed car. Quentina wrote the ticket, put it on the windscreen, took the photo. You had to be careful with photos of permits, to make sure the relevant detail was visible on the digital image.

Homesickness, Quentina found, was a strange sensation. Some at the hostel felt it as a constant nag or pang. It was what kept some of them silent, held them inside themselves. Like the feeling that makes people go quiet when they're starting to feel sick. Quentina didn't feel it like that. For her, she had specific bursts of homesickness, tied to specific sensations and specific memories. Today, turning the corner of Pepys Road, she caught the smell of burning wood, of hot ash, and was suddenly back on the outskirts of Harare, the smoke either from their own yard or from the neighbours', a cooking fire or a cleaning fire or just a fire, the smell seeming to seek you out so it could cling to you. An odd time for someone to be burning wood in London; it must be a fire someone had held back because of the terrible weather. The wood was wet, which made the fire smell like autumn, and something other than wood was burning too – there was a chemical note. Plastic melting perhaps. Mother, father, my country, my exile: all this rushed in on Quentina. For a moment she could feel her home around her, the warmth, the dry high air of her home town, the wonderful knownness of the place which held her from her first memories to the day she was forced to leave. She stopped and closed her eyes for a moment. Exercise could take place later. The smoke gathered around her.

When she opened her eyes, Quentina could see two police-men at the other end of the street, on her side of the pavement, walking in her direction, not quickly but not slowly. Without any conscious thought taking place, she felt her stomach turn over. It was a consequence of her condition: police made her nervous. She wanted to have nothing to do with them; no good could come of it. I'll gently make myself absent. She turned and made to go down Lindon Road, and as she did so a man crossed the street towards her, a smartly dressed young man in his middle twenties, clearly heading for her, and Quentina was, with a grow-ing sense of alarm, wondering why he seemed to be looking at her, when she suddenly realised: it's another policeman. She thought: change direction! Run away! And her body, seeming to act independently, began to cross the road, the other way from the plain-clothes policeman, so they would cross over without meeting; but he changed course again and stopped two yards in front of her. He was holding up a wallet with a card in it, in front of her face, and smiling slightly, giving an ironic edge to his words, as he said, 'Ms Kwama Lyons?'

74

From Zbigniew's point of view, it would be silly to take on extra work at the Younts'. He was struggling at number 42. There was no one aspect of the job which was in itself too much for him, not once he had subcontracted the specialist work to the people he was borrowing from Piotr's crew – but the fact that all the responsibility devolved on him made the work more stressful than he had imagined. When things went wrong, there was no back-up. The fact that he was sitting on half a million pounds of someone else's money in an old suitcase made the sense of stress and alienation worse. It was lonely and weird, and then he very nearly had a bad accident. Stripping wallpaper off the second-floor landing, Zbigniew had been horrified to find that chunks of the actual wall were coming away with it   whole lumps of plaster, one of them a ten-kilo chunk which only just missed his head.

It would have been an ugly death, killed by a piece of falling plaster in a house he was supposed to be renovating; his body wouldn't have been found for days, rats would have eaten him, it would have been a horrible end, and then they would have found the £500,000 in cash, and God knows what they would have thought . . . When the adrenalin of the near miss wore off, and the thought of how long it would have taken to find his body took hold of him, Zbigniew began to feel ill. Who, in truth, would have found him? He worked alone. He stayed in the house alone. He had no girlfriend. Mrs Leatherby lived in Essex and came down to London only at monthly intervals. Zbigniew called her once a week to keep her informed of progress – part of his do-what-British-builders-don't-do strategy – and she would probably notice the absence of that call, but it would take at least a week for her to become concerned. Piotr would have called his mobile and got no answer, then he would have left it another day or so, then he would have tried again, then he would have started to get worried, and then, finally, perhaps he would have gone to the house, a little reluctantly and prepared to be angry at Zbigniew for forgetting to charge his mobile, and then he would have peered through the letter box, and then, only then, perhaps, he might have thought, I wonder what's that smell . . . ?

The thought was slow to get into Zbigniew's head, but once it did it made him feel shaky. He took a break and went downstairs, stopping at the turn of the landing to look back at the place from where the chunk of plaster had fallen. Motes of dust were still drifting down. It had been a close one. He had the feeling he sometimes had, of envying people who smoked, because they had something to do at moments such as this. Instead Zbigniew simply sat at the bottom of the stairs for ten minutes before trudging back up them and returning to work, ready to leap backwards the moment he sensed anything untoward.

That same day, he went over to number 51 and told Mrs Yount he would do the decorating work for her. He had always half-wanted to do it, not for the money but for the chance to see that sexy, distant Hungarian girl again. It was the revelation of his cut-offness, his isolation in his London life, which made him act. Poland was real in a way that Britain was not, but he had to live here for now, so while he was living here, he might as well try to have a life. That was the idea.

'Bogdan, I'm thrilled to bits,' said Mrs Yount. He told her he would start work the following week – it was, he estimated,

about a four-day job. It would be a break from his work at number 42, but he would stop in there at the start and finish of each
day, just to keep an eye on things, and also to keep his conscience
clear. So he would have four days to make an impact on the Hungarian. After that he could leave a couple of tools and brushes
there and he would have other opportunities to make contact –
but his best chance would be in those four full days.

Day one was a disaster. Zbigniew had not allowed for the fact
that because it was summer, Matya and the children spent most
of their time outside. Add to that the fact that his painting job
was at the top of the house – the third time he had painted these
particular walls – and it was a perfect recipe for spending an
entire day failing to speak to her. He could hear movement in
and out of the front door downstairs, and there was one time
when Matya and the children seemed to have come back from
their lunch date. Aha! thought Zbigniew. This is my chance! I'll
go down to the kitchen for a glass of water! But by the time he
had checked himself in the bathroom mirror and wiped some
paint off his face and straightened his hair, and started downstairs, he heard the front door close again. It was unfair. Weren't
these children allowed any rest?

Some builders and painters he knew would have got depressed at going over work they had already done, effectively
undoing their own labour, but Zbigniew didn't allow himself
those sorts of feelings. If he wasn't doing this work, someone else
would be; if someone was going to be paid for it, it might as
well be him. So he got on with the job and waited for his opportunity. Matya got back at five and Zbigniew recklessly went
downstairs to try and start a conversation – only to find that the
boys had friends over, and she was cooking tea. She was making
what seemed to be an entire restaurant service's worth of meals:
a baked potato with beans (one of the Yount children had baked
beans at least once a day), another baked potato with cheese,

a carton of chicken and sweetcorn soup to be divided between the visiting children, a portion of spaghetti and pesto which she had planned to share with the other nanny until it emerged that she couldn't eat anything containing flour, so Matya was eating the pasta herself and had made an omelette for her guest. At the same time, two of the boys were making mess with finger-paints. Matya, doing ten or eleven things at the same time, had the look of a woman who did not want to be courted; who would regard any flirting as somewhere between an irritation and an outright provocation. He got a good view of her bum as she bent over the table to mop up some spilled food, J-cloth in right hand, mobile phone in left. The effect on him was such that Zbigniew forgot to get the glass of water he had come downstairs pretending to want. At six, she left. He heard the door close. At five past six, he left too.

Day two was very similar. Matya and the boys were out, briefly in, then out again. Zbigniew felt he had to be careful – if he did the same accidentally-popping-downstairs manoeuvre, she might see through him and he might begin to seem desperate. The outcome of this sensible strategy was that he didn't see or speak to her all day. He spent it painting and – since he'd brought his laptop, which still had the Younts' wireless password on it – intermittently checking on his stocks. He stopped at five thirty, wrote an email to his brother back in Warsaw, and went back to the house.

Day three began promisingly. Zbigniew arrived at eight, while the children and their nanny and their mother were all still at breakfast, so he went straight upstairs and got on with the work. He was ahead of schedule and if this had been a different kind of job might have contemplated a flat-out fourteen-hour day to get it all finished – but that would disrupt his nanny plan, so instead Zbigniew was budgeting for two days of steady progress. He had worked here before and knew the sounds of the house, so he could interpret the noises when Arabella called out her farewells, then went upstairs to shower and get dressed, then went out with more farewells, then came back in again a minute later to collect her car keys, then went out again. It was about nine o'clock. Zbigniew could hear the crashing, scuttling, and laughing noises which meant that Matya and the children were downstairs. There was no evidence that they were about to head out – that took a good twenty minutes, so there would be warning. Excellent. Finally. Today was the day. He would give her a few minutes, then go down and initiate . . . whatever there was to be initiated. He would make no special preparations for what he should say – something natural, spontaneous, perhaps something based on whatever it was the children were doing. Yes – the children. Ah! Such energy! Something like that. One day, I hope to have children of my own, and hope that they have a nanny just as beautiful, who would bend over the kitchen table and – no, that probably wasn't the way to go. Small talk about the children, a joke, a drink after work. Yes. And then just as Zbigniew was about to act on his audaciously brilliant plan, disaster. There was a car horn from outside, the doorbell rang, the door was opened, two women's voices were speaking a loud foreign language at each other – from its unrecognisability, Zbigniew recognised it as Hungarian – there was the noise of a loud car engine, probably an SUV, there were rapid orders, a rapid gathering of coats and toys, and in an unprecedentedly brief time, less than two minutes at most, Matya and the children had been swept out. As for where, Zbigniew didn't know and didn't care. It had been a stupid idea taking on this job. Mrs Yount would change her mind about the colour again in a matter of weeks. Matya was out all day every day, she obviously couldn't stand to be in the house. By the time he left she still hadn't come back.

By day four, Zbigniew had more or less given up. It had been a moronic idea and he didn't fancy her that much anyway. The real reason he had taken on the work was that he felt he owed it to Mrs Yount. He felt responsible because it was his paint job that he was redoing. No other reason. Matya, who he didn't want to speak to anyway, was out all day, just for a change. He heard her and the children leave the house at about nine o'clock, the usual drama with clothes and shoes and last-minute trips to the toilet, and then they were gone. He made steady progress with his painting, finished the dado rails by late morning, then went on to the final details and was done by five o'clock. The Hungarian nanny, who he hadn't liked much anyway, and her charges still weren't back. Zbigniew cleared up the paper and cloths he had used to protect surfaces, and wrote a note for Mrs Yount saying that he was done, that he would be round in a day or two to see if everything was all right (and to collect his cheque, though he didn't say that). He took his brushes and paints downstairs, then went back up to get the note and the coffee mug, and as he did so heard the door open and a stampede of children and nannies come into the house, the nannies issuing orders, the children voicing protests. Zbigniew came down into the mayhem with his note for Mrs Yount and his dirty mug.

'Aha!' said the second nanny, another Hungarian from her accent, shorter than Matya, with short hair cut to curve under her chin and bright flirting happy eyes. 'A man! Perhaps he will eat pizza!'

'Pizza is horrible!' said the younger of the two Yount boys, who, like the other three children, was hiding under the dining-room table.

'They said they wanted pizza. Now they say they don't want it,' said Matya, addressing herself to Zbigniew, the first time she had spoken to him. Zbigniew put his set of house keys and the note for Mrs Yount on the table by the telephone, where messages and letters were left, and saw, sitting next to the lamp, a set of car keys and Matya's phone, a Nokia N60. He had the same model phone. They were meant for each other. Zbigniew had an idea.

'We want baked beans,' said a voice from under the table.

'Perhaps you can help us eat all this pizza?' said Matya's friend.

He made gestures to indicate polite refusal and then, since both the girls were eating, said, 'Just a slice.' Then he introduced himself.

'I thought your name was Bogdan,' said Matya.

'Bogdan the Builder. A little joke of Mrs Yount's.' He saw this register with her.

'My name is Matya,' she said, 'but the children called me Matty.' She had a nice undertone to her words and eyes – lively and a little sad at the same time. That body too. Zbigniew was convinced. He made some chat with the girls, helped joke the boys out from under the table, and left with his brushes and paints and, in his jacket pocket, Matya's mobile phone.

75

There was no clock in Shahid's cell, and no natural light, and he wasn't wearing a watch when he was taken to jail, so his sense of passing time was limited to the point when his lights were turned out and then turned on a stretch of time later – which, he assumed, meant that a day had passed. That had happened five times now, which meant that five days and nights had gone by. Shahid had not spoken to anybody apart from – he presumed this is what they were even though the thought of what it meant was difficult to process – his interrogators.

Not that they called themselves that. They did not call themselves anything. They were all men and there were four of them, two significantly older than Shahid – in their fifties or so – and two about the same age. One of the thirtysomething men was Asian, a police inspector, and he was the only one of them who wore a uniform. The others all wore suits. They all of them kept asking the same set of questions, over and over again, mainly about Iqbal, but also about his own past, about Chechnya and people he'd known there. Sometimes they showed him photographs, and asked him if he could recognise any of the people in them. When he truthfully said that he couldn't, they looked as if they didn't believe him.

Iqbal, however, was the main subject, and the question they asked most often was 'Where is he?' Today, the sixth morning after he had been arrested and therefore his seventh day in prison, was no different. It began with the lights being turned on and with breakfast being pushed through a hole in the door: a single poached egg, cold burnt toast, and the most over-sugared tea he had ever tasted. He had a shit, which was the most humiliating thing about the whole experience since it was degrading and de-filed to have the open toilet so close to the bed. There was an inspection hole in the window, so anybody could look at him on the bog, which was bad enough. The smell was worse. It wasn't a chemical toilet, but it had a persistent chemical smell, and the metal washbasin also gave off a faint scent of industrial perfume. He had had an upset stomach, surely caused by stress, and his bowels were loose. The frequent semi-liquid shitting and the toi-let and the sink combined together to make a shaming cocktail of odours, which hit him hard when he returned from interrog-ations.

Shahid washed his hands, brushed his teeth, and waited. About fifteen minutes later, a police officer came in and took the tray, and then another two policemen came in, put handcuffs on him, and led him along the corridor and round two corners to the interrogation room where the Asian policeman and one of his colleagues were waiting. The white policeman was a man who gave an impression of heaviness. It wasn't that he was fat, but he sagged as if with a moral or psychic burden; his shoulders sagged, his eyes sagged, his suit sagged and he sat sagged in his chair, as if his disappointments with the world were bearing down on him. He made it clear that Shahid was one of these dis-appointments.

'Well rested?' asked the Asian officer. Shahid, who had not lied about a single thing as yet, saw no reason to answer with anything other than a shrug. The interrogators had a varying set of props and tools; sometimes they read files that came in plain brown folders, over the top of which Shahid couldn't quite see. They might be looking at their horoscopes – you couldn't tell. Sometimes they had turned on the tape recorder, sometimes they took notes. Sometimes they had cups of coffee, bottles of water (always Volvic; there must be a dispenser somewhere). Once one of the older officers came in drinking a Diet Coke. But the times Shahid found most disconcerting were the occasions, like today, when his interrogators were entirely empty-handed: no folders, no drinks, nothing. They just sat there with their hands in their laps and asked questions. The fact that they made no attempt to record his answers made it seem as if they weren't listening to him. His answers were being discounted. So he was being grilled and ignored at the same time; Shahid found that hard to take.

The two policemen just sat there and looked at him.

'I want to see a lawyer,' said Shahid.

'Tell us how you know Iqbal Rashid,' said the other officer.

'I've told you about three hundred times already. I want to see a lawyer. I'm entitled to see a lawyer and I want to see one now.'

'Iqbal Rashid,' said the other officer.

'I want to see a lawyer.'

'There were just a couple of details we wanted to check.'

'I want to see a lawyer.'

'It was in Chechnya, wasn't it?'

'You know perfectly well, because I've told you a hundred times, that it was on the way there' – and Shahid was, because it was finally easier than having the same fight all over again, telling the story. They kept interrupting, checking details, going over things, and whenever he resisted or showed how sick he was of going over the same ground, they kept asking the same question over and over again until he gave in and answered. With part of him, Shahid knew that the whole point was that he be as demoralised and shamed and tired and compliant as possible; but this knowledge didn't seem to help him fight his interrogators. He knew he was innocent. He knew that his intentions were

432

good and that that should be enough. For what felt like the thousandth time he recounted the details of the trip to Chechnya and the people he'd met there and had the sense that he wasn't being listened to – that nothing he said would ever be listened to.

'. . . and no he didn't always go to mosque or if he did I didn't see him there.'

Without showing any sign that he was changing gear or changing the subject, without sitting up or showing any increased attention, the policeman said,

'So where were you going to get the Semtex?'

At which Shahid was so surprised he found he couldn't speak. They waited for him.

'What Semtex?'

'The Semtex you're planning to use to set off an explosion in the Channel Tunnel.'

76

At the offices of Bohwinkel, Strauss and Murphy, Mrs Kamal sat on a straight-backed chair with her handbag in her lap, her sari tight around her, and the gleam of battle in her eye. Rohinka, whose feelings about her mother-in-law were what they were, was impressed. Ahmed and Usman were both also present but were making only occasional contributions. There was no ambiguity about the fact that Mrs Kamal was in charge.

'. . . and as for the idea that Shahid chose to waive his right to see a lawyer, this is a conscious, deliberate, open attempt to insult our intelligence. He has not just come down from the hills. He is not some Urdu-language monoglot from the tribal areas who's never seen a knife and fork. Do they really expect us to believe that he has signed away his right to legal representation? This is a young man who was offered a place to read Physics at Cambridge University. He is lazy and he has his faults but he is not an idiot and I simply do not believe what the police are asserting in this matter.'

Fiona Strauss was not a natural listener, but she knew how to listen to a client. She sat behind the desk, her fingers arched together, frowning, her mouth pursed. On the wall to her left, there was a photograph in which she could be seen shaking hands with Nelson Mandela. Behind her was a view of Montagu Square, with the plane trees in full bloom and a light spattering of rain hitting the window in intermittent gusts. She was good at pausing: when people stopped speaking she always waited for a moment before saying anything in reply. Even the way her patterned scarf was tied seemed designed to express principled concern.

'Shahid has been in custody for seven days now, yes? Because he is being held under the Terrorism Act, they can keep him for twenty-eight days without charge. That is a deplorable fact, but it is a fact.'

'But he hasn't done anything!' said Ahmed. 'It's ridiculous! Shahid's no more a terrorist than . . . than I am!'

'I believe you. But that doesn't affect the legal position.'

Everyone in the room could sense that Fiona Strauss was holding back. She was a famous human rights solicitor, and was the first name to come to mind in cases of this sort. She was so well known that Rohinka's first thought, when she went into her large office and saw her, was that she knew her already: a side effect of her appearance being well known. It was a bit like seeing Mel Gibson in the street and waving at him because you thought he must be an old friend. They expected to have to do no more than tell her what had happened to Shahid, and the blue flame of her indignation would be lit. Then suddenly there would be action, press conferences, an interview on the steps of the police station, and Shahid's immediate release. The wrong done was to them so flagrant that it was astonishing to find it did not automatically seem so to everyone else. But it didn't appear to work like that. The lawyer was resisting them, was requiring to be seduced; was requiring – and this was hard to take – to be interested. She had her pick of the world's injustices, and liked to choose carefully. The Kamal family had expected to be meeting a crusading avenger who wished for nothing more than to pick up a flaming sword of truth and wield it on their behalf, and instead found that they were having to make a sales pitch.

Ahmed began to talk about how his brother was a good boy

and wouldn't have anything to do with terrorism of any kind, about how they as a family were well aware of the virtues of Britain as a free society (Usman was shifting in his chair at this point) and how they were good citizens, a family of practising Muslims who were respectful of other faiths and other paths. The others could hear that he was rambling, in the effort to get the full attention of Fiona Strauss. When he wound down, Usman had a go. He was hunched forward and looked as if left to his own devices he would be wearing a hoodie. For reasons of his own, he roughened up his accent and deepened his voice while talking to the solicitor.

'The thing is, we know we got rights. We supposed to have rights. So where are they? Who's gonna help us' – and then giving the word a flourish – '*exercise* them?'

Usman gradually got angrier and angrier, and as he did so, made steadily less sense. It was clear that he was possessed by a furious sense of the injustice that had been done to his brother, but he was spluttering and going round in circles and his accent kept shifting from his normal educated voice to some version of South London which seemed like a new personality he was trying on specially for the occasion. Ahmed had never seen him so agitated; it was as if he had gone slightly mad.

By way of showing that she appreciated the effort they were making, and also that they had not yet succeeded, Fiona Strauss said,

'Unfortunately, I say again, the legal position is clear.'

Mrs Kamal gathered a silence around her. Her power of projecting her mood, very often a great burden in family life, became an asset here. She said:

'Well, this is all very good isn't it? We are in the country which regards itself as the cradle of liberty. What happens? We are all woken at dawn with a gun stuck in our heads, in a manner which would embarrass a police state. My middle son is dragged off to jail. He is completely innocent of anything and he had never been arrested or charged with anything in his life, not once, not ever, but that doesn't seem to matter to anyone, and he is held without any information being allowed out, without any contact with the outside world, his signature is forged to claim he is waiving his rights, and that's it. Shahid would never waive his rights, that is the exact opposite of the kind of boy he is. But never mind. Nobody cares, nobody is willing to do anything, he's just gone. Why not just bundle him off to Guantanamo and have done with it? That's what you seem to be saying, Ms Strauss, am I not right?'

'Mrs Kamal, the legal facts of the case are what they are. In relation to the judicial realities of the matter, my opinions have no status. They have no traction. Merely as a point of fact, you should know that there is not the slightest possibility of Shahid being extradited to Guantanamo Bay.'

This speech made something clear to Mrs Kamal. With her instinct for a weak point, she realised that what the lawyer was seeking was an appeal to her vanity. It wasn't that she needed to be made to feel important, but that she needed it to be made clear that her clients understood that she was important. Everybody who came into this office was convinced that they had experienced a level of injustice without precedent, and they always thought that their story would do the work of convincing for them – that the story was all it took. So it was as if the story was the most important thing. But for Fiona Strauss, the important thing was herself, and she needed this to be acknowledged before she would take an interest in a case. Then the story could have its due. Mrs Kamal saw this, and acted on what she had seen.

'But we need you, Ms Strauss. We are lost without you. We have rights on which we cannot act. The door is closed to us. We are excluded from justice. Without your help we don't even know where to begin to seek it. The legal position may be as clear as you say – I am sure it is as clear as you say – but the moral position is clear also. We know that the fight against such injustices is your whole life. We know that. And all we can do now is ask for your help for us and for Shahid. He is in a dark place. You must help us bring light to him, Ms Strauss, because there's no one else we can turn to.'

The lawyer separated her arched fingers and briefly, silently, drummed on the desk in front of her. Then she sighed, a sincere sigh, and said, 'Very well. I will do what I can.'

'You have no idea what this means to us,' said Mrs Kamal, seizing her hands. The Kamal family were loud with relieved thanks, with exclamations, with gratitude and approval.

They spent another twenty minutes talking about what to do next. The lawyer promised to make representations to the police, and to explore the possibility of a press conference – exactly the thing the family had wanted all along. The Kamals left happy, except for Usman, who still seemed furious.

In the car on the way home – there had been extended discussions about how to get in to the appointment, and the non-desirability of paying the congestion charge, versus the unthinkability of Mrs Kamal taking the Underground – Rohinka said, 'Well. That lady lawyer is quite a piece of work.'

Mrs Kamal said, 'I liked her.'

77

Doctors and lawyers. Lawyers and doctors and men from the insurance company. That, now, was Patrick and Freddy's life – and because Mickey always came to meetings with them, it was his life too. For the doctors – doctors plural, because they saw several different specialists – they went to surgeries in and around Harley Street. For the lawyers they went to three different sets of offices. The club's lawyers were in a tall block in the City of London, with a view of other tall City blocks. The fittings were modern, steel and glass and sophisticated coloured plastic. The insurance company's lawyers were in offices in Mayfair, a Regency building with, again, modern fittings, except in the big conference room where the two sides met, Freddy and Patrick and Mickey and one or two of their lawyers at one end of an oval oak table, which was polished so brightly that the gleam of reflected halogen spotlights made it hard to look at. As for Freddy, his lawyers were in Reading: it was a firm Mickey had briefly worked for and still trusted. The drive out of London to the lawyers' offices was a relief, even if the only countryside they saw was the fields on either side of the M4.

The whole process felt like a form of torture. It didn't begin that way – in fact it had begun with a strong sense of optimism-in-the-face-of-hard-times. After the first meeting at the insurance company, Mickey had turned to Patrick and Freddy and had said, 'Well, that went well.' He ought to have known better, he thought now, he really ought to have known better. He ought to have known that any case which had so many lawyers and doctors in attendance was a carcass, around which the professionals were clustering to gorge like vultures. But he had allowed himself to believe in the atmosphere of confidence, the sense given that all those present were men of good will whose only interest was in solving the unfortunate problem to the mutual satisfaction of all parties. What had happened to Freddy was tragic, but the system existed to provide a remedy, and only the details were left to be determined.

But what had happened to Freddy? That was the first problem. The doctors didn't agree. Doctor number one, an orthopaedic surgeon, was a very formal man in his middle fifties with enormous dark-framed glasses who always seemed to be passing judgement on whoever he was speaking to. He had the weirdest body language of anyone Mickey could remember seeing, because he had so little of it: talking or listening, he sat completely immobile. He had done the initial remedial surgery and therefore was the only person actually to have looked not just at Freddy's knee, but inside it. He was, they were told, the leading specialist in this kind of surgery not just in London or Britain but in Europe; there were, arguably, men his equal or superior in America, but only arguably. He was Mr Anterior Cruciate. His judgement was that Freddy would never play football again; he would never again run or kick a ball with intent. The very best he could hope for was that he might, if he were lucky, walk without a discernible limp.

The second doctor, visited at the insistence of the insurance company, was much nicer. He was a younger, more casual man, handsome and confident and not more than forty, and they saw him on a warm day when he'd taken off his jacket and tie. When they came into his office, he'd been listening to a Bob Dylan CD that he turned off by remote control. He took care to put Freddy at his ease, to smile and say how sorry he was for his trouble. Even his hands, touching and very very carefully manipulating the knee, were gentle. He told them that he had looked extensively at X-rays and at the surgical notes of his distinguished colleague – for whom he had the highest regard – and that in his opinion, Freddy had a 50 per cent chance of being able to play professional sport again. At that point, he gestured to a photograph on the wall behind him of a professional cricket player, a bowler in mid-delivery stride, jumping half a metre in the air, his whole weight – and to Freddy's eye, he looked a bit fat – about to land on his left, front, leg. The doctor said that he had used a new technique to operate on the cricketer's left anterior cruciate ligament, which had been in the same condition as Freddy's after he broke his leg, and that photo, taken over a year ago, was the result. The cricketer was still playing cricket, and bowling quicker than ever. He did not say that the other doctor was wrong but he made it very clear that he believed he himself was right.

So they had to go and talk to a third doctor, one agreed on by both of the other two – a third opinion which both of them could see as an acceptable second opinion. This involved a train trip to Manchester, Freddy playing *Championship Manager* on his PSP, Mickey driving everyone within earshot crazy by making calls on his iPhone until the battery ran out, and Patrick looking out the window at this country he knew so little about. The countryside looked so empty, the city- and townscapes so old, so crowded, so thick with history and long habitation, and so impossible to know.

This third surgeon was amiable, crisp, and made it evident that in his own judgement he was the clear first choice to provide the opinion and when time came to do the surgery. He had light-coloured hair and fair skin and seemed to have been freshly scrubbed; he radiated cleanness. He listened briskly, asked questions briskly, and examined Freddy's knee with a brisk air too, as if he thought Freddy might be malingering. Then after all this briskness he would not give them a verdict then and there, not even a provisional one, not even a hint. He would think about it and write to them in a day or two's time.

The letter, when it came, agreed with the first surgeon. Freddy in his judgement would never play football again. He said that he was very sorry.

All that was the positive, practical, forward-moving part of the experience. It got worse from there, because it was at this point that the insurance company and the lawyers took over. Mickey couldn't believe it. He knew perfectly well that if you left the taps running in the bath, and water came through the ceiling of the downstairs flat and trashed it, the insurance company would niggle and carp and look for exclusions and exemptions and generally seek every way they could to weasel out of paying. Everyone knew that, it was a fact of life. Or they would screw you so hard by raising the premiums that you would have been better off not claiming in the first place. No-claims bonuses, no-fault car insurance: all these were giant conspiracies against the public. Everybody knew that. But seeing that this was a young man's whole life – not just his livelihood (though that as well) but his whole life, the thing which was at the centre of his seventeen-year-old existence – Mickey thought they might have shown a bit of ordinary human decency. He thought they might have had the common humanity to treat the case on its merits and pony up. The insurance was for a rainy day, and Freddy's knee was that rainy day. It was as rainy as it fucking well got.

Well, you might have thought that, but if you did, you were dead wrong. It had become clear that the insurers had no intention of simply paying up. Every letter was answered with the maximum possible delay, every phone call was bounced around between the various senior executives who were 'handling' the case, and every opportunity was taken for pissiness or evasiveness or stalling. They sought to explore the possibility of a legal challenge against the player who had tackled Freddy; that was a whole series of meetings between them and their lawyers and Freddy's lawyers and the club. They then sought to look into the possibility that Freddy himself had been reckless, that his own behaviour – which meant reaching for the ball after he'd turned and spun and flicked it on – was a piece of contributory recklessness. Then they tried to look into the possibility that the first piece of surgery after the tackle, done by Mr Anterior Cruciate himself, had been botched, and had made things worse, and therefore that it was the surgeon – or rather his insurer – who was legally responsible for paying for the damage to Freddy's knee. They did anything and everything they could to stall, frustrate, delay, and block any resolution of Freddy's case. The fact that Freddy's case wasn't a case, it was Freddy, his whole life, seemed to weigh on them not at all.

78

Roger was sitting in his office, not thinking about anything much, which these days meant he was half-entertaining a half-fantasy about what it would be like to go off with Matya and live somewhere else, Hungary even, her home town, him the exotic sexy British man who had thrown it all up to go and live with his hot sexy Hungarian, eating goulash and making love all morning . . . or somewhere warm perhaps, yes, that was better, somewhere with palm trees and a hammock, he'd run a little restaurant out of a shack serving nothing but grilled fish, everyone had always said his barbecues were brilliant, yes, that was the one, serving his lovely grilled fish, living in a bungalow near the beach, the shutters open, Matya not wearing anything much except a T-shirt and a bikini and maybe a grass skirt, which was a cliché but what the hell it was his fantasy, and making love all morning, and then a nap in the hammock after the lunchtime rush . . . and then his deputy Mark appeared framed in the doorway of Roger's office. This was no mean feat, given Roger's field of view over the rest of the open-plan trading floor, but Mark seemed to pride himself on his ability to creep up on Roger when he wasn't expecting it. Roger's attention came back to the day and the place he was actually in: a set of figures needing to be prepared, a Wednesday morning in the City of London, of course raining, every built and living thing in sight a different shade of grey.

Mark tapped the door frame with his knuckle, a gesture he made into a kind of fidget, and asked, 'Am I disturbing you?' This was something he always asked at the start of any conversation at work, and its ritual nature was borne out by the fact that he did not wait for an answer and came straight into Roger's office.

'The figures,' said Roger, not meaning to make it sound like a sigh but finding that he had.

'The figures,' said Mark, who came round to Roger's side of the workstation – this was their routine – and laid out a spread of papers. He began to talk and to go through the numbers, which were neither good nor bad, pointing things out with his red marker pen. Roger grunted and let Mark talk through the data. His attention faded in and out and he kept his end of the analysis up with grunting, nodding, and occasionally pointing at some numbers. He was more and more like this at work these days. It wasn't a desperate need to be somewhere else, or someone else, it was more a mild longing, a gentle absence; he was partly not there, more or less all the time. After Mark had talked and crunched numbers and made points for about twenty minutes, Roger looked at his watch and said, "Time for the show.' The two men collected their papers and left for the conference room. Roger knew that if there were any difficult points at the meeting, he could bounce the questions over to his deputy.

And as for that deputy, and what he was thinking, well . . .

79

Mark, looking over Roger's shoulder while he himself, as usual, did all the work – Mark whose great preoccupation was, and had been ever since childhood, his feeling that he needed the world to acknowledge him as the heroic main character in his own story – Mark was thinking that he, Mark, had been a naughty boy. In fact those very words would sometimes run through his mind, like a nursery jingle or a pop-music ear worm, a tune you'd got stuck in your mind and couldn't get rid of. I've been a naughty boy, I've been a naughty boy . . .

The fright with Jez, when he had nearly been caught at his monitor, had been a real fright. It still wasn't something Mark liked to think about. Jez might have gone to his boss; might have done anything. And physically, at an animal level, Mark was frightened of Jez. But a strong man with a definite purpose did not over-dwell on such minor setbacks, and all Mark had done was lie low for a month or two and not do any rummaging around other people's desks or terminals – though, because he was a strong man acting on a plan, he stuck to the plan, and kept on coming in to the office before anyone else. That way there would be no change in his behaviour when he went back to his scheme. This was how you had to think if you wanted to get things done.

After six weeks, Mark had gone back to work on his plan, and had immediately had a breakthrough. One of his old mates from back-office days now worked in Compliance, the section of the bank which monitored staff's adherence to the various laws and codes of practice and risk-control models. Dropping in to visit him one day, Mark found him out of the room, having left behind on his desk a Post-it pad covered in numbers. The string of digits was, Mark guessed, the strongly encrypted password to something. Taking a big risk, Mark came round to the terminal and checked the log-in and found that while his colleague had a weekly changing password he also – because those passwords were impossible to remember – kept a file of passwords, to which he now, he found, had the key. It was really as easy as that, if you knew what you were doing. Mark had already found an old account which had once been used to balance trades at the end of the day and which was supposed to be for short term, twenty-four-hour-only use; but precisely because it hadn't been used in so long, he was now able to delete it from Compliance's systems without any discrepancies appearing. So now he could log on to colleagues' accounts without their knowledge, trade, park the profits (and losses, if there were any, though that was unlikely) in the no-longer-dormant account. The system was supposed to flag anything which seemed statistically anomalous – but he could use his access to Compliance to track any alerts, and sign off on them, before anyone else noticed. He was in business.

The plan was simple. Trade, not on his own account, obviously – he was no thief, thank you very much! – but on the bank's, until he had made, say, £50 million. Serious money. An amount which didn't risk the bank but which was irrefutable evidence of his talents. Then, fess up. Tell them what he had done and let them draw the obvious conclusion: that he was a risk-taker with a proven talent for delivering spectacular returns, and there were fifty million reasons for giving him what he wanted – which, in the short term anyway, was Roger's job.

Mark had this very week made his first trades. The City was going through an anxious phase, with rumours of all sorts of nasties emerging from the US derivatives market, but Mark had always believed that it was during bad weather that you found out how good a sailor you were. He had bought some derivatives taking a long – optimistic – position on the Argentine peso, measured against the yen. Within seventy-two hours, there had been a 6 per cent movement in the currency in the right direction. Thanks to the magnifying effect of derivatives and leveraging, Mark had come close to doubling this bet, which meant doubling the bank's money. He had closed the position and hidden the profit in the no-longer-dormant account. Then he had gone on to make a big bet on the dollar, the highly out-of-fashion dollar, against a basket of other currencies, and that was going so well that he was still running an open position, and was well on his way to doubling his money again. This was not mere evidence that he might have a talent for this kind of thing: it was not an indication: it was the thing itself. This was what genius looked like.

It had been difficult getting to the position where he was able to do what he wanted. That was fine with Mark, the difficulty was part of the point. This wasn't supposed to be the sort of thing most people were capable of thinking of, or capable of doing. His face, his mask, his Thomas Pink shirt and Gieves & Hawkes suit and Prada shoes might not be exceptional (though to the person who studied them, there were signs that this City uniform was more carefully put together, more thought through, than most), but the person inside them was a once-in-a-generation talent. Given that, it had to be admitted that Roger was a grievous disappointment. Mark deserved a better figure to outwit, surpass and overtake. He had once seen Roger as a worthwhile antagonist, someone who merited his efforts to outdo. But it was increasingly clear that his boss wasn't that person. He just wasn't up to the role of Mark's enemy; he wouldn't even be a footnote in his biography.

'Bring the paperwork, would you?' said Roger, proving the point, as he drifted in his airy, athletic way towards his own office door. For such a tall man he had an indecisive, soft manner of movement, as if his determination to get where he was going might fail him at any moment. He had a folder under his arm, which for Roger, clearly, was good enough reason to let his junior colleague carry everything else. He was just so oblivious, that was the thing about Roger which really irritated Mark – which properly got under his skin. What would it take for Roger to notice what was going on around him? A bomb under his chair? Mark wouldn't put it past him to not-notice. Well, he'd certainly notice when his deputy turned around and told his bosses – Roger's bosses – that he had just made fifty million quid while Roger was looking out of the window thinking about how to pay for his wife's Botox, or whatever it was he thought about. Maybe the inside of Roger's head was like one of those *Simpsons* cartoons depicting what Homer was thinking about: tumbleweed drifting past, a mechanical monkey doing somersaults, a hamburger. Yeah, that's probably what it was like to be Roger. Like being Homer Simpson, except taller and richer and working in a bank. For now, anyway.

Roger, with his thin folder, and Mark, with his armfuls of paperwork, arrived at the meeting room. Lothar was sitting there already at the head of the table, red-faced and fit-looking, his own single folder on the table in front of him, beside a large plastic glass with a bright green liquid inside, presumably one of his nasty-smelling health drinks. Lothar said what he always said at the start of meetings, one of the few words which made his German accent fully apparent:

'Chentlemen.' He made it sound halfway between a statement and a question.

80

Shahid had taken to sitting on the floor in the corner of his cell. He wasn't sure why, and it wasn't part of a conscious plan; it wasn't as if it offered him a more interesting view of his bed and his toilet. But since he had found out that the police thought he and Iqbal were part of a plot to use stolen Czech Semtex to blow up a train in the Channel Tunnel, he had lost his earlier confidence that things were somehow going to turn out all right of their own accord. Up until now, although what was happening to him was ridiculous, he had never lost a basic trust that there was a larger justice working in his favour. Now, however, that belief was fading. The plain fact was that the police did not believe him. They thought Iqbal was a bad guy, which as far as Shahid knew might well be true – 'You know a lot more about him than I do,' as he kept telling all four of his interrogators, over and over again – but they also thought that he and Shahid were closely involved with each other. Instead of Iqbal, Belgian semi-nutter from more than a decade ago who self-invited, it was Iqbal-and-Shahid, co-conspirators, peas in the pod, two halves of the same naan. It turned out that his internet use was being monitored and that Iqbal had visited jihadi websites, corresponding in encrypted emails, and reading and downloading all sorts of terrorist how-to information – which was nowhere to be found on Shahid's computer. What that meant was that Iqbal had been doing things on his own laptop. But none of that had anything to do with Shahid. It had nothing to do with him! Nothing! To do! With him! NOTHING TO DO WITH HIM!

'OK, he's been using my wireless broadband,' said Shahid. 'You know when he came to stay with me. Look at the dates. You can obviously do that. You won't find a single jihadi site anywhere on the records before Iqbal came to stay. It's not that hard to work out, is it? Two and two, meet four.'

'Tell us again about the last time you saw Iqbal,' replied the heavy, sagging policeman, who was the very worst of them for never seeming to have heard what Shahid said. And they began, all over again, again and again, the same true stories, the same interruptions. It was a small comfort that even his interrogators were beginning to look bored and tired, though not nearly as bored and tired as Shahid himself felt. On and on and round and round and now Shahid was back in his cell, sitting on the floor, which he had come to like doing as he found he lost his belief that things were going to be all right; the contact with the floor and the wall, the fact that to sit like that he had to be curled in on himself, was comforting. Everything else might not make sense, but at least gravity was still gravity.

There was a knock on the door of the cell. This in itself was not routine. When they came to take him for interrogations, they just opened the door; when they brought their terrible bland food, they just shoved a tray through the hatch. Nobody ever knocked. Shahid sat there for a moment, then said, he hoped sounding ironic,

'Come in.'

The door opened and a policeman came in, followed by a middle-aged woman in a trouser suit, carrying a slim briefcase in brown leather. The policeman nodded at her and then went back out. The woman was smiling in a way which did not indicate any particular emotion other than a desire to indicate that she was well-meaning. She held out her hand to point at the floor beside Shahid and said,

'May I?'

He nodded. She sat down, cross-legged, in the same position as him.

'Fiona Strauss. Your family have hired me to be your lawyer.'

Shahid felt his eyes fill with tears. For a moment he could not speak.

'I'm surprised we can afford you,' he eventually said. Without knowing it, Shahid had said the perfect thing, because the remark gestured gently in the direction of the lawyer's importance; and at the same time Fiona Strauss, who was a sincere fighter against the things she thought were wrong, felt that this young man sitting on the floor of his cell needed her. She was a complicated person who took a simple view of things. He was the victim of an injustice, and he needed her.

'I'm working pro bono,' said Fiona Strauss, with a faint smile. She took a spiral-bound notebook out of her briefcase, opened it, and held it up in front of Shahid. On the page was written:

'Assume we are being listened to.'

'Right,' said Shahid.

'I'm told you signed a waiver of your rights.'

'Excuse my bad language, but that's crap.'

'They have the piece of paper, I've seen it.'

'Well, then it's a forgery. They faked my signature.'

'OK. I believe you. But for now we must assume it doesn't matter. Have you been ill-treated? Are you being adequately fed, are you being allowed to sleep, are you being physically abused, are your religious beliefs being respected, are you being threatened, physically or in other respects?'

As she was talking, she turned the notebook over to another page which said:

'Don't tell me anything they can use.'

It was a lot for Shahid to take in. What he mainly felt was a sudden sense of connection with his family outside: chubby Ahmed, irritating Usman, sexy Rohinka, and Mrs Kamal, driving everybody nuts and – Shahid had always felt this, even when he had heard nothing, knew nothing about what was happening – doing more than anybody else to try and help him. His eyes teared up again. The lawyer, feeling him struggle, put a hand on his shoulder.

'Don't worry, we don't have to do everything in one go. I'll be coming back.'

His voice choked, Shahid said, 'They brought me a bacon sandwich. The first morning. Then they realised.' And he broke down and began to cry, deeply and fully, the sensation close to one of physical pain, and it came accompanied, even as he cried, by the sense that things inside him were breaking up, like an iceberg cracking or a huge sheet of glass shattering into fragments. It's all got to me, Shahid told himself, as he cried, it's all got to me much more than I realised.

Fiona Strauss stayed for an hour and when she left, she took something out of her handbag and handed it to Shahid, wrapped in a piece of silk: his copy of the Qur'an.

81

From that moment on, Shahid's time in custody divided into two. The first part of it was formless and blurred and, afterwards, he couldn't remember how it was partitioned into days, or the sequence of what happened before what, or anything to give it shape or order. He had specific memories – the diarrhoea, the time he spilled tea on himself, the inedible fish fingers which were so hard he could have used them to drum on the table, the time all four interrogators had had a go at him – but the overall way in which the time had passed now seemed vague and dreamlike. Then Fiona Strauss had come, and time had shape again. He waited for contact with her, looked forward to it, and his days were now oriented around specific events. It was the weirdest thing.

Now, too, he had his Qur'an. It was wrapped in the gold and green silk shawl that his father had given him over twenty years ago, unannounced, for no reason, just coming home from work and pressing it into his hands. Shahid was not, and never would claim to have been, devout – even when he had been off on his adventures it had been more out of a feeling of solidarity, of brotherhood in the *umma*, than of pure religious feeling in and of itself. He was an OK Muslim in a B-minus kind of way. He wasn't going to claim that he had suddenly turned into a devout believer, but the day after Fiona Strauss came he prayed five times, after asking the guard who brought him his breakfast the direction to Mecca – and the policeman had instantly told him, as if he had known all along and been expecting to be asked. Shahid learned something: it turned out that there was a huge difference between washing your hands in the nasty metal sink because there was nowhere else to do it, and washing them in the sink because you chose to do so as part of the ablutions before prayer. The space in the cell, as demarcated in Shahid's head, changed. It was now his space and he chose to use it to pray in. He had for the first time since his arrest a feeling that he was not just someone who was acted on, passive, done-unto; he could decide what to make of what was happening to him. In his own head, he was free.

Facing his interrogators that day, going over the yet-again questions, Shahid felt different. He felt that it was his questioners who were trapped, who were bound within the narrow circuits of their own suspicions. All they could do was repeat themselves; he was more at liberty than they were. It was almost funny. They had a script that they had to stick to. He was alone – alone in front of Allah – but free. They were all in it together, and they had no choices of their own to make.

Brotherhood in religion had always been an easy emotion for Shahid to locate. This was more elusive, but it had always been this more difficult feeling that Shahid had liked best about Islam: the aloneness before God. Not the imam, not the rest of the *umma*, but you standing on your own before Allah. No one to mediate the contact. Shahid felt that more purely than he ever had before: the contrast between the human world of institutions and the awful singleness of Allah. On the one hand, Formica table tops, policemen and their questions, plastic cutlery on a shatter-proof plastic tray, rules and human smallness all around; on the other, nothing but you, on your own before the infinite. The religion Shahid had grown up in never reached more deeply into him than when he caught this feeling, the exhilarating bleakness of the desert faith. I am here for a maximum of twenty-eight days, he told himself; after that they have to charge me, and there's nothing they can possibly charge me with. OK, so Iqbal was up to something. Maybe he wasn't organised enough to be up to the thing they were accusing him of. But he was up to something. And OK, Iqbal had been staying at his flat. But no British jury would send him to jail for that, so there was no prospect he would be charged with a crime. And even if he were, because he was innocent, and because he was alone before Allah, he didn't care what happened. No, that wasn't right: he did care, he cared deeply. But there was a part of him where the events, the what-happened-next, did not reach. A part of him apart.

82

If Shahid had known, there would have been another source of comfort close to hand. The policemen interrogating him did not agree about whether he should be there at all.

Iqbal Rashid had been a person of interest to the security services for some time. He was an associate of Brussels-based radicals who had trained in Afghanistan and who were known to have dealings with Al Qaeda groups in Pakistan. When he first came into Britain he was not subject to close monitoring by MI5 and Special Branch, but they had an eye kept on him, as part of the general penumbra of concern around Al Qaeda affiliates and wannabes. Then police in Belgium intercepted a plot to blow up a bomb and sink a cross-Channel ferry, and because the people involved in that were known associates of Iqbal Rashid, the level of attention given to him was raised. He was subjected first to a raised level of surveillance for two weeks, to see what, if anything, he was up to. During that two weeks he had contact with a number of persons of interest to MI5 and it was decided to make the watch on him permanent while he was in the UK. It was around this point that Iqbal got in touch with Shahid, who was at first completely unknown to the security services. When they looked into his case they found that he had been to Chechnya and had there met people who went on to train in Al Qaeda camps. They began monitoring both Shahid and Iqbal and it became clear that the Belgian was involved in something that was either a sinister and sophisticated plot, at a late stage, to blow up an important piece of infrastructure, thought to be the Channel Tunnel – or it was just a whole load of loose, blabbermouthy talk by angry young idiots showing off to each other. The normal procedure would be to wait until someone actually did something overtly terrorist in intention, and then to arrest all the conspirators; this was the historic preference of the British police, as opposed to the American bias, greatly intensified in the wake of 9/11, to thwart plots by arresting their members at an early stage. But British juries were showing a reluctance to convict people arrested on the basis of these early-stage, putative plots, so the police were strongly minded to stick with their method of arresting as late as possible. Then someone linked to the group had been seized trying to buy Semtex in the Czech Republic and the security services had been faced with the choice of waiting to see what the plotters did next, or stepping in and seeking convictions with the evidence they had. After debating the point, and reluctantly, they had decided to go ahead with the arrests after Iqbal Rashid had left Shahid's flat and disappeared; and it was as a result of this that Shahid now found himself in a cell at Paddington Green Police Station.

Iqbal's involvement in the plot, if there actually was one, was clear. Shahid's wasn't, at all, and the only evidence against him was the internet use at his flat during the period Iqbal had been staying with him. Jihadi websites had been visited, and encrypted emails exchanged – the encrypted emails being a fingerprint-clear proof of something amiss, since no one without a dark purpose would bother with the necessary weapons-strength secrecy. It seemed entirely obvious to some of the security services – Amir the Asian interrogator, and Clarke the tired heavy Special Branch man among them – that Shahid had nothing to do with whatever was being planned and that he was at worst a kind of useful idiot, willing to give shelter and accommodation to a man he knew was up to no good. To some others, including the MI5 officers who had been in charge of the initial surveillance, nobody could be that naive. His semi-jihadi past combined with his association with the terrorist Iqbal made it self-evident that he was a central member of the plot, and if there was little direct evidence that was nothing more than a sign that he was careful – in other words, the absence of evidence was an important and sinister piece of evidence.

'Bullshit,' said Amir. 'Total bullshit. Catch-22. The fact that there's nothing on him is proof that he's a trained operative? Bullshit.'

'He has the history,' said the MI5 liaison.

'No he doesn't. He has the archaeology – more than ten years ago. So he went to Chechnya. Big deal. There's nothing else here. There's no form. Nothing from our people at the mosque, nothing on his record of travel, no pattern of any kind. He would have to be some weird kind of sleeper agent who does nothing for a decade. When he was in Chechnya, Al Qaeda didn't exist. All bullshit.'

'Until we find Iqbal Rashid, he's not going anywhere,' said the MI5 man. And that was where the situation rested. Shahid had been held in prison for ten days, and did not have to be charged for another eighteen.

83

'I feel a little bit sick,' said Matya. 'What's it called? Like being in a car. Or on a boat. Sick from the movement.'

'*Cierpiący na morską chorobę*,' said Zbigniew. 'I don't know what it's called in English.'

They were on the London Eye, more than halfway up. Stepping onto the wheel had been, to Zbigniew's surprise, slightly disconcerting: the implacable way it couldn't be stopped or slowed. Matya, obviously feeling the same thing, put a hand above his elbow as they stepped on. That was good. Up they went in the clear capsule. They weren't alone: a number of tourists – seven Japanese and a few southern Europeans – were in the same bubble. The Japanese were jockeying to take mobile-phone photographs of themselves and the view.

The city spread out around them and Zbigniew started by pretending to look at the views – because his real reason for being there was to be with Matya, and he wasn't that bothered about anything else – and then found himself getting genuinely interested. He had worked in London for three years now but had no idea about most of what he was looking at. London was big and low in the middle, with a higher edge in both directions, like a gigantic saucer. North and south weren't where he expected them to be and the patch of green, higher, but not much higher, say twenty metres above the river, three or four kilometres away, must be the Common. Zbigniew, who had no feelings about

London that he was aware of, was nonetheless impressed. One thing about London: there was a lot of it.

The mobile phone thing had worked perfectly for Zbigniew. He waited for two hours: went home, checked his portfolio at the kitchen table, ate the beef stew which one of Piotr's crew had cooked, and then, just as he thought he was going to have to take the initiative, the phone rang. The ringtone was 'Crazy' by Gnarls Barkley – which might mean that she was a girl who liked her music. Interesting. The number being shown on the screen was his number and it took him a moment to get his head around it: that meant not that he was calling himself but that Matya was calling him, i.e. calling herself, using his phone. The moment of confusion was useful because it meant he didn't have to act confused.

'Um, yes, who is this?' said Zbigniew.

'Who is that? Why do you have my mobile?' said Matya.

'Why do I have your mobile? Why do you have my mobile?'

They sorted it out from there. Bless Nokia for the popularity and ubiquity of the N60. Zbigniew knew that this was a moment to be gallant, and made no secret about the fact that it was all his fault, so he would make everything all right by bringing the phone to her, right now. So she would go to the pub about two hundred metres away from her and he would meet her there in about half an hour.

Zbigniew knew the pub, a cattle market just off the Common. He got there in twenty minutes and took up a position at the bar; she was on time.

'Completely my fault,' said Zbigniew, raising his hands. 'A hundred per cent. Didn't think, didn't check.'

'Well, it doesn't matter, thanks for bringing it back straight away,' said Matya, who had changed out of her daytime jeans in-to a slimline dress which Zbigniew found he both wanted to look at and couldn't bear to look at, at the same time. She really was lovely. He wished he could think of clever or funny things to say, but all he could come out with was 'Can I buy you a drink?'

'No,' she said, but smiling, looking down and up, before adding, 'Not tonight.' And Zbigniew, understanding what that meant, felt a flash of real happiness for the first time in a long time. So they made a date for a week later, she left, and he floated home. Perfect. Could anything be more perfect?

Zbigniew thought long and hard about what to do with Matya on their first date together. Zbigniew's sense of himself, in the privacy of his own mind, was that he was about as unromantic as it was humanly possible for a person to be. Matter-of-fact, practical, unemotional, temperate, sane. There were few activities which could not be approached as if they had a secret user's manual. Attraction to the opposite sex and the need to find a mate were practical realities of life and it would be better if they were approached as such. Zbigniew had noticed, however, that this was not the way the world worked. Besides, something about Matya made him feel as if there were perhaps something in this idea of romance after all . . . And he knew for sure – he could detect – that the right way to treat her was as if she were special. She was not like other girls.

Lurking in this was his memory of Davina. She had been an education in the truth that people did not, in practice, come with a user's manual. He would not go down that route again; he would not use Matya. He would feel for her what he felt and would not let things get away from him again. He would try to be more like a man. He wasn't sure exactly what that meant, but he felt that the idea imposed obligations on him.

The simplest way of treating Matya differently would be to do the things he had never bothered to do with anyone else – the things he had not exerted himself to do. Going to a film would be too easy, not romantic enough, and it was something he had tried before. Restaurants were romantic but also expensive and he did not feel at ease in the kind of places Matya would want to be taken to – French places, Italian places. She would be able to feel his concern about money. Women could sense that kind of thing. A long walk in the park? Too romantic. Too like something out of a film. He would seem desperate, as if he were on the verge of proposing marriage. A trip to the seaside, to Brighton, would be something he had never done before himself, therefore romantic, with the thrill of discovery, but also with much potential to go wrong, and expensive too.

So he took her for a walk along the South Bank. This was something Zbigniew knew people did but had never done himself and when he suggested it, over the phone, Matya paused for a moment and then said Yes, sounding surprised and pleased. He had won points by coming up with something she had not expected from him. (Polish men – very unromantic. That was what Matya's friend had told her.)

The river scene gave Zbigniew, for the first time, a feeling of being in the middle of London. It was like: London? Here it finally is! He had seen heaving pubs and bars, bodies strewn all over the Common during the freak intervals of good weather, packed Tube carriages, the high streets of South London in their full Saturday-night mayhem; but this was different. This was people from all over the world, in the middle of the city, because they had come there to be there, with Parliament across the dark grey river, tourist buses coughing diesel on the access road, the theatres and museums and concert halls, the railway bridge, road bridge and pedestrian bridge, all busy in both directions, the restaurants packed, jugglers and mime artists wasting everybody's time and taking up space, children running about, a skateboard park for the teens to show off to each other, couples holding hands everywhere, a policewoman walking up and down with a horse with a child protection phone number written on a cover on its back, presumably because this area was riddled with pimps on the lookout for girls to exploit, street stalls selling tourist junk and portable food, musicians, and lots of people not doing anything much, just being there because they wanted to be there. For once it wasn't raining and there came a time when the clouds even parted.

'What's that yellow thing in the sky?' said Zbigniew. 'I feel as if I have seen it before. Not in London. Somewhere else. It burns!'

They argued over whether to buy an ice cream or a Dutch waffle and in the end got one of each; except she was right, the waffle tasted as if it was made out of grilled cardboard. Matya giggled at him as he tried to eat it and then had to chuck it away. As for the sight of her eating the ice cream, chocolate with mint chips, Zbigniew didn't know where to look. They stopped and listened to a man playing the clarinet, a piece Zbigniew recognised as Mozart. He said so and she was, he could see, impressed. Then – his master stroke – he announced that he had pre-booked tickets for the London Eye. And here they were.

One of the Japanese girls had come over to Matya and by sign language and mime offered to take a photograph of Matya and Zbigniew on Matya's mobile phone. So they huddled together and the smiling Japanese girl held her hand above her head to indicate, here it comes, and then took the picture. Then Zbigniew (clever Zbigniew) had the idea of asking her to do the same thing with his phone, so that he and Matya would have near-identical Zbigniew-and-Matya-on-the-London-Eye photos on their phones. Then he took her home, in time for the tea date with a girlfriend that she'd warned him about – a clever way of setting a limit to their date; he wasn't the only one who'd given some thought to stratagems and how to play it – and he took her back to the Tube, giving her, as they parted, a single kiss on the cheek. Well, Zbigniew thought, how perfect was that? And then it was time to think about something else, but to Zbigniew's great surprise, he found that he couldn't.

84

On the morning of Monday 15 September, Roger got the sack. He had no preparation, no build-up, and he did not, not even in the faintest way, see it coming. It had been an ordinary morning, with the only noteworthy thing being the fact that a busker was kicked out of the Underground by two policemen, who had clearly moved beyond the stage of negotiating reasonably by the time Roger arrived, because they had picked the musician up and were carrying him bodily out of the station, their hands under his armpits, his feet wildly pedalling. A third policeman, following behind, carried the man's violin case. It looked like a piece of slapstick out of a silent film, and Roger was still smiling to himself about it at eleven thirty, when he had a message to say that Lothar would like to see him in his office immediately.

Roger sauntered through the trading room, slaloming around the desks, his crew hard at work, the noise levels satisfactorily high – because a loud trading room is a busy trading room. Mark was nowhere to be seen, as indeed he hadn't been all morning: that was a good thing also. Roger had long since tired of his efficient but shifty and hard-to-read deputy, with his air of aggrievement or underappreciation, or whatever it was; Roger had never been interested enough to find out.

One of the tricks to managing Lothar – managing upwards, that crucial skill for the modern corporate employee – was to always do what he asked immediately. Even if, especially if, the task had no particular urgency, Lothar liked the idea that his will was always turned into action as soon as he expressed it. So Roger felt that this meeting, or chore, or whatever it was, had already got off to a good start when he arrived in Lothar's office a mere ninety seconds after his phone had rung. Lothar was sitting at the meeting table rather than behind his desk, and he did not look well: he was pale, indeed he was about the same colour as his white shirt. It was as if he'd decided to give up all that skiing-sailing-orienteering-triathlon nonsense and had taken up sitting in libraries, and, over the weekend, he had acquired the complexion to go with it. Next to Lothar was Eva, the head of human resources, an unsmiling Argentinian whose complete devotion to corporate correctness in all forms made Roger nervous. This will be some bullshit thing about a complaint, or a hiring and firing issue. It couldn't be about Roger discriminating against female colleagues; he hardly had any. Somebody had gone behind his back about something. Such was life.

'Ah, Roger,' said Lothar. 'We seem to have a little problem. When I say "we" I mean Pinker Lloyd. What do you know about the fact that your deputy has been practising criminal embezzlement under your nose?'

Lothar's voice was cracking slightly and he was, Roger could see, shaking. He realised that his boss was not pale because he had given up outdoor sports; he was pale because he was angry. He was as angry as Roger had ever seen him; he was as angry as Roger had ever seen anyone. Roger had the strong feeling that something had gone very, very wrong.

'What are you talking about?' said Roger.

And they told him. He found it hard to take in, but the gist was that someone in Compliance had found something he wasn't expecting in the records of his own computer use. This was Mark's mistake: he hadn't allowed for the Compliance and security people monitoring not just everybody else's computer use, but their own as well. That was on Friday afternoon, three days ago. The Compliance guy had looked into it, and found that unauthorised – probably illegal – trading had been taking place, had alerted his department head, and a whole group of people had worked all weekend. Mark had traded tens of millions of pounds of stock, and was at first about £15 million up, but then took a hit and was now trading about £30 million down. A team of traders was at this very moment unwinding his remaining positions. As of six o'clock this morning he was in police custody, charged with fraud. He had been doing his unauthorised and/or illegal trading right under his boss's nose. That was the phrase Lothar used – 'right under his boss's nose' – referring to Roger in the third person, so there was a moment when Roger wasn't sure if Lothar meant his boss's or his bosses'. It was the former, because Lothar went on to say:

'This constitutes gross negligence. You are dismissed immediately, for cause. You have fifteen minutes to empty your desk and leave the building.'

At this moment, the door opened and a large black man in a security uniform stood there with his hands folded in front of his waist.

'You're joking,' said Roger.

'Fifteen minutes.'

'This is bollocks, Lothar. Even by your standards this is bollocks.'

'Goodbye,' said Lothar. Eva looked up and nodded at Roger, the only time they had made eye contact. She stood up and passed him an envelope.

'You'll be hearing from my lawyers,' said Roger, hearing a tremor in his voice.

'Details are in this letter,' she said. For an instant, Roger wanted to say something about the Falklands.

'Clinton?' said Lothar. The security guard took a step forward.

Roger raised his hands in a don't-touch-me gesture and led the guard back to his office. Those moments were so horrible that afterwards Roger found it hard to remember them. He had to fight an overmastering wish to look at nothing other than his feet. Finding your way in between these desks is tricky! Must look down! No – Roger tried to keep his head up. But it was hard, because every single person in the room was staring at him, and the trading room, which had been its familiar raucous self only a few minutes ago, was now so quiet Roger could hear a faint electronic hum, coming perhaps from the lights, or from somebody's hard drive, a sound he had, despite years spent in and around this room, never heard before. He had never seen them, his crew, his colleagues, his soon-to-be-ex-colleagues, looking like this: Slim Tony literally had his mouth hanging open, tough Michelle looked as if she was about to cry, Jez was sitting with a phone handset held up to his ear, but was ignoring it, moon-faced, to stare at Roger. Jez's eyes moved sideways to look at the security guard for a moment. Then they switched back to gawking at Roger. Then back to the guard. Then back again. It was like he was watching tennis. Never had so many screens of data been ignored by so many traders for so long.

In his office, Roger had a decision to make. Do I close the electronic blinds, or do this with the blinds open? Seem ashamed, or let people see my shame? Luckily, the choice was made for him by Clinton the security guard, who hit the switch, and turned the room opaque – which was thoughtful, or experienced, of him. But there nonetheless was a small humiliation even in that, because right up until this moment no security guard at Pinker Lloyd would ever have dreamed of touching any button, of making any adjustment, in Roger's office, unless told to do so. Clinton felt right at home here. Clinton was in charge. That was how bad this was. That was how real this was. His passwords would already have been changed to lock him out from the bank's computer systems.

The door opened. Another security guard, who was also black, came in, carrying an empty cardboard wine carton. He put it on Roger's desk.

'For your stuff,' said Clinton. The guard who had brought in the wine carton – a Sancerre, Roger noticed – helpfully opened the cardboard flaps on top. The guard stepped back but did not leave the room.

Roger went round to the other side of his desk. My stuff. Right. The desk had a photograph of Arabella and the boys in winter clothes, taken two years ago at Verbier, the nanny who had just wiped Joshua's nose out of shot except for a patch of shadow at the bottom of the frame. Arabella hadn't liked the picture because she thought the light unflatteringly bright but everyone looked so glowing and healthy that it was one of Roger's favourite pictures of them. He put it in the bottom of the cardboard box, then followed it with his pen. Then his desk diary. He opened the drawers of the desk, and Clinton came round to stand behind him. Roger knew why: to stop him taking anything belonging to the bank. In theory Roger knew the whole drill, because it was standard operating procedure whenever anybody was sacked. But there was, it turned out, a big difference between theory and practice, and it was this: theory was when it happened to other people. Practice was when it happened to you.

There wasn't much in his desk, except – and this was something he'd entirely forgotten about – a spare shirt he'd taken in for some meeting a few months before but never bothered to put on, and a pair of trainers he'd taken in to work when he was thinking about using the bank's gym. There was a Moleskine notebook Arabella had put in his Christmas stocking one year when they gave each other stockings (hers had a spa voucher and a pair of earrings). The notebook was empty apart from a set of numbers which Roger took a moment to recognise. They were the sums he had done back when he was calculating his expenditure and how much money he needed from last year's bonus. The non-appearing million-pound bonus. He started to put his BlackBerry in his pocket, but Clinton held out his hand and coughed. He and Roger looked at each other.

'What?' said Roger.

'That's bank property,' said Clinton. He was matter-of-fact about it. Roger put the BlackBerry back down on the desk. He was almost done. He put in a bottle of wine that a member of his crew had given him as a thank-you for something a couple of months back. His desk diary, largely unused, was the last thing to go in his box, which was about a third full. Roger picked it up.

'OK,' said Clinton, now clearly in charge. He opened the door, and Roger went through it, the two security guards trailing behind. This time one or two people pretended not to stare; one or two of them looked as if they wanted to say something but weren't sure what to do. Slim Tony, bless him, held his hand up to his ear with thumb and index finger extended like a phone: call me, or I'll call you. Then he made a drinky-drinky gesture. Roger smiled at everyone he made eye contact with, because after all, you had to act as if you could see the funny side.

At the edge of the lift lobby, he stopped. Clinton and his colleague stopped too. Roger straightened his back and, with his box in front of him, raised his head to address the whole room.

'Well,' he said, 'it's been real.'

Then he turned and went out to the lift. It took a very long time to come. Everything seemed too loud: the whirr of the cable as it ascended, the ping of the button announcing its arrival, the faint grinding as the door opened. Down they went. At the ground floor Clinton opened the security gate for him.

'Do you want my pass?' asked Roger. Clinton shook his head.

'It won't work any more,' he said. 'Goodbye.'

And Roger walked out of the door of Pinker Lloyd for the last time.

85

Arabella had her good points. She was, in her way, resilient. She had the toughness of her obliviousness. So if he had had to guess, Roger would have guessed that she would be brave and strong about what had happened. Her stronger, stuff-the-world side would kick in and she would be realistic and practical. She would be a rock.

That turned out not to be the case. Wrong, hugely wrong, mega-wrong. Arabella went to pieces, and did so in the most direct way possible: by bursting into tears, falling onto the sofa, and saying, over and over and over again, 'But what are we going to do?'

The right move for Roger would obviously have been to sit down on the sofa beside her, put his arms around her, and tell her that everything was going to be all right. But Roger found that he didn't have it in himself to do that. Wasn't the first stage supposed to be denial? Roger felt a distinct lack of denial. What had happened wasn't nearly deniable enough.

'I don't know,' said Roger. 'I have no idea.'

He had been feeling pretty shitty when he walked in, and Arabella's reaction was making him feel even worse. The trip home had been hell. Not as hell as it would have been if he'd had to take the Tube; that, carrying his box of personal effects, would have killed him. So no, not that bad. But still pretty bad. The cab ride had been nauseating; the driver was one of those cabbies addicted to side roads and back-doubles, and he seemed to pride himself on never travelling in a straight line for more than fifty metres, with a special penchant for targeting streets featuring sleeping policemen, so the cab's swaying, bouncing motion left Roger feeling physically sick. He also found himself, for the first time ever, thinking about the cost of the cab. All those other times he'd taken taxis, and never given it a thought . . . the time sweeping through the dark with Matya in the seat beside him, watching her reflection in the glass, looking at her smile, imagining giving her one right there on the wide back seat . . . and now here he was, his cardboard box and his rising nausea, one eye on the meter. Jesus it was expensive. When had the prices gone up so much? It was going to hit thirty quid, for God's sake!

And now here was Arabella, making him feel worse. Maybe that was what she always did; maybe she always made him feel worse, and he'd never really noticed before. Maybe what seemed like the ordinary rough-and-tumble of marriage, combined with hard work and London, was something simpler: the fact that added to any equation, Arabella made it worse. What don't you need, when you've just, completely out of the blue, lost your job? What's literally the very last thing you need? A spouse convulsed with disbelieving grief. That'll do it.

Arabella was now rocking backwards and forwards.

'What are we going to do, what are we going to do, what are we going to do?'

'I don't know. Where are the children?'

'What are we going to do? I don't know. How should I know? Out somewhere. With Matya. What are we going to do?'

'Well, for a start, we're going to have to cut back on expenditure everywhere. Everywhere,' said Roger. 'No child-support money to spend on frocks, not any more' – because that was where that £1,500 a year went, a fact he knew she didn't know he knew. Ha! Take that! Screw you very much! Arabella blinked. He'd got her! Yeah! Take that!

'Gym membership . . . lunches out . . . all that stuff will have to go.'

Arabella kept rocking.

Sod this for a game of soldiers. Roger needed to get some air. He turned and went out the door thinking, I know what I'll do: I'll go for a walk. In the five years he'd been living in Pepys Road, this was something he had never done, not once, in the mid-week. He had never not been at work and in the holidays they'd always been expensively elsewhere.

Roger strode out the door and down the road. He dodged an Ocado van backing into a parking spot, and then had to pause to allow a dog-walker to sort out a crisis with tangled leads and a large poodle which, from the way it was sitting immobile on the pavement, seemed to be on strike. It didn't help that the dog-walking man was trying to use one of his hands to send a text. Down the road, Roger could see Bogdan the builder, the Pole Arabella used sometimes, throwing a piece of plaster into a skip. He saw Roger and the two men nodded at each other. Maybe I could be a builder, thought Roger. Do something a bit more physical. It would suit me. Always liked to do DIY, back in the day when I had the time for it. Still got the energy, the physique, the va-va-voom. Life in the old dog yet . . .

He turned the corner and headed out on the Common. This again was something he'd only ever done on the way to or from work, or wheeling the boys out at the weekend, a time quite a few other bankers could be seen, all in their various tribal uniforms, their pushchairs so big and unwieldy they were like infant SUVs. Weekends were all about the Euro bankers with their sweaters over their shoulders, the yummy mummies on their mobiles, the British military fitness crowd shouting at their idiotic punters, unable to believe that they were being paid for yelling at people to do sit-ups. On sunny days, huge numbers of young people would remove as much of their clothing as was legally possible and sprawl on the grass drinking alcohol. Simple pleasures are the best. There had been far less of that this summer than usual, a fact you could tell just by seeing how green the grass was. The sprawlers looked like yobs and proles, but Roger knew that appearances were deceptive; just because they had their kit off and were getting drunk didn't mean that they weren't web designers, secretaries, nurses, software engineers, chefs. It was a rule of London life that anybody could be anybody.

The Common demographic was different in the middle of the day, middle of the week. It was more underclassy. Four homeless men were sitting on a park bench drinking Tennent's Super, while a woman, looking just as rough as they did, harangued them about some injustice. They were nodding, agreeing, feeling her pain and at the same time feeling no pain whatsoever.

Three truanting teenagers were practising skateboarding on the pavement and into the road. It was as if by the energy they put into not caring about the traffic they could make the traffic go away. Roger thought about saying, hope you've filled out your donor cards, lads – then thought better of it. There were three of them, after all. A few yards away, a scowling skinhead, in his late thirties so old enough to know better, was letting his pit bull shit on the path, and visibly daring anyone to say something to him about it. A couple more truanting teenagers were playing basketball on the netless court, and beyond them, the skateboarders who could actually be bothered to use the skateboard park were practising their stunts and moves. Roger had done a little skateboarding in his youth, but in those days the emphasis had been on what you could do with the board when its wheels were in contact with the ground, whereas now the emphasis seemed much more on lifting the board in the air, or shooting the bottom of the board on the edge of the ramp, or grabbing it with your hand while airborne. A man in a red bandanna rode up to the top of the ramp, flipped up into the air, grabbed the bottom of his board, and came back down with the board on the top edge of the structure, which had the effect of making him fall over backwards onto the wooden floor. Some of the other skateboarders applauded – ironically, Roger assumed.

Actually, Arabella's question had been a good one. What are we going to do? What am I going to do?

An ice-cream van had set up beside the duck pond, and Roger felt that a large ice cream, a seriously childish one like a double scoop of vanilla with two chocolate flakes, would be the ideal way to celebrate his new-found independence/unemployment/disgrace. But, he realised on consulting his pockets, he didn't have any money: his cash was in his jacket. He was a man in pinstriped trousers, a City shirt and a tie, walking across the Common with no money.

The sky began to spit. Time to get back home before he got drenched. Roger turned and picked up the pace to beat the squall he could see coming in from the west, the clouds dark and rainy. Other people were having the same idea, and the Common was staging an informal evacuation. By the time he came back past the skateboard ramp, everyone had melted away. The rain abruptly became heavy and vertical. Roger realised he wouldn't make it home without getting drenched, so he detoured sideways across to the row of shops that ran towards the high street, and took cover under an awning. Other people had had the same idea, and every awning had a small huddle underneath it. Next to him a pair of goths had taken the opportunity to start snogging. Next to them, a cross-looking Indian lady in a shalwar kameez was fighting a losing battle against a folding umbrella which would not unfold. She kept pushing the top back down into the handle and trying to release it, but hadn't mastered the wrist technique to make it snap open. Roger took pity on her.

'May I?' he asked. She handed the umbrella over and Roger click-flicked it into position. As he did so, the rain began to slow down.

'They're tricky,' said Roger as he handed the umbrella back.

'They're badly designed,' said Mrs Kamal. 'But thank you anyway.' She headed off into the rain. It was clear that it wouldn't slow down much, so Roger decided to take the plunge. He hunched his shoulders and got ready to move off, and as he did so, he saw the billboard advertising the *Evening Standard*, and his heart momentarily stopped. It said

'Bank Crisis'.

And Roger thought, oh God no. But then he picked up a copy of the paper and his racing heart eased: it wasn't about the scandal at Pinker Lloyd but about Lehman Brothers. The subhead said 'US Giant On Brink Of Collapse'. The front-page details of the piece were fantastic. Basically, Lehmans were sitting on a pile of assets which weren't worth anything, and no one wanted to buy them or bail them out, so they were going to go under. Roger put the paper back, smiled, and set out home through the rain at a slow jog. Nice to know he wasn't the only one having a supershit day.

86

Shahid had noticed that the police used a variety of different techniques to start their interrogations. Sometimes they would be waiting for him when he went into the interrogation suite; other times they would make him wait before they came into the room; sometimes they would come in and just sit there for a bit looking over notes; other times they would be barking questions at him as soon as he was through the door. They would be friendly or less friendly, they would try to make him want to please them or they would act as if they had long since given up on him. He assumed it was all a game for them, a set of manoeuvres, and did his best to ignore the inevitable emotional turmoil he felt. He often found himself wondering who was on the other side of the mirrored wall in the suite; what kind of running commentary was happening there.

He went into the room on his fourteenth day in custody and saw that today there was a different policeman, one he hadn't seen before. Or had he? He wasn't one of the regulars and yet he didn't look completely unfamiliar. He was a young man, younger than Shahid, fresh-faced and slim-shouldered, in a nice suit. He was on his own, which was not standard practice.

'Hello,' said DI Mill, 'I'm Detective Inspector Mill.'

It came back to Shahid.

'You were at that public meeting, the one about the creepy website and cards and stuff,' said Shahid. 'I went to that.'

'I know you did,' said Mill. He dropped his eyes to the folder in front of him and looked as if he were reading it – a copper's trick Shahid had got used to by now. The silence stretched.

'You haven't turned the machine on,' said Shahid.

Mill didn't answer. He gave the impression he was thinking about something else. Eventually he said,

'Hardly any of my friends understand why I want to be a policeman. They think all you do in the police is go round banging people on the head and arresting drunk drivers. Or something – they don't really know what they think, they just know they're against it. But the real problem with the job isn't anything to do with it being violent or difficult or with what the other coppers are like. The real problem with it is the sheer amount of routine. The drudgery. Most of it's routine and detective work is no different. It's not TV. Most of the time you know what's going to happen. Surprises are rare. Nice surprises are even rarer.'

He fell silent again. Shahid felt no need to say anything.

'And then something comes along which is a little bit different,' said Mill, 'and it reminds you why you wanted to do the job in the first place. Like being here, for instance. I'd never been here before. Paddington Green. It's where they bring terrorist suspects, as you know. Been doing it for years, since the IRA days. I've seen it on the news all my life. But this is the first time I've ever been inside. That counts as something new. It's pretty cool. I like new things.'

Mill went quiet again and seemed to be following a train of thought.

'I'll tell you what else is cool. Terrorism is cool. I mean, it's very uncool as an activity, obviously. But the thing about terrorism is, the resources given to it. From a policing point of view. Antisocial behaviour, all of that, it's not such a big deal for us. People mind about it and all that but it's not what gets you up in the morning. Somebody's nicked your bike? Good luck with that. Somebody's planning to stick a bomb somewhere? Different story. So that's what's cool. The amount of resources you get on terrorist cases. The kinds of things you can do with those resources are amazing. Like, getting somebody's internet service provider to hand over the records of what sites they've been visiting over the last couple of years. That's part one. Part two is getting the manpower to go through that stuff and see where it leads you. And this is where we get to the surprising thing. Surprising to me anyway. You following me so far?'

Mill was looking closely at Shahid. He was looking for signs that Shahid knew what was coming. He didn't see any. Shahid looked the same way he had all the way along – like an irritable and, it had to be said, not very guilty thirtysomething. He nodded to Mill's question.

'What we found was this: that all the initial traffic setting up that blog We Want What You Have – the one which you came to the meeting about – came from your IP address.'

Mill folded his arms and sat back to watch. It was unmistakable: Shahid Kamal's first reaction was total shock.

'What?'

'Yup – it came from your IP address. It didn't come from your PC, or if it did, you've had it professionally cleaned up to target just those files and no others, which my colleagues tell me is unlikely. But it definitely came from your IP address.'

Shahid looked away and thought for a few moments.

'This is a trick. The reason you aren't taping this is because it's all a lie and you're trying to entrap me into something. You lot have come across no evidence of anything so you're using this thing which was going on in the street and just chucking it at me.'

In response, Mill reached out and turned on the tape recorder that was always present in the suite, attached to the side wall. He said:

'DI Charles Mill, 16 September 2008, interrogation of Shahid Kamal, tape starts at' – he glanced at his watch – '14.17, no others present. So Shahid, I've just told you that there is a proven link between your IP address at your flat and the blog We Want What You Have, whose proprietor is under investigation for charges of harassment, trespass, obscenity, vandalism.'

'Vandalism?'

'Yup, that was when the clever clogs went down the street and keyed every car in it, all the way down one side and back up the other. That's a lot of damage in a street of fancy cars. Call it ten grand. Custodial sentence, right there.'

Shahid shrugged. He did not look unduly troubled by the thought of people's SUVs being messed up. Mill went on:

'And there's another one, animal cruelty. Dead birds, someone's been sending them to houses in the street. Blackbirds. Not all of the houses, just some. In A5 envelopes. Bit sick, if you ask me. Know anything about that?'

'That's disgusting, but it's nothing to do with me.'

What Mill did not say was that the dead birds had been sent in the last fortnight – in other words, while Shahid was already in Paddington Green. The link between We Want What You Have and Shahid's internet access had been found two days before, after the latest wave of activity. By the time they knew about the link with Shahid, they already knew that he couldn't have been responsible for what was now going on; at best he might be involved with somebody else. But there was a strange pattern to the way the site had worked. When it began, it had been photos of houses taken, Mill had long since concluded, by someone with a strong local interest. Then it went away for a while. Then it came back again, much darker, with abusive labels on the site, abusive postcards sent to the houses, graffiti in the street, cars being keyed. Now dead blackbirds had been sent through the post to seven different addresses. It seemed much angrier. The shift in tone and behaviour was baffling.

Shahid's eyes were moving from side to side. He was thinking hard.

'I know nothing about this,' he eventually said. 'Try the Belgian, if you can find him.'

'It began some time before he came and stayed with you. Have you changed the encryption on your wireless internet at any point in the last months?'

'No,' said Shahid, unthinkingly – before realising he had just been tricked into giving up a perfect defence. If his internet access had been open, the traffic might have been nothing to do with him. He sighed. 'It is encrypted and I am the only person who had the password. As you know, I let the Belgian use my internet access but not my computer.'

'You'll understand why this looks strange to us. You're under arrest as a terrorist suspect, now it looks as if you've been making all sorts of menaces on the internet, threatening your neighbours, scaring the living daylights out of them. Doesn't look too great, does it?'

'I'm starting to get used to being accused of things I didn't do,' said Shahid. 'I have no reason to believe you.' He crossed his arms and looked over at the one-way glass. Yet again he found himself wondering who might be on the other side and what they might be thinking.

'So who did this?'

'No idea,' said Shahid, and for the first time in their meeting, it seemed to Mill that he wasn't telling the whole truth.

87

The London centre for asylum and immigration tribunals, where cases concerning the immigration status of asylum-seekers to the UK are decided, was near Chancery Lane. Hearings took place in the complex of court rooms, where the judges shared offices and picked up their weekly paperwork, the whole building having the inconsistently decorated air and too-bright colours of underfunded public-sector work. There were times when the whole building seemed to smell of instant coffee. This was the place where the fate of Quentina Mkfesi was to be decided.

The hearings had a standard format. On the Monday, the judges – a separate inquisitorial service inside the Ministry of Justice – would cold-read a brief and hear evidence from the witnesses, represented by their lawyers, with the government's case for refusal of asylum being made by another lawyer. On Tuesday they would have more hearings. On Wednesday they would go home and begin to read up on the case. On Friday they would make a decision and write up their judgment, which would determine whether or not the applicant would be allowed to remain in the UK.

It followed from this that the allocation of judge for an asylum applicant was crucial. So although Quentina Mkfesi didn't know it, her entire future – the next few years of it anyway – hung on the identity of which of two members of HM

Government's immigration and asylum service would be assigned to deal with her case.

On Monday 22 September, Alison Tite and Peter McAllister, both of them immigration judges, arrived at work within thirty seconds of each other. They shared an office on the second floor of the building, clumsily partitioned so that it shared a window with another office. Both of them were carrying coffee, hers a cappuccino in a styrofoam cup from the small Italian deli down the road, his a gigantic milky drink from the Starbucks by Chancery Lane Tube station.

Alison Tite was a thirty-seven-year-old barrister with two small children, married to an actuary, who had initially practised family law, but who had then drifted into immigration work because she wearied of the set cast of characters in her former field, and of the intensely personal bitternesses involved. Immigration work felt more connected to the larger currents of history, which she found more satisfying. Her favourite part of the cases was always the two days she spent reading background information on the specific case files. A recent example: she read *The Kite Runner* as background to a lurid case about a would-be Afghan refugee whose brother had been stoned to death and whose family shop had been firebombed and then confiscated. Or so he said; there was something convincingly Taliban-like about that sequence, arson before confiscation, and Alison allowed his appeal. Alison liked the feeling that the man in front of her, or woman or child, came as the representative of a world, of a way of life, and she needed to understand that world to make a judgment about whether that man/woman/child should be allowed to stay or had to be deported. Her favourite book was *We Wish to Inform You that Tomorrow We Will Be Killed with Our Families*.

The great flaw in the system was that deportation did not mean deportation. In almost all cases it was not legal to return the asylum-seeker home to Sudan, Afghanistan, Zimbabwe, or wherever. In most instances, the asylum-seeker packed off on a plane would face torture or death or both. That was wrong and, more importantly to the system, illegal under European human rights law. So failed asylum-seekers couldn't be allowed to stay legally: they could not work or claim a full range of citizens' benefits from the state. And yet they couldn't be sent back to the country they had come from. Even from the most realistic, least idealistic perspective, it could not be seen as an ideal solution. In practice, what happened to the failed asylum-seekers was that they were sent to detention centres.

Alison knew that the main thing about the system was not her opinion of it, and within the constraints of her power, she did what she could to be as fair as possible. If she was the judge on an applicant's case, that applicant stood a much better than average chance of winning the right to remain legally in the UK. She had one other thing going for her: she could write very well. That meant that although the percentage of her cases granted PRR (permanent right to remain) stood out as high, when her judgments were read, they were difficult to challenge. When her name was on the docket, the asylum-seeker's barrister cheered up, and the Home Office's groaned, and reached for the Red Bull.

Today it was Alison who was groaning. She had period pains, her youngest child had earache and had woken her three times the night before, her sister had invited herself down to stay for the weekend and in consequence had inflicted a double load of everything – cooking, cleaning, washing up, commiserating, hand-holding, and complaining about schools and husbands. The result of all this was that for Alison, in a way she would have admitted to almost nobody, being at work was a relief, verging on an outright pleasure. Gang-raped Somalis, tortured Syrians, genitally mutilated Kikuyu activists, Chinese gangmasters claiming to be political dissidents: bring 'em all on. Not a single one needed to be given Calpol, or told that they still didn't look a day over thirty. When she arrived in her office, a fat file, tied with the traditional ribbon – the ribbon that always made her think of other people's fingers, and all the things those fingers must have done – was already on her desk.

Peter McAllister sat on the other side of the same desk, with the same degree of non-view out of the semi-window. He was stretching his arms as far back and up as they would go, and his pinstripe suit was riding up. He was looking a bit porky, Alison felt; as if whatever horse-riding-type exercise he was taking at the weekend was not keeping at bay the effect of his eating and drinking during the week. Her first impression of him, two years earlier, was that he looked like a privileged man passing into early middle age with his early assumptions and prejudices entirely intact. That impression was accurate: that was exactly who Peter McAllister was. He had been to Radley and St Andrews, had been a pupil under an old friend of his father's, had gone into commercial law but had disliked using his brain quite so ferociously, so had ended up here, where his moral certainty was useful. He was a member of the Tory party and he and his wife, who was the one with the money, were back-and-forthing about whether he could put himself up for a constituency at the next election: realistically, he would probably do best to fight a Labour safe seat this time, then bag a winnable one next time round. He'd be in his early forties then; with a following wind, he'd be a minister within a few years, and after that, you never knew. In the mean time, he was fighting the good fight by injecting the traditional values of Englishness into an immigration system which was always in danger of 'producer capture'. The people who worked with immigrants always ran the risk of coming to believe that they worked for the immigrants. That was a mistake Peter never made. He remembered who paid his salary.

He did not rule for the government (he would have said, for the taxpayer) in every case, but he did often enough to mean that his and Alison's judgments more or less cancelled each other out. They got on perfectly well, discussed work in neutral terms and mainly when it concerned technical points of law, and never socialised.

'So what have you got?' said Peter, unwrapping his own brief, after he'd finished the yawn induced by his stretch. 'I'm not at all in the mood today, rode ten miles cross-country at Josie's dad's place last night and I'm so stiff I can hardly move. Getting too old for it. So what's on?'

Alison had scanned the first page of her brief.

'Saudi dissident. You?'

'Some Zimbabwean woman. Quentina something.'

88

Roger came downstairs in the late morning to find that the post consisted of three bills and a mysterious A5 envelope. It had something in it, something that wasn't a book or a CD. He pulled the envelope open and his head jerked back when he saw what was inside: a dead blackbird, rigid with rigor mortis. The bird was starting to smell. With it was a card with the usual words written on it: 'We Want What You Have'. He threw it in the kitchen bin. The perfect start to the day.

The sheer unfairness of life. That was the thing that Roger couldn't get out of his mind, couldn't stop thinking about. The sheer unfairness of life.

He had done his job. He hadn't been flaky or negligent. If he were to be completely honest – if you were to strap him down and pull out his fingernails – he might admit that there had been a passage of time when he was a tiny bit absent minded, a tiny bit floaty, a tiny bit prone to spending the odd hour here or there thinking about how nice it would be to be bending Matya over his desk and taking her from behind. But that had only been for a while and was in any case no worse than anyone else. It was all as if he was being punished for a crime – and what had he ever done wrong, apart from having a deputy who was a crook and a sociopath? It just wasn't fair.

The worst of it was the maths. The Younts' outgoings were still what they had been. Two houses to run and maintain, neither of them cheap, clothes and holidays, Arabella's completely out-of-control discretionary spending – he'd given her a semi-lecture on the subject a few days after he was sacked, and the net effect of that was that she went out with Saskia, got drunk and came back in a taxi with four colossal bags of new clothes, to cheer herself up. Talking to Arabella about money was like trying to talk to a child about nuclear physics. There were the cars, the service costs which seemed to bleed out of them – by chance he'd just had the car insurance and travel insurance bills in the last few days, which had caused him to go and look at the house insurance contracts, which were apocalyptically expensive, even given the fact that they'd shelled out for the also-apocalyptically-expensive burglar alarm and home security – laundry and haircuts and taxis and piano lessons for Conrad and swimming lessons ditto, and food and wine and Arabella's personal trainer and a constant haemorrhage of house bills for carpets and chairs and kitchen equipment and who knew what, and nursery fees for Conrad in the mornings combined with Matya who was lovely, who was the incarnation of loveliness, but who was not cheap, when you drilled down into what she cost the Younts and allowed for the fact that if they let her go they would be saving some serious cash.

Money coming in, money pouring out had been a source of anxiety to Roger even back in the days when money actually was coming in. This, though, took that to another level. This was Apocalypse Now. The money was still going out – gushing out like a bust tap – but it wasn't coming in. Zero. Zilch. Nada. The big egg. Zip. Sweet FA.

The other possibility was going to get a job. Of course that was the first thing Roger had thought of. He wasn't going to just sit there on his arse, not him. That wasn't the stuff the Younts were made of. He called an old chum from school who now ran a headhunting company, and tried to put a few feelers out. But that experiment in testing the water had gone badly; very badly. The first warning had been just how hard it was to get Percy on the phone. He'd called five times in two days. Finally he'd rung and the phone had been answered by a different secretary – Percy's PA must have been away from her desk – and he'd said 'it's a personal call' with just enough negligent public-school authority for her to put him straight through. When he got through, Percy had been reserved. No, strike that: he'd been outright shifty. He had treated Roger like a down-and-out trying to touch him for money.

'Old boy,' said Percy. 'Always so good to hear from you.'

'I won't beat about it, Perce – I'm looking for work. I've had a spot of bother with Pinker Lloyd. You might have heard some chat. Somebody stuck his fingers in the till and because he worked in my department, they're trying to stick it on me. My plan is, get another job and then sue the bollocks off them. I mean, really take them to the cleaners. The advice I'm getting is, we'll be talking seven figures.' This was a flat lie. Roger had been so demoralised and taken aback that he hadn't even spoken to his solicitor about what happened – and the fact was that the bank's employment contracts were drafted in such a way that he would be unlikely to see any cash at all. Another of life's lavish unfairnesses, but not one he was about to share with his old school semi-friend. 'Anyway, I don't want to spend the rest of my life on my rear end counting out the settlement and living off the interest on the interest, so I thought perhaps we'd have a chat, see what's knocking around out there?'

'It's good to have a plan,' said Percy. 'Absolutely. Very good.' Then he paused. He was doing that thing of pretending to have answered Roger's question, even though he knew perfectly well that he hadn't.

'So I was wondering if we might put something in the diary,' said Roger, advancing over the parapet of his own desperation.

'Quite so, quite so. Absolutely,' said Percy. 'Only – well, I hate to play this card. May I speak to you as an old pro?'

'That's why I've come to you.'

'Experience teaches that there are some times when it's best to let the market come to you. I know you're a trader at heart, Roger' – he knew nothing of the sort, not least because it was entirely untrue – 'and I know you're a go-and-get-'em type. Like to make your own weather. Create your own reality. A strength, a great strength. Really. In normal times. But – well, there's a bit of a but knocking around at the moment. Not just the Pinker Lloyd thing but the market in general. Lehmans was a horrible shock. It's pandemonium out there. People are wondering who's next. They're wondering what's going to jump out of the cupboard and shout Boo! And this doth not for a hiring climate make. Nobody's taking anybody new on. Nobody feels too sure about being kept on themselves. You follow me? Bad time to go looking for work – don't want to seem desperate. Very off-putting. I tell my clients, it's like sex. More desperate you are, more likely you are to have to pay for it! See my point? In your shoes, best course of action is not to act. Not just now. Let it shake down a bit. Dust settles. I tell my client, dust always settles – though it can take longer than you think. Best all round, eh?'

'I thought that in this case—' Roger managed.

'That's just it, though, Roger,' said Percy. 'This is the case. It's all a question of timing. Long and short of it, speaking both as a pro in the field and as your old mucker, best to lie low for a bit. Trust me.'

And that was that. Percy hadn't so much given him the brush-off as picked him up bodily by his belt and collar and slammed him head first into a wall. This was made much, much worse by the fact that while Percy was an utterly obnoxious excuse for a human being, exceptionally vile and greed-crazed even by the standards of City headhunters, than which no form of life was generally agreed to be more low – he did know his field. If what he was saying, in effect, was that no one would touch Roger with the nozzle of a septic tank suction hose, then no one would touch Roger with the nozzle of a septic tank suction hose. He wouldn't be wrong about that.

This meant that Roger would be ill-advised to send out his CV and start touting for work. There was nothing for it except to make massive cuts in expenditure and try and make the cash in their current and savings accounts last as long as possible. Those balances stood at around £30,000 and Roger knew – was horrified to know it, but knew it nonetheless – that at current rates of expenditure the money wouldn't last two months. Then they would be into his savings, the various assets wrapped in various tax-free devices over the years, and then into his pension fund. In the City, there was a term for this. It was called 'being completely fucked'.

So there was nothing for it except massive cutbacks in expenditure, starting right now. Action this day! Right now meant today, meant this very hour. Preferably this minute. Showdown with Arabella and then full-scale lockdown on expenditure. The thing was, though, that Roger felt that he didn't want to do that; couldn't face it. What he wanted to do, it turned out, was to log on to something called the White Shirt Specialists, which had a new offer where you could order three gorgeous white shirts for £400, a considerable saving from the normal price of nearer £500. Roger had been thinking about this saving, holding it back for a rainy day, and now here was the rainy day and Roger felt himself browsing a range of subtly different collar and sleeve and button and cuff designs, and also the question of monograms, which often struck him as vulgar but which in this case could be made delightfully understated, white on white. He found himself wondering if it were really true that the shirts could be made to fit perfectly with only the requested measurements of height, age, weight and collar size. There was something depressing – or maybe it was liberating? – about the fact that your physique boiled down to just these four measurements. That was all it took to sum you up: 41, 96 kg, 1.90 m, size 17 collar = Roger Yount.

The internet was, in these days when he was getting used to the numb shock of being sacked, unemployable and on the way to broke, Roger's salvation; or if not his salvation, exactly, it was what he did with most of his time. His favourite thing was reading pieces about the implosion of Lehman Brothers – the amazing idiots, the total fuckwits – and his second-favourite was playing poker online. When he had been in work, supervising a room full of traders all week and therefore responsible for tens of millions of pounds of, in effect, bets, this had had no appeal. Now, though, it was as if the gambling side of his personality needed an outlet, and found it here. He had put £1,000 from his credit card into his Poker Stars account, and was already up by £500. He was loose and aggressive against a lot of amateurs who played tight-weak. It was fun.

Then, five days after talking to Percy, Roger pulled himself together. He went for a walk on the Common, had a double espresso, got his spreadsheet and reran the numbers. Then he called Arabella on the house phone and asked her to come into his study to see him. That, they both knew, meant a Money Talk. It helped that the room had two leather armchairs and a (largely token) cigar humidor, and a vintage nude print of a Parisian whore kneeling on a chair facing away from the viewer, exposing her temptingly large, temptingly white behind. Once his wife came in, Roger simply gave her a sheet of paper with a list of things on it – all her discretionary spending, from shoes to Botox to one-on-one home-visit Pilates instruction.

'These are all the things which are going to have to go,' said Roger. It was satisfying. Arabella went pale.

'We're broke,' she said.

'No. Or yes. As good as, in some respects.'

In a deep dark part of Roger's brain, one he was reluctant to admit to himself, this felt great. Felt fantastic. It was payback – hard to work out exactly why, but it definitely felt as if it was – for what she had done at Christmas.

And then a thought came to Arabella.

'What about Matya?' she said. Roger had known this was coming and had prepared for it. His countess, his lost countess. A masochism strategy, but one that would hurt Arabella more than it would hurt him.

'We're going to have to let her go,' said Roger. 'It's clear from the numbers. Matya is a luxury' – a voluptuous, silky, heart-lifting luxury, a sexier woman and a better mother to our children than you will ever be and the woman I would happily have made love to twice a day for the rest of my natural life – '... a luxury we can't afford.'

'Oh,' said Arabella.

'Yes, that's right,' said Roger. 'So you're going to have to be mummy. All night, all day. The whole deal. It's in the numbers – we have no choice.'

'Oh,' said Arabella again. In his head Roger was dancing a gloating, jeering tarantella of victory.

89

It happened very quickly. The Younts gave Matya her notice. The agreed period was a month; Matya said she was sad, but understood. So in a few weeks' time she would stop working for them, and Arabella would be a 24/7 solo mother for the first time.

When she heard the news – Roger and Arabella sitting across from her at the kitchen table with cups of tea that she had made, while the boys sat in the media room watching a DVD of Shaun the Sheep – Matya felt nothing at all. She had known that Roger had lost his job. It would have been impossible not to know: from one day to the next he had gone from being invisible at home to being omnipresent. Roger's size made him hard to ignore: in the most basic way, he took up a lot of space. His noise footprint was large. The house seemed immediately smaller. He was constantly in the kitchen, crashing up the stairs to his study to listen to his punk compilation CD at a too-high volume. From wearing, in the week, nothing but classic suits, he was now never to be found in anything except a dressing gown or horrible knee-length khaki shorts with huge sagging pockets. He was always offering to help, and, Matya could not fail to notice, never missed an opportunity to check her out, especially from behind, and especially especially when she had to bend over to stack the dishwasher, load the washing machine, or do anything with the children. It was a bit much.

Knowing that Roger had suddenly and dramatically lost his

job, it wasn't hard to work out that her job was likely not to be long in following. So as soon as Arabella had asked her for 'a little chat', Matya had suspected what was coming. It was later, in the course of the afternoon, that she began to think about what it really meant. She would be traipsing around looking for work – something she hadn't done for some time, and about which she had no illusions. It would be a boring ordeal of smiling and making nice while trying to work out if the prospective employers were sane and reliable and whether their children were the kind she could imagine looking after for nine hours a day. That was a chore but she knew it was one she could do, because she had done it before. The thing which made it worse was that her flat-share had finished and she was having to look for somewhere new to live. That, in London, was more than a chore – the actual physical process of looking, the Tubes and buses and the trudging around, the small ads and want ads and Craigslist-surfing and free-sheet-poring, the texts and appointments and interviews, the vetting of addresses and then rooms and then flatmates, all of it, was exhausting, depressing, remorseless, one of those things which made you feel the oppressive scale of London – but again, it was something she knew. She had done it before.

What she hadn't done before, what was unknown, was leaving Joshua. All day she tried not to think about it; all day it was on the edge of her mind. She could feel a great pit of gloom opening up beneath her. Who could resist a three-year-old, bursting with love, whose idea of complete happiness was to come and snuggle up with you? Their love affair wasn't in the early stages any more – it wasn't quite in early-dates territory; her heart didn't skip a beat when she saw him – but she was happier with Joshua than she had been with anyone else she had ever known. Matya was aware that this was connected with her childhood: she was redis-covering her lost parents through the love she was able to express for Joshua. It was a way of getting her parents' love back, of re-incarnating them inside herself. But so what? Who cared what the reasons were? What was real was the feel of his hand in hers when they went out in the afternoon to pick up Conrad from primary school. Or the calm, measured way in which he would look upward and say, 'I love you, Matty' – and the words had more impact than they ever had from a boyfriend.

So that was what hit her when she got home to the flat at half past six. Unusually, she closed the latch on the door behind her. She sat on the small odd leather sofa – a gift from Arabella, who had bought it for her dressing room and then gone off it – and put her head in her hands and cried. Not for her job or for the other changes in her life, but for Joshua, who she knew she would miss so unbearably much.

90

There was a rattle – a now-familiar rattle – and Shahid's breakfast was pushed through the slot in the door of his cell. Shahid
had been sitting on the floor, not thinking about anything much,
since saying his dawn prayers. He had a watch now, but 'dawn'
here meant whenever Shahid woke up. That usually wasn't much
after six. Breakfast arrived at seven, so there was a decent gap to
sit and think.

Shahid thought about Iqbal and how stupid he'd been to let
him into his flat. He wondered where he was. He hoped that
when the police found him they would kick the living shit out of
him.

He thought about what he would do to the person responsible
for We Want What You Have when he got hold of him.

He thought about the cell, how he had never known any room
he had been in as well as he knew this one. He wondered if a
time would come when it wasn't still imprinted on his mind,
every detail of it: a crack in the corner of the ceiling and small
fibrous marks on the walls which spread down and outwards so
that they looked like the map of a river delta. A patch of damp
to the left of the sink which was sometimes cold and wet to the
touch. The pipes, which made a rackety clanking noise that at
times almost fell into a rhythm, a syncopation – clunk BANG,
clank clunk BANG.

He thought about Mrs Principle the solicitor, as he called her to himself. She had the kind of upright, strict, buttoned-up and clipped British manner which made it impossible not to speculate about her sex life. It would be something kinky, definitely, it had to be. Spanking perhaps. Or she dressed up in leather and wielded a whip and made men crawl around the floor saying 'Yes, mistress.'

Shahid thought about his own sex life – whether he would ever have one again. He had never felt his sex drive so absent. Maybe it was true, maybe they did put something in the food. But he knew that when/if he got out, he would like to have A Girlfriend. He didn't have anything more specific in mind than that. A nice well-brought-up Muslim girl, a virgin, incredibly keen on sex, would be ideal. But it was more a question of someone to hang out with, to wake up with, to watch TV with, to go clubbing with, to go to Gap and pick out T-shirts with. A girl. That girl from the Underground, the one he'd tried to find via 'Lost Connections', the one he still sometimes thought about.

He thought about Ahmed and Rohinka and Mohammed and Fatima and was able to admit that he envied his fat, slow, sedentary, cautious older brother.

He thought about Mrs Kamal and was almost able to smile at the idea of what she must be putting everyone else in the family through. Also any policemen or lawyers or anybody else who got within earshot.

He thought about what he was going to do with the rest of his life when/if he got out of here. Sue them for wrongful imprisonment, for abusing his rights, for locking him up for no reason . . . that was one thing he could do. But Shahid knew that he wouldn't. He felt time passing here, felt it strongly, more sharply than he ever had. Time going past, purely going past. It was a paradox of the place. You were locked up, and every day was the same, and nothing happened except the same questions being put to you and you giving the same answers back, so every day was a slow-motion wallow in itself, every hour felt days long – it was so far beyond boring that it was a whole other state. And yet it made you aware, cruelly aware, of how time was shooting past. Shahid could feel his life slipping away. He was thirty-three, and what had he done? How big a hole would there be in the world if he never got out of here? He needed to do something – get back into proper work, not the shop, but go back and finish his degree and get a real job, have a real life.

He thought about the fact that this was his nineteenth day in jail, the nineteenth day since he'd been arrested.

And then he thought about breakfast. It would be cold by now, but then it was never much more than tepid when it came through the door. Today it was scrambled eggs and toast. The eggs had been overcooked, so they were granular and smelled faintly of sulphur. One piece of toast had a very thin layer of butter, barely a scraping, and the other had a compensatory smear of butter about half an inch thick. The tea was undrinkable even when it was hot, so Shahid ignored it as he ate the cold food, much more slowly than he would have done at home.

Some police and warders you heard coming, others you didn't. This was the second kind. There was a scraping and the cell door was opened by a policeman with a huge circular keyring, a cartoon-like keyring, in his left hand.

'Ready?' said the policeman.

Shahid shrugged. 'For what?' This was his new thing – wherever possible, to answer a question with a question.

'Got your stuff together?'

'For what? What are you talking about?'

'Didn't they tell you?' Now the policeman seemed to be playing the same question-with-a-question game.

'Does it look like they told me? Whatever it is?'

'Oh.' The policeman gave a short bark-like laugh. 'Now that,

that really is typical. You're getting out today. In fact, right now. Your brief and your family are here to pick you up.'

Shahid did not think it was possible for a thought, a feeling, to be so strong a physical sensation. He felt his heart race, his head fill with blood, he jerked upright and knocked the table, hard, with his thighs. The undrinkable tea spilled on the floor of his cell.

'You're joking.'

But the policeman was enjoying the fact of the cock-up so much that there was no possibility he was joking. The cock-up had confirmed his world-view, and in the process made him very happy.

'Typical, that is. Whatever it is, whoever it most concerns, that's the person they never tell. Don't get around to telling. Typical. Classic. That's this place all over.'

Shahid picked up his prayer shawl, his prayer mat, his Qur'an, his toothbrush, and his sweater. He pulled on his shoelaceless trainers.

'I'm ready,' he said.

'Typical,' said the policeman one last time, not to Shahid but to the air at large, still happily shaking his head. He led Shahid out of the cell, down the corridors Shahid was starting to know so well, and to the lift. They went down four floors to an office with a counter, on top of which Shahid's tracksuit bottoms – the ones he'd been wearing when he was arrested – were sitting. The custody sergeant, a fat man with cold eyes, gave him a clipboard with a form to sign, and he signed it. Then the other policeman led him through a glass-metal-mesh door and there were Ahmed, Usman, Rohinka, Mrs Kamal and Mrs Principle, all of them jumping to their feet as soon as they saw him and all of them looking worried, happy, shiny-eyed. Then Shahid's own eyes began to blur too.

'Who's running the shop?' he tried to say, but his voice

cracked halfway through and it came out as a sob, as Shahid burst into tears.

91

It sometimes seemed to Rohinka as if she got no sleep at all – literally none, ever. She knew that she must, of course, because if she didn't – if she literally never went out, not for a second – she would by now have died or gone mad. But there were times when those two states didn't seem all that far away. And as for the fact that she never slept, well, one sign of it was that whenever Fatima came into the room in the morning – any time from half past five – Rohinka could hear her coming. Perhaps it was only that she was so attuned to her daughter's waking that the first footfall woke her from her shallow, expectant sleep. That was more likely, Rohinka supposed. Not that it felt as if it made much difference: either way, all day and every day, she was on the ragged edge of exhaustion.

She was always already awake by the time her daughter came in the room and began her patented three-step process for rousing her mother: first, for about a minute, simply stand beside the bed – very very close to the edge of the bed, ideally about a quarter-inch or so – and wait for the first sign of life. Second, begin to tap her mother on the shoulder with the flat of her hand, a cross between a tap and a pat, not violent, respectful even, but firm, insistent. Third, she would simply clamber over Rohinka, using her as a climbing-obstacle-cum-plaything like something at the recreation centre, and launch herself into the gap in the bed beside her. By that point there was no longer any mileage for Rohinka in pretending to be asleep.

Today was the same. She heard Fatima coming from the landing, her feet light but purposeful, in no hurry – she knew what she was doing. Mohammed, in his cot in their room, showed no sign of waking, as he tended not to do – a blessing, Rohinka supposed. At 5.30 a.m., one child was enough.

So today was the same as always. But today was different too, because today was the day that Mrs Kamal was taking a plane back to Lahore. Usman would be travelling with her, a trip with several overlapping agendas: he would help Mrs Kamal with the journey (though anyone less in need of help Rohinka couldn't think of – still, her notional frailty had sometimes to be deferred to); he was himself claiming that he wanted to 'chill out in Lahore for a bit'; and he had succumbed to his mother's bullying to go and meet some potential marriage partners. Well, maybe it would work out for him. Usman had not been quite himself recently. Not that he spoke more, or showed more interest in the children, or anything like that, but he was less angry and more preoccupied. He had trimmed his beard and stopped irritating Ahmed by pretending to refuse to serve alcohol. Perhaps it was no more than that he was growing up a little.

As soon as Fatima came in the room and stood by the bed, Rohinka did something which amazed her daughter: she got up.

'Mummy!' said Fatima. 'What are you doing?!'

'Mamaji leaves today,' said her mother. 'There's lots to do. You can help me.'

'Shall I go and wake her up?'

Fatima, for all her indefatigability, her unstoppability, her take-no-prisoners approach to life, was very wary of her grandmother. (Who, predictably, doted on Mohammed.) She did not go into her room uninvited. It was tempting to let Fatima be Mrs Kamal's early-morning alarm call; tempting, but probably not a great idea. Woken up in the wrong way, Mrs Kamal could start her last day in a bad mood and colour her departure for everyone. For a moment, Rohinka allowed herself to think about how nice it would be to get her home back: to get past that sense of always having somebody in your space. No one to encounter on a midnight trip to the bathroom, no one to hide birth-control medication from, no one extra to have to cook for or wash up after or do laundry for; it would be nice to have Mohammed back in his room, nice to just have their home back to themselves. Normality had never seemed more attractive. Only the four of them – even the thought felt like a long, relieving exhale.

'Best stay with me. Or go downstairs and see what Daddy is doing.'

Fatima nodded, her expression serious: she had a mission. She moved around to her father's side of the bed and got in.

An hour and a half later and they were all in the kitchen, good to go. Even Shahid, who under the circumstances could be forgiven for lying in and giving the occasion a miss, was there. He had been out of custody for three days and was still giddily happy – the main symptom being that he couldn't stop talking. He had lost weight in jail, five or six kilos, and what with the fresh shave and haircut he'd had on getting out, was suddenly much more handsome. In fact he now looked like someone out of a film, a lean dark good-looking stranger with a past. If it had been him going to Lahore, Rohinka would be willing to bet that he wouldn't come back single. Now he was sitting next to Fatima, coaxing her to eat her breakfast cereal by pretending to take huge mouthfuls of it himself, then flying it to her mouth making aeroplane noises. Mrs Kamal was sitting next to him, arranging her passport and plane ticket and other documentation on the table in front of her. On the other side of her was Mohammed in his high chair, barely awake. He was not cranky, but he was also not fully conscious, and he was making no attempt to eat or to interact with anyone: sitting there slumped sideways, chubby and skimpy-haired, he had the air of a Sultan recovering from a heavy lunch. Next to him his father too looked tired, and the coincidence made them look very alike; the resemblance, which Rohinka sometimes could and sometimes couldn't see, was unmistakable. They looked like twins with a thirty-five-year age gap.

Mrs Kamal snapped her handbag closed.

'It's time,' she said.

'Usman's brought the car round,' said Ahmed. The two brothers would take their mother to the airport; Shahid had an appointment with Mrs Strauss the solicitor. They went into their farewells, and then came out in front of the shop, where Usman sat at the wheel of the Sharan with its hazard lights blinking. Ahmed loaded Mrs Kamal's bag into the back of the people carrier. She had two suitcases and the biggest wheelie carry-on bag Rohinka had ever seen: with its handle extended, it was almost as tall as she was.

Standing in front of her mother-in-law, Rohinka felt a wave of the very last thing she had expected: affection. She had seen what Mrs Kamal had been like when Shahid was locked up, and would never forget it. She hoped Fatima and Mohammed would never be in trouble of that scale; if they ever were, she hoped she could live up to her mother-in-law's example. But this wasn't easy to put into words, and she made no attempt to begin. Perhaps she didn't have to. Mrs Kamal stood in front of her, gripped her arm and said with an amused, knowing look, like a character actor taking applause at a curtain call:

'Daughter. It has been eventful.' And then Mrs Kamal turned to get into the car, saying, 'And now time to see about that upgrade.'

Part Four

November 2008

92

What's the worst that can happen? Roger had always thought that was a stupid question. If you had difficulty imagining how bad things could become, all that meant was that you didn't have much imagination.

There was no need to ask Roger's former colleagues at Pinker Lloyd what was the worst that could happen. It was fantastic: the entire bank had gone under. The scandal about the rogue trader in Roger's department had not been huge, but it had been just big enough to start rumours about the bank, which had caused people to take a sceptical look at the books just at the moment when capital markets were freaking out after the implosion of Lehman Brothers. People began to wonder about Pinker Lloyd's exposure to short-term loans and its reliance on borrowing money cheaply, easily and quickly on the international money market. Credit dried up overnight: lenders withdrew their loans, clients withdrew their money, they had to ask the Bank of England for help, the Bank dithered and bingo, Pinker Lloyd was out of business. The bank had gone into receivership; its assets were being parcelled out and sold off; and everybody lost their jobs. Lothar had been publicly humiliated. Roger was thrilled. It couldn't have happened to a nicer group of people.

So he ought to have been in a good mood, but now 51 Pepys Road was on the market. The asking price was £3.5 million. The estate agent, Travis, had told him that the price was a little 'toppy', but that 'they might as well go for it', on the basis that 'what's the worst that can happen?'

Roger found that he hated everything about selling the house. He hated Travis, especially his voice – not his accent, he was used to all sorts of accents in the City, but his voice, which was flat, scratchy, affectless but wheedling. Most of all, he hated him for the fact that he felt entitled to have opinions and give advice – he announced that he was loving the way you've done the kitchen, praised the clever use of natural light in the sitting room, said there was something a little bit tired about Roger's study but that that wasn't such a bad thing given how nice the rest of the house was – it left them something to improve and gave it a bit of a blank canvas feeling. Travis was an avid fan of TV property programmes and felt at ease with the culture of wandering around other people's houses and passing judgement on them.

As did most of the people who came to look at 51 Pepys Road – not that people said things out loud, except in the most egregious cases, but Roger could tell that they were thinking them, and that was bad enough. They looked, they snooped, they ogled, they judged. Roger could hear their little brains whirring. Why are they selling? Wonder why the husband's around the house. Wonder where they're moving to. Wonder what price they'll accept. Wonder whether those pots are Lucie Rie. Snoop snoop whirr, went their little brains. Many, a significant minority, perhaps even a majority, were blatantly there to do nothing except sniff around the house out of vulgar curiosity. Travis claimed that he 'weeded out the time-wasters', but this was clearly not true, and when the obvious non-starters came to peek into his life, Roger struggled with the temptation to tell them right there on the doorstep to just fuck off. There was even a couple from down the street who came one day to poke around. They clearly hadn't been expecting to be recognised by the owners. Travis was showing them around, but just to freak them out,

Roger followed behind them, glaring, arms crossed, while the estate agent did his spiel. They were in and out of there in ten minutes flat.

'Travis, those people already live in this street,' Roger said, biting back something much ruder.

'Oops, my bad,' said Travis, clearly not thinking it any fault of his. 'Some people, eh? Still, got a couple of good 'uns for you this afternoon.'

It was not that the house did not get offers. It did, immediately – meaning on the first day, from the very first people to look at it. Not that the offer was real, of course. Or rather it was real in the sense that its intention was sincere, but the money simply wasn't there. These were people who would a. have to sell their own house for a lot more than they'd paid for it and b. have to arrange a gigantic mortgage before they were in a position to even think about offering for 51 Pepys Road – in fact they shouldn't, given the realities of the situation, even have been looking. Travis, full of nonsense as he was in almost every respect, turned out to be surprisingly tough about the question of what offers to take seriously. No doubt because it bore on the question of whether he'd actually get paid his commission. 'Don't even think about them,' he'd told Roger. 'Unless the money's real, it's not worth it.'

Maybe they could actually afford it though . . . and that truly was a galling thought. Roger's earlier, pre-Christmas-2007-bonus-fiasco, pre-sacking self was not far from being that person who could unthinkingly afford a £3.5 million house. That person felt as if he had died a long time ago; or rather like Roger's long-lost and not much missed younger brother.

What Roger hated most about all this house fandango was that it was insane. No one could make a rational judgement about a decision of that size so quickly, after a twenty-minute viewing. But this air of madness seemed to be general. The whole process had a frenzy to it – everybody seemed in a rush, everybody was somehow heated up. It verged on the sexual. The thoughtful ones – the ones whose caution stood out, who were obviously more deliberate and grown-up – came and looked at the house twice for maybe a total of forty minutes. For the biggest financial decision they were ever likely to make in their lives – forty minutes. It all made Roger think about those postcards that said 'We Want What You Have'. He'd like to track down whoever it was who sent them, jam the postcard into his mouth, and say, OK, fine, I'll swap your life for mine, sight unseen – just to see the look on the little shit's face.

Arabella, on the other hand, was rather enjoying the house being on the market. There was something very satisfying about the business of making the house nice as a way of adding to its value. Doing things to prettify the house was a sensible and practical necessity – it was a way of 'maximising the value of their most important capital asset', a phrase Arabella remembered from the time Roger had used it to justify pulling up the floorboards to put in new wiring for his home entertainment system. It went without saying that no house was perfect in and of itself. There were always little things to be done. Arabella bought a new bedside table and took the old one to the dump, and in her opinion made the bedroom much nicer, more saleable, just by doing that. Obviously she did that without telling Roger; equally obviously he didn't notice. She longed – longed – to get rid of the Christmas sofa, a grey modern piece which looked lovely at the showroom but was just somehow wrong in their drawing room; but Roger would probably spot that change. Nothing could have irritated Roger more than seeing Arabella take a bizarre kind of pleasure in primping and tarting up the house prior to selling it. If her behaviour had been specifically designed to drive him round the bend – which in some moments was what Roger suspected – it couldn't have been more perfectly calculated.

'The plan is,' Arabella said to Saskia over drinks in the bar at a restaurant where the bar was called The Library, 'flog the house, move to Minchinhampton for a bit. That's on the market too but it'll take longer to sell – so we're told, anyway. Then the plans diverge. Official plan, by which I mean Roger's plan, is that we sell Minchinhampton too, take the money and go and look for a' – she made quote marks with her fingers – '"small business opportunity" for Roger to set up shop then "do something real" by which he means . . . well, your guess is as good as mine. It has to be somewhere with good schools, primary anyway, and where the transport isn't too much of a nightmare.'

'Doesn't sound too much like you. Green wellies with Chanel, Audi four-by-four on the gravel, flirting with the stable boy – I suppose I can see it, just about.'

'Well, quite. The real plan, my plan, is, we go to the country, I get Minchinhampton looking nice, and take my time over it, and Roger gets enough of a chance to get the walking through the fields breathing fresh air out of his system, and realises he's going to die of boredom, and all the guff about somewhere the children can run around is absolute crap because the country's just as full of dangers as the town, more so, and then he notices that I'm so bored I'm about to run off with the Bikram Yoga teacher in the nearest market town, and he snaps out of it and by then all the Pinker Lloyd fuss has died down, and he sends out his CV and gets another proper job. None of this rubbish about moving to Ludlow to make widgets – a City job. Six-figure basic, seven-figure bonus in a good year. The way it's supposed to be.'

Saskia gestured for two more lychee martinis. The waiter bowed and glided.

'That sounds more sensible,' she said.

'Yes, and the good thing about this is that it's made my parents wake up a bit. They always thought that because Roger did what he did and because we live like we do – correction, we lived like we did – we were made of money. They thought we were rich instead of your typical London struggling well-off. So they've woken up to the realities a bit, and the fantastic thing is, they've offered to pay the boys' way through school – boarding school – we're resolved on that. At least I am. So all we have to do is get them through to eleven, and then Mama and Papa will do all the rest – prep school first and then somewhere decent. It's all a long way off but you do need a plan, don't you?'

The martinis arrived and the two women toasted each other. Across the room there was someone Arabella thought she recognised from TV. Or did she?

This lunch was a rare moment of luxury for Arabella, a rare glimpse of her old life. Josh was at his nursery, pick-up at 3.30, and Conrad was on a play date with a woman Arabella knew from NCT classes, who she'd reconnected with when bumping into her in the coffee shop. They hadn't seen each other for years. There was something of an ideological difference, or at least a certain human stickiness, about the fact that Polly had chosen to give up work while her children were young, whereas Arabella didn't work but also had full-time childcare. The thing about looking after young children was, you had to be cut out for it, and Arabella, quite simply and quite frankly – she said so herself – wasn't. Her boys were lovely, but they were all-consuming, and Arabella did not want to be all-consumed. And now here they were again, both pushing Bugaboos containing sleeping three-year-olds.

The first play date at Arabella's house had been a bit of a disaster because little Toby had had an incident in his knickers within ten minutes of being left there, and Arabella hadn't been able to face the prospect of wiping his bottom – so when Polly got back from the hairdressers two hours later, he was pretty ripe. Arabella said, 'Oh my God, that only just happened,' but Polly would, once she saw the evidence first-hand, have reasons to strongly suspect that wasn't true. Arabella's next text to Polly had been ignored and she'd thought she'd blown it, but a fortnight later she'd called up and set up this play date. They were, for all the minor differences, from the same tribe. Arabella was due to collect Conrad just before she had to pick Josh up.

It felt like the first treat she'd had in months. The full-time-mother thing was hard.

'Mrs Yount, so nice to see you again,' said the head waiter, arriving at the side of their table. He made to pick up the two menus, which neither woman had touched. 'Two set lunches?' he asked. Saskia nodded, and then he again bowed and glided.

'£34.50 for six courses,' said Saskia. 'You're practically stealing from them.'

93

It had got to the point where Patrick could no longer bear to go to any of the meetings concerning Freddy's future. Freddy's injury, Freddy's prognosis, Freddy's insurance claim, Freddy's future – they were all the same thing. If there were to be a single meeting which he knew in advance was going to be decisive, that would be different: Patrick could clench his teeth and get through it. But it was never like that. The insurance company's lawyers were always there, stalling, dodging, and driving up the wall even the other professionals who were supposed to be used to this kind of thing.

The result was that Patrick asked Mickey to go to the meetings on his and Freddy's behalf. He trusted Mickey. It was the man's evident upset over what was happening which had caused this. Patrick could see that Mickey felt just as miserable as he did and with that could see the truth, which was that however he might have begun his relationship with the Kamos – seeing Freddy as a club asset to be exploited and milked and cashed in on to the maximum possible extent – he had now come to the point where he loved Freddy. Patrick finally had someone he could be completely open with about his son's circumstances. So the strangest of things had happened and Patrick and Mickey had become, sort of, friends. They were not fully at ease with each other, and never would be – but on the subject of Freddy, they could be fully honest and open. Their relations had the freedom-within-boundaries of friendship.

'I have a favour to ask of you,' Patrick said. The two men were sitting downstairs watching Barcelona play Majorca in La Liga on a Sunday evening, while Freddy was upstairs in the games room. All three of them found it painful to watch football, and all three of them were continuing to do so out of principle and also out of the fear that if they ever gave the habit up, they might not get it back. 'I must ask if you will represent Freddy alone at these meetings. I find them too difficult. I can't go any more. Until there is real news.'

Mickey understood straight away what was being asked of him and what it implied.

'Of course I will do that, Patrick. It would be an honour.'

And so that's what Mickey had been doing – going to the meetings and soaking up the bullshit. In doing this, he had also been dishing out some stick. The absence of the Kamos allowed him to show just how upset he was, which meant it allowed him to be much angrier and much more explicit.

'Who the fuck do you think you are?' he said to the most senior of the four executives from the insurance company present at their last meeting. The senior one was the skinniest, as in corporate affairs these days was often the way. Next to him were two plumpish middle-manager types, Tweedledum and Tweedledee, one of whom was in charge of medical mumbo-jumbo and the other responsible for legal bullshit, and the fourth was a subordinate who, to judge from his contributions to meetings thus far, might have been deaf-mute. 'What the fuck do you think you're doing? You think Freddy Kamo's some jungle bunny who should piss off back to the bush and still be grateful he's got one good knee left? Is that it? You think he's some unfortunate loser who's so thick he isn't going to realise he has a valid, legally binding contract with you?'

'I find this extremely offensive,' said the man, starting to get up from his seat.

'Good. And you'll fucking well sit still and listen to it unless you want to be reading all about your refusal to pay out in the *Daily Mail* tomorrow morning. You move from where you're sitting and I'll take this as a sign that these negotiations are no longer proceeding in good faith. And I have to tell you that my sense of your good faith is pretty fucking tenuous. Which part of "legally binding" don't you understand?' Mickey picked up one of the folders of doctors' reports and waved it. 'This says, translated into English, "his knee is fucked". Which part of that don't you understand? How plain do you want it to be? His knee is fucked, there's a legally binding contract, and it's time for you to FUCKING PAY UP.'

Mickey felt better. He knew that the bluster would have no effect, but the threat to go public might. The negotiations were protected by a non-disclosure agreement, but if the insurance company could be shown to be behaving unreasonably he would be able to go public. What was happening behind the scenes, almost certainly, was that they were putting together the final details of the settlement they were prepared to make. This would involve Freddy not being allowed to play football ever again. His pay-out would be conditional on his retiring from football permanently – for the obvious reason that if they shelled out a huge amount of money to compensate him for not playing, he shouldn't subsequently go on to be paid for playing. Mickey had mentioned this to Patrick, who seemed to have taken it in, but he wasn't really sure: he didn't want to labour the point. People who knew him might laugh at the idea of Mickey trying not to labour a point, but the truth was, he didn't want to, because he didn't want to seem to be patronising Patrick. Who after all was not stupid, and who would realise what this meant: no more football for Freddy. Ever. He would be being paid not for doing the thing he loved, but for never doing it again. It was a hell of a thing for the boy to have to face, and Mickey was morally certain Patrick wouldn't have alerted his son to what might happen. The news itself would be hard enough to take: no point building up the badness too far in advance.

'I suspect you are well aware the medical evidence is much more complex than you are giving us leave to understand,' said the insurance man. 'Expert opinion about the condition of Mr Kamo's knees is not unanimous. As you know, these settlements often impose conditions on the subsequent career of a player and it would be cruel and reckless to see such conditions imposed on a man as young and talented as Mr Kamo without feeling certain that such constraints were warranted.' In other words, the man had guessed what Mickey was thinking. He was a complete bastard but he wasn't a stupid bastard.

Mickey stopped listening. Nothing was going to be decided today. What all of them were really doing was nothing but waiting for the meeting to be over. It was grey and damp outside, not cold, a typical English non-autumn day. Mickey loved football, and football had been good to him, but as he got older there were moments when he felt the cruelty of the game, its emphasis on luck, the brevity of its careers, the long afterlife of its heroes outliving their fame; the way a single bad thing could happen, and then everything was over. As it had happened to Freddy. He wasn't sure how much more of it he could take. Maybe something like property development was a cleaner racket after all.

94

Rain spattered against the window of the two-bedroom flat in Hackney where Parker French lived with his girlfriend Daisy, his perfect girlfriend. Where he lived with her for now, anyway. Parker didn't know it, but he was right on the verge of being dumped. The reason he didn't know it was the same reason he was on the verge of being dumped: because he was obsessed, oblivious, lost, locked-in, reckless, deaf. Daisy didn't know how to get through to him. She was sitting listening to music with a cup of tea and a list divided into two columns, Yes and No. The Yes column was full of negative items and featured words like 'blank', 'absent', 'down' and 'not here'. The No column had only one item in it: 'He used to be lovely'.

When Daisy went back over the chronology – which she often found herself doing, just to check and recheck her sense that she wasn't imagining things – there had been three phases. That was excluding Normal Parker, the boy she had been going out with ever since they kissed at a sixth-form dance on a hot June night back at sixth-form college. Normal Parker was her boyfriend's habitual sweet, boyish self; her boyfriend who needed more looking after than he realised, was more fragile in his confidence than he knew, was determined to make a mark but never quite clear how or when. He was a boyfriend but he was also at times a little like a younger brother; that wasn't a complaint, she liked that, and it went with his looks, his narrow dark looks, and it somehow also went with the fact that he was the exact same height as her. She knew that Parker was completely sincere about his desire to Get Away – meaning Get Away from Norfolk, from the world of their childhoods. That she had always believed in, utterly.

As for Parker's art, well . . . the important thing was that Parker believed in it. Parker would do something with his life, she felt sure about that. Whether that thing would be art was less plain. It wasn't clear to Daisy that Parker had any real feeling for the art world. This wasn't so much an issue about his talent, but his ability to read how that world worked; it was a long way away from Norfolk and it wasn't about being able to execute nice collages and your art teacher telling you you're the most gifted pupil in the class. Daisy's sense of the art world was that it was much more like a game, a deadly serious adult game, and that Parker hadn't quite realised how that game worked. But none of that really mattered to Daisy, his naivety was all part of Parker's Parkerness, and it was that about him that she loved and trusted. If he didn't do art then he'd do something else. All that was Normal Parker, Parker who she hadn't seen around for some months and whose existence took a conscious act of effort to recollect.

That was because there had been three successive different versions of Parker since. The first of them was Speechless With Grief Parker, the one who had emerged after he had suddenly been sacked – suddenly in his version of things, anyway, though in Daisy's experience there was no such thing as an entirely unforeshadowed dismissal, not unless you accidentally reversed your car over the boss's dog. But his sacking was sudden to Parker, and that was the main thing. For weeks he had been lost, gone, buried under his sense of grief and grievance. That had been sad, of course, and she had felt for him, but it had been ir- ritating too, not least because to Daisy, who was tougher than

Parker, the final responsibility for not getting sacked lay with the person doing the job. If you did get sacked there was, finally, no one to blame but yourself, so the best thing to do was to suck it up and get on with it. The fact that she couldn't say that made it all the more irritating, so she was pleased when, having taken Parker away for the Cotswold weekend in the spring to try and make him snap out of it, she found that he had, indeed, snapped out of it. Just like that: an idea or plan had hit him, and he had been like a different person. He was bouncy, he was full of vim and jokes, he was hopping up and down.

That was the birth of Manic Parker. This was someone she didn't recognise at all. He was fizzing with . . . with . . . Daisy didn't know quite what it was, but he was fizzing with something. She would wake up in the morning to find Parker already awake beside her; which was strange enough in itself, since Parker was never awake before her, and certainly not awake like this, staring at the roof, sometimes smiling but not with his usual cheeky look, instead looking like a not very nice person relishing a private joke at somebody else's expense. Once or twice she had even been woken by Parker tapping his feet or jiggling his legs in bed – which was so strange, so not-Parker, that she hardly knew what to think. She was confident that she knew him well enough to be able to read the signs if he was having an affair, or had run out of money gambling on the internet, or something specific like that; but this she couldn't decode. When she asked, he was brisk about saying that there was nothing wrong; equally brisk the one time she had asked him about when he was going to start looking for work. More than brisk: he'd said, 'I've still got savings left, but if you don't feel I'm contributing enough, I can move out.' That meant, don't ask again. So she didn't, but she wasn't happy. Manic Parker kept about his business, visibly scheming and making plans and cooking things up and, it sometimes seemed, cackling to himself in entirely private, entirely secret glee. She once or twice had the thought that she preferred Speechless With Grief Parker.

As if in answer to that thought, or in punishment for having had it, another version of Parker then turned up. This version was the one with whom Daisy was still living. This was the one who had Daisy making a Yes and No list while listening to Joni Mitchell's *Blue* on her iPod. He did not appear overnight, but Manic Parker first had moments, then hours, then days, when he transformed into what he was now, Dostoevsky Parker. This version of Parker first arrived in the form of nail-chewing, distraction, and an appearance of shifty preoccupation during times when he was supposed to be doing something else – paying attention to her, for instance, which had formerly been one of his strengths, but had for some months now seemed something he'd either forgotten to do or had lost interest in. She would go into the kitchen where he was supposed to be cooking the dinner, and find him just standing there gnawing the inside of his lip while the vegetables he was supposed to be stir-frying turned to charcoal. One of Dostoevsky Parker's new pieces of body language was to sit at the table with his head in his hands. Instead of waking up early, Dostoevsky Parker couldn't sleep: he had trouble falling asleep (which Daisy knew was a sign of anxiety), he woke up early and couldn't go back to sleep (which Daisy knew was a sign of depression), and during the rare middle bits when he was asleep, he thrashed around like a breakdancing dervish. Dostoevsky Parker even looked different from Normal Parker: he was heavier and paler and more earthbound. He looked as if he subsisted exclusively on carbohydrates and ill feeling.

So what was going on? Daisy had no idea. But one big difference between this Dostoevsky Parker and Grieving Parker was that this one didn't seem to be mourning a specific loss so much as suffering a general and all-consuming sense of gloom and, unless Daisy was mistaken, guilt. He was fretting not about something which had been done to him, but something he'd done.

'I wish you'd tell me what's the matter, baby,' Daisy said to him one evening in November, when she'd got home knackered from work and had wanted nothing more than to have supper cooked for her, maybe a back rub, and then to watch some junk TV with her boyfriend of long standing. Instead here she was sitting in silence over a ready meal she herself had microwaved, acting as the equivalent of an unpaid psychiatric nurse. She wanted to yell, but that didn't work with Parker; he would just retreat further. So she did her best to gentle him out of himself. She also knew that there wasn't much more of this she could take, and that she couldn't face doing it for much longer. She couldn't think of any more things to list under No.

What she didn't know was that Parker was longing to tell her, was desperate to tell her. He wanted nothing more than to confess. He wanted to break down all the barriers he had artificially built up, to knock down his jerry-built edifice of silence and secrecy and false self; to blurt and blub and let it all out. The need to confess rose in his throat like a nausea. And yet he couldn't speak, and so the two young people who loved each other stayed stuck and miserable.

95

If Quentina had been asked what she expected from the detention centre, she might have got several things right straight away.
She could for instance have guessed that there would be no privacy, that male guards would feel free to barge into women's
rooms and search their belongings whenever they felt like it, and
that many of the women, some of them devout Muslims, would
be outraged. No surprise there. She would have expected the
food regime to be poor – not that they couldn't get anything to
eat after five o'clock, or that the children, of whom there were
many, would sometimes be crying with hunger. She knew that
the place was a prison and would feel like one. But what she
hadn't expected was the politics – the internal politics. When she
arrived, she found that a large group of prisoners was on hunger
strike to protest against conditions at the prison and they had a
list of fifteen demands, including that the authorities give back
the birth certificates that they'd taken away from children born
in the UK, and also that they reinstate the daily allowance of 71
pence. And they wanted access to legal information, since the
majority of them had no legal representation.

Quentina agreed with all fifteen of the demands. But she had
only just got there, was still dazed and bewildered from the immigration hearing, and just didn't feel ready to pitch straight
into a hunger strike. The causes were all right, all just, but they
weren't honestly her causes – she was a new girl and hadn't even

known about the existence of the 71p allowance. Quentina felt that she hadn't been in the detention centre long enough to get really angry about the conditions. For the moment she was just trying to survive.

That wasn't the general feeling. The atmosphere at the Refuge in Tooting had been low, verging on depressed, with the emphasis on survival and endurance. Thrown in with that was an unspoken emphasis on the need to acknowledge the good intentions of their benefactors, who were keen to send the message that not all British people were as cruel as their government and their newspapers. That was not the mood at the detention centre. Here people were angry, fumingly angry, all the time. They hated the government, hated the press, hated the administrators of the detention centre. There had been riots the previous year, when warders had tried to prevent detainees from watching a documentary about conditions at the centre. It was easy to imagine that there could be riots again. In the mean time there was the hunger strike.

Quentina's guide to this was Makela, a Nigerian doctor who had run a clinic for victims of female circumcision. Her application for asylum had been rejected because the authorities believed, or claimed to believe, that her life was not really at risk back in Nigeria. She was angry, but not with Quentina; she agreed that Quentina as a new arrival couldn't pitch headlong into the centre's politics. She also made it clear that in her view, over time, the politically aware detainees had a responsibility to make trouble, especially if they didn't have children.

That would be in the future – perhaps a long time in the future. Quentina, for the first time since she had arrived in the UK, felt defeated. The air here was hard to breathe; it was thick with resentment and the lack of hope. That was why people were so angry: it gave an alternative to being completely beaten, broken, finished. All Quentina wanted to do was sit on her bed and look at the ceiling. Nothing seemed to have any point or purpose.

The immigration tribunal hearing had been a disaster. In her first sighting of the red-faced judge presiding over it, she had felt a flicker of hope: he looked like a man whose natural state was to be reasonable. But as the first morning went on she saw that this was misleading. When he did ask questions they were pointed and implicitly sceptical. How exactly had she got into the UK? How exactly had she been supporting herself? When the government's lawyers got on to the fact that she had been working illegally, she saw his manner harden. The pretence of friendly impartiality melted away. At that point, noon on the Monday morning, she realised that her application was going to be rejected.

At the end of his day's hearing, her lawyer, a mild-mannered woman in early middle age, turned to her and made a grimace.

'That was terrible,' said Quentina, to save her the trouble.

'I didn't want to say anything,' said the lawyer. 'But he's one of the toughest ones. I'm sorry. Don't worry, if we lose, which we haven't done yet, there's still every chance for an appeal.'

They hadn't lost yet – but they might as well have. Tuesday was just as bad as Monday, with the judge dwelling much more heavily on the subject of Quentina's illegal employment than on the prospect of what had happened to her in Zimbabwe before she left, and what would happen to her if she was sent back. He moved through all those details briskly. It was no surprise when his judgment, as they received it on the following Monday, was that she should be deported. In practice that meant being sent to an immigration removal centre to await the result of her appeal.

She had been here now for two months. The drive down was in a minibus owned by the private security company that ran the detention centre, for a profit, on behalf of the government. Under other circumstances Quentina would have enjoyed the trip: a chance to admire the famous green fields of England, which she'd never actually seen before, unless you counted the Common. There were arable fields, cows, tractors. So England was not just London after all. Quite funny to find that out just before being forced to leave. Her first sight of the detention centre's main building had given her a flash of optimism: a three-storey modern structure with a car park in front. To anyone familiar with the vernacular of contemporary British buildings, it looked like a motel or a conference centre, or maybe a sixth-form college. But as with the judge, first impressions turned out to be deceptive. The immigration centre was a prison, with the twist that when people were discharged from prison they went somewhere better, but when they were discharged from here they were sent back to the place they had risked everything to escape.

Everybody was obsessed with the food. One of the fifteen de-mands of the inmates on hunger strike was for 'edible food we can eat'. It was no joke. Quentina had not eaten like a princess at the Refuge, but that was a seven-star holiday resort compared to this. The meals did not merely fail to look appetising, they actually stank. The meat smelled off. There was no spicing to the food, no flavour. The desserts were even heavier and lumpier than the savoury courses. The only edible thing Quentina saw in her first two weeks at the detention centre was fruit – tired and bruised fruit, but nonetheless fruit, as welcome as a gift dir-ect from heaven. She lost far more weight than she had ever lost when she was walking ten miles a day as a traffic warden.

When she said this to Makela, the Nigerian woman had smiled.

'That's how it begins,' she said. 'The first thing that makes people crazy is always the food.'

96

It might be today. Might it be today? Or not. It possibly wouldn't happen at all. It might be better – no, it certainly would be better – if it didn't happen. There was no reason to think that it would happen and even less reason to want it to happen so, on balance, it wouldn't happen. But what if it did?

Matya was getting ready to go out on a date with Zbigniew. She was at her new shared flat in the bit of Brixton which was sort-of Herne Hill or vice versa, depending on whether the person you were talking to wanted to sound cool or posh. Her discovery of the place had been that rare thing, a positive experience of flat-hunting in London. The tip-off had come via a Hungarian friend. She had a colleague with a spare room who was looking for a sane, solvent, non-smoking female lodger, not allergic to cats, content not to have a television, willing during the owner's work-related absences to check on the well-being of her widowed mother downstairs. The interview and checking of references took ten minutes: she offered Matya the flat on the spot, and she moved in the next day. Zbigniew borrowed Piotr's van and brought round her stuff.

Zbigniew. He was the issue. Matya was dressing for a date with him, and by some process she wouldn't analyse this had in her mind become the date on which he was going to make a pass and she either was or wasn't going to go to bed with him. It was hard to examine exactly how they'd got to this point, how he'd gone from someone who she positively, definitely wouldn't go out with, to someone she really liked. He ticked such a large number of negative boxes. He was a Pole, and Matya thought Poles complacent and self-absorbed. He wasn't rich, and if there was a single box she definitely wanted ticked it was that a serious boyfriend would have serious money. He worked with his hands and – this overlapped with the money issue – Matya was keen to have a white-collar, desk-job boyfriend, someone as unlike all the boys she knew from home as possible.

And yet . . . there she was putting on her best knickers, pink ones with black trim, and her most effective bra, and the jeans she knew that men liked, the ones that got her most looks in the street or bar – the ones that were the most reliable indicator of whether she was carrying an extra kilo, because that made them instantly go from sexily snug to too-tight. She was putting on the beaded shirt Arabella had given her after a shopping splurge and was going to wear the suede jacket that made her waist look small and her tits look big. So why all this, if all these other things about Zbigniew were true? Well, it was the fact that his liabilities were also assets. His Polishness meant that he knew who he was. There was nothing fake about Zbigniew, no false notes to his talk or personality. It was refreshing, oddly so; most men these days felt as if they were trying to sell you something, some version of themselves, to try and get into your pants by pretending to be someone they were not. You were always trying to look beyond, look past the act, to see the real self. It was tiring, and Zbigniew wasn't like that at all.

He wasn't rich. That meant he knew the value of money: you could trust him with money, trust him to get the point of it. A rich boyfriend might make her own economies, her choices, her triumphs, seem petty. There were people in London who earned ten, twenty, fifty, a thousand times what she did – lots of people. How much did she really have in common with any of them? How would a boyfriend from that world feel about her flat-sharing, or know what to say when she lost her Oyster card with a full £30 on it? No problem of that kind with Zbigniew. His money values – his sense of what things cost – were completely in alignment with hers. That meant that their dreams were similar too. To people who are rich by London standards, the idea of a rose-covered cottage in the country with a garden seemed silly – they could buy one with half an annual bonus. But that wasn't the way it seemed to Matya or to Zbigniew.

And then there was that question of working with his hands. Matya paused as she put on her eyeliner. If there had been anybody else present, she would have blushed. The plain truth was that Zbigniew's work gave Zbigniew his body, and Zbigniew's body was one of the things she liked best about him – put plainly, she liked its hardness. Zbigniew was not pumped up like some bodybuilder, some action hero on the television; he did not burst out of his clothes. But his body was firm and taut and whenever Matya had touched it or bumped into it she had always noticed that it was, simply, very firm. He was muscled and compact and clean and she could tell that his skin would feel lovely to the touch, smooth on top but taut underneath. It was not hard to imagine what he might be like in bed . . . He had a real sense of humour too, not like those English boys who would tire you out by always putting on a show, barely able to speak without trying to make a joke, but quiet and dry and quick to see the ridiculous side of things. He could do an impersonation of Mrs Yount changing her mind about the colour of the bathroom which made Matya cry with laughter.

And yet there were still things which added up to reasons for not fancying him. She had a vivid memory of what it felt like to consider Zbigniew unthinkable. This remembered Zbigniew would intermittently rise up and blot out her feelings for the Zbigniew who was in front of her at that moment. If he had known, he would have been very taken aback to learn that his biggest obstacle with Matya was her memory of the time when she had found him ridiculous. Because she had seen him first in a menial capacity, doing jobs for the Younts, a trace of that hung around him – he was in some sense, like her, servant-class. The fact that she was too made it worse, not better. Also, he was not good-looking: he had a broad flat blank Slavic face and hair a shade of brown that you couldn't quite remember, so next time you saw him it was either a shade darker or a shade lighter than you expected. He wasn't ugly, but he wasn't good-looking. You just didn't notice his looks.

97

Zbigniew had no idea that his deadliest rival was Matya's former impression of him. He might have been relieved to hear it. As he saw it, his deadliest rival was the suitcase which, before going out on their date, he had taken out and dumped on his mattress at number 42 Pepys Road. The case had flipped open, and he was now sitting beside it. By some trick of memory, the amount of money in the suitcase looked bigger every time.

Perhaps the notes were expanding. Or perhaps it was because he was willing the money to be less of a problem. He was trying to squeeze it down in his mind. As a mental device this had some success, and he was able to go for stretches of time without thinking about what to do – except the actual money could not be compressed so easily, and looked bigger every time he checked on it.

Zbigniew was not prone to irrational fears, and he felt there was nothing irrational about his anxiety. He had held on to the money for far too long and now, whatever he did, he felt he had compromised himself. Not giving the money to Mrs Leatherby straight away had been a form of fault. At 5 per cent interest, £500,000 invested for three months was more than £6,000: that was how much money he had cost her in cash by not acting. By not doing anything he had stolen from her. He sold all the stocks in his modest portfolio, as a way of . . . as a way of . . . he wasn't sure what it was a way of. The money he had invested in the course of his time in London had, thanks to the turbulent market conditions, shrunk by about 15 per cent.

He should give the stolen money back. And yet . . . and yet what? There was the cottage, his father's cottage, his parents' golden years of retirement, the thing in all the world he most wanted for them, bought with stolen money. That was the problem. He would never be able to tell his father what he'd done; which meant that what he'd done would never seem right. It would be a lie, it would poison everything. He couldn't do it. Yes, he should definitely give the money back. But he felt he couldn't do that without telling someone. It must be the residual imprint of Catholicism. He had to confess. He had to have absolution. The weight of the secret was just too great to bear. And also there was a glimmering, flickering thought that he was reluctant to admit too directly, but which was certainly there. If he confessed to someone about the suitcase with half a million pounds in it, the suitcase which had never been missed, the suitcase whose owner had died long ago and which now belonged to someone who knew nothing about it and whose life would not be affected by its absence in any way, someone whose house was worth millions already, so someone (just to get this crystal clear) who was already rich, who didn't need or know about or miss or suspect the existence of this money; and in the mean time the money was in the possession of him, Zbigniew, whose life it would transform utterly, whose many ambitions would be immediately fulfilled just by taking ownership of this cash – the years of ease and comfort for his parents, the chance to set himself up in life, the sudden access of capital which would let him move on, employ people, create wealth, share happiness, give his father one rose-covered cottage and give Matya another one, and a bed with a good firm mattress too – so there was on the one hand oblivious richness and on the other deep desiring and deserving need – well, maybe, if he confessed to a person about this predicament, this dilemma, maybe, just maybe, the person to whom he confessed would say, don't be an idiot, you have to take the money for yourself, are you crazy? It would be an injustice not to. It would be theft – theft from yourself. That's what the person to whom he confessed might say. Perhaps. He hoped. On the other hand – and Zbigniew had come to feel that this was more likely, even as he had grown resolved on his confession – she might think there was nothing to discuss. She might go the exact other way. She might say that it was so obvious that he had no choice but to hand over the money – that it was so morally clear-cut – that he had in effect stolen the money. She might conclude that Zbigniew was not the man she had thought he was, that anyone who could do such a thing as sit on a suitcase containing £500,000 of someone else's money – she might think that a man who would do that could not be trusted. The conversation in which he told her about the suitcase might be the last conversation they ever had.

With these thoughts, full of apprehension, Zbigniew got dressed and went downstairs. Number 42 Pepys Road was almost finished. The paintwork downstairs needed touching up, then Mrs Leatherby had to look around and point out things that weren't satisfactory, and then they were done. The Pepys Road era of Zbigniew's life would be over. Maybe another part of his life would begin; he certainly hoped so. It all depended on what Matya said.

98

'What, now? Right now? You don't mean right now?' said Zbigniew.

They were in a café on the high street, leaning with their heads close together. The agenda for the date had been coffee, film, dinner, and then who-knew-what. She had never looked lovelier. Now, though, it seemed there was a different plan.

'Right now. This minute. From here – you take it from here and you go to see her. Call first. But you go to see her.'

'But it's Sunday afternoon!'

'So what?'

Zbigniew blew out his cheeks.

'Right now,' he said. That was Matya's solution to his problem. She had not judged or criticised or second-guessed – which, he realised, was what he had both expected and feared. She wasn't the type to say, take the money and run. And he was glad that she wasn't like that. He was even gladder that she hadn't done a Piotr and denounced him or told him off. But she had been clear and firm on what to do next, and it wasn't what Zbigniew had expected to hear. He had been braced for more of the agonising that had been going on inside him. Instead, she simply told him to take the suitcase to Mrs Leatherby straight away: right now.

Moving slowly, as if daring Matya not to stop him, he fished his mobile, the Nokia N60 which had changed his life, out of his pocket. She watched. He found the number, held it up in front of Matya so she could see. Matya made no gesture. So Zbigniew pressed the dial button.

The phone rang six times. OK, she was out. Zbigniew moved to break the connection and then –

'Hello?'

'This is Zbigniew. The builder. I need to come and see you. Now, today.'

'Oh! What's wrong?' said Mrs Leatherby.

'Nothing but I need to come and see you. I can't say over the mobile. You are at home?' Of course she was, that was where he had called her. Sounding about as worried as a person could possibly be, Mary confirmed that she was at home. Zbigniew said he would be there in about an hour and a half, depending on the train times.

'And now you have to come with me,' he said to Matya. This was his revenge.

'Why?' Matya folded her arms.

'I can't go to this place I've never been before, and by the way I have no idea where exactly it is, carrying a suitcase with half a million pounds in cash, on my own.'

That was his excuse, anyway. She had grumbled a little, and pretended to prefer the idea of sitting alone in her flat, listening to the radio, before giving in. They had left the café and gone back to Pepys Road, Matya's first time there since leaving the employ of the Younts. Zbigniew had taken her up to the room where he was sleeping – which stank of paint, something he always noticed when he came in from outside – and showed her the suitcase. Matya had looked at it, then looked at him, and said, a little sadly:

'This is probably the only time in our lives we'll ever see that amount of money in cash.'

And now Matya sat across from Zbigniew in the rattling carriage of the train to Chelmsford. The train kept seeming to have got out of London into the countryside, before being reswallowed by the suburbs. At one point there was a stretch of green fields, and Matya thought they'd got out of the city, but then there was a long sequence of tower blocks. Some sections of the journey were as beautiful as anything in Hungary, and some were as ugly as anything in Hungary.

The trip was supposed to take forty-five minutes, but at one point the train stopped in a field, without explanation, for a quarter of an hour, so now it was late. The compartment was full. Across from them sat a young man, wearing a baseball cap pulled down, staring straight in front of him while he listened to music over headphones and chewed gum. There was a can of lager on the table in front of him. Zbigniew had thought about putting the suitcase on the overhead luggage rack, but then found his head filled with pictures of the train braking or jolting and the suitcase being thrown down and bursting open and the air filling with ten-pound notes, the passengers gaping at him while he crawled around scrambling to pick up the cash . . . so no, not the overhead rack. Not the space for luggage at the end of the compartment. In the end he put it in front of his seat with his legs folded over it and every time Matya looked at him she had the impulse to laugh.

They pulled into Chelmsford station. Outside there was a car park and a café. A solitary taxi was waiting at the rank. The cab driver had his eyes closed with a newspaper folded over his stomach. Matya pointed at the café.

'I'll wait for you there. If it looks like you're going to be more than an hour or so, call me,' she said. Then she leaned over, kissed him, and set off across the car park.

The cab driver gave a jolt when Zbigniew opened the door, then shook himself awake. The trip to Mrs Leatherby's house took ten minutes, past houses which to Zbigniew's eyes all looked very similar, bungalows and near-bungalows. He had thought it would be more like a village but this was just a different sort of town. Zbigniew took the cabbie's mobile number and paid him – five pounds, much cheaper than London. As he got out of the taxi he moved to shut the door, then realised, just as he was about to slam it closed, that he'd left the suitcase on the back seat. That would have been a very good way for the story to end.

99

Mary had been trying to keep herself busy since Zbigniew's strange phone call. She was at the kitchen sink, washing up some pots which were in theory clean but which hadn't been used for a bit, when she saw Zbigniew step out of the taxi and start walking up the drive.

Since her mother's death, Mary had not been miserable all the time, but she had been flat. That was the word for it – flat. Of course she knew that what had happened was in one major way a relief: her mother had been set free of her suffering. Some people died lingeringly, horribly, for a period stretching into years. Petunia had suffered, and it had been too slow, but it wasn't the worst of all deaths, and Mary was glad of that. And there was one kind of good news in her death – or what would have been good news if it could be considered in the abstract. The house had been valued at £1.5 million and the estate agent was bullish about the figure. Mary would never have to worry about money again. Indeed, if she didn't want to, she'd never even have to think about it again. Alan's garages did nicely and they were already well-off – exactly how well-off, she didn't know, because it wasn't the kind of question she liked to ask.

That was, for Mary, the trouble. The equation was too plain and too depressing. In the debit column, she had lost her mother; in the credit column, she now had a gigantic pile of cash. It felt as if her remaining parent had been taken away and in return she'd been given lots of money. Nothing else about her life had changed. Alan was still solid and dependable and, in his solid dependable way, a little distracted. Ben was still behind his wall of preoccupations, either in his bedroom doing God-only-knew-what on the internet or out doing God-only-knew-what with his friends; it wasn't at all obvious to Mary which she liked less. The great positive addition to her life was her dog Rufus, a Yorkshire Terrier who was now three months old, and who was friendly, good-natured, not very bright, and the only living thing who seemed excited at the idea of being in Mary's company. Now, as Zbigniew came up to the door, Rufus first ran to it, then back to Mary to check that she was aware of what was going on – come quick, developments! – and then back to the front door to yap at the prospective intruder. Keeping Rufus in position with her foot – which wasn't hard, since the dog was mainly showing off his keenness – Mary opened the door.

The Polish builder was carrying a battered old brown suitcase. As he usually did, he shook Mary's hand very formally. 'I am grateful to you for agreeing to see me with so little warning,' said Zbigniew.

'Come in,' said Mary. The roof has fallen in. One of my co-workers has been killed in an accident. I stayed the week at my girlfriend's house and squatters have taken over your property. I have forged your signature on legal documents and 42 Pepys Road is now mine. The house has burned down in a fire and I wanted to tell you in person. Over the months working at your mother's old house I have come to know you and love you as a person: please run away with me. But the builder's manner did not correspond with any of those propositions. He looked preoccupied, but he did not look like the bearer of catastrophic news.

'Tea?' said Mary, gesturing towards the sitting room.

'Is there a possibility of coffee?'

'Coffee,' said Mary. She went out and bustled in the kitchen while he waited in the sitting room. When she came back he was still standing by the window, looking at the largely featureless driveway, still holding the suitcase. Mary poured the coffee, sat down, and gestured for him to sit too. Then she waited.

'Mrs Leatherby,' said Zbigniew. 'This is not easy to explain. It is better if I simply show you.' He turned the suitcase to face her and opened it. Zbigniew watched her face.

'Five hundred thousand pounds,' he said.

Afterwards, Mary always remembered how quickly she had realised what had happened. It was not a process that took time. She just simply and immediately knew. It helped that she recognised the suitcase. Yes, that was it, it all flowed from the suitcase. Dad, cash, suitcase, hiding place, sudden death, builder finds it, not sure what to do, fesses up. She got it straight away. It was obvious what had happened – he'd found the money and had then had no idea what to do with it. Mary knew what that felt like.

It had been interesting to hear about the secret compartment. Her father had of course been handy, in his miserish way. He had no enjoyment of DIY but his passion for saving money was so keen he did it anyway. So he had evidently built himself this hideaway. It would have been in character for him to plan a big revelation, almost certainly as a way of winning an argument. No doubt his fantasy went something like this: Petunia would say something about the need for security in old age, some money to supplement the pension which would be not all that generous during his life and would be less so after his death. She would say something about his needing to make more provision, he would goad her by talking about how you couldn't trust anyone in the financial services industry, how they were all thieves, she would grow upset, he would then produce the suitcase and make his big revelation: see how I have provided for you. I may be cranky, but I'm not stupid. He would show her the money, the savings he had squirrelled away in cash, under the bed or somewhere, over years and years. And Petunia would be tearful and forgiving and apologetic and furious, all at once. That was the effect her father had had. Except that it hadn't happened like that. It was lucky he hadn't lived to see what happened after his death. He'd have been furious.

After the Pole went, Mary just sat there. It was a nice day, getting dark around five, and Alan made full use of it, coming home from the golf course only after nightfall. He had found Mary sitting downstairs with all the lights off, so much in the dark that she'd given him a shock, a hell of a shock, when he saw her.

'Crikey,' he said. 'What's up?'

'Good game?' asked Mary.

'Not bad. Got a bit stuck afterwards, he was droning on about his bloody in-laws again. It's amazing the way he can repeat himself word for word and not think you're going to mind. But don't change the subject. What's up?'

'Sit down,' said Mary. Then she opened the suitcase.

'Christ on a bike,' said Alan.

'Half a million,' said Mary. 'My dad. Case in a secret compartment. The Pole found it.'

'But—' said Alan. Then he stopped. It was funny for Mary to see him at such a complete loss for words.

'I know,' she said. 'They're old tenners. Worthless. He hoarded it for so long it turned into waste paper.'

'Not quite,' said Alan, beginning to recover. He went over to the table where they kept the spirits and poured himself a gigantic Scotch, half of which he drank at a swallow. 'Christ. You gave me a hell of a turn. I don't think I've ever seen that much cash in one go. Anyway, you're half right. You can't just take them somewhere and spend them. That tenner was withdrawn in the early nineties and it's not legal tender any more. But the Bank of England still has to honour it.'

'So we take it to the Bank of England. I can really imagine that, can't you?' Mary would wear a little hat and maybe a fur coat and would plonk the bag down on the counter and then pop it open to see their expressions change.

Alan drank the rest of his Scotch and poured a refill.

'What happens is, you can't use it yourself, but once the Bank's issued it it's still valid, always and for ever. The trouble is, a lot of the time, if there's a fair bit of money, they want to know where it's come from. So they ask lots of questions, income tax, inheritance tax, all that, and if you can't show that it's all legit, they investigate you, and the next thing you know they're claiming tax plus fines. The fines can be up to a hundred per cent of the full amount. And then there's lawyers' and accountants' fees to pay, and most of the time you end up with hardly any of the money left.'

'So it is waste paper after all, more or less,' said Mary.

'Give or take maybe a hundred grand.' Alan finished his second whisky and started to pour himself another. Then he thought better of it and came across to Mary and gave her one of his super-powerful, rib-cracking hugs.

'You all right?' he said.

'I'm glad my mother never knew,' said Mary. 'She'd have killed him.'

100

At number 27 Pepys Road, Patrick and Freddy Kamo were both loafing around, killing time, waiting for Mickey Lipton-Miller to call or to visit to report on what was supposed to be the conclusive meeting with the insurance company. This was meant to be It – the final offer. The settlement. The meeting had begun late the previous afternoon and Mickey had said that he would either call before nine in the evening or first thing the next day. Father and son had woken up early, waiting to hear from the agent, and now didn't quite know what to do with themselves. Freddy had a go at *Halo 2*, but it didn't take, and now he had put a CD of Fela Kuti on and was sitting at the table jiggling his legs, not really listening to the music. Patrick had been out to the newsagent and bought a newspaper, but found he couldn't read it. The combination of fatigue, worry, and the English language made the letters dance on the page, failing to resolve into words whose meaning he could understand. He could ring home – Adede and the girls would certainly be up already – but that would be such an unsettled, anxious-seeming thing to do that it would make Freddy even more uncomfortable. So there was nothing to do except trust Mickey to be in touch as soon as he could.

It had been two months of misery for both of them – though the misery was of different sorts. For Freddy it was primarily physical. He had had the second, major operation on his knee. It went well, according to the surgeon – the senior and most pessimistic of the three specialists – but convalescence was still drawn-out and painful and boring. Freddy's exercise regime was much duller and much more repetitive than training for football had ever been. He did not feel in full control of his body, and hated that. The whole process was a physical sinking-in of the reality he was facing: his injury might never get better, he might never be the same again, his life in football was almost certainly over. The thing he lived to do, he wasn't going to be able to do any more. Freddy was not prone to depression, but even he sometimes felt that what had happened to him was a form of death sentence.

Patrick's misery was in his head rather than in his body. He was possessed by a sense that, in addition to everything that had already gone wrong, yet more would go wrong: the insurance company would find what they were so clearly looking for, a loophole to avoid paying out, and yet Freddy would also be unable to play football again, so they would lose out in every way: no insurance, no livelihood and no chance for Freddy to do the thing he loved. They had come to London full of hope and would be leaving it stripped bare. The only thing left to them would be going home – but that, to Patrick, was a consolation so large that it too was now becoming a kind of torment. Home, Africa, Senegal, Linguère, their house, their bed, waking up next to Adede, the weight of his daughters when they jumped up on him and demanded a hug, an evening in the police bar with his old colleagues, the food that actually tasted of something, the bite of cold beer on a hot night, the sweat on the bottle rolled over your forehead, the sense of being known in a place you knew; that you were taking up your allotted space on the earth. Speaking your own language, all day. Home. All of it – home.

Both Kamos twitched at the noise of a key in the lock. Mickey did what he always did, which was to put the key in, turn it and open the door an inch, then ring the doorbell to announce his presence, then come in. Well, it was his house – which was presumably the unconscious point. He came bouncing in, which with another man would have been a good omen, except Mickey on purpose kept his energy levels high when he had bad news, as a way of being hard to read.

'Sorry I couldn't call last night. We went on a bit after ten and I didn't want to break our arrangement. And anyway, I wanted to tell you in person. So here I am,' said Mickey. He knew Patrick wouldn't think to offer him a cup of tea – he was hospitable, but sweetly, laughably bad at things he was used to thinking of as female work. So Mickey just sat down at the table and dumped his briefcase down on it, looking across at the two Kamo men. They were grey with anticipation.

'Ready?' said Mickey. They nodded. 'OK. Here it is. The good news is that the insurers are offering to honour the value of the contract. They were legally obliged to do that, since that's what's being insured, but you know what they're like. So that promises a single payment of five million pounds, tax-free both here and in Senegal.'

'Five million pounds,' said Patrick. He looked at Freddy, who showed nothing.

'Five million pounds,' said Mickey. 'Which is the good news. Bad news, or any rate less good, is that there are certain conditions. Which we knew there would be, but still. The main one they asked for is that Freddy is not allowed to play football again. Ever.'

'Never,' said Freddy. 'Not with friends?'

Smiling a little, Mickey said, 'No, they can't stop you having a kick-about with your mates. What they mean is, playing any kind of football for which you get paid. Or representative football for that matter, where you can earn money from image rights or sponsorships or whatever.'

'Never,' said Freddy.

'Yes. As I say, that's what they wanted. That's what we were arguing about. And that's why the bad news isn't entirely bad news, pure and simple – because it turns out, I won't lie to you, to my surprise, they were more imaginative than I thought. They saw the point. The deal we ended up with, finally, is that Freddy can't play football anywhere in Europe or the Americas or Asia. But he can play in Senegal. He can run out on a football field again. If he gets in the national team or something and there's sponsorship rights, they might want some of that money. But anyway, that's the headline news. No football in Europe, but he can play in the league at home.'

Mickey had fought hard for this: to be able to say to Freddy that his life in football was not over. It was to his complete amazement that he first sensed possible flexibility on the part of the insurers, and then detected actual movement. It hadn't taken him long to work out why. It was partly that the amounts in question were so small they wouldn't feel cheated – Freddy would be lucky to earn the equivalent of ten grand a year in Senegal, even fully fit and at the height of his powers. However mean and pissy the insurers were, not even they could worry about defending that to their shareholders. That was one thing. But the more important thing, he gradually realised, was that they thought the whole issue was moot. For all their stalling, they believed the gloomiest medical prognosis. They didn't think Freddy would ever kick a ball in anger again. Allowing him to play pro football back home was like giving him permission to be the first man on Mars – it just wasn't going to happen.

No need to tell Freddy that, though. Mickey watched the news sink in, and Freddy reached for his father's hand.

'I get to play football again?' he said.

'And five million pounds. And,' said Patrick, looking for the first time in months like a man with something to look forward to, 'we get to go home.'

101

At number 42, the garden which had been Petunia Howe's great joy in life, her hobby and her solace, was being dug up and replaced. Zbigniew stood at the window of the main bedroom on the first floor, the room in which Petunia had died, and watched.

He had come back to fix some wall sockets in the bedroom. The wiring was a little loose and so the power supply was intermittent. He had promised a year's guarantee as well as the work he'd done, and he was happy to come back and fix it, even though the house no longer belonged to the Leatherbys. It had been bought by a City banker and his American wife, a childless couple in their early thirties who had paid £1,550,000 for it. The house was as yet unfurnished; the new people were going to get a team of painters in. Zbigniew didn't mind that, part of doing up a house to sell it included the assumption that the new owners would change stuff. It wasn't his house anyway. But he did find that he disliked seeing the garden torn out. The new owners wanted a more modern look. The crowded, profuse, overgrown, over-living plant beds of old Mrs Howe were to be replaced by a geometric pattern of decking and gravel and pavings, with a water feature at the end, and four small square formal beds of low shrubs. So now four men from the garden design company were ripping out Petunia's garden and bodily carrying the debris through to the skip at the front of the house, over the plastic sheeting they'd put in to protect the carpet.

The Sunday on which Zbigniew had taken the money and giv-en it back to Mrs Leatherby had turned into the best day of his life. The first reason: Mrs Mary Leatherby had rung him up in the early evening and had told him about the money. It had been worthless, or all but worthless, all along. If Zbigniew had tried to spend it, he would have had no explanation of how he had all this out-of-date currency and he would have been caught as a thief. He would have lost his honour, and for nothing. He felt the way a man feels when he's been about to step out into the road without looking, then caught himself at the last moment and just avoided a speeding car.

But that wasn't the main reason it was the best day of his life. The main reason was that when he had got back to the train sta-tion and found Matya sitting outside the café, he had said, 'What shall we do now?' and she had shrugged and said, 'Let's go to bed.' For a moment he had thought he was undergoing an aural hallucination. But the look she gave him told him he wasn't. That was the single happiest and best and most surprising moment of his entire life to date. They had spent the trip home kissing, car-ried on snogging on the Tube, kissed all the way up the stairs to her flat, and then stayed in bed until it was time for both of them to go to work on Monday morning. It would be an exaggeration to say that they had been in bed ever since. But it wouldn't be all that much of an exaggeration. He simply couldn't get enough of her, her body and her company – it wasn't just the sex (though it was, obviously, that too) and the amazing thing was that she seemed to, said she did and acted as if she did, feel the same way about him. She said she liked the way he was truthful and the way he stood in his shoes. Zbigniew wasn't quite sure what that meant so was happy to take it as a compliment.

It happens quickly when it happens, and it had happened to Zbigniew and Matya. Now they were looking for a flat together. They were spending two evenings and one weekend afternoon a week flat-hunting – they had agreed to do it that way, and take as long as they needed to find a place which felt right, rather than blitz it and be worn down and give in to the first plausible thing they saw.

Zbigniew, who could see that work was beginning to dry up, had once or twice mentioned Poland, how cheap it was, how beautiful the countryside was, how warm and open-hearted his family were; to which Matya would reply by talking about the glories of Hungarian food and culture and landscape. And there was a serious language question over her learning Polish or his learning Hungarian. So it was London, now and for the foreseeable future, and for Zbigniew that was about as unexpected as finding Matya had been. The fact that this had come to be the place where he lived, not just where he was passing through or cashing in, had not formed any part of his plan. Matya had a new job as a translator – one of her employers was a senior executive at a building firm which employed many Hungarians and had just lost its former interpreter to a better offer from someone else. So Matya now spent her day in a yellow hard hat, earning twice what she'd earned before, with the prospect of taking that career forward and/or applying for a desk job. From what she said, they loved her and were desperate to keep her. Zbigniew did not find that at all hard to understand.

Even Piotr liked Matya. No, that was wrong – of course he liked (and fancied) Matya: who wouldn't? What was remarkable was that even Piotr was willing to show pleasure in Zbigniew and Matya being together. They'd all been out to Sunday lunch at a Polish pub in Balham, and it had been a success. Piotr had brought his girlfriend, a girl from Krakow who worked as a teaching assistant in a primary school, and the whole occasion had been like a version of the old days which hadn't actually happened like that the first time round, since they'd never lazed around and hung out with girlfriends in that way. Piotr's view of Zbigniew seemed to have undarkened, and they would now spend time together without it feeling as if they were constantly having an unspoken argument.

A man with a clipboard came into Petunia's garden. It was clear that he was in charge of the other four men: he stood and held out the clipboard and compared it to the evidence of work in progress in front of him. It was apparent that something wasn't quite right. Two of the men straightened and came over, and a discussion between the three of them began, all the men nodding and pointing as they talked about what they would do with the garden once they had got rid of all the plants and greenery that Petunia Howe had loved. Zbigniew turned his attention away from the window and bent to his work.

102

Many things can go concealed in the hurly-burly of family life. Shahid and Usman had not spoken or interacted in any way for months – and nobody else in the family had noticed. For the last two of those months, Usman had been in Lahore with their mother, taking a break from London, reacquainting himself with Pakistani life, and very nearly arranging to get married to a lawyer's fourth daughter. He had been so close to deciding to do it that he had had to go away to think it over, so here he was in London again, and much more relieved to be back than he wanted to admit. Usman was coming to think that your roots were not necessarily the same thing as your home, but he didn't yet know what to make of the thought.

On the morning after he got back, he went to see Shahid at his flat. He noticed that his brother had installed a CCTV camera over the door; there was a pause and he was buzzed in. Shahid was standing at the top of the stairs. It's not easy to look dignified and outraged while wearing an open dressing gown with a pair of Y-fronts clearly visible, but Shahid was managing to do it.

'You little shit,' he said. 'I know it was you.'

'This is the part where I'm supposed to say, "Please let me explain,"' said Usman.

'Fuck you. Fuck your explanation. I was in a cell for nineteen days because of you. And don't for a moment, don't for a single moment, think I didn't know right from the start who was to blame for that stupid stunt. In fact the only thing I blame myself for is not having realised the first time I saw those stupid postcards. "We Want What You Have". I should have thought, let me see. Who's stupid enough to think this is interesting, lazy enough so he doesn't have a proper job so he has the time to do it, enough of a political cretin to think it's a significant gesture of some sort, retarded enough to keep doing it even after it starts to get people worked up, and just enough of a geek to do it on the web? Stupid, lazy, politically cretinised, retarded, spends all his time wanking on the internet. Oh of course! My younger brother!'

Shahid was still standing at the top of the stairs.

'Can I come up now?' said Usman. Shahid stepped back from the stairwell and Usman took that as a yes. He trudged up. Shahid was stood at the sink with his arms folded. Usman sat down and took a breath.

'Look, I know it makes no difference, and I know it's too late, but I'm sorry. I'm genuinely and deeply sorry. When you were arrested I assumed it was to do with that idiot fake jihadi. It was only the day before you got out that the lawyer said something to mother and Ahmed about the blog and I realised that was involved. But it didn't make any sense! I stopped doing that stuff back at the start of the year! I took the site down, everything. And then someone must have screen scraped all the pictures because someone puts them back up again and starts doing that extra-freaky shit with dead birds and trashing cars and everything and I didn't know what to think. I had no idea what was going on. I didn't mean things to get out of hand. I didn't think people would get themselves in such a twist. And all because they thought it might affect property prices! You make a point about Western obliviousness and they think it's about property prices. You tell them they're in a condition of complete moral unconsciousness and they worry about whether their house is still worth two million quid! Unbelievable. Then they decide you're a terrorist.'

'It wasn't you who—' began Shahid, and Usman held up his hand.

'I know – it was you who ended up in Paddington Green. But that wasn't the idea, they got it all wrong, it was that idiot Iqbal, if he hadn't . . .' Usman trailed off. Shahid just sat there.

'You had my password,' he said. 'You were logged on through my IP address.'

'I got it in the café downstairs,' said Usman. 'They get your wireless pretty much full-strength. I worked out your password.'

Shahid's password, as it happened, was Shakira123.

'I don't believe you,' he said.

'Remember when you got the broadband put in? That summer? All the time you were singing and humming that Shakira tune. The one about "I'm on tonight" and "hips don't lie". For about six weeks it was all you talked about. I was going through a . . through a strict phase and you did it to wind me up. So the first time I tried your password I guessed Shakira. But that didn't work. So then I thought for a bit and remembered back when we were kids. Remember when you were about ten and I was five? You had a little electronic safe. Dad gave it to you not long before he died. Birthday present I think it was. And you and I spent a lot of time together at that point, you sort of looked after me and we were very close. And you told me your password was Usman123, so I remembered that and I tried it on Shakira. Shakira123.'

There was a long silence.

'Fuck you,' Shahid eventually said again. Usman smiled and got up. He fished out his wallet, took out a card and gave it to Shahid. It had a mobile phone number on it.

'What, I call this and I get to go to jail again, this time for drugs?'

'Remember that girl you met on the Underground? You liked

her, got her number, then lost it, you put an ad in "Lost Connec-tions", she never saw it, that was the last you heard of her?'

'How do you know she never saw it?'

Usman shrugged. 'She told me. That's her mobile number.' He made for the door. 'And in case you're wondering, no it wasn't easy.'

'Fuck you,' said Shahid to his brother's back, though with less conviction this time.

103

In the days after his visit to Shahid Kamal at Paddington Green
station, DI Mill had come to a conclusion about the enquiries he
had been making into the Pepys Road harassment campaign. He
had talked it over with the DC who'd been working with him,
and they agreed: We Want What You Have was two different
series of events, run by two different people or sets of people. For
the first few months, the postcards and website and the DVDs
were the work of a person or persons with a local interest but
no particular animus at any individual. There was something almost abstract about it: no people in the photos, no abuse, no
criminal damage. That person, whoever he or she was, had a link
to Shahid Kamal; at the very least, he or she had hacked into his
internet access; more likely, it was someone known to him. Then
the whole thing went away for a while. Then it came back with
someone else behind it, someone who did not have that link to
Mr Kamal – or if he or she did, he or she was for some reason
now eager to conceal the link. This person was much angrier
with the people of Pepys Road. He or she had a darker sensib-
ility. His or her acts began with graffiti and abuse and turned
to vandalism, criminal damage against property and the use of
dead animals. This person or persons seemed to be escalating
his or her or their campaign. The first person(s) had arguably
not broken any laws; you could probably slap an ASBO on them,
get them to promise not to do anything similar again, and leave

it at that. The second person(s) had certainly broken several laws, probably enough to earn a custodial sentence. But the blog was registered behind several layers of anonymous identity, and there were no fingerprints anywhere. Now that police patrols were taking an extra interest in Pepys Road after the cars were vandalised, there had been no further activity. The blog had been taken down. So Mill was closer to knowing the sort of person he was looking for without knowing who it was.

He wasn't worried. Mill was sure something else would happen. Most detective cases are solved by hard routine work, or by luck – the latter category including stupid mistakes by the criminal. Experience taught Mill that he would have to wait for a piece of luck. Until it came, he mentally parked the issue and got on with other work. His feeling was that he wouldn't have to wait long, and he was right. The break came out of the blue, two months after Shahid Kamal was released from prison. His DC came up to his desk, smile lines etched deep around his eyes, and without comment passed him an issue of the *Evening Standard*, folded open to page three. The headline said:

EXPOSED: ARTIST KNOWN AS SMITTY

His artworks are controversial, his stunts infamous. His provocative graffiti have travelled the journey from Underground station walls to prestigious art galleries. He makes collectors' pieces which sell for millions. But nobody knows who he is. His name is Smitty, but his identity is one of the art world's best-kept secrets. Until today, when an *Evening Standard* investigation reveals that Smitty's real name is Graham Leatherby, a 28-year-old Goldsmiths graduate who lives in Shoreditch, the son of Alan and Mary Leatherby, whose home in Maldon, Essex is worth £750,000.

There was a large photo of Smitty, wearing jeans and a hoodie with the top thrown back.

'Sweet Jesus!' said Mill.

'That's right,' said the DC.

'The Leatherbys owned that house at number 42. The mother died and they inherited it. There must be something to this,' said Mill. 'It's too much of a coincidence. I know this guy's work. Janie has a book by him and she made me watch a documentary. He's always doing this, you know, art stuff, installations and pranks and practical jokes. This is right up his street. If you'll forgive the expression. We've got to go and have a word. No way this is just a coincidence.'

The red light on Mill's phone was winking: a sign that the switchboard was asking if they could put a call through. He picked up.

'Switchboard here. We've got someone wanting to talk to you. Says he has information relevant to an inquiry. Wouldn't give his full name, but said to say to you that he's the artist formerly known as Smitty.'

Mill and the DC just looked at each other.

104

No one was answering the buzzer at Smitty's warehouse studio, so Mill buzzed another of the entryphones, identified himself as a policeman, and he and his DC were let in. They clanked up the metal stairs to Smitty's floor and walked into a huge, high-ceilinged workspace with a blackboard all across one wall, an enormous wooden desk, and a young man sitting in front of a PC.

'He's not here and anyway he's not talking to the papers,' said the young man, without fully taking his attention away from the screen in front of him.

Mill held out his warrant card.

'Oh. OK. He said there might be police. He's in the office. His other office. The Bell. Off Hoxton Square, yeah?'

The two policemen went back down and out. The pub was about a five-minute walk away, through the mixture of semi-gentrified and still-slummy streets. Mill shoved through the heavy door into the saloon bar. It was empty apart from three or four people sitting at the bar and, at a table facing the entrance, the man who was recognisable from the newspaper photograph as Smitty. He sat to the left of the dartboard, beneath a huge old Watneys mirror. In front of him was a mobile phone, a pint and a packet of crisps. The two policemen went over and stood in front of him. Smitty looked up.

'Hello. You look like coppers,' he said.

Mill held out his warrant card. Smitty gestured at the seats opposite him.

'You ever watch *The Simpsons*? Bart. I love Bart. You know one of Bart's sayings? "I didn't do it. Nobody saw me do it. You can't prove anything."'

'We're not here about anything in that *Standard* article. I don't care what you've done in the course of doing your, er, stuff,' said Mill. 'In the course of your legitimate art work. Actually, I have your book.' That wasn't strictly true, since it was Janie who owned a copy of *Smitty*, Smitty's lavishly illustrated book about himself. But he thought that would be gratifying to the artist, who indeed did look a tiny bit pleased. 'I'm not talking to you under caution. I just want to ask about something. Another pint?' He pointed at Smitty's drink. Smitty thought for a moment.

'IPA,' he said.

'Pint of IPA, bottle of Kaliber, and whatever you're having,' he said to the DC, who headed off to the bar. Smitty stretched his arms out and looked around the pub.

'I love this place. Know why? It's what I call PM. Proper Manky. Hasn't been cleaned up and tarted up like most of London. I love this mirror. When did Watneys go out of business, what, twenty years ago? And they've still got the mirror. Formica tables. Beer towels. Everywhere else round here, it's caipirinhas and Perrier-Jouët. See those regulars at the bar? See any of them move or speak? Exactly. They never do. Fancy some food? They've got crisps, pork scratchings, or if you're feeling really flash, pickled eggs. That's Proper Manky. In another few years, there won't be anywhere like this left anywhere in London. It'll all be lychee martinis, decaf vanilla lattes, and complimentary Wi-Fi.'

The DC came back from the bar and put down the drinks. Mill took a swig of his no-alcohol lager.

'So, this is about Pepys Road,' Smitty said. 'Where my nan lived.'

'Exactly. And where there's been a long-running campaign of harassment, postcards, graffiti, videos, a blog, and now acts of damage and vandalism and animal cruelty.'

As he had done with Shahid Kamal, Mill was looking very closely at Smitty while he said this. The artist's reaction didn't seem to be one of guilt or concern. Mill opened his briefcase and took out a folder with photocopies of the inquiry's Greatest Hits, mainly postcards and stills from the DVD but also pictures of the graffiti and the defacements and a series of photos of the dead birds and scratched cars. Smitty looked at the pictures.

'I remember this stuff starting, what, must have been about a year ago. Before my nan got ill. I went around there, she'd had a few cards with pictures of her house. And then she'd just had a DVD which she hadn't played because she didn't have a DVD player. I passed them on to my mum and that's the last I heard of it. I assumed it had just stopped. My mum did the place up and then she sold it. We Want What You Have. A good line, I remember thinking. Funny that it kept going.'

'We wondered if it might have something to do with you. It feels like your kind of thing.'

Smitty snorted. 'My arse it does. Animal cruelty? I was a vegan for five years and I still hardly ever eat anything with a face. And I assure you I'm very bloody careful about not breaking the law. I have quite a lot to lose, guys. I can see why this feels arty and see why you made the connection but trust me, it's two plus two equals eleven.'

He kept on looking through the pictures. Smitty's mind went back to the time he had gone and seen his grandmother, the last time he had seen her in full health – if indeed she had been in full health, because in retrospect he'd thought that she seemed a little weak, a little peaky. If he'd only known, then . . .

then what? Then, not necessarily anything different. But he still would rather he'd known than not known, and just gone back to his studio, back to work, just like on any other day, back to his desk, his known surroundings, his incredibly annoying assistant whom he'd sacked not long after.

'Anyway, when it started up again, I didn't hear about it at first. My nan had died and there wasn't anyone in the house except the builders. But then my mum went to a meeting and found out it had been going on and getting worse. Then I saw something in the local paper. I start wondering about who's behind it, and it hits me, an idea comes to me. And I'm pretty certain I know who it is. I don't know how he got started, but I had a folder of stuff about the cards and the blog and the DVD at my studio, and I'm pretty certain that's where he saw it. My former assistant, who I sacked, just before all this stuff started getting nasty. A nasty little toerag trying to get back at me. Trying to get into my head. Trying to be an artist. And all without realising that I didn't even know it was going on. Silly little shit. But I can't come to you because I can't say who it is without saying who I am, and who I am is the single biggest thing in my life – the fact that people don't know it's what gives my work its edge and purpose. Which has now been taken away, thanks to our wonderful media. Which is the worst thing which has happened to me in years, thanks for asking. But it does mean I could come and tell you what I know.' Smitty puffed out his cheeks and sighed. 'Anyway, that's his name.' And Smitty slid across the table a piece of paper with his ex-assistant's name and address.

105

All the internees said that it was an important moment when you had grown used to the food. Some said this was a bad moment, a sign that you had been there too long; others said it was a good moment, a sign that you had become philosophical about your fate. People did not stop complaining about the food when they passed through this moment but they did not complain in the same angry way; they were more resigned, and the big change was that they now ate. For Quentina, the moment came with a jelly. She had been eating nothing but bread and fruit for about a month and was feeling gassy, bloated and unhealthy, and then she saw this jelly. It was red and had pieces of fruit in it. It was the fruit which convinced her. It wasn't that the jelly looked especially tempting; but it did look edible. She ate it: it was sweet. It tasted like jelly. She managed to get it down. The moment of defeat or of acceptance had occurred. There was a sense of psychological discomfort when she swallowed the first mouthful but after that it was OK.

Quentina had found a mental trick to help herself to get through her days in the detention centre. It was simple in its way. All she did was say to herself, over and over, whenever the need or occasion arose, the same words: this will not last for ever: this is the hardest thing you will ever do. This will not last for ever: this is the hardest thing you will ever do. She found herself saying it after she woke up in the morning and had a few seconds of not knowing where she was – and sometimes, in the happiest version of those seconds, she was back at home with her mother and father in their bedroom, except the door wasn't where it should be, and the window was on the wrong side of the bed, and there was something strange about the light, and then she would come fully awake to the reality of the detention centre, England, internment, statelessness, being a non-person in a non-place waiting her way through non-time.

These things were not harder than each other. They were all equally hard. It was very difficult being in the same place as the hunger strikers. Some of the first hunger strikers had given up, one or two of them, in particular a Kurdish woman with two children whose husband had been killed by Saddam, coming right to the very edge of death, her eyes huge and their irises a strange grey colour, bizarre against the sallow near-yellow of her slack but stretched skin. If it hadn't been for her children she would have starved herself to death, Quentina was sure; in the event she went too close to the edge, had kidney failure and nearly died anyway. Others had joined the hunger strike, so there were different internees at different stages of this war of nerves with the authorities. It was like the boys' game of chicken – except that it wasn't like a game at all.

One of the hardest things for Quentina was the sheer blankness of passing time. That was, after all, what had driven her to get the job as a traffic warden in the first place, the incredible temptation of having something to do, combined with the chance to earn a little spending money. Here, though, she found herself wondering why people were so agitated about the restoration of the 71p daily allowance. It wasn't that the sum was so small, it was that there was nothing to spend it on. Visitors were allowed, but they weren't allowed to bring anything in. There were charities which arranged visits so that internees had some point of contact with the outside world – for some internees these were the only British people they had ever spoken to who were not agents of the state. But Quentina couldn't be bothered with that. She didn't want to make small talk with a stranger and she even less wanted to complain to someone who had nothing to offer but sympathy. Makela the Nigerian doctor urged her to sign up for friends' visits, as they were called, but Quentina resisted.

'You're making a mistake,' said Makela, the kind of person who prided herself on her own frankness. 'You're turning in on yourself. I've seen it happen before.'

'I thank you for your advice,' said Quentina, and Makela knew enough to stop there.

There was a small library, mainly put together by donations from charities, presided over by one of the warders and by an Egyptian intellectual whose husband had been tortured in prison. The warder and the inmate got on well, the only instance of any such relationship in the internment centre. Quentina took out some books and tried to read, but this was yet another activity whose point she couldn't see. The non-fiction stories were too boring or too depressing – a history of the International Monetary Fund, a book about a young woman suffering abuse from her stepfather – and the fiction suffered from an irredeemable fault: it was all made up. Quentina couldn't, in her current frame of mind, see the point of anything that was made up. Makela said that books helped her to escape, but that didn't make any sense. A book couldn't get you out of the detention centre, or land like a helicopter and carry you off, or magically turn into a UK passport which gave you the right of residency. Escape was very precisely, very specifically what a book couldn't help you do. Not in any literal sense. And the literal sense of escape was the only one that interested Quentina.

The one thing that did help was doing shifts in the crèche. It wasn't that Quentina had any special liking for children, or special gift for them, or they a special liking for her. But it was, in a basic and straightforward way, something to do. She would help out for three hours in the morning on every second day – that was all the opportunity there was, because people were so desperate for activity that the competition for places to work in the crèche was ferocious, and there was a waiting list: Quentina only won her start when a detainee was sent back to Jordan. She helped set up little play zones, tidied up bricks of Duplo, refereed at the small sandpit and indoor dollhouse, and sat in story corner to read stories to any child who would listen. Those nine hours a week, ten to one on Monday, Wednesday, Friday, went past quicker than any other hours – which only made the rest of the time seem slower, heavier, like glue.

It might have been enough to break her, and without one crucial ingredient, it probably would have been. But Quentina had a secret weapon: she knew things could not be like this for ever. The tyrant could not live for ever. In Quentina's view, the rumours that he had syphilis were true, and explained his descent from tribal partisanship to outright evil; even if he didn't die, he was old and getting older, his country was desperate and getting more so, and he was going to die or be deposed one day, perhaps one day soon. When the tyrant goes, everything changes. Quentina had promised herself that the very day she heard news of that she would volunteer for deportation. She would go home. And it was that thought which kept her sane, and kept her functioning, in this no-time, no-place, which was designed to be, and succeeded in being, unbearable. This is the hardest thing I will ever do. But this will not last for ever.

106

'You do not have to say anything,' said DI Mill, 'but if you do say anything it may be taken down and used in evidence against you. It may harm your defence if you do not mention anything on which you later come to rely in court.'

It was difficult to get through the formal warning. The young man Mill was talking to was weeping uncontrollably. It was less like arresting someone and more like telling someone they'd been bereaved. If you're this upset, thought the DI, why the hell did you do it in the first place?

With another part of his mind, he knew the answer. Mill's experience was that while it was true that some people wanted to be caught, there was another category, less well known, of people who wanted to have been caught. In other words they did not go out of their way to be nicked, but once they had been, they went to pieces with guilt and relief. This looked like being one of those. Mill took out a packet of paper tissues and, catching the eye of his DC who was sitting next to him with his notebook out, handed them over to the suspect. Mill said, 'There, there.' The man took out a tissue, blew his nose loudly and at length, then looked around for a bin, couldn't see one – even though this was his own flat – and dropped the tissue on the floor.

'I didn't mean any harm,' said Parker French, Smitty's ex-assistant. 'It got out of hand. I really didn't mean to upset anybody.'

'Start at the beginning,' said Mill. While the kid had been crying, Mill had had a good long look around the room. It was a sitting room/dining room/kitchen with one bedroom and you could see that it was shared with a girlfriend. The flat was in Hackney and could not be cheap-cheap so either she worked at a paying job or one of them had some family cash. Parker's accent was neutral educated middle-class, very similar to Mill's, though just for a pleasant change he both was and looked younger than the DI. There were more CDs than usual for someone his age, and there were quite a few books too, all of them shelved in an orderly way. The TV was a couple-sized normal TV rather than a single man's monster flat-screen. The biggest piece of decoration was a poster for the Tate's exhibition of Picasso and Matisse.

'I hadn't been thinking about it until Smitty . . . until he sacked me. I'm sorry but he was such a total . . . he was just horrible to me. Treated me like all I could do is go out and get his coffee. I'm an artist too! I've got the same training he has! He didn't run around making people coffee, did he? If he wants respect, he should give respect. It's got to be earned. But no, he's Smitty, he doesn't have to do any of that. And then, without warning, I mean completely without warning, he tells me I'm fired. Like, totally assassinates me. I'm supposed to just go off and crawl into a hole and die.'

Parker took out another tissue and went through the same routine of blowing his nose on it and then dropping it on the floor.

'I got so angry. Not so much that day but later. I got really furious. The disrespect, you know? The disregard. I didn't matter. Like that thing they call it in Iraq, collateral damage. I was just collateral damage. I was barely shit on his shoes. Well, I got angry, and then I thought about it, and I decided that I wasn't having it. I decided I was going to do something to get back at Smitty. And make a name for myself at the same time, you know? Do something with a bit of edge. Smitty was always giving these sermons about how the art world worked, how commodification worked, how you had to do something so strange that people noticed it but that didn't make it look like you were desperate to sell stuff. So that's what I decided to do. And I wanted it to be something which messed with his head as well. His meaning Smitty's. I wanted to get into his head and make him feel he was being messed with and he didn't know why.'

'Pepys Road,' said Mill. Parker nodded.

'Where his granny lived. There had been these postcards. He was freaked out by them, I could tell. But also fascinated. It was like an art project, it was his kind of thing. He had this folder of stuff on his desk and kept looking at it. It was there for weeks. I looked at it too. The idea didn't come straight away. But I was looking at the blog and then I saw it hadn't been updated for a bit and I thought, bugger it. I screen-scraped all the stuff that was already on there. You know what that means, right? I copied it so I could repost it. And then the site was taken down, just like that. Disappeared. So I thought, sod it, and started it up again. Put it on a different blogging platform but gave it the same name. Then I put back up the original material. Then I began adding, with the graffiti and all that. I started with Smitty's house.'

'His grandmother's house,' said Mill. Parker looked uncomfortable.

'Anyway. I started with that. But I wanted it to get darker. To have more edge. These wankers, who do they think they are, you know? Do they think they're, you know, the kings of the world, or something? People are like, starving. People haven't got jobs. Children haven't got medicine, you know? And there these posh wankers are . . . I just wanted to say something, you know? Make a statement.'

'Was Smitty's grandmother a posh wanker?' asked the DI.

'Well Smitty was a posh wanker, much more than he let on,'

the boy snapped back. 'It was him I wanted to mess with. I didn't think his nan would be that bothered.'

'Did the fact that she died in May make no difference to you?'

Parker was visibly startled by that. His head jerked up. He didn't reply.

'The house has been empty for months. Those cards, DVDs, all that, have been going to a vacant address. We talked to Smitty. He had absolutely no idea about what had been going on.'

And now his mouth was flapping open and closed like a fish. A sense of sadness washed over Mill; the boy was about to pay very severely for his misplaced energies.

'Did someone help you with the graffiti?' That was the first edge to cross: criminal damage.

'No. Just me,' he said in a very quiet voice. 'I only did it once. I thought the risk of being caught was too high. It's the cans, the way they rattle when you shake them. It's hard to do in an occupied area. Once was enough.'

'The time in May,' Mill said, while his DC kept writing.

'Mm,' said the boy. This would appear as a declarative statement by the time his words had been written up.

'And the birds, that was you too?'

Now the kid did look embarrassed. He dropped his gaze and muttered something.

'I missed that,' said Mill.

'The first one came from home. My parents' place. In Norfolk. It had flown into the window, killed itself. I went there for the weekend, it happened that morning. My mum was upset. I said I'd dispose of it but then I was taking it to the compost when I thought, I don't know what I thought, I thought about Joseph Beuys, you probably don't know him, he's an artist and a big hero, I wondered what he would have done, I thought it would be a strong statement. Then the other ones I got from a taxidermist. I don't know where he got them from. There were only six or seven of them, anyway . . . It was stupid and I shouldn't have done it, I saw that afterwards.'

Mill caught the DC's eye while he kept writing. If the parents confirmed that account there would be no animal cruelty charge. There would be something to do with misuse of the post, maybe. As things stood the kid was guilty but probably wouldn't go to jail. One big issue left, and Mill could tell that the DC was thinking along similar lines. Occasionally, very occasionally, Mill found himself wishing that suspects did what was right by their own interests rather than what was right by the law. That was what he felt now. This kid needed a lawyer and a few minutes to think what was the prudent thing to say, rather than just to go on relieving his soul. If Mill had been on his own, he might not have pressed the issue; he might have given the boy time to collect himself. The irony was that a real criminal in this position would never, under any circumstances, have said the wrong thing. The law is a brilliant mechanism for catching people who don't know what to say and do when they are in trouble. With more seasoned criminals it works much less well. Mill said, as gently as he could,

'And the cars? Was that you on your own too?'

There was no direct evidence linking the vandalism of the cars to the rest of the campaign. Nothing on the postcards or blog had mentioned the incident in which a set of keys had been scratched down the side of cars in the street – an act that had stood out as by far the biggest criminal incident of all in Pepys Road. One probably big enough to guarantee a custodial sentence for the person who had done it, in the very very unlikely event the police caught him. Mill wanted to catch this kid, but he didn't particularly want him to go to jail, which is why his heart sank when he heard the whispered words,

'Just me.'

107

The gigantic red removal lorry of the Younts' possessions had left at about eleven o'clock, heading down the M4 to Minchinhampton. Arabella and the children had gone down to the country the day before, and now only Roger was left in the empty house, with nothing left to do but drop the keys off at his solicitor's. Then he too would drive down to the country and their Pepys Road years would be over and their new life would begin.

Roger was looking forward to it. That was what he told himself. The new new thing. He was done with the city and with the City. He was done with the commute to work, with pinstriped suits, with City boy subordinates and Eurotrash bosses and clients like Eric the barbarian; done with earning twenty or thirty times the average family's annual income for doing things with money rather than with people or things. He was done with London and money and all that. It was time to do or make something. Roger was completely sincere in this conviction, even though he wasn't quite sure what he meant – wasn't quite sure what he meant to make or do. But, something.

In his last fifteen minutes in Pepys Road, Roger went right to the top of what was still legally his house, to the loft which had been converted, after discussion, into a 'spare room'. Arabella had wanted a study, but been forced eventually to admit that she never actually did any studying so didn't need one, and while Roger had been tempted to claim it as his den in the end he'd settled on a smaller, snugger room on the second floor, one which by taking up less space was likely to be easier to defend as his territory ('But the boys *need* another room'). Then down through the boys' bedrooms, the only evidence of their former presence the bright wallpaper, cowboy (Josh) and spaceman (Conrad) – and also, for the observant, the scratched pencil marks indicating how the boys were growing. Their bathroom was bright orange. Then down, Roger's den, the fitted bookshelves still there and the space where his Howard Hodgkin had sat (a present from Arabella when she was trying to make him seem more cultivated), Arabella's dressing room with her little built-in writing table and the fitted cupboards, the small second spare room with marks on the carpet from the bed frame, the loo, then their master bedroom, where, Roger had estimated, he and Arabella had made love about sixty times, once a month for five years, not that high a figure really, but a nice room for all that, the brightest in the house, painted cream, and empty now except for yet more cupboards, and lighter than it had ever been because the blinds and curtains were gone.

Going to the window, he looked down into the front garden, where the Sold sign was nailed next to the front gate. Roger sat on the floor for a moment to drink in the feeling that all this was no longer his. Let it sink in. It was strange being in the house when it was completely empty. It made it obvious that a house was a stage set, a place where life went on, more than it was a thing in itself. The emptiness wasn't creepy; there was no *Mary Celeste* vibe here that Roger could detect. More as if they had finished with the house, and the house had also finished with them. They had moved out and now the house was expecting the new people to move in. The house too was waiting for the new thing; waiting to stage a new production.

The change to their life had sunk in with him. It was sinking in with people everywhere, as it gradually dawned on them that hard times were moving in like a band of rain. He wished it had sunk in with Arabella. Roger had been waiting for a moment when she got it: when she looked around and realised what was happening. He had been hoping that a giant penny would drop, a light bulb would go on, Arabella would have a 'moment of clarity' and see that this just couldn't go on. Not only for economic reasons – for them of course but not only for them – but because this just wasn't enough to live by. You could not spend your entire span of life in thrall to the code of stuff. There was no code of stuff. Stuff was just stuff. You couldn't live by it or for it. Roger's new motto: stuff is not enough. For some months now his deepest wish had been for Arabella to look in the mirror and realise that she had to change. He wanted this more than he wanted his bosses at Pinker Lloyd to be publicly humiliated, more than he wanted his deputy Mark to go to prison, more than he wanted to win the lottery. She couldn't go on like this.

But it hadn't happened. Arabella showed no sign of thinking that she couldn't go on like this. On the contrary, she showed every intention of going on as she was for ever. No Plan B. It was labels, logos and conspicuous consumption all the way. If anything, looking after the children so much of the time seemed to have made it worse. It gave an edge of longing to her dreams of labels and holidays and treats, where before there had been a more straightforward greed. It was a mystery to Roger how someone he knew so well could be such an impervious, impenetrable stranger. Roger wasn't quite clear whether she had always been the way she was now, or whether what had happened was that he had moved in one direction and she had gone in another. Whatever the reason for the shift, it was real, and he now, and increasingly, found her crushingly shallow and wearingly, suffocatingly materialistic. He had worked in the City, among the biggest breadheads on planet Earth – and he was married to a bigger breadhead than any of them.

Now Roger was downstairs. First he went down further to the children's playroom. If his nose were super-sensitive, if he were a dog, he could probably just get a last whiff of Matya, her perfume, her hair, the way she'd come in from walking around with the boys smelling of the cold, the winter air, the outside, smelling of freedom, of other lives . . . Roger hadn't come down much when she was here; he hadn't trusted himself. But now this was just an empty room.

He went back up to the ground floor. The last time he would ever stand in the sitting room, the last time he'd ever flick off and on the lights in the kitchen, the last time he'd stretch out his arms in the dining room and twirl around, his last look at the garden, his last time in the corridor, the last time he would close the front door and then lock it. They say the best thing to do is walk away quickly and not look back, but instead he leaned his head against the door for a moment, a last few seconds of physical contact with the biggest and most expensive and most significant thing he had ever owned.

The car was parked immediately outside. He got in, started the engine, pulled out into Pepys Road, and then stopped. He turned and stared at what was now no longer his front door. Time for goodbye. Roger had deliberately not found out anything about the buyers. He'd been out the first afternoon they viewed the place, and then had chosen to be out the second time they looked, because he'd been worn out by all the time-wasters, idiots, fantasists and ne'er-do-wells who came and made offers and then melted away. But these people were serious, cash buyers, whose offer came in at full price, was accepted and went straight through, all without Roger knowing or wanting to know a single thing about them. Now as he took his last look at his old house, Roger allowed himself a moment to wonder who they were. Then he pulled out into the road. At the end of the street he turned and caught one last glimpse of his old front door, and as he did so all he could find himself thinking was: I can change, I can change, I promise I can change change change.

Also by John Lanchester

ff

Mr Phillips

One warm July morning Mr Phillips, a cautious middle-aged accountant, climbs out of bed, leaving Mrs Phillips dozing. He prepares for his commute into the city – but this is no ordinary Monday. It is the day on which Mr Phillips will chat with a pornographer, stalk a TV mini-celebrity, have lunch with an aspiring record mogul, and get caught up in a bank robbery. So why is Mr Phillips not at work?

'Absolute blinder of a book; hysterically funny, very moving, sooo elegantly done. Rather wish I'd written it meself.' Zadie Smith

'To read this book is the greatest of fun. It is as easy to read as it must have been difficult to write.' Barbara Trapido, *Independent on Sunday*

'Wonderful – an inspired daydream about sex, statistics and the strangeness of ordinary London life.' Theo Tait, *Guardian*

ff

Fragrant Harbour

It is 1935, and Tom Stewart, a young Englishman with a longing for adventure, buys himself a cheap ticket aboard the SS *Darjeeling* – en route to the complex and corrupt world of Hong Kong. A shipboard wager leads to an unlikely friendship that spans seven decades as Hong Kong endures the savagery of the Japanese occupation before emerging as a crossroads of international finance, warlords, drug runners and Chinese triads.

'There's a depth and emotional candour here that, long after you have finished the book, is hard to forget ... Redolent with the bright shine of romance and nostalgia.' *Observer*

'A wonderfully compelling work. Lanchester anatomises our infinite human corruptibility...but he also celebrates integrity, courage and life-long love.' *Sunday Telegraph*

'Exoticism, a powerful narrative, intelligence, goodness and villainy. A heady and compelling mix.' *Scotsman*

ff

Faber and Faber is one of the great independent publishing houses. We were established in 1929 by Geoffrey Faber with T. S. Eliot as one of our first editors. We are proud to publish award-winning fiction and non-fiction, as well as an unrivalled list of poets and playwrights. Among our list of writers we have five Booker Prize winners and twelve Nobel Laureates, and we continue to seek out the most exciting and innovative writers at work today.

Find out more about our authors and books
faber.co.uk

Read our blog for insight and opinion on books and the arts
thethoughtfox.co.uk

Follow news and conversation
twitter.com/faberbooks

Watch readings and interviews
youtube.com/faberandfaber

Connect with other readers
facebook.com/faberandfaber

Explore our archive
flickr.com/faberandfaber